Mindless of her state of
'Oh, I am so overjoyed to

Trelawney interrupted
muffled laughter.

He held her a little awa
suggestion of a frown; instead, his eyes glinted at her in an
appreciative look that also held mocking amusement.
'Flattered as I am by your—er—enthusiasm, ma'am,' he
said in that slow, intimate voice she remembered so well, 'I
am rather at a loss to account for it, considering the nature
of our relationship.'

She flushed, bewildered and confused, and then humiliated as she realised that he felt she was reading far more
into his interest in her than he cared for.

'Our relationship?' she echoed stiffly. 'Apart from our
one previous meeting, the only relationship between us is
the fact that we are both prisoners of the Corsairs.'

The twin grooves appeared beside his mouth in a wry,
sardonic look. 'Oh dear! I very much fear that you will
withdraw whatever tempting offer you were about to make
when you learn that you have mistaken me for someone
else. I am Rais Trelawney Grant, the captain of this ship.'

Born of Afrikaans-speaking parents in Johannesburg, South Africa, Christina Laffeaty describes her education as 'erratic'. Between the ages of seven and fifteen she attended twelve different schools where her attendance depended on whether or not she was needed to help out with the ploughing or harvesting. She attributes the fact that she acquired any kind of education at all to her own obsessive reading.

She was nineteen before she learned English—from her husband, who brought her to live in England—and she started writing professionally shortly afterwards. Her work includes short stories for the BBC, the *Evening News* and various women's magazines; radio plays, serials and about seventy books. Mrs Laffeaty has a son and a daughter and lives in the West Country. *Trelawney's Woman* is her seventh Masquerade Historical Romance and she has also written a longer historical novel, *Illicit Obsession*.

TRELAWNEY'S WOMAN

Christina Laffeaty

MILLS & BOON LIMITED
ETON HOUSE 18–24 PARADISE ROAD
RICHMOND SURREY TW9 1SR

First published in Great Britain 1987 by Mills & Boon Limited

© Christina Laffeaty 1987

Australian copyright 1987 Philippine copyright 1987 This edition 1988

ISBN 0 263 75967 9

Set in 9½ on 10 pt Linotron Times 04–0188–86,600

Photoset by Rowland Phototypesetting Limited Bury St Edmunds, Suffolk Made and printed in Great Britain by Cox & Wyman Limited, Reading

CHAPTER ONE

GENEVRA BOWED HER head as she listened to the captain's voice, which was intermittently torn away by the breeze and sometimes drowned by the creaking of the ship's timbers or the flapping of the sails.

'. . . We therefore commit her body to the deep . . . to be turned into corruption . . .'

The passengers attending the service could hardly have been called mourners, for few of them had exchanged so much as a word with Ellen Grey, the dead woman. She had come on this voyage as a poor relative and unpaid companion, and Genevra had a bleak feeling of fellowship with her, for she herself would soon be joining the ranks of that unfortunate band of females who depend on the charity of their kin. Her thoughts wandered away from the funeral service. Heaven knows, she had explored every other possible avenue that she had hoped might be open to her! In the end she had been forced to write to Uncle John, who as her only family connection was her legal guardian until she came of age in a year's time. She had explained the situation to him, and had added:

> If you would be prepared to lend me a sufficient sum to make it possible for me to attend an Academy, I am sure I would quite quickly gain the qualifications needed for me to hire myself out as a governess, and my first concern would be to repay you.

John McDonnell had written back, pointing out that as the British Consul in an unimportant post like Algiers, his capital was limited, and besides a grown-up daughter of his own to support there was also his second wife and a baby son. While he could not lend her the money she required, he would be happy to offer her a home in the Consulate in Algiers. 'I am sure you would wish to make yourself useful to your new aunt in every way,' Uncle John had added, thus making it very clear that she would be occupying a position of servitude in his household. 'Reliable help is hard to come by in Algiers.'

In fairness, she had to admit that he owed her nothing. He was not her true uncle, and if the two of them had ever met it must have been when she was too young to remember. His first wife had been Genevra's mother's sister, of whom she did retain faint memories, for Aunt Clare with their daughter Sophie had paid visits to the Rectory in Sussex many years ago, leaving Uncle John alone for a while in whichever country he happened to be Britain's representative at the time.

So she had no real claim on him, and he had been appointed her legal guardian by the Court only because there was no one else. Since the death of Aunt Clare, followed just a year later by that of her mother, there had been very little contact between their two families, apart from desultory correspondence. Genevra could not remember what her cousin Sophie looked like and had never met Uncle John's second wife Harriet, but she did not imagine that the latter would have been very pleased at having her predecessor's relative thrust upon her.

Genevra sighed, and gave her attention to the funeral service again, and thought compassionately of the dead woman. Since Ellen Grey's mistress had spent most of the voyage confined to her cabin, the companion had seldom appeared in public either. If she had not died of a heart seizure, so that she had to be buried at sea, it was doubtful whether any of the passengers would even have known her name. Somehow, she thought fiercely, she herself would not come to her end like the dead woman, unknown, unloved and unmourned.

She peeped through her lashes at Abigail Pascoe. Certainly there was no grief on her beautiful face, no tears in her blue eyes. It had been rumoured among the passengers that Miss Pascoe kept to her cabin because she was a poor sailor, but her appearance did not betray the ravages of sea-sickness. It did, however, reveal that she had been very dependent upon Ellen Grey, for underneath her black lace cap, some of her piled-up fair hair was coming down; it had obviously been clumsily pinned by someone who had only the sketchiest talent for attending to her own toilette.

Although she was said to be twenty-six or twenty-seven, Abigail Pascoe still retained the looks which ship's gossip claimed had proved to be her fortune. There were few passengers, for *Kite* was principally a cargo vessel carrying supplies destined for the garrison at Gibraltar, and mail, newspapers and official despatches for the British Consulates along the Barbary Coast. But among the handful of passengers were officers' wives who had met Abigail Pascoe in her youth or who knew of her by reputation, and from them Genevra had heard how she had overcome the twin handicaps of having no dowry at all and of possessing a scapegrace as a father.

She was beautiful enough to have made a respectable match in spite of being poor as a church mouse, the gossips had said, but her father frightened suitors off. There was no knowing what future scandals he might plunge them into. Then she caught the eye of a merchant who possessed a vast fortune. He was old, and in trade, but so hopelessly besotted with her that he did not care about constantly having to rescue her father from disaster. She played a calculating game by insisting that he should make a Will leaving her his fortune if he should die before they could be married. Since she kept on postponing the ceremony, Fate took a hand in her schemes and he did succumb before the knot could be tied. She inherited all his money, just as she had hazarded.

'*I* heard,' someone else had put in, 'that the experience of having been poor all her life made her extremely miserly after she came into money. Her chief interests began to centre on ways of saving it, and of expanding her fortune. She also wants the respectability denied to her while her father was alive and constantly plunging the two of them into scandal. She has aspirations of marrying into the nobility.'

'But what could she be doing on this voyage?' Genevra had asked.

'They say she is going to Gibraltar to trace a distant cousin. Apparently he served in the war against France, and now that it is over he will be returning to the garrison on the Rock.'

'If she is indeed searching for a long-lost relative,' a

woman had remarked spitefully, 'I'll lay odds that she wishes to press him into her service in some way. She has found that it is cheaper to surround herself with poor kinsfolk than to pay for the services of outsiders.'

Genevra, who disliked malicious gossip, had decided to reserve her own judgment. But it was impossible, looking at her, to guess what her feelings were regarding the death of poor Ellen Grey. The funeral was over, and people were returning below. Genevra stared at the undulating ocean which had closed, as if it had never been disturbed, over the remains of the dead woman. Seagulls wheeled overhead, and the increasing number of vessels they passed implied that Gibraltar would be reached within a day or so.

She watched, curious, as one of the other vessels put out flag-signals, and wondered what the message had read. Then she dismissed the thought and went below to the cabin she shared with three service wives. They were constantly decrying their cramped conditions, complaining that the end of the voyage could not come soon enough. To Genevra, the shared cabin was the last bulwark against reality, a place in which she could still dream optimistic dreams that some miracle might occur to save her from having to live in an alien land with distant family connections she hardly knew and on whose charity she would have to depend.

The women were discussing Abigail Pascoe's lack of emotion at the death of her companion.

'If she felt anything at all,'' one of them was saying, 'it was probably annoyance at the thought of having to hire a replacement for Miss Grey.'

'She'll not have an easy task to find someone in Gibraltar . . .' The speaker was interrupted by a knock on the door. It was a ship's boy, who announced,

'Cap'n wishes for to see Miss Shaw in his cabin.'

Genevra stiffened with astonishment. Why on earth should she have been singled out for attention by Captain Dunne? Then excitement coursed through her. Perhaps he had learnt something of her circumstances through ship's gossip, and knew of some respectable position in Gibraltar, maybe, for which her limited qualifications might be suited.

'Please wait a moment,' she told the lad, and borrowed a

mirror from one of the women to confirm that she looked
tidy. Her nose was small and straight, her mouth too wide
for her liking, and her eyes, slightly slanted at the corners,
were liberally flecked with gold so that they looked more
amber than green. Cat's eyes, Papa had called them
teasingly. She wished her winged eyebrows did not give her
face such a look of wondering innocence, so that she
appeared to be younger than her twenty years. But most of
her attention was reserved for her hair, a source of dis-
satisfaction and even embarrassment ever since she could
remember.

As though it were not enough that it should defy most
laws of nature by being almost jet black and therefore at
odds with her creamy complexion and light-coloured eyes,
it also curled in the most wayward manner so that tendrils
were always escaping about her face. But what she had
been most sensitive about since early childhood was the
streak of pure white that grew in a widow's peak from the
centre of her forehead. Although she knew it was a family
trait and that her mother had possessed a similar streak, this
did not console Genevra at all. She considered it so peculiar
that she took great pains to hide it, brushing the front of her
hair so that it fell in curls over her forehead to cover it.
Satisfied that no white showed, she tucked a few of the
unruly curls behind her ears and returned the mirror to its
owner. She smoothed her blue cambric gown over her slim
hips and straightened the modest fichu of white lawn about
her throat. The gown looked what it was—a made-over
garment donated to the Rectory's Poor Relief Fund that
she had had no qualms about appropriating. Since her
parents' deaths, she had become as poor as any of their
parishioners. Deciding that her appearance would have to
do, she followed the boy to the captain's quarters. He rose
when she entered, and bowed. 'You must be Miss Shaw,' he
said, which struck her as puzzling and unnecessary, since he
had sent for her.

Captain Dunne was a man of middle years with a somewhat forbidding face, but his expression softened as he
studied her. He was looking at her in a fatherly way, as
though he felt sorry for her while disapproving of the fact
that someone as young as she, even in such obviously

straitened circumstances, should be travelling alone. He had evidently completed his compassionate study of her person. 'Sit down, Miss Shaw,' he invited her. 'I am waiting for Miss Pascoe to join us, for what I have to say concerns her also.'

'Oh?' Genevra's bewilderment was increasing, and her surmise that he might be going to suggest a situation for her began to fade.

He nodded. 'With the death of Miss Ellen Grey, you and Miss Abigail Pascoe are the only two passengers who will be continuing on to Algiers.'

'I thought she was disembarking at Gibraltar!' Genevra exclaimed.

Captain Dunne did not comment. If the gossips had been wrong about the heiress's destination, Genevra was thinking, they could also have been wrong about her character. But what on earth could be taking someone like Abigail Pascoe to such an obscure, foreign port as Algiers?

He had obviously been wondering the same thing about Genevra, for he said, 'May I ask why you are bound for Algiers?'

She hesitated. In his letter to her, Uncle John had written: 'For complicated reasons of diplomacy, I would prefer it if you did not disclose your family connection with the British Consul in Algiers. If asked, it should suffice to say that you are travelling to join the household of relatives in the city.' She had supposed it to mean that if she committed some indiscretion during the journey it would reflect badly on his position, but it had also struck her chillingly that it might mean, instead, that he did not wish to acknowledge her publicly as his niece. But the captain was waiting for her answer. 'I am going to make my home with relatives there,' she said.

He gave her a brief smile. 'Algiers is very cosmopolitan, with a sizeable British community. Presumably Miss Pascoe is also travelling to visit friends or relatives.' He looked quizzically at her. 'I am acquainted with several members of the British community in Algiers, and it is possible that I know your relatives. What is their name?'

She cast him a hunted look. Since he was calling at Algiers to deliver diplomatic despatches among other things, he could not fail to know the name of the British Consul. She would just have to ask him to keep her uncle's identity to himself. 'My uncle is John McDonnell . . .' she began.

But it obviously did not even occur to Captain Dunne that someone so shabbily dressed could have any connection with the British Consul, for he cut in by saying, 'I often carry mail for a Mr J. McDonald in Algiers, but I am not personally acquainted with him or his family.'

Genevra suppressed a sigh of relief. She wanted to change the subject and ask him many questions about Algiers that had been exercising her mind ever since she had realised that there was no choice for her but to accept Uncle John's offer. All she knew about the city was that it would be utterly different from the sleepy Sussex hamlet where she had been born and grown up. But before she could frame her questions, a knock came on the door.

Abigail Pascoe was shown in, and Genevra noticed that she had made an ineffectual attempt to pin up her wayward curls again. She had changed into a light blue crepe gown that earned her own envious admiration, although it struck her that Miss Pascoe wore styles more suitable for someone younger than a girl in her late twenties. But, then, her figure was so good and her complexion so youthful that only a malicious person would have criticised her for it, and no one ignorant of her true age would have given it a second thought. As Miss Pascoe turned to address the captain, Genevra saw that she had failed to secure one of the fastenings at the back of the gown. Such small tokens of incompetence made her seem rather vulnerable, and she warmed to her.

'You wished to speak to me?' Something in Abigail Pascoe's voice suggested that she would have expected the captain to request an audience of her at her own convenience rather than be summoned to his cabin, and Genevra became less certain of her vulnerability.

'Yes, Miss Pascoe.' He drew out a chair for her. 'Allow me to present Miss Genevra Shaw who, like yourself, is bound for Algiers.'

'I see.' She sat down and examined Genevra. There was no compassion in *her* glance; it was detached and analytical, and seemed to assess Genevra's circumstances precisely.

'A short while ago,' the captain said, 'we received from a passing vessel a message that affects both of you ladies. It merely said that we should be on our guard against Corsair vessels from Algiers. No doubt I shall receive fuller details when we arrive in Gibraltar tomorrow, but this can mean only one thing. There is a dispute between Britain and the Dey of Algiers—probably over the matter of the tribute we have to pay him annually—and while it lasts, we cannot venture into the waters along the Barbary Coast. It will mean a delay in Gibraltar until the matter has been resolved.'

Miss Pascoe frowned. 'It will not suit me at all to kick my heels indefinitely in Gibraltar!'

'I am afraid it cannot be helped, Miss Pascoe.'

Genevra leant forward in her chair, her brow furrowed. Abigail Pascoe had appeared to understand precisely what the captain had been saying, while she herself was totally in the dark. 'Would you please explain, sir,' she asked, 'what you meant about a tribute which has to be paid? Isn't a tribute a—a kind of compliment?'

Captain Dunne said drily, 'In this particular case, the word "tribute" is a polite term for a blackmail payment which the Barbary Regencies demand from other countries. It has been the custom for over three hundred years that countries whose shipping use the waters along the Barbary Coast pay such a tribute.'

'But what would happen if we did sail to Algiers in spite of this dispute?'

The captain pursed his lips and appeared to be considering his reply to Genevra. It was Abigail Pascoe who explained with a short laugh, 'The vessel would be boarded by Algerian Corsairs. They would seize the cargo and take everyone on board prisoner.'

Giving her a look of curiosity, he said thoughtfully, 'You appear to know a good deal about Algiers, Miss Pascoe.' There had been a question in his voice, but she did not answer it.

'What are Corsairs?' Genevra persisted.

'They are highly-skilled navigators . . .' Captain Dunne began, but Abigail Pascoe interrupted him in a flat voice.

'They are wolves of the sea, who go raiding the ocean and plundering the shipping of those countries which have failed to pay protection money. Their ambition is to take home as many prisoners as they can cram into their holds.'

'Good heavens!' She stared at her, wide-eyed. 'But what use can such prisoners possibly be to them?'

Abigail Pascoe uttered a humourless laugh. 'The Algerians hold them to ransom, and until it has been paid, the prisoners are kept as slaves!'

Genevra's head rocked back. Why on earth had Uncle John mentioned none of this in his letter? He had warned of excessive heat and urged her to bring light clothing; he had asked her to pack as much reading matter as she could, for they had to rely on the occasional ship bringing back issues of English newspapers. But he had said nothing of Corsairs, or of people kept as slaves.

The captain was addressing Miss Pascoe with disapproval in his voice. 'I must ask you not to alarm the other passengers by sharing with them your knowledge of Algiers. It is very unlikely that we shall encounter an Algerian vessel so close to Gibraltar.' He stood up, indicating that the interview was over. 'I thought it only right to give the two of you warning of the delay ahead. You will have to disembark with the other passengers at Gibraltar, and put up in lodgings until the affair has been resolved and we can safely sail for Algiers.'

Genevra tried to hide her dismay. 'Could we not remain on board while we are waiting?'

'That would be impossible, Miss Shaw. There is no way of knowing for sure how long we shall have to remain in Gibraltar.' He added in a kindly, reassuring tone, 'Lodgings are to be had there quite cheaply, you know.'

She swallowed. Even the cheapest of lodgings would be out of the reach of someone who had no money at all. Everything she had been able to amass, added to what had been donated by her father's parishioners, had gone on the stage fare to Plymouth and on the ship's passage. Deep in anxious thought, she left the captain's cabin. If she had known how long she would be delayed, she might have tried for a temporary post of some kind, however menial, but it would be unfair to expect anyone to employ her when she might, at a moment's notice, have to leave on *Kite*.

Intending seeking the comparative privacy of the deck again while she wrestled with her problem, she stepped on to the companionway to hear Abigail Pascoe saying abruptly, 'Just a moment. You are unable to pay for lodgings in Gibraltar, aren't you?'

Genevra stiffened, and returned with what even she herself recognised as an unconvincing show of defiance. 'What makes you think that?'

Abigail Pascoe made a gesture, dismissing her tattered pride. 'It's perfectly obvious. Come to my cabin; I wish to speak to you.' The invitation was brief and to the point. She added, 'I may be able to help'.

No offer of help in her present predicament could possibly be turned down out of hand, so Genevra inclined her head and followed. The private cabin they entered a few moments later was quite as large as the one Genevra shared with three others, and was furnished with a fixed dressing-table and two armchairs besides the single bunk.

'Sit down,' Abigail Pascoe said. 'I have a suggestion to put to you, but first I need to know why you are bound for Algiers.'

Genevra folded her hands in her lap and tried to gather her thoughts. Abigail might look younger than her years and at times even appear vulnerable, but there was an inflexible core to her and an authority which could not be denied. *She* would not be content to be fobbed off with the bare statement that Genevra was travelling to Algiers to join the household of relatives. In return for any help she had it in mind to offer, she would want to know as much as possible about her background.

'My father died a few months ago,' she began to explain. 'He was a clergyman, and he had never been able to save anything from his stipend, which of course came to an end with his death. Because my mother died when I was fourteen and I was needed to keep house, I had never acquired any skills which would have made it possible for me to earn my own living.' She smiled ruefully. 'Papa taught me French, but I found that it is of little use to be fluent in one foreign language when I do not have any knowledge of the other accomplishments necessary to become a governess.

And even though I managed the Rectory after my mother's death, I soon discovered, when I tried to apply for work as a professional housekeeper, that I was considered far too young for such a responsibility. My situation became quite desperate when the new Rector arrived, for he had a large family and there was no room for me. Neither had I any relatives to go to . . .'

'Strange,' Abigail put in with something hard in her blue eyes. 'In my experience, there is almost always a relative or two lurking in one's background.'

'My father had two sisters,' Genevra explained, 'but they were both sickly and died while still quite young and unmarried. My mother had one sister, who also died some years ago, and her husband is the only family connection I have left. He and his second wife and their family are . . . They live in Algiers, and when I wrote, asking him . . .' She broke off, and continued, 'When he learnt of my father's death and that he had been appointed my legal guardian, and he realised how I was situated, he invited me to make my home with them.'

'I see,' Abigail commented, in a tone which suggested that she was only too aware of the role Genevra would be playing in her uncle's household.

'I know we had not been corresponding very regularly with my uncle,' Genevra went on with a frown, 'but I'm surprised that he has never mentioned the Corsairs of Algiers.'

Abigail shrugged. 'The Algerians are very sensitive to any suggestion that they are pirates who enslave people. They refer to those they capture as prisoners-of-war. No doubt your uncle judged it prudent not to write anything critical in a letter which might be tampered with by officials in Algiers.' She changed the subject. 'Well, Miss Shaw, I have a proposition to put to you. As you know, my companion has died. I am prepared to pay the cost of your lodgings in Gibraltar if you would agree to take Ellen's place.'

Genevra looked doubtfully at her. 'Do you mean, until we arrive in Algiers?'

'Initially, yes. If we find that we suit one another, and living in Algiers with your relatives does not appeal to you, it could become a permanent post, with wages to be decided later. What do you say?'

'You—You will not be remaining permanently in Algiers?'

'No,' replied Abigail without elaboration. 'Well, what do you say?'

With relief and hope, Genevra replied, 'I have to accept with gratitude, Miss Pascoe.'

Abigail nodded. 'If you are to stay with me permanently, you will have to learn such skills as dressing hair in modern styles and fancy sewing. But, in the meantime, all I shall mainly require is that you look after my clothes and dress my hair neatly.'

'I shall do my very best, Miss Pascoe.' Genevra hesitated. 'May I ask what takes *you* to a place like Algiers?'

Abigail's eyes rested on her, their expression cold and remote. 'You will move into the cabin next door, which Ellen used to occupy.'

Genevra flushed, and said stiffly, 'I was not trying to pry into your affairs. I was merely expressing interest.'

'The only interest I shall expect you to show is in your duties. By the by, what did you say was the name of your relatives in Algiers?'

Even in the unlikely event that Abigail should know the name of the British Consul, Genevra could easily have seized upon Captain Dunne's mistake and said that they were called McDonald. But she was still smarting under the snub she had received, and pride made her say politely but pointedly, 'While the arrangement between us remains a temporary one, I do not consider the identity of my family in Algiers to be of any relevance, Miss Pascoe.'

Abigail appeared not to be aware of the discourtesy, for she shrugged, and said, 'You are probably right. Unless and until I should decide to offer you a permanent position, your family are of no interest of me. Go and collect your things now.'

Genevra withdrew from the cabin, chiding herself for that reckless flash of pride that could so easily have ruined everything. Abigail Pascoe was a cold, enigmatic person, but she herself could not afford to take offence so easily. If she did go on to be gainfully employed by her, she would be receiving practical experience that could be put to use in finding other, more congenial, employment later.

The women with whom Genevra had shared the voyage were so agog at the news that she was to attend Miss Pascoe that they did not ask her why the captain had sent for her.

'Be sure to find out whether it's true that Abigail has her sights set on a baronet!' one of them said.

'Miss Pascoe is not someone who would allow anyone to ferret out her secrets.' With this firm reply, she dismissed Abigail from the conversation, and went on, 'Has any of you ever heard of Algerian Corsairs?'

'Lord, yes!' replied the wife of a naval officer. 'Those bearded Turks with their scimitars have been striking terror into Christian sailors for hundreds of years! And they are not only from Algiers, but also from Morocco and Tunisia. But they would not interfere with the shipping of any country with whom they have a treaty.'

Genevra decided not to tell them that the treaty between Algeria and Britain was under dispute, and after she had packed her possessions, she took a fond leave of the three women with whom she had become friends. Scarcely had she moved into her new quarters when Miss Pascoe required her attention. Her hair required brushing and putting up, and afterwards it was time to go and fetch dinner, for she insisted on taking her meals in the privacy of her cabin.

It was a difficult time of adjustment for Genevra, because although she was used to hard work, her labours had always hitherto been given voluntarily, and she had not had to bow the knee to anyone. But paid employment of any kind seemed so vastly preferable to being the poor relation in Uncle John's home that she would have to learn to put up with anything.

The arrival of *Kite* in the harbour at Gibraltar provided a welcome diversion. Genevra had spent most of the day below, packing, and it was not until the vessel had tied up and a crewman had carried her luggage on deck that she, too, was able to go up top and stare at the view. The huge mass of rock towering over the sprawling town was awe-inspiring, and almost took her breath away. The waterfront was crowded with people who had come to meet relatives, with strange vehicles drawn by a single mule, apparently touting for custom, and by seamen loading and unloading cargoes.

Miss Pascoe insisted on waiting until everyone else had gone ashore and there was no longer such a press of people before she and Genevra disembarked. The driver of one of the mule-drawn vehicles offered his services, and when their luggage had been loaded aboard, the two females were driven up a steeply sloping, narrow cobbled road and deposited at a tavern with the very English name of the King's Head. Indeed, if one disregarded that ominous rock, the British influence in Gibraltar was so strong that one might almost not have been abroad.

The King's Head seemed to be popular with ships' officers, for Captain Dunne and colleagues of other nationalities were drinking and gossiping in the saloon. Miss Pascoe gave them a reflective glance, and announced that she would take luncheon in the public parlour. After two rooms had been engaged for them, Genevra helped her employer to wash and change her gown, and dressed her hair.

'You will have the unpacking to finish,' Abigail said, 'so I shall ask for something to be brought up to you on a tray.'

'When I have finished my tasks, may I go out and see a little of Gibraltar?' asked Genevra.

'Just make sure that you are back in plenty of time to attend to me before dinner,' Abigail told her.

Genevra completed her duties, and selected from among her meagre wardrobe a bonnet of unadorned chip-straw that covered her hair completely and would shade her face from the sun, hot enough here to scorch a delicate complexion, even though it was still early in the year. She had been working for Abigail Pascoe for less than two days, and already she felt like an uncaged bird as she left the tavern and began to stroll down the street towards the waterfront. She was beginning to have serious doubts about the desirability of a permanent post in Abigail's employ, because she was tight fisted as well as cold, curt and secretive. Genevra thought with indignation of the room she had been given at the King's Head. It was poky and dingy, and she felt certain that its usual purpose was to house a resident chambermaid. It just happened to be unoccupied at the moment, and she suspected that its rent had been much reduced. Also, she thought resentfully, instead of a proper luncheon, she had been provided only with a mutton pie and a mug of chocolate on a tray. Was someone so miserly likely to pay her an adequate wage, and might she not be better off, after all, in Uncle John's house?

If only, she thought, Uncle John's home had been in Gibraltar, with its air of friendliness, its reassuring British architecture and the sound of familiar English voices hailing one another in the street. She might then have been able to find respectable employment in the town, instead of being a drain on her uncle's resources.

She tried to consider life in Algiers with her relations in an optimistic light. Her Uncle John must be a kindly man, for he could easily have washed his hands of her and ignored the fact that the Court had appointed him her guardian. Then there was her cousin Sophie, who would now be eighteen, and she did have a blood relative after all, for Sophie's mother and her own had been sisters. The thought led her to that curious remark Abigail Pascoe had made about everyone having a relative in the background. Gossip had said she was going to look for a long-lost cousin, but it was curious, all the same, that she should be so very secretive about her affairs.

Genevra's wandering had brought her to the waterfront. A long mole jutted out to sea, and vessels of all kinds were tied up alongside it. Small craft, which looked to be fishing-boats, plied the waters, and all along the quay seamen were busy, loading cargo on to some of the ships or unloading others. Well-dressed gentlemen with their ladies also promenaded along the waterfront, and several Naval officers in uniform appeared to be supervising the sailors.

Then Genevra saw the man. He had been engaged in conversation with a group of seamen, but as they went on their way he stood there alone and apparently deep in thought. She studied him with covert interest. He was wearing a deep blue coat of superfine with several shoulder-capes, unbuttoned at the front, so that she could see that it was lined with silk of the same colour. His long muscular legs were encased in tightly-fitting breeches tucked inside light-coloured Hessian boots, and beneath the high points of his white shirt-collar he wore a silk cravat that matched the blue of his coat. He was too far away for his features to be defined, but he was clearly young, powerfully built, and very much in command of himself. She could not have said why she had noticed him so particularly, for he was certainly not the only splendidly dressed gentleman to be seen.

His gaze flicked over her in a look that suggested that he was not really seeing her at all as she continued towards him. He was taller even than he had at first appeared, and his broad shoulders stooped slightly, as if it had become second nature to him to avoid low ceilings. In an involuntary action he straightened them, displaying a powerful chest. His hair fell in a wayward untamed lock across his forehead, and its colour was only slightly less dark than her own.

He gazed out to sea, and then glanced around him. Suddenly, in place of the lack of awareness with which he had dismissed her before, he was looking straight at her, and moved towards her. He was clean-shaven, his skin honey-brown from exposure to the sun. His colouring ought to have struck her as being as incongruous as she had always regarded her own, and yet it did not. His eyes, set beneath straight well-marked dark brows, were an unusual shade somewhere between deep blue and grey, and reminded her of storm-clouds. No, she amended, they were the colour of smoke, and there was something sardonic in their depths, as though he regarded life as a wry joke.

As he approached, he smiled, and twin grooves appeared beside his mobile mouth with its generously curved lower lip. In a less compelling face, the grooves would have been called dimples. To Genevra's fancy he had assumed an oddly predatory look, like that of a dangerous wild animal that had finally manoeuvred its prey into position and was moving in for the kill. Which was nonsense, of course . . . She had averted her gaze and was moving to pass him, but he shot out an arm and caught her by the shoulder.

'How very fortunate that we should meet like this,' he said in a slow, lazy drawl with an intimate undertone.

'You have made a mistake . . .' Genevra began, forcing an icy edge to her voice.

The next moment she was in his arms, with his hands against her shoulder-blades crushing her to himself and his mouth invading hers with an intimacy that astonished even as it undermined her, so that she could not think coherently. This could not be happening! Total strangers did not behave with such utter lack of propriety or inhibition in broad daylight, and with numerous spectators looking on. But the slow confirmation that it was happening gave her the impetus to start struggling, and suddenly she was free, and two gentlemen in a uniform that suggested that they belonged to some form of policing patrol were holding the man's arms. 'You come along of us, sir,' one of them growled. 'Molesting of a young lady like that!'

The man shook them off, unperturbed. He appealed to Genevra, his eyes glinting at her. 'Would you say I was molesting you, ma'am?'

His cool insolence momentarily took her breath away. Before she could respond, one of her rescuers said with outrage in his voice, 'We seen you ourselves, sir! And we ain't fools. With our own eyes we seen the lady kicking and fighting!' He turned to Genevra. 'Is this here gentleman known to you, miss?'

Shaking off the renewed state of bemusement that had been creeping over her, she found her voice. 'Certainly not! I never saw him before in my life! He—He just pounced on me!'

'Ah, well.' Her assailant shrugged, his smoky eyes laughing at her. Then he made her a bow. 'My name is Trelawney, ma'am. Next time, you won't be able to claim that we are strangers.'

She watched, still shaken, as he was led away by the two uniformed men. He went willingly, even cheerfully, and she could not escape the certainty that there had been something wholly calculated about the whole incident. He had, she sensed, wanted to create a diversion for some reason of his own, and she had just happened to provide him with the means of doing so. She could not even begin to guess why such a striking-looking man should apparently have wanted to get himself arrested.

But he had been right about one thing. If they met again, they would not be strangers. Not after that kiss.

CHAPTER TWO

As she retraced her steps to the King's Head, Genevra's mind was filled with thoughts of the mysterious, disturbing and outrageous Trelawney. Who and what could he possibly be? What had been behind his bizarre behaviour? And how could a man kiss a complete stranger with such intensity and apparent passion? The memory that she herself had responded to that intensity and passion from a complete stranger caused her to abandon this particular line of thought with shame. But on her return to the tavern, she discovered that there was almost no likelihood of her encountering Trelawney again.

She had carried a jugful of hot water to Abigail's room so that she could wash before changing for dinner, when she said casually, 'I want you to pack up our trunks again, Shaw. Snatch a quick supper in the kitchen when you have finished here and tell them to add the cost to my account. We leave for Algiers on the morning tide.'

Genevra stared at her in surprise. 'The dispute with Britain has been resolved?'

'No. That might take weeks, even months. I wish to complete my business in Algiers and return to England and civilisation as soon as I possibly can. I fell into conversation with some ships' officers during luncheon, and I discovered that a Portuguese vessel is sailing tomorrow and will be calling at Algiers. Captain Dunne has agreed to refund the remainder of our passage-money, and I have secured berths for us on *Caranguejo*.'

'Oh.' Genevra studied her doubtfully. 'Will we be safe?'

'Perfectly safe. Portugal is not in dispute with the Dey of Algiers, and her shipping will not be harassed.'

'That is not precisely what I meant, Miss Pascoe. When we arrive at Algiers and are questioned, it is bound to come out that we are British and not Portuguese . . .'

'It won't matter,' Abigail said shortly. 'Britons visiting Algiers are perfectly safe, provided they observe the laws of the country. It is only on the open sea that they may be taken prisoner.'

Genevra frowned in perplexity. 'Why should that be so?'

A grim smile twisted Abigail's mouth. 'Because, by custom, the sea-raiding of the Barbary Regencies has acquired a kind of legality. World acceptance of the Corsair system has given them the right to take prisoners who sail their seas. The world would not accept their imprisoning visitors who arrive in peace on their shores.'

Genevra shook her head in bewilderment at such distinctions. 'Have you visited Algiers before, Miss Pacoe?'

'No,' Abigail said, in a voice that totally discouraged further questioning. She added, 'A fool of a serving-girl spilled port wine all over the skirt of the gown I wore at luncheon. Sponge out the stain before you retire for the night.'

Genevra tried to hide her bitter anger. Abigail Pascoe had made very sure that she herself would get by far the best of their deal. In return for no more than one night spent in a dingy, cheap room and two inadequate meals, she was demanding continued servitude until they reached Algiers.

However, the deal had been made, and Genevra conquered her resentment and made a start on her tasks. She worked until late, repacking the garments she had so recently unpacked and placing them in careful layers in Abigail's trunks. She paused, and held one of the gowns up in front of her, admiring the effect in the mirror. It looked as if it would fit her with very little adjustment, but it was highly unlikely that she would ever own anything half as fine. For an instant, as she studied her reflection, reality and logic deserted her and she found herself indulging in a fantasy in which, dressed in the gown, she was attending a glittering social occasion. A tall figure shouldered his way towards her, and Trelawney said in his low, intimate voice, his smoke-coloured eyes laughing at her, 'So we meet again, ma'am, and *this time* you cannot claim that we are strangers . . .'

She shook her head, banishing the fantasy, and continued with her work. She wondered why Abigail had decided to take so many beautiful and obviously costly clothes on a visit to a city as barbaric and uncivilised as Algiers appeared to be. Perhaps it was simply that, having had no money at all in the past, she now rejoiced in the luxury of acquiring beautiful garments for their own sake, and liked to keep them in her possession wherever she happened to be. Her glance fell on a leather valise, the key to which Abigail carried on her person. Even if one might account for the clothes, how did one explain that the woman was taking to a ramshackle country a fortune in jewellery? Abigail had unlocked the valise in Genevra's presence earlier, presumably to check over its contents, and even to her unpractised eye, the pieces had obviously been genuine. Truly, her employer was an enigma.

Everything had been packed, apart from the smart travelling clothes Abigail intended wearing in the morning and the gown she had worn at luncheon that day. Genevra had tried to sponge out the stain, without success.

Abigail entered at that moment, followed at a respectful distance by two swarthy, brawny men. 'These are crew members of *Caranguejo*,' Abigail explained. 'I could see no reason why we should encumber ourselves with the luggage in the morning, so I have arranged with Captain Perreira that it should be taken on board tonight. If they are ready, Shaw, lock the trunks.'

Genevra did as she had been instructed, and hurried to bring down her own trunk. The two Portuguese sailors had just left with their luggage when Abigail's glance fell upon the stained gown, and Genevra explained, 'The stains would not budge, Miss Pascoe. I am afraid the gown has been ruined, and I could see little point in packing it.'

Abigail scowled, and then her face cleared. 'I shall hold the tavern-keeper responsible, and refuse to pay our account! The gown need not be wasted entirely, for you may have it.'

Genevra flushed with anger. This woman did not possess an ounce of grace. When she could trust herself to speak, she said woodenly, 'Thank you, Miss Pascoe, but you have been far too generous already. And if anyone is entitled to the gown it is the serving-maid, for without a doubt she would be made to reimburse the tavern-keeper.'

Abigail appeared to have noticed no irony or contempt.

'It does not much matter to me who has the gown, now that it is of no use to me,' she said. 'You may retire now, Shaw.'

That incident sealed matters irrevocably as far as Genevra was concerned. She could not possibly work for a woman like Abigail Pascoe.

The next morning, while she packed their overnight garments and toilette articles, Abigail went to confront the landlord of the tavern about her stained gown and his account. Genevra was thankful not to have been present, but the grim, resentful expression with which the landlord regarded both of them later as they sat down to breakfast, the reddened eyes of the serving-maid and Abigail's air of triumph told their own story.

Genevra felt uncomfortable, and wished that Abigail would hurry with her breakfast. 'The captain of *Caranguejo* cannot afford to miss the tide,' she hinted.

Abigail helped herself to more scrambled eggs, and replied, 'With the breeze which has been blowing since dawn, he will have no need of the tide. In any event, he would not dare to sail without us.'

At last breakfast came to an end, and Abigail hailed a passing mule-cart in which they set out for the harbour. With a feeling of loss and of depression, Genevra looked back at Gibraltar. Its steep cobbled streets and brooding rock would be her last link with England. When she next stepped on land it would be foreign soil. She would just have to learn to fit in in Algiers, both in the Consulate with Uncle John's family and in a city whose ruler prospered by demanding blackmail payments from other nations. A glimmer of hope flickered in her heart. Algiers was a cosmopolitan city, Captain Dunne had said, with a sizeable British community. It was not altogether impossible that she might be able to find a paid position there . . .

Her thoughts were interrupted by the discovery that they had reached the waterfront. This was a different bay from the one in which *Kite* had arrived, and was not the same as that on which she had met Trelawney . . . Deliberately she quenched the thought of him. She had enough to contend with in the uncertain future stretching before her, without rendering herself even more helpless by dwelling on memories of a reckless, audacious, mesmeric stranger whom she would never see again.

While Abigail paid the driver of their vehicle, Genevra looked about for *Caranguejo*. But the Portuguese vessel was not only no longer at anchor; her gang-bridge had been hauled up and she was clearly preparing to sail. At the same moment as she realised the situation, she saw their own trunks piled neatly together on the waterfront.

The captain of the Portuguese vessel had not, after all, been prepared to wait indefinitely for them, and Abigail's complacency had been misguided. Stifling an unworthy but human feeling of malicious satisfaction, Genevra turned and called out to Abigail, who cast one look at the scene and came hurrying towards the waterfront, her eyes blazing. In a ringing voice, she called out to the crew members at work on the deck, ordering them to lower the gang-bridge immediately and to take the luggage aboard. It was clear that they did not understand her angry commands, but her obvious fury and imperious voice led one of them to fetch the captain.

The gang-bridge was lowered and a rope thrown round a bollard on the harbour. A few moments later, a man with a dark weathered skin hurried towards them. Before he could speak, Abigail demanded with frosty rage, 'What is the meaning of this, Captain Perreira? If we had arrived five minutes later you would have sailed without us! And pray do not pretend that you were concerned about missing the tide, for the breeze is more than sufficient . . .'

'No, no, *minha senhora*!' He gave her an anxious, perplexed look. 'I do only like your brother say.'

'My . . . *brother*?' For a moment Abigail appeared to be bereft of words. Then she collected herself. 'Pray explain, Captain!'

Genevra was as bewildered as she knew Abigail must be as the captain began his account in hesitant English. Early that morning, it appeared, a young gentleman had visited *Caranguejo* and asked to speak to Captain Perreira. His story was that his headstrong young sister with her companion planned to sail to Algiers to join a totally unsuitable young man with whom she fancied herself in love. But after a long talk, she had been persuaded to remain in Gibraltar, and had asked him to have her luggage removed from the vessel.

For the first time since Genevra had met her, Abigail's self-assurance appeared to have deserted her. 'This—This man,' she said at an obvious loss, 'What name did he give you?'

Captain Perreira frowned in thought. 'He tell me he is brother of young English lady, *minha senhora*, and so when I speak to him I call him *o senhor* Pascoe, because I believe it is his name.'

Abigail was beginning to recover her assertive air. 'There *is* no Senhor Pascoe, either in Gibraltar or anywhere else! What did this—this mischief-making imposter look like?'

'He young man, *minha senhora*, in very fine clothes and with—with aplomb. What I think the English would speak of as a "milord" and what we call *Vossa Excelência*. You understand me?'

Abigail nodded slowly, her expression grim. 'I understand what you are saying, but that is all. I am not related to, or acquainted with, anyone in Gibraltar, and I can think of no one with any motive for trying to prevent me from sailing for Algiers, or interfere in my affairs in such an utterly outrageous and baffling manner!'

Genevra's heart had begun to thud in her breast. *Trelawney!* It was precisely the kind of audacious meddling he would be capable of, and it had not been Abigail whom he had wished to keep in Gibraltar, but Genevra herself. And that must mean that he had been sufficiently interested in her to have made it his business, after their meeting yesterday, to discover who she was and what her plans were, and to take such brazen, calculating steps to overturn them. It was the only possible explanation. Whoever he was, whatever he was, *he*, too, had felt it—that certain something between them that had been born of a kiss that had occurred, on his part, for calculating reasons of his own. He would have learnt of Miss Pascoe's miserly nature and acted recklessly to frustrate her plans so that he could rescue Genevra.

Standing on tiptoe, peering around her, Genevra searched in vain for his tall figure. In the meantime their trunks were being loaded on board *Caranguejo* once more,

and the captain was inviting herself and Abigail to precede
him along the gang-bridge. Oh, Trelawney, she thought
with desperation, hurry and rescue me before it is too late!

'Come along, Shaw!' Abigail sounded impatient. 'Quite
enough time has been wasted by some malicious stranger
with nothing better to occupy his time or his attention!'
Slowly Genevra began to climb the gang-bridge, turning
her head constantly for a sign of Trelawney. Abigail continued, 'There were a number of young men, no doubt
off-duty officers, taking dinner in the parlour of the King's
Head last evening. It seems that one of them must have
overheard my conversation with Captain Perreira and
conceived the notion of playing a warped, pointless joke on
me.'

Trelawney, Genevra thought again, all hope withering as
she realised that he would be waiting at the King's Head,
confident that she would be returning there with Abigail at
any moment.

The captain expressed the hope that, in spite of an
unfortunate start, they would enjoy the voyage to Algiers,
but she barely heard him as she stood on the deck while they
sailed away. The sunlight turned the tears on her lashes to
prisms of colour. The rock receded into the distance and,
with it, her hope of ever seeing Trelawney again.

She tried to tell herself that a man who had behaved as he
had done was not worthy of a single thought, let alone such
a disproportionate feeling of loss for someone who was a
complete stranger. And if, as intuition insisted, it *was* he
who had tried to prevent them from leaving Gibraltar,
there was not a scrap of evidence that his intentions towards
herself had been in any way honourable. What little she did
know about him, after all, was totally to his discredit. He
had approached a completely strange girl and kissed her
with no apparent motive other than the bizarre one that
he had wished to be arrested. Why? A probable reason
suddenly occurred to her, and it began to make more and
more sense as she considered it, damning him further.

In a place like Gibraltar, smuggling would without
doubt figure prominently. It was only too easy to imagine
Trelawney as a smuggler. If he had wanted to divert attention from a craft carrying contraband in the process of being

unloaded by his underlings, what better way than by kissing a perfectly strange girl, knowing that she was bound to struggle, and so divert the attention of anyone policing the waterfront to the two of them? Yes, she decided forlornly, she had probably been spared a great deal of future grief by being carried beyond Trelawney's reach. He was clearly not a man to be trusted in any way.

As the distance between themselves and Gibraltar grew, Genevra concentrated with all her might on rooting out any stray thoughts of Trelawney, but the voyage itself continued to defeat her efforts. Captain Perreira's hope that they would enjoy it was turning out to have been exceedingly hollow. There was nothing to cushion their boredom and discomfort, and even the miserable conditions which they were forced to share did not alter the relationship between them.

Abigail did not unbend in the slightest from her secretive and imperious attitude: she volunteered no confidences and invited none, apart from saying in a matter-of-fact voice, 'I have decided that, under my guidance and training, you would make a passable personal maid. But if your uncle in Algiers is also your legal guardian, his permission would be needed. What is his name?'

Genevra hesitated. Intuition warned her that if she were to state at this stage that nothing would induce her to accept the post, Abigail would find ways of making what already promised to be an uncomfortable voyage well-nigh unendurable.

'My uncle is called John . . . McDonald,' she answered at last. She would wait until the ship had docked before she spurned Abigail's offer, and, she reassured herself, she would be far too angry and outraged to track down the J. McDonald of whom Captain Dunne had spoken.

Abigail did not leave the subject there. 'From what you have told me,' she said, 'it seems clear that your uncle's second wife would welcome the chance of being relieved of responsibility towards you. Your uncle, however, may have reservations. Was he particularly fond of you in the past?'

Genevra tried to hide her resentment at the way in which Abigail was taking it for granted that she herself would welcome the post. She also wished that she would drop the subject of Uncle John, but since she seemed intent upon probing the matter, Genevra considered it wise to volunteer some judicious information instead.

'As far as I know,' she said, "my uncle and I are strangers. I dare say he might have met me when I was a small child, but I have no memory of it. He has spent most of his adult life abroad, and since his first wife, my Aunt Clare, died, we have exchanged only a few letters.'

Abigail nodded. 'Good. He is not likely to be greatly interested in your affairs.' To Genevra's relief, she did not pursue the matter further.

As the voyage got under way, the smell of the spicy, greasy food being prepared in the galley began to permeate their cabin, and both Abigail and Genevra were forced to flee up on deck for much of the time. Four days after they had sailed from Gibraltar, they were on deck one morning when they saw a vessel approaching, flying the Portuguese flag. Her deck was completely deserted apart from one man at the tiller, and when she came into hailing distance, he began to engage the captain of *Caranguejo* in what sounded like friendly banter. The voyage was so uncomfortable and tedious that any diversion was welcome, and Abigail and Genevra watched with detached interest. Whatever had been agreed between the two men on their respective vessels, the three-masted ship hauled up on *Caranguejo*. At the same time, the man at the tiller made vigorous gestures to her captain.

'He wants us to heave to,' Abigail remarked with annoyance. 'I hope we are not going to waste time here at anchor while the two Portuguese captains exchange gossip!'

The captain of *Caranguejo* was responding, and the two ships drifted to a stop close together. Genevra noticed that several brass cannon positioned in the ports in the other vessel's side were pointing directly at them, and this would have been an alarming sight had the ship not been another Portuguese vessel stopping for a friendly exchange.

The next moment she froze in disbelief as the air was split with noise, and the deck of the other ship was no longer deserted but swarming with men who had leapt up from the gunwales. At almost the same time the Portuguese flag was being hauled down, and the masts and the poop were being emblazoned with flags of exotic colours, embroidered with stars, crescents, crossed swords and, most ominously of all, the head of a turbanned Turk.

'Is—Is it a Corsair ship?' Genevra faltered, hardly able to believe in the reality of the men who were swarming over their own deck. There was no sign now of the helmsman, dressed in European clothes, who had hailed the captain of *Caranguejo* in Portuguese.

'Yes.' Abigail's face was pale, with a look of intense concentration. Her hands were clenched, their knuckles showing white. 'Come. We must hurry below!'

But terror kept Genevra rooted to the spot. A small rowing-boat was being swung out from the Corsair ship, and after it had been launched, a number of men climbed down a rope-ladder. She stared in fascinated fear as two of them plied the oars while the others brandished their swords above their heads in a menacing manner as they approached *Caranguejo*, all the while uttering blood-curdling shouts.

'Come below!' Abigail commanded in a tense voice, turning back and taking Genevra by the arm. Together they hastened to the companionway, and Genevra was propelled down and inside their cabin. Abigail locked the door behind them.

'I—I thought you said we would be safe aboard a Portuguese vessel,' Genevra began, trying to control the fit of trembling that had seized her.

'We should have been. Something has gone wrong.' Abigail was clenching and unclenching her hands. She appeared to come to a decision. 'Open your trunk.'

'Wh—Why?' Genevra stammered, as Abigail reached for the valise containing her jewellery.

'Because we have to hide my jewellery inside your trunk. Quickly, now!' Genevra stared at her. What had been happening seemed like a kind of nightmare, and this command appeared to be the most bizarre twist of all. 'You dolt!' Abigail raged. 'Unlock your trunk this minute!'

'I—I don't understand. . .'

'*Then don't try to!* Just do as you are told. I am ordering you to hide my jewellery inside your trunk, Shaw!'

The angry arrogance and the curt use of her surname

penetrated Genevra's shock and helpless disbelief. She flung up her head. 'I don't know what you have in mind, Miss Pascoe, but from what I've learnt about you, I'm sure it must be something which would benefit *you* . . .'

Her voice was blotted out by the sound of footsteps clattering down the companionway, accompanied by unintelligible shouting. Genevra swallowed hard, and felt her scalp prickling. An image rose in her mind of those wild-looking men, who were banging on the cabin doors now, and it would not be long before they arrived here.

Several different expressions flickered across Abigail's face—rage, frustration, and then desperate urgency. 'Listen to me, please, Shaw,' she said tensely. 'We only have a few minutes. We are about to be taken prisoner, and only payment of a ransom would free us. If the Corsairs found the jewellery in my possession, they would realise the extent of my probable wealth and would bleed me white before they let me go!'

'So—you wish them to attempt to bleed me instead?' Genevra stifled rising hysterical laughter. Unbelievably, with the Corsairs almost at their door, Abigail still thought she had the right to use for her own ends the maid-servant she had acquired so cheaply.

'No!' Abigail gripped her by the shoulders. '*Think!* They would take one look at you and realise that you are penniless. They would not even waste time on a careful examination of your trunk. *My* trunks, on the other hand . . .' Her voice took on a taut, frenzied edge. 'You fool, haven't you understood? If we could keep them from looting my jewellery, it could be used to pay a ransom for both of us! You would benefit equally! Or do you expect your uncle to ransom you? From what you have told me about your relationship, I would doubt it!'

The taunt about Uncle John struck home. Even if he were willing and able to pay a ransom for her, she could not possibly face him with a situation in which it would be expected of him. Realising that there had been more than self-interest in Abigail's command, Genevra hurriedly pulled out her trunk, flinging its contents on the floor.

The jewellery was tipped out of the valise, and Genevra began to stuff the pieces inside her only spare pair of boots.

She placed them at the bottom of the trunk, and had begun to cover them with her worn, made-over gowns and underclothing when she realised that Abigail was rooting feverishly through her more personal belongings.

'What are you doing?' Abigail had taken an untramed water-colour sketch of Genevra's father and placed it to one side with some faded flowers pressed between two thin sheets of parchment, a memento of her mother. Abigail added a small bundle of letters, most of them notes of sympathy written after the Rector's death. 'Those are private and personal!' Genevra objected.

'Kindly use your common sense!' Abigail rapped. 'An empty valise would immediately arouse suspicion. One would expect it to contain *something*—if not valuables, then items of sentimental worth. I do not possess anything of that nature.'

Even if Genevra had wanted to argue, there was no time, for Abigail had hardly finished throwing the few mementoes inside the valise and shut the catch when there was a rapping on the door. Genevra stood transfixed with renewed terror at first, and then tension gradually began to drain from her as the rapping was followed by a man's voice from outside with a reassuringly refined accent.

'Oblige me, ladies, by opening the door!'

'An Englishman!' she exclaimed, dizzy with incredulous relief. 'A British ship must have spotted the Corsairs and come to our aid . . .'

Abigail interrupted her by shaking her head, saying in a staccato whisper, 'A renegade! A treacherous European turned Turk. Algiers is riddled with them.'

Genevra gave her a blank stare, understanding nothing. The notion of an *Englishman* throwing in his lot with what were little more than marauding pirates was too fantastic to be entertained. No, that cultured voice outside could belong only to a friend who had come to assure them that they were safe.

But the next moment the door crashed inwards, and a coal-black man waving a scimitar catapulted into the room. Behind him came a young man dressed in robes and with his head partly covered by a loose hood that left one side of his face in shadow. Genevra had an impression of blue eyes and tawny-gold hair beneath the hood, but then her attention was drawn by the sword tucked inside the folds of the Englishman's waistband. He turned towards Abigail. The side of his face which was visible showed finely-chiselled features of classical beauty, a high cheekbone and lips as generously curved as that of any girl.

'My name is Rupert Runcorn,' he said, making Abigail a bow. 'My apologies, ma'am. It is a matter of deep regret to me to find myself in a situation such as this, involving a young Englishwoman of breeding as well as of beauty.'

To Genevra his pretty speech, delivered in cultured accents, and his obvious charm only added to the nightmare. Her feelings were further heightened by Abigail's wholly unexpected reaction to the man. She appeared to be mesmerised, and made no move to object as he reached for her hand and brought it to his lips. But as he dropped it and lifted his head she recoiled, making a sound of shock.

Runcorn tossed back his head, and as the hood fell to his shoulders Genevra saw, for the first time, what had caused Abigail to cry out. In cruel contrast to the classical, almost perfect, beauty of one side of his face the other, hitherto cast in shadow by the hood, bore a jagged scar running from his cheekbone to the corner of his mouth, lifting his upper lip slightly in what appeared to be a permanent sneer.

He made Abigail another bow, and said in a hard voice, 'Quite so. I had forgotten for a moment to see myself as others—particularly genteel young Englishwomen—must see me.'

Turning aside, he spoke rapidly in a strange tongue to the black Corsair, who picked up their trunks and removed them from the cabin. Genevra stared unblinkingly at Runcorn, who had not paid her the slightest attention.

Because the entire scope of the situation in which they found themselves was too grotesque to be taken in fully, her mind started to fix upon relative trivialities. What must it have been like for a young man to come by the scar, and was it the very kind of reaction he had received from Abigail that had caused him to throw in his lot with seafaring brigands? Genevra caught herself almost feeling sorry for him, and reminded herself forcibly, He is a Corsair, come to take prisoners for their ransom value.

Still ignoring Genevra, Runcorn spoke to Abigail.
'*Caranguejo*'s captain was only too ready to volunteer
information about the wealthy young Englishwoman and
her maid on board. He realised that if this raid netted a
prize like yourself, we would be unlikely to claim that his
Mediterranean passport is a forgery and so relieve him of
his entire cargo. I have to ask the two of you, Miss Pascoe,
to follow me on to the deck . . .'

'*I am not Miss Pascoe!*'

Abigail's vehement voice, with a note of genuine-
sounding distress in it, reverberated through Genevra's
mind, making little sense at first. It was only when Abigail
pointed an accusing finger at herself that a glimmer of
understanding began to dawn. The escalating horror of the
situation struck her fully as Abigail went on, '*She* is Miss
Pascoe. My—My mistress forced me to change clothes with
her, sir, when we learnt that Corsairs were aboard.'

Genevra was struck dumb. Too late she was beginning to
understand the ruthless treachery behind Abigail's insist-
ence that the jewellery should be packed inside her own
trunk. There was a very good chance that it would not be
discovered after all; if it were, it would simply provide
added evidence that Genevra was not the impoverished
maid which she seemed, and *she* would be the one who
attracted an impossibly high ransom. If the jewellery were
overlooked altogether, Abigail, posing as the maid, would
regain possession of it and find some way of using part of it
to pay a ransom for herself, leaving Genevra to her fate.

'I—I am . . .' Genevra began in a whisper, passing her
tongue over her dry lips, unable to go on as other implications of Abigail's betrayal began to crowd in. If the Corsairs
believed her to have untold wealth in England, what would
they do to persuade her to have it handed over to them? She
made another attempt to force out the words to tell Rupert
Runcorn what had happened, but he was still paying her
no attention. He had noticed the valise, half concealed
beneath one of the bunks, which the black Corsair had
overlooked. He picked it up and opened it.

'They—They are my few precious mementoes,' Abigail
said in a tremulous voice as he began to inspect the contents. 'You will see, sir, that the letters are addressed to

Miss Genevra Shaw—and that is who I am, companion and maid-servant to Miss Abigail Pascoe.'

'Indeed?' He spoke absently. 'Exchanging clothes with one's servant is, of course, a trick tried many times before in these circumstances. The ransom for the so-called servant is set low, and he or she arranges for it to be paid. The *real* servant languishes in Algiers, living in hope of a ransom being paid by a grateful employer who, more often than not, conveniently forgets about the poor wretch and dooms him or her to remain a prisoner for life.'

Genevra's blood froze. What a fool she had been to trust Abigail! She heard her say with convincing distress, 'She —She did promise to pay a ransom for me, sir, but I did not believe her.'

'Nor I you, ma'am,' Runcorn interrupted. He gave Abigail a smile, which the scarred corner of his mouth turned into a grimace. 'Distasteful as I find it to cast doubt upon the word of a lady, I believe you are the mistress and the other young woman the maid.'

'You are wrong!' Abigail's voice had risen. 'The evidence is staring you in the face!'

'So it is,' Runcorn agreed, glancing at the valise. 'Would a poor serving-maid transport her mementoes inside a valise made of the finest leather? A valise, moreover, bearing her monogram embossed in gold? The monogram will require close scrutiny to decipher it, but I am confident that among any other initials there will also be revealed an *A* and a *P*.'

Dismay showed on Abigail's face, followed by rage. She opened her mouth to speak, but at that moment they were interrupted by the arrival of another Corsair, who addressed Runcorn. He nodded, and turned to Abigail. 'Please, Miss Pascoe, let us not waste time in further, futile, argument. You and your maid are to join the other prisoners on deck immediately.'

Now that the trap that Genevra had perceived closing about her had so unexpectedly been demolished by Rupert Runcorn, she found her voice, and also experienced a faint return of spirit. 'This is a Portuguese ship,' she said defiantly. 'There is an undisputed treaty between Portugal and Algiers.'

'Maybe so.' For the first time Runcorn fixed his attention upon her with speculation in his deep-set blue eyes. 'You are uncommonly well spoken for a poor serving-maid! I am wondering whether you, too, are precisely what you appear to be.'

'I have told you,' Abigail began in a high, desperate voice. 'She is . . .'

'I am Genevra Shaw, and in spite of being well spoken I am quite as poor as I appear,' she interrupted firmly. 'There is no one in the world who would be able to pay a ransom for me.'

Runcorn appeared to have lost interest in her. 'Your mistress, Miss Pascoe, will be held liable for your ransom also.' He dismissed the matter.

Her face contorted, Abigail screamed, 'I am not Miss Pascoe! *I am not!*'

Runcorn's mouth twisted in that grimace which made it impossible to define the nature of his smile. 'There, ma'am,' he told Abigail. 'You have no need to distress yourself. You clearly possess the means by which to ensure your own freedom and that of your maid. Go up top now with her before my patience, like that of my Turkish friend here, becomes exhausted.'

Abigail began to move automatically towards the door where the Corsair was waiting, but Genevra stood her ground and addressed Runcorn. 'You have no right to take us prisoner! We are sailing on a Portuguese vessel!'

He shrugged. 'Times are hard, now that British ships are avoiding our waters. You and your mistress may have been sailing on a Portuguese ship, but you are not Portuguese nationals, and neither are the Genoese and the Sicilians, so you are the legal prisoners-of-war of the Dey of Algiers, and I must ask you to go on deck immediately.'

It was clearly useless to continue arguing. Outside the cabin, Portuguese passengers stood in their doorways and looked on with a mixture of pity, and gratitude that they themselves were not in any danger. On deck, Genevra and Abigail joined the others who had been rounded up. Many of the Genoese and Sicilians were weeping hopelessly. The crew stood by in attitudes of fear and impotence as the Corsairs flung the possessions of the prisoners into the rowing-boat and ferried it to their vessel, where it was hauled aboard before the boat returned for the prisoners, who were taken on board in batches.

Waiting their turn on the deck of *Caranguejo*, Genevra looked at Abigail. 'I—I can scarcely find words to express my feelings about what you tried to to,' she began.

Abigail ignored her. She was clutching the valise and staring unblinkingly ahead. Genevra glanced at the Corsair ship, and suddenly Abigail's treachery paled into insignificance before the unknown fate which awaited both of them. 'What will happen to us?' she asked. 'You seem to know so much. Will they . . . ill use the women?'

Abigail did not answer, or give any indication that she had heard. Her face was a mask behind which her feelings were concealed. Or perhaps, Genevra thought, it was simply that she was in a state of deep shock.

Batches of prisoners were being forced, with threatening swishes through the air of scimitars and swords, to climb down the rope-ladder to the rowing-boat. Surrounded by Corsairs, there was no hope of escape, but even so Genevra found herself instinctively following Abigail's example and holding back so that they were among the last of the prisoners to be ferried to the Corsair ship.

Runcorn brought up the rear, and tried to relieve Abigail of the valise. 'You will need both hands free for the descent,' he pointed out.

'No! I shall manage!' She pushed one wrist through the handle of the valise so that she would be able to grip the rope-ladder with both hands.

'Now, I wonder,' Runcorn mused, 'why you should insist so obstinately on keeping hold of a valise that contains someone else's mementoes. Can it be because it contains something else far more valuable? A negotiable bank draft, perhaps, tucked away inside a secret recess?'

As Genevra preceded them down the rope-ladder, she thought she understood what Abigail had in mind. By making the valise appear to be important, she was hoping that their trunks—and Genevra's in particular—would not be searched too closely. It had to be something like that, for it was difficult to negotiate the ladder even while unencumbered.

Genevra boarded the rowing-boat without mishap and obeyed the gestured command of a Corsair to sit down. As she took her place, she watched first Abigail and then Runcorn climbing aboard also. Abigail still had the valise threaded upon her wrist and he appeared content to allow her to retain temporary custody of it.

The men at the rowlocks had just lifted their oars when Abigail suddenly reached out for the rope ladder still hanging from the side. Several of the Corsairs bellowed at her and one of them stood up, rocking the boat, and tried to dislodge her fingers. But with seemingly demonic strength she hung on by one hand, and at the same time she swung the valise at the head of the Corsair, who tripped and fell, so that the boat rocked violently. She took advantage of the moment by swinging one leg over the side as the boat tilted, her foot scrabbling to find a rung on the ladder.

Runcorn shouted at her not to be foolish, for there was no hope of escape. She ignored him, and succeeded in heaving her other leg over the side also. He leant over to grab at her, but she began to struggle like someone possessed. With a mighty heave, he succeeded in prising her away from the ladder, but the boat tilted at a crazy angle. The air was rent with screams and oaths as prisoners and Corsairs were spilt into the water.

Genevra flailed about wildly for a few seconds, her skirts billowing and helping momentarily to keep her afloat until, inevitably, they became sodden and began to drag her into the cold, churning depths.

Her last coherent but idiotic thought was, Now I shall never know who Trelawney is, and why he kissed me that day.

CHAPTER THREE

HER LUNGS FELT as if they were bursting and there was a roaring in her ears. Genevra knew instinctively that she was about to perish. Then, suddenly, she was no longer being borne downwards. Strong, rough hands were pushing her towards the surface, and as her head emerged above the water she began to splutter and cough. She could see nothing, for her eyes seemed to be on fire. An arm enclosed her waist and she began, mindlessly, to struggle. But its owner was stronger than she and retained its grip, and she found herself being heaved and pulled along the surface, sometimes swallowing great draughts of sea-water in her unreasoning resistance. She was caught by the shoulders, and other hands hauled her from the water. Choking and coughing, blinded by the stinging effect of the salt on her eyes, she was not fully aware that she was back on the rowing-boat until someone was supporting her while she retched violently and vomited over its side.

Slowly, as her shock and terror and confusion diminished slightly, Genevra took in the reality of the situation. Like herself, three male prisoners and one woman were soaked to the skin, shivering and coughing as they recovered from their ordeal. Some of the other women prisoners were weeping and a Genoese girl was being heaved aboard the boat in a state similar to her own.

Caranguejo had made no preparations to sail, and her crew and some passengers were standing by the rail, watching as the Corsairs emerged from the water for several seconds to draw breath before diving again, and she recognised Rupert Runcorn from his tawny-coloured hair as among those still in the water. They were searching for someone who had not yet been rescued . . .

Abigail! For the first time Genevra realised that she was not on board. Runcorn had obviously lost his grip on her as they were plunged into the water. Floating away in the

distance, she could see the valise which contained everything she had possessed to remind her of her parents and
her own past: the valise which had been threaded upon
Abigail's wrist when she made her desperate, futile attempt
to climb back on board *Caranguejo*. Having decided to
make the attempt, why had Abigail kept such a stubborn
hold on it when it could only have hampered her? Was it
possible that Runcorn had been right, and that it contained
a hidden bank draft? As she sat there, shivering, she
saw the men diving in a pattern which made it clear that they
were following the drifting course of the valise in their
search for Abigail.

Frowning, Genevra tried to make sense of what had
happened. Could the buoyant, almost empty valise possibly
have enabled Abigail to keep her head above water while it
remained attached to her wrist? That certainly seemed to
be the reasoning of the Corsairs who were searching for
her. But if the valise *had* supported Abigail's weight for a
while it was quite clear that it was no longer doing so, for it
was floating freely. It had worked itself loose from Abigail's
wrist, and was sinking visibly. When it finally disappeared
beneath the surface, the Corsairs gave up their search for
Abigail, and only Runcorn swam on and dived in an
attempt at retrieving it. He came up again, empty-handed,
and was clearly spent as he began to swim back to the boat.
The oarsmen cleaved through the water to pick him up, and
he was hauled aboard, his breath coming in rasping gasps.

Genevra was trembling as violently as if she had a fever,
and it was only partly because of her wet clothing. She
looked at the Corsair ship which they were approaching,
and she almost envied poor drowned Abigail, who had died
because any risk had seemed preferable to her having to
part with her fortune. Abigail had been spared whatever
terrors the future was to hold.

If only Trelawney's outrageous, self-indulgent scheme
had succeeded, and she and Abigail had been prevented
from sailing on *Caranguejo*! No matter how dishonourable
his intentions, at least Abigail would not now be dead, and
the only dangers facing Genevra herself would have been of
a moral or emotional nature. An entirely different notion
occured to her. Could there have been more behind

Trelawney's interference than a desire to keep in Gibraltar a stranger who had stirred his interest? Could he have guessed, or feared, what awaited them if they sailed on the Portuguese vessel? As the smuggler she suspected him to be, he would know these waters intimately. He would be aware that the Corsairs did not scruple to harass even vessels of those countries with which they had undisputed treaties.

She gave a ragged sigh, and dismissed the thought. None of it mattered now. Rupert Runcorn's eyes were red from the sea-water, the scar on his cheek showing livid. That scar rendered the grimace which he gave her unreadable. Did it express a tinge of remorse, or was he solely concerned with the loss of a valuable prisoner, and of the valise he had believed to contain a bank draft? Or was he, perhaps, thinking that now her mistress was dead and unable to ransom her, Genevra had become utterly worthless to the Corsairs? The fact that she *was* worthless now gave her the only spark of hope in what was becoming an increasingly spine-chilling situation.

The rowing-boat had reached the Corsair vessel, and the prisoners were made to climb on board. The sun scorched down on the deck, so that Genevra ceased shivering with cold, and her main physical discomfort was the heaviness of her wet outer clothing that steamed in the sun. But she felt shocked, terrified and still filled with the horror of knowing that Abigail had drowned. She stood on the deck with the other prisoners and looked around her. The Corsairs appeared to be an astonishing mixture of races. Apart from obvious Moors and Turks, there were men with blond Nordic looks and several with ruddy complexions and blue or grey eyes.

She remembered that Abigail had talked about Algiers being riddled with European renegades, and she suddenly became aware that, apart from the Portuguese who had hailed the captain of *Caranguejo* and lulled him into a sense of false security, there must also have been someone among the boarding party who could communicate with the Genoese and Sicilians in their own language. The Corsairs' forethought was grimly impressive, as were their preparations for any nationalities among their victims.

Rupert Runcorn had disappeared, presumably to change out of his wet clothing, but the prisoners who had been tipped into the water were accorded no such consideration. Some of the other Corsairs indicated that they were all to follow them to the poop. A canvas awning had been rigged up to provide shade, and beneath this, seated cross-legged on a richly patterned rug and smoking a curious long, bent pipe partly submerged in a glass container of water, was a dark-skinned man dressed in a white cotton robe and a red turban. At one side of him a Negro wearing a heavy chain round an ankle was brewing coffee on a small oil-stove, and at the other side stood a man with an abacus. As the prisoners filed past, they were counted.

The man with the pipe then addressed them, his meaning translated in turn by interpreters so that all the prisoners would understand. They would be well treated, he said. The Algerians were honourable men who behaved fairly towards their prisoners-of-war. As if to illustrate this, he snapped a command at the Negro slave, who began to fill tiny cups with very sweet, strong coffee and offered them to the captives.

Genevra turned to Rupert Runcorn, who had re-appeared wearing dry pantaloons, a collarless shirt and a red cap. 'Tell the captain that my mistress has drowned', she urged. 'Tell him that there is no one in the world, now, who would pay for my release, and I am not worth keeping as a prisoner . . .'

'Every prisoner,' he interrupted, 'has a way of turning out to be worth *something* to *someone*.'

'I assure you . . .' she began desperately, but was cut short by an urgent shout from somewhere else on deck.

The sails of another ship had been sighted, and suddenly everyone was bustling about and the Corsair vessel changed course. It was obviously another potential victim, and the decks had to be cleared of tell-tale prisoners and Corsairs, and a friendly flag run up to deceive the other captain. The prisoners were herded down below, separated into sexes. The half-dozen or so women were gestured, with respectful bows and no signs of salacious leers or other familiarity, to enter a small compartment with tiers of bunks. The door was locked upon them.

While some of the Genoese and Sicilian women fell, weeping and keening, upon the bunks, others began to search through their luggage, which had been thrown, higgledy-piggledy, into a pile at one end. There was no sign of Genevra's trunk, or of those which had belonged to Abigail. No doubt, she thought with numb resignation, they were being kept aside for special scrutiny and the jewellery stuffed inside her boots would inevitably be discovered.

The few other women who had also been pitched into the water found dry clothes and changed into them. When they became aware that Genevra's luggage was not there, several of the Genoese offered her a change of clothes from their own meagre wardrobes. Gratefully she accepted, and promised, by means of mime, to return the borrowed garments as soon as her own had dried sufficiently for her to change back into them. But as she began to divest herself of her sodden gown and petticoats, she discovered that the combined effect of the sea-water and the rough handling she had received from her rescuer had had a devastating effect upon the already worn fabrics, and as she struggled out of them the material all but disintegrated. Dismayed, she decided not to try to remove her shift in case that should also fall apart.

With sympathetic gestures, the donors of the dry clothes indicated that she was welcome to keep them. She indicated her thanks and put on the peasant garments, which consisted of a kilted skirt in a drab shade of green, a plain white cotton blouse and a sleeveless jacket of figured cotton in muted colours. A pair of sturdy but clumsy boots replaced her own, which she knew would be rock hard and useless when they dried out. The donated skirt was too short and far too wide at the waist, and someone offered her a frayed neckerchief to use as a belt to hold it up. The sleeves of the blouse were also too short and had to be left unbuttoned, and the jacket hung dispiritedly to below her waist. But the clothes were dry and clean, and in the circumstances in which they all found themselves, her appearance was the very least of Genevra's concerns.

As the other women settled down to bewail their fate, Genevra sat in wretched silence on the edge of one of the

bunks and contemplated her own future. At least the
Corsairs did not appear to harbour immoral designs on
the female prisoners, and that was one small comfort. Also,
the Negro slave who had offered them coffee had looked
well fed and even cheerful in spite of the heavy chain round
his ankle, so it was probably true that prisoners were
treated reasonably. All the same, it was grotesque that, in
the enlightened year of 1816, ordinary passengers could
be forcibly removed from the vessels in which they were
sailing and taken prisoner by the arbitrary command of the
ruler of such a ramshackle country as Algeria obviously
was.

Abigail had said that it was specifically to raise revenue
from the ransoms that the Corsairs sought prisoners in
the first place. While Abigail was alive and a prisoner,
Genevra's fate had been bound up with hers, for she could
well believe Runcorn's statement that the Corsairs would
have forced Abigail to pay her maid's ransom as well. But
now Abigail was dead, and he had said that every prisoner
was worth something to someone. And who in the world,
Genevra wondered despairingly, would or could pay even a
modest ransom for herself? Certainly not Uncle John, who
owed her nothing and who had asked her not even to reveal
the fact that there was a family connection between them.
From now on, if questioned, she would have to adhere to
the story that she had no personal reason whatever for
sailing to Algiers. She had simply accompanied her mistress, Abigail Pascoe, who had kept to herself her motive
for making the voyage.

Genevra could sense that the ship had hove to, and there
was a good deal of noise going on, but if more prisoners had
been taken, none of them was a woman, for no one came to
the cabin until after the vessel was in motion again. Then
the door was unlocked, and Rupert Runcorn stood framed
in the opening.

'Miss Pascoe, please come with me,' he said.

For a moment Genevra failed to respond. Then she
realised that it had been a slip of the tongue on his part. She
stood up. 'I assume you are addressing me?'

He bowed perfunctorily. 'Yes, indeed.' He inspected
her, dressed as she was in her ill-fitting clothes, but the

permanent sneer at one corner of his mouth made it impossible to tell whether he found amusement in the sight. He went on, 'I have to take you to see the Rais, so that he may calculate your market value.'

She blenched. It was almost unbelievable and deeply degrading to be assessed in order to establish what she might be worth to someone else in terms of pounds, shillings and pence. 'What is a Rais?' she asked as she followed him from the cabin.

'It is the title by which the captain of a Corsair ship is known, ma'am.'

She supposed that the Turk with the bubble pipe wished to question each prisoner separately, and had begun to move to the companionway leading to the deck where he had been seated under an awning. But Runcorn took her arm, and halted her.

'In here, please. I am sure you will wish to change out of those clothes into something of your own before being inspected and questioned by the Rais,' he said.

He had thrown open the door of another cabin as he spoke, but Genevra turned upon him, fear and despair temporarily blotted out by anger. 'If you imagine that I care a snap of my fingers for what your ruffianly Rais might think of my appearance . . .'

He interrupted her with what was obviously false sympathy in his voice, since he was one of the human predators responsible for her capture. 'I am afraid that your own wishes do not enter into the matter. In order to judge your value, the Rais must inspect you dressed in your own clothes and not in bits and pieces borrowed from others.'

He had been urging her inside the cabin as he spoke, closing the door behind them. Set out on one of its two bunks were Abigail's open trunks. Their contents had obviously been subjected to scrutiny, and she glanced around, searching for her own battered trunk.

Runcorn said, 'I shall wait for you outside, Miss Pascoe, while you change into something suitable.'

She turned slowly to face him. This time it could not have been a mere slip of the tongue! 'I don't know what you are about,' she said with emphasis. 'But you are perfectly well aware that I am *not* Miss Pascoe.'

'Are you not?' Once again, the scar on his face made it impossible to define his smile. 'The dead woman said you were.'

A tingling sensation travelled along Genevra's spine. 'She was lying! You knew it as soon as you saw my personal mementoes inside *her* expensive valise—where she had placed them against my wishes!'

'A valise,' he murmured, gazing up at the bulkheads, 'which is now at the bottom of the ocean. There is nothing whatever to prove that the dead woman had been lying, and I no longer believe that she was. The valise was probably a gift presented to Miss Genevra Shaw by a former employer. There had been sufficient time for the two of you to exchange clothing, and I believe that is what happened.'

'It did *not*!' Genevra cried, appalled at the trap which was, once again, yawning at her feet. 'Whatever you may believe, I am quite penniless, and there is no one in the world who would pay a ransom for me!'

'The Rais will be the judge of that. And since he owns fifteen per cent of you, it will matter very much to him whether he will be placing on the market wealthy Miss Abigail Pascoe or her penniless maid.'

Genevra sucked in her breath, overwhelmed by the hideous enormity of the statement. 'He—He owns fifteen per cent of *me*?'

Runcorn nodded. 'The other eighty-five per cent is owned by a group of merchants and Janissaries who invested money in the raids.'

She stared at him in horror. It was one thing to know that, by custom and world acceptance, the ruler of Algiers was able to take prisoners and demand ransoms for them. It was quite another to be told that she was an investment, with shares in her person held by a group of men who had, as a business transaction, financed the raids and expected a profit.

Runcorn became brisk. 'Now, Miss Pascoe, kindly change your clothes so that I may take you for an audience with the Rais.'

'I am not Miss Pascoe!' she cried, close to hysteria. 'If I change into anything, it will be into clothing of my own! Where is my trunk?'

'If you are referring to the battered one that belonged to Miss Shaw,' Runcorn shrugged, 'I am afraid that, by an unfortunate accident, it was dropped overboard when the baggage was being loaded on the ship.'

'I . . .' she began, and stopped. The full force of what had happened, and why, was beginning to sink into her mind. As the only English-speaking Corsair who had boarded *Caranguejo*, Runcorn would have been responsible to his Rais for her own capture and that of Abigail. After she had drowned, Runcorn had realised that he would be held accountable for the loss of such a prize. He must have decided, even while they were still on the rowing-boat, to pass Genevra off as her wealthy mistress and so avoid the wrath of his Rais. When he had disappeared to change his own wet clothing, he must have taken the opportunity to throw her own trunk overboard so that she would be forced to wear Abigail's clothes in order to appear, from the outset, to be wealthy . . .

The jewellery! Even if he had taken the time to make a swift inspection of her trunk, he must have missed the jewellery, or he would surely have mentioned it when she told him she was penniless. So he was hoping to placate and befool his Rais by presenting her as Miss Abigail Pascoe, whose clothes made it clear that she possessed wealth —and, in his efforts, he had thrown overboard a fortune in jewellery! Hysterical laughter bubbled in Genevra's throat and overcame her. Runcorn hesitated for a moment, and then he slapped her cheek. Her laughter changed to tears, and dimly she heard him mutter an apology and urge her to stop crying and change her clothes.

'L—Leave me alone!' she sobbed.

He cursed under his breath. She was aware that he was rummaging through one of Abigail's trunks and that he had taken out a gown of lilac silk. 'Put this on, Miss Pascoe.'

'No!' she cried through her tears. 'I won't! I am not . . .'

'Then you leave me no choice.' He moved, pushing her into a corner of the cabin, flinging the lilac gown down on a bunk. He held her fast with one hand while the other divested her of the sleeveless jacket. Then he began to pull at the laced-up fastenings of the blouse, and fury halted Genevra's despairing tears. She lowered her head, sinking her teeth into his hand. He let out a yell of pain but did not stop. She kicked at his legs and twisted her free hand in his hair, and he responded by pinning her head under his arm while he continued to undress her by force. Her wet hair had come loose and was blinding her. She could hear the fabric of the neckerchief-belt tearing as he pulled it from her waist. She had begun to weep again, but this time with rage and humiliation as she felt the skirt falling to the floor, leaving her clothed in nothing but her still slightly damp shift.

The door of the cabin opened. Runcorn's body was between it and herself, and he was so preoccupied with trying to manoeuvre her into a position where he would be able to dress her forcibly in Abigail's lilac gown that he seemed unaware of any intrusion. But a moment later there came the sickening thud of bone crushing against bone, and she was free and reeling drunkenly on her feet while Rupert Runcorn's body lay slumped on the floor.

Her vision clearing, she blinked in numb disbelief at her rescuer. He looked as striking and as immaculate as when she had first seen him, with only that wayward lock of his dark hair suggesting that he had recently been engaged in anything as physical as knocking a man down. Trelawney's smoky eyes surveyed her, travelling from the mass of jet-black curls tumbling about her face to her shoulders and lingering on the clearly visible curves of her body beneath the thin, clinging damp shift.

At first Genevra could not bring herself to believe in the reality of him, when she had so often conjured up a vision of him in her imagination. But gradually the truth came to her. That latest vessel that the Corsairs had attacked must have been his smuggler's ship, and he had been taken prisoner, too. A breathtaking thought struck her. Could he have been following *Caranguejo*, to make sure that the girl he had kissed in Gibraltar remained safe? And had he deliberately allowed himself to be captured so that he could rescue her? It did not surprise her at all that he should have escaped from where the men were confined, for if ever there was a man who would retain control over his own destiny it was he, and Fate had clearly ordained that her own destiny should be linked with his. His appraising look had changed to a slight frown, as though he were contemplating how best to free himself and her from the clutches of the Corsairs.

Mindless of her state of undress, she flung herself at him. 'Oh, I am so overjoyed to see you! I never dreamt . . .' She broke off, remembering his frowning look, and continued feverishly, 'If we waited until dark, perhaps you and I could . . .'

She was prevented from completing the suggestion that darkness might give them a chance of stealing the Corsairs' rowing-boat, because Trelawney interrupted her with a disconcerting sound of muffled laughter.

He held her a little away from him. He no longer wore a suggestion of a frown; instead, his eyes glinted at her in an appreciative look that also held mocking amusement. 'Flattered as I am by your—er—enthusiasm, ma'am,' he said in that slow, intimate voice she remembered so well, 'I am rather at a loss to account for it, considering the nature of our relationship.'

She flushed, bewildered and confused, and then humiliated as she realised that he felt she was reading far more into his interest in her than he cared for.

'Our relationship?' she echoed stiffly. 'Apart from our one previous meeting, the only relationship between us is the fact that we are both prisoners of the Corsairs.'

The twin grooves appeared beside his mouth in a wry, sardonic look. 'Oh dear! I very much fear that you will withdraw whatever tempting offer you were about to make when you learn that you have mistaken me for someone else. I am Rais Trelawney Grant, the captain of this ship.'

His eyes narrowed in an expression of rueful humour. 'In the circumstances, I won't be so tactless as to welcome you aboard, ma'am—whoever you may be.'

CHAPTER FOUR

'WHOEVER I MAY BE,' Genevra echoed, her mind discarding for the moment everything else Trelawney had said and fastening on his clear implication that, until now, he had never set eyes on her. Why should he put up such an inexplicable pretence? 'You—You must remember me,' she began.

The corners of his mouth flickered as he surveyed her. 'Believe me, ma'am, if I had met you before I would not have forgotten.'

She shook her head in confusion. 'You tried to prevent me from sailing on *Caranguejo*. You posed as the brother of my employer, and had our luggage removed, and the vessel almost sailed without us . . .'

'My dear ma'am,' he interrupted, one eyebrow in the air, 'we are clearly at cross purposes. You must have someone else in mind, because I assure you that I have not the slightest notion of what you are talking about!'

The blinding truth struck her with devastating force. Why on earth had it never occurred to her before? There had been nothing more than malice behind the removal of their luggage from *Caranguejo*, and the malice had been directed at Abigail—by the incensed landlord of the King's Head! He must have bribed an impecunious young officer to pose as Abigail's brother for the sole purpose of avenging himself by causing her the maximum inconvenience.

Trelawney went on with amusement in his voice, 'Why should you imagine that I would wish to *prevent* potential prisoners from entering the waters of the Barbary Coast? It would be akin to the owner of a gambling hell closing his doors to young blades with more money than sense!'

Blotting out everything else to which she had been subjected was an overwhelming feeling of disillusionment and pain. What a fool she had been to weave such romantic fantasies about him, even imagining that he had followed *Caranguejo* and allowed himself to be taken prisoner—all on her behalf! While he had filled her mind, Trelawney had had so little interest in her that he did not even remember having met her!

With a shock, the belated knowledge of what he had proclaimed himself to be registered fully in her consciousness. He was the captain of this unspeakable pirate ship! In spite of his magnetic physical presence, he was a contemptible renegade Corsair, and even worse than Rupert Runcorn, for it was by his orders that she and the others had been captured. She remembered that he owned fifteen per cent of her person, of her entire human identity, and the enormity of what she had discovered about him flooded her mind.

Because she would otherwise have burst into tears of betrayal, she lashed at him in repugnance instead. 'Of all the despicable turncoats one might possibly imagine . . . Of all the *villains*! It is not even as if you could have been driven to it by deprivation or lack of advantages, for you are clearly a man of breeding and education! Rupert Runcorn, at least, has the excuse that his disfigurement has hardened and embittered him. But it's obvious that nothing but evil drove *you* into becoming what you are, and that you revel in it, and feel not the slightest twinge of conscience or shame!'

His eyes laughed at her. 'A sermon, my dear ma'am,' he drawled, 'would be so much more effective if the preacher were not a deliciously half-naked young woman with her hair falling in glorious disarray about her face.'

Genevra flushed, remembering for the first time her state of undress. She looked at Runcorn's figure lying on the floor, and exclaimed bitingly, 'You have very likely killed him; and if you have I'm glad!'

'It would take more than a blow to the head to kill Rupert Runcorn,' said Trelawney. 'Since I have already seen you in your shift, you can have no false modesty about getting dressed in my presence and coming with me. I wish to speak to you.'

He leant against the doorway, his attitude making it clear that he would not move until she had obeyed him. It was not false modesty that caused her to hesitate. Foolishly, in spite of the shock and disillusionment of discovering what he was, some illogical and purely female instinct rebelled at the thought of him seeing her in the ill-fitting peasant clothes. At the same time, she could not bring herself to put on one of Abigail's gowns. She would have to come to it soon enough, through necessity, but she had been drowned too recently, and it seemed indecent to start wearing immediately the clothes she herself had admired so enviously. She compromised by selecting a satin robe in pale cream, and pushed her fingers through her hair in an attempt to tame it, automatically pulling some of the curls down so that the white streak would not be visible. She stepped across Runcorn's body and, with a flourish, Trelawney stood aside for her to precede him.

She was guided to another cabin, which immediately proclaimed itself to be that of the Rais. It was spacious and sumptuously appointed, with embroidered silk rugs on the floor, and besides a comfortable-looking bunk, there was a deep, low sofa upholstered in rich brocades. At one side was a desk scattered with papers and ledgers, but what held Genevra's attention were robes and pantaloons spread out on the bunk, as if they had been placed there for Trelawney to change into.

'I see that you, too, have turned Turk,' she said with scorn. 'You wear Western clothes only to trick people. I suppose the last ship you raided was thought to be British, and so you quickly turned the respectable Englishman again—just as you did when you visited Gibraltar!'

Momentarily, his eyebrows had drawn together, and wariness flickered into his face. Then he collected himself. 'How did you know that I had lately visited Gibraltar?'

'I was walking along the waterfront there, when you grabbed hold of me and—and forcibly kissed me, ignoring my struggles. I wondered then what kind of man you were. Had I known that such things as renegade Corsairs existed, I would have guessed your profession!'

Her insults had been completely wasted upon him, for his expression cleared, and he said, '*Now* I understand! You were the one who saved my face! I wish you would tell me your name, ma'am, so that I may thank you properly.'

She flushed deeply with mortification. He had insulted her in Gibraltar by using her and assaulting not only her person but her senses. He could not know, of course, that the biggest insult was the revelation that he had not even recognised her, and that the kiss that had affected her so profoundly had meant less than nothing to him. And now he was offering her further insult by claiming that she had, somehow, helped to save a villain like himself from an unknown fate, and he seemed to think she would welcome thanks for having done so!

'My name is Genevra Shaw, and if I indeed helped you in any way, I am extremely sorry!'

'Oh, but you did help me,' he assured her. 'You see, I spied someone coming towards me who knew my face; a slave who had recently secured his freedom. Fortunately I am blessed with excellent sight and could recognise him before he had spotted me. So when you came along, Genevra Shaw, I saw how I might escape notice by playing the ardent lover.'

She stared at him. There had been something about that explanation which did not ring quite true, but she could not pinpoint it. 'Why were you in Gibraltar?' she demanded.

'Questioning the seamen, of course,' he returned readily. 'I pretended to be looking for a vessel to carry a cargo to Algiers for me. The truth, of course, was that I was trying to discover which vessels due to sail from Gibraltar would be worth boarding. Osman Pasha, the Dey of Algiers, is particularly interested in acquiring British prisoners at the moment, in the hope that a sufficiently large number of them would be a bargaining counter in a dispute between himself and the British government. But I found that the most I could hope to bag were two English ladies who had acquired passages on a Portuguese vessel.'

And I, Genevra reminded herself with pain and mortification, was stupid enough to imagine that you had tried to prevent us from sailing for Algiers!

'And now I understand,' Trelawney went on, 'that one of you has met with an unfortunate and fatal accident.'

'It was no accident . . .' she began, and stopped. Honesty compelled her to acknowledge that it had been an accident, caused entirely by Abigail's frantic determination not to be parted from her fortune. 'It was an accident,' she amended, 'which would never have happened if you and your fellow scavengers had not set out to plunder human beings. I cannot think how you can square with your conscience what you are doing!'

'It is not easy,' he assured her earnestly, 'but it can be accomplished with practice.'

She flushed. This man, about whom she had once been foolish enough to weave romantic dreams, was not only totally contemptible and without shame, but could make mocking jests about his unspeakable profession. She sat down on the sofa and glared at him. 'Are you remotely interested in what your underling was trying to do when he tore the clothes from my body?'

The smoky eyes roamed over her in intimate appraisal. 'Rupert Runcorn will be punished for what he did, because female prisoners are to be treated with respect and are certainly not to be physically molested. However, it does not require great imagination to guess why he forgot himself on this occasion.'

Genevra's flush deepened. 'Well, it was not in the least what you think! Miss Abigail Pascoe, who drowned, was a very wealthy young woman and I was her maid . . .'

Trelawney interrupted with a nod. 'Yes, I have been told of the relationship between the two English female prisoners. What was Miss Pascoe's business in Algiers?'

'I don't know. She did not discuss her affairs with me. I supposed that she was going there to look up relatives.'

'And you were her maid.' Trelawney's expression was curious. 'You are very well spoken to be a servant, Genevra Shaw.'

That was, more or less, what Rupert Runcorn had said. She decided that it would be judicious to offer some kind of explanation. 'I am well spoken because I am a poor relation.' She hoped it would sound as if the relationship had been between herself and Abigail. 'And now that Miss Pascoe is dead, there is not a soul in the world who could be called upon to pay a penny to ransom me, so the fifteen per cent share you own in my person is totally worthless!'

His laughing gaze assessed her. 'I would not entirely agree with that,' he murmured. 'Tell me, how did you know that I own fifteen per cent of Genevra Shaw?'

'Because Rupert Runcorn told me so. He obviously feared your anger if you were told that wealthy Miss Pascoe had drowned while in his custody, and he wanted me to wear one of her gowns so that he could pass me off as her when he presented me to you.'

'I see . . .' Trelawney's eyes had narrowed. He stood up. 'Allow me to return you to your cabin. I think you will find that Rupert Runcorn has regained consciousness and removed himself.'

He pulled at a tasselled cord, and a moment or two later a young Moor with splendid dark eyes and a face the colour of honey appeared in the doorway and salaamed. 'This is Ahmed,' he explained. 'My personal servant.'

Genevra accompanied them to the cabin. As Trelawney had predicted, Runcorn had recovered, and removed himself. Trelawney's gaze flicked over the cabin, taking in Abigail's opened trunks, the lilac gown on one of the bunks, and the peasant clothing strewn upon the floor. He issued an order to Ahmed, who replaced the gown inside one of the trunks, closed all of them, and made it clear that he was about to take them away.

'Wait!' Genevra protested. 'My own clothes were ruined when I fell into the sea, and I have only a few garments donated to me by the other women. I shall need Miss Pascoe's clothes because Runcorn claimed that my trunk had fallen overboard, but I think he tossed it over the side himself.'

'Yes, I rather imagine that he did,' Trelawney agreed. His voice was very smooth, his eyes mocking as he continued, 'What a contradictory creature you are, Genevra Shaw! You fought so hard to avoid being dressed in your mistress's clothes, and now you are *asking* to be allowed to do so.' He stooped, picking up the peasant blouse, jacket and skirt and tossing them on a bunk. 'Change into these, and await a summons from Ahmed. You will do me the honour of dining with me in my cabin.'

Several different reactions seethed through her. She could not begin to guess at his reason for having Abigail's trunks removed, and she felt mortified at the thought of being forced to continue wearing the ill-fitting and ugly clothing. As for the thought of joining him for dinner, dressed like that . . . 'I do not have the slightest wish to dine with you,' she told him.

'It was not an invitation. It was an order.' He was smiling, but this time there was steel in his eyes.

After the two men had left, she examined the peasant garments with angry rebellion in her heart. She had been, and still was, grateful for the gift, but she had not foreseen that her own trunk might be lost, and it was outrageous and inexplicable that she should be forced to go on wearing them when Abigail's clothes could have been put to use. Since she could not go on wearing nothing but the silk robe, she slipped out of it and dressed in the peasant garments again. The neckerchief had been torn in half by Runcorn and was now useless, and she had to use the belt of Abigail's robe instead to hold the skirt up.

She sat down on one of the bunks afterwards, wishing that Trelawney had not impinged upon her life again and shattered all her illusions. Apart from everything else, there was danger of a very subtle kind in the fact that he was the Corsair Rais of this dreadful ship. Because of his compelling presence and because he treated everything as if it were a wry joke, he did cause one to minimise, and at times even forget, the hideousness of the situation. While responding to his provocative banter and his male magnetism it was very difficult to keep in mind the reality of being a prisoner, to be held as a slave in an alien land.

A ragged sigh shook her. It would have been far, far better for her if the unprepossessing Turk with the bubble pipe had turned out to be the captain, so that constant fear would have kept her on her guard, and for Trelawney to have remained a once met, intriguing stranger about whom she could have continued to spin fantasies with which to comfort herself in the unknown but dreaded future. There was nothing comforting at all about the real Trelawney; even knowing him for what he was, he still had the power . . .

She stifled the treacherous admission of her vulnerability, and jumped as someone knocked on the door of the cabin. Surely it could not be Ahmed already? She judged the time to be somewhere after noon, and Trelawney had ordered her to join him for dinner.

But when she opened the door, Rupert Runcorn stood before her. She was about to close it hurriedly in his face, but he stopped her by saying with humility, 'Ma'am, I have come to apologise, and explain, and to throw myself upon your mercy . . .'

'*Mercy!*' She gave a bitter laugh. 'Because of you I am a prisoner, and not in a position to dispense mercy to anyone, so I cannot see why you should beg it of me!'

'You could speak up for me to the Rais, ma'am, if only you would allow me to explain . . .'

'What you did, and why, requires no explanation at all! I know perfectly well what you were about!'

He said nothing, but turned his head slightly, so that only the unscarred side of his face was visible. Genevra could not help catching her breath. It was like looking at a beautiful work of classical art. Then he gazed directly at her again, and the renewed shock of such cruelly flawed perfection stirred her to compassion.

'Very well,' she gave in. 'Say your piece, and have done.'

'Ma'am, after the other lady drowned, I honestly began to wonder whether she had not told the truth when she said that you had exchanged clothing. If she was wealthy Miss Abigail Pascoe, why had she made such a foolish, doomed attempt to escape? After all, she would have been able to buy her freedom with a ransom. On the other hand, if she were penniless Miss Genevra Shaw, tricked into having a false identity thrust upon her, doomed to spend perhaps the remainder of her life as a prisoner while impossible ransoms were being demanded for her release . . .' He spread his hands.

What he had said sounded so reasonable that she almost forgot how he had forcibly undressed her. She gave herself a mental shake. 'And so you decided to impose your own beliefs, from the outset, on the mind of your Rais! Well, Rupert Runcorn, let me tell you that in your excessive zeal you probably did me a service without realising it! Miss Pascoe and I did not exchange clothing. What she did, however, was to trick me into hiding her jewellery inside my trunk. It represented a fortune, and if you had not taken it upon yourself to throw my trunk overboard, and the jewellery had been discovered, I've not doubt that everyone would have believed that we had, in fact, exchanged clothing. Miss Pascoe, while posing as the maid, had been determined to retain custody of her jewellery in case the two of us were separated.'

Runcorn had blenched, so that the scar appeared even

more prominent. 'Dear God! Miss Shaw, I beg of you—don't tell the Rais about the jewellery! If you did, I would certainly face being severely bastinadoed!'

Genevra frowned. 'What is that?'

'It is a form of punishment, ma'am, which involves being beaten on the soles of the feet, and apart from being put to death by some horrific means or another, the bastinado is most feared by all of us who are slaves.'

'Slaves?' She stared at him. 'You—You cannot be . . .'

He stooped, and pulled up one leg of his wide pantaloons to display a thin chain enclosing his ankle. 'The mark of all slaves, ma'am. Those of us who . . .'

He was interrupted by the arrival of Ahmed, who indicated that Genevra was to follow him. Runcorn cast her a look of desperate appeal, but she did not respond. She could not believe that he was a slave, for that slim, inadequate chain did not impede his mobility in any way, and sea-raiding would surely give a slave ample opportunities to escape. As she walked along with Ahmed, other Moorish men passed by, carrying baskets of black bread and casks filled with oily fruit giving off a strange and pungent odour. She supposed that it must be destined for the other prisoners, and that what Trelawney had referred to as dinner was obviously served at this early hour.

If the clothes she was wearing had transformed her into a Genoese peasant, the transformation of Trelawney was striking and breathtaking. He had changed into Turkish clothes, which added an exotic quality to his undeniable appeal. He wore wide, draped pantaloons of white silk which were tucked, just below the knee, into blue close-fitting stockings. On his feet were embroidered slippers with upward-pointed toes. Into a swathed cummerbund of blue silk was tucked a curved knife with an ornately-jewelled handle. He wore a white silk burnous draped about his shoulders, its edges embroidered in scarlet and blue, and in the centre of the intricately folded turban which now covered his head a large sapphire glowed.

He salaamed when he saw her, secret laughter lurking in his eyes. 'Try not to be overwhelmed, Genevra Shaw, and sit down.'

'I am not in the least overwhelmed by your heretical

trappings!' she lied, making her voice as withering as she could. 'And I am sure I have read somewhere that Muslim men do not share meals with females.'

'Ah, but my heart was not in it when I abjured! It was done for convenience only, because a Christian cannot become a Rais. I would not wish you to think that I have gone completely native,' he added earnestly, mocking her.

'How contemptible you are! You could not even be sincere about your conversion to Islam!'

He laughed. 'You would find few Mussulmen in Algiers more sincere than I am—merely more hypocritical. They pay lip-service to their religion, but after prayers you will find them frequenting the taverns and the bawdy-houses that are there supposedly for the exclusive use of the prisoners.'

Genevra could not begin to comprehend a society which provided taverns and bawdy-houses for its prisoners, and did not pursue the subject. Instead, she asked, 'Did Runcorn also turn Turk?'

'No. He is a *paga lunar*.'

'What does that mean?'

'It is one of the categories of prisoners in Algiers.'

'A slave!' she exclaimed. So the man had been telling the truth . . .

'A prisoner-of-war,' Trelawney corrected smoothly. 'And while we are on the subject of Runcorn, you may be sure that he will be punished.'

'No!' she objected swiftly. 'Now that I know him to be a slave, I do not wish to add to his miseries! I am sure he genuinely believed me to be Abigail Pascoe, and that was why he acted as he did.'

Trelawney gazed thoughtfully at her. 'I find your sudden defence of Runcorn somewhat surprising, considering his assault upon you.'

'I would not have defended him at all if I had continued to believe him to be a despicable Corsair! Now that I know him to be a slave, I can understand why he did not want to risk your anger. And so, believing me to be Miss Pascoe, he wanted me to be dressed in her clothes when he presented me to you.'

'His efforts were doomed to be wasted,' Trelawney

observed, 'since I had met you before, and I knew that you were the maid and not the mistress.'

Genevra stared at him. He had noticed so little about her in Gibraltar that he had not even recognised her, so how could he be sure that she was not Abigail Pascoe? Perhaps he had retained an impression of the girl he had kissed as someone dowdy and shabby and highly unlikely to possess wealth.

She decided that she had done what she could to spare Runcorn punishment, and changed the subject. 'It goes against the grain to claim possession of Miss Pascoe's clothes, but I need them, and I cannot see why I should be forced to go on wearing these ill-fitting garments . . .'

She was interrupted by Ahmed entering the cabin with a folded trestle table which he set up. It was very low to the ground, and she wondered how they were possibly to sit down to it when she realised that the large, plump cushions stacked in a corner did duty as seats. He spread a white cloth upon the table, and two other young Moors entered with covered dishes.

Trelawney said something to them in a tongue in which she recognised several words as being English or French, and she concluded that it must be a form of *lingua franca* employed in Algiers. She had understood enough to know that Trelawney had given orders that they were not to be disturbed.

'You are probably wondering,' he said after the servants had withdrawn, 'why we dine at this hour. The day in Algiers starts so early that the main meal is usually eaten at or before noon, and we continue the custom while at sea. Would you care to start with a dish of olives?'

She recognised them as the berry-like fruit the Moors had carried below for the other prisoners, but in all other respects dinner with the Rais was a far cry from that of black bread and olives. There was something called couscous, which Trelawney explained was a mixture of ground millet and rice flavoured with spices, and served with a fiery meat stew. The bowls of strange-looking fruit he said were figs and dates. Genevra was surprised to discover how very hungry she was, and when she looked up after having helped herself to more dates, she found that he was studying her with an intent expression.

'I am afraid,' he said, 'that charming as you would look in Miss Pascoe's gowns, I cannot allow you to wear them. At least, not for the moment.'

'Why not?'

'Because,' he said calmly, 'I have a fancy to own a one hundred per cent interest in you, and naturally I wish to buy the remaining eighty-five per cent from the other investors for as low a price as possible. Miss Pascoe's expensive gowns would serve to give an inflated impression of your value.'

Genevra looked at him in speechless outrage. He might have been talking about buying a pedigree cow! It would have been bad enough to hear a Turk or a Moor say such things; on the lips of a refined Englishman they were bizarre, and bordered on a fantastic nightmare.

'I—I refuse to be owned by you!' she spluttered.

'*Someone* has to own you,' he pointed out.

The simple words sent a chill through her. She had been forgetting that people had put up money to finance the sea-raids, and that they would want a return on it by selling the prisoners as dearly as they could.

'I have never heard of anything as evil as what you and the Algerians do! The modern world is supposed to be civilised.' She went on, swallowing hard, 'What—What would happen to me if you did not buy me?'

'You would be put up for sale, with the rest of the prisoners. As penniless Genevra Shaw, you would not command the high price Miss Pascoe would have fetched, but bidding would still be brisk, for even if you were never to attract a ransom, you are young and healthy looking. Your new owner would then place you in a harem where you would be fattened up by being fed sweetmeats and cakes dipped in syrup, for the Moors and Turks favour plump women. Strenuous attempts would be made to persuade you to abjure and turn Turk, so that you might be sold as a wife to a rich man. If you refused to embrace Islam, you would still be sold, at a much reduced rate, as a concubine for someone's harem.'

A long shudder tore through Genevra's body. 'You must be very proud,' she said fiercely, 'to have abandoned England for such a grotesque, barbaric country!'

He shrugged, unmoved. 'In England, I would long since have been shot. I served in the war against France, under the command of Sir Edward Pellew.'

Genevra interrupted with an involuntary cry, for she recognised the name. The husband of one of the women with whom she had shared a cabin on board *Kite* had also served under Sir Edward Pellew. Then she remembered what Trelawney had started to say, and asked, 'Why would you have been shot?'

'Because I did not agree with the orders of my immediate superior,' he said coolly, 'and so I stole the vessel of which I had command and slipped away from the fleet in Toulon harbour.'

'So you are a thief and a deserter, as well as a renegade!' she cried with contempt. 'I would believe anything of you!' Smiling, he inclined his head, as if she had paid him a compliment. She clenched her hands together. 'Why do you wish to buy me?'

He have her a long, enigmatic look. 'No doubt I shall find some use for you.'

Hot colour suffused her face. 'As a concubine for your harem?'

He grinned at her. 'Since I do not have a wife, I have no harem either.' He stood up. 'Thank you for your company, Genevra Shaw. The one thing I miss about England is the stimulating contact with members of the fair sex. The Christian Europeans in Algiers are zealous in protecting their womenfolk from contamination with me, while Muslim women, of course, are kept in a state of purdah and one has to marry them in order to enjoy their company. Yes, I am looking forward to owning you.'

She rose, giving him a look of loathing. As she moved to pass him, he caught her hand in his and brought it to his mouth. Parting his lips, he touched them to the fleshy cushions at the base of her fingers, and she felt a tingling spasm, for she would not have believed that such a simple feather-light caress could have such a tumultuous effect on her senses.

He dropped her hand, and lifted his head, his eyes laughing at her. 'That was for my fifteen per cent,' he murmured. 'Only wait until I own the full one hundred!'

CHAPTER FIVE

SHAKING, GENEVRA blundered to the door, and with mocking gallantry Trelawney took her arm to escort her. They found Ahmed waiting outside, and as soon as he saw them he addressed Trelawney, speaking so rapidly that in spite of the sprinkling of English and French words in the *lingua franca*, Genevra could not follow it. But there was urgency in his voice, and she concluded with revulsion that another possible victim ship had been spotted, and that the charade of approaching it under a friendly flag was about to be repeated. Trelawney still kept a firm hold on her arm as he shot questions at Ahmed, but it seemed to be a purely automatic gesture for he gave every indication of being totally engrossed in the exchange with his servant. A look crossed his face that she could not identify, but certainly this was not the man who delighted in turning even the most outrageous circumstances into a jest.

She was reminded bitterly of her own situation. Had he merely been playing a cat-and-mouse game, enjoying another bizarre joke at her expense, or did he really aspire to buying her cheaply from the other shareholders? If so, why did he wish to own her? *To own her!* The idea in itself was insupportable, quite apart from what his motives might be. With any other man those motives, so clearly hinted at, could have been taken at face value, but with Trelawney, she sensed, one could never be sure of anything. The only certainty was that he was capable of asserting an insidious mastery over her senses . . . Such a discomforting thought intensified her gloom, and she reflected on how she had once dreaded the future as a drudge in her uncle's household. How infinitely desirable such a fate seemed now! With even more bitterness, she wondered how she could ever have been foolish enough to imagine that Trelawney might save her—first from servitude to Abigail, and then from the Corsairs. She became aware that the conversation between him and Ahmed had ended.

Trelawney turned to her, and said with heavy irony, 'It appears that I have been lucky enough to acquire a second Genevra Shaw.'

She stared at him without comprehension. 'Wh— Whatever can you mean? A second . . .?'

'Ahmed informs me that while you and I were dining in my cabin, *Caranguejo* appeared within sight and hove to. A small boat was lowered and two oarsmen approached us, bringing with them a passenger securely tied up. The passenger was a young Englishwoman who claimed to be Miss Genevra Shaw, and the two oarsmen—even if they had been able to contradict her story—did not wait to be questioned.'

'*Abigail!*' Genevra whispered in stunned disbelief.

'So it would seem. Apparently she had remained submerged within the cover of the hull of *Caranguejo*, clinging to the lower end of the rope-ladder and coming up for air briefly at intervals. After the search for her had been abandoned and we had sailed away, she climbed aboard, but the captain did not wish to court future trouble for himself by allowing her to remain. She had been claimed by Corsairs as a legitimate prisoner-of-war, and so he made all haste to have her delivered to us.'

'Where is she now?' Genevra asked in a dazed voice. She had only just begun to accept that Abigail was dead, and now to learn that she was alive after all, and, in spite of all her efforts, a prisoner somewhere on board the Corsair ship . . .

Trelawney replied sardonically, 'Where else would one expect a second Genevra Shaw to be taken other than to the cabin of her namesake?' He rapped a command at Ahmed, and propelled Genevra towards the cabin.

Abigail appeared almost unrecognisable at first. She was seated on the edge of one of the bunks, weeping, and such uncharacteristic tears in themselves made her seem like an entirely different person. But whereas the water had caused Genevra's hair to frame her face and fall to her shoulders in a wild disarray of curls, it had turned Abigail's coiffure into straight, lank strands that plastered themselves against her skull. Unlike Genevra's own percale gown which had soaked up and retained water, the elegant creation of mousseline-de-laine into which she had helped Abigail only that morning had dried in the sun, but limp and crumpled and stained by salt, it had shrunk and now resembled a rich woman's ill-fitting cast-off. Genevra could not help acknowledging with unease that at the moment Abigail looked far more like a poor relation than she did herself, and she had to hide her relief when Trelawney said in a brisk voice,

'Miss Abigail Pascoe, I believe. I am the captain of this ship, Rais Trelawney Grant.'

She looked up, her lids puffy and her eyes red. Genevra, who had grown to know her rather well, recognised the expression that flitted across her face. Self-interest, it said, was of paramount importance and had to be served. In a piteous voice, Abigail cried, 'My name is Genevra Shaw! My mistress forced me to change clothing with her . . .'

'Yes, that story has been recounted to me,' Trelawney cut her short. 'I have very good reason not to believe it. Now, Miss Pascoe, I recommend that you abandon this charade. I'm sure you will wish to change into some of your other clothing. Your trunks will be brought to you . . .'

'I am Genevra Shaw, and the only trunk I possess is the shabby one which was taken from *Caranguejo*!'

'The trunk to which you are referring was lost overboard,' Trelawney observed drily. 'I am afraid you will have no choice but to appear in your true colours, Miss Pascoe.'

'*Lost overboard!*' The colour had drained from Abigail's face and she began to weep again, but this time the cause of her tears was obvious and genuine. At least one of the reasons why she had wished to cling so desperately to Genevra's identity was the knowledge that her jewellery was hidden among the dowdy clothes inside her shabby trunk, and might well have escaped detection.

'It—It is a conspiracy,' Abigail sobbed. 'You are together in this. She has bribed you with a promise of her fortune! I am nothing but a poor relation, who had been on the way to join my uncle in Algiers when Miss Pascoe persuaded me to take a temporary post as her maid, and now she has stolen my identity . . .'

Trelawney interrupted her by turning to Genevra, and

asking with a frown, 'Is there an uncle in Algiers belonging to either of you?'

Genevra had frozen as soon as Abigail mentioned the existence of an uncle. At all costs Uncle John had to be kept out of this nightmare situation. Her mind working rapidly, she decided that if Abigail wished to claim kinship with the unknown Mr J. McDonald in Algiers, nothing could be done to stop her. For herself, she resolved to brazen the matter out and deny steadfastly that she was connected with anyone there.

'I know nothing of Miss Pascoe's reasons for going to Algiers,' she replied firmly. 'As for myself, I simply accompanied her as her maid, and for no other reason.'

'She is lying!' Abigail screamed with legitimate outrage. 'Can you not tell that she is lying?'

'Miss Pascoe,' Trelawney pointed out with weary patience, 'if she is indeed lying, and you are Genevra Shaw, then this uncle of whom you have spoken will identify his niece and settle the matter once and for all.'

'No, he—he won't,' Abigail sobbed, 'because he has not seen me since I was a very small child, and will not recognise me.'

'What is your uncle's name?' he demanded.

Abigail stopped weeping, and now her attitude was mutinous and wary. 'I shall say no more about him, other than that he is a wealthy man and an important member of the British community in Algiers. Though I am only his poor relation, he will make a great deal of trouble for you.'

Trelawney gave her a long, searching look, and then he addressed Genevra. 'Let us return to my cabin. I wish to speak to you.'

With a sick feeling at the pit of her stomach, she accompanied him. Abigail must have convinced him of the existence of an uncle who was expecting a poor relation, and he meant to worm his identity out of her. She could not, she *would* not, involve Uncle John. It had been bad enough that he had felt himself forced to offer her a home; she could not embarrass him professionally, socially and financially by making it known that his niece-by-marriage was a prisoner of the Corsairs! Inside Trelawney's cabin she waited, steeling herself for his questions.

Instead, he stood close to her and studied her for a long moment. At last he broke the silence between them. '*One* Genevra Shaw,' he observed, 'promised intriguing possibilities. *Two* threaten to be a positive embarrassment.'

'You—You know that Abigail is lying,' she began.

He inclined his head. 'Very probably. But I need to be certain that the financial investment I intend making will not be in the wrong Genevra Shaw.'

She flushed, bewildered and disconcerted. 'You really do intend buying me?'

'If you are the true Genevra Shaw, yes. I thought I had made that clear.'

'But why?'

He sighed, as if she were a child persisting in repeating the same tiresome question. 'I have told you that I can perceive several uses for you.'

She bit hard on her lip, and then burst out, 'Surely it would profit you to pretend to believe Abigail, and buy *her* cheaply, knowing that she is worth a large fortune?'

'True,' he agreed with a glint in his eyes, 'but I suspect it would not prove to be nearly as entertaining.'

Her flush deepened. 'I do not believe you are the kind of man who would sacrifice profit for entertainment.'

'I wish you were not so adept at penetrating my façade!' he protested with mock-dismay. 'You are right, of course. But the real Miss Abigail Pascoe obviously has connections in Algiers or she would not have set out for there. The truth about her wealth and her identity would not remain a secret for long. It would certainly come out before I could offer an option to the other shareholders for her purchase by private treaty, and the bidding for her at auction would be well beyond my reach.'

Genevra shuddered. 'What a fiend you are, to talk so casually about *options* and *bidding at auction* where a human being is concerned!'

'Would you have me weep crocodile tears instead,' he returned lightly, 'and pretend to bewail the cruel fate that has forced me to become a Corsair Rais? Whatever else I may be, you have to concede that I am not a hypocrite.'

She was silent for a moment. Then, striving to hide her

anxiety, she asked, 'You do believe there really is an uncle in Algiers?'

He nodded. 'The statement had a ring of truth about it. And the reason why she refused to disclose his name is obvious. If she is Abigail Pascoe, she would want him to learn, in advance, that she is posing as her penniless maid, Genevra Shaw.'

'If she *is* . . .' Genevra echoed. 'You know perfectly well that I am Genevra Shaw, because you met me on the waterfront in Gibraltar!'

'Ungallant as it may sound,' he said apologetically, but with a hint of amusement, 'I was somewhat preoccupied at the time. It has occurred to me that the young lady who saved my face might well have recounted the story of our meeting to her companion, in which case either of you might be the true Genevra Shaw.'

'I certainly did not . . .' she began, and stopped, realising that he had moved purposefully closer to her. Her heart began to drum as he buried his hands in her hair, drawing it away from her face so that she could feel the warmth of his fingers against her scalp and forehead.

A surprised look entered his eyes as he discovered the white streak. 'That is something which, once seen, I would not have forgotten,' he murmured.

'I . . . take pains to hide it,' she muttered, mortified that he had not only discovered it but was drawing attention to it.

'You shouldn't. It is distinctive and intriguing.'

She swallowed, trying to fight the weakness which was invading her at his touch, and at last managed to protest, 'My—My hair was covered by a hat when we met in Gibraltar.'

'Indeed?' He moved away, and pulled at the tasselled cord. Ahmed entered almost immediately and Trelawney issued an order. Salaaming, he withdrew, but returned within moments, carrying a peasant-woman's cap made of cotton, with a narrow, limp brim and bands by which to tie it underneath the chin. After Ahmed had handed it to Trelawney, he was dismissed.

Moving towards her again, he jammed the cap on her head, bundling her hair underneath it, and once again his touch rendered her powerless to resist. He stared down at her, his lips pursed, and after a moment he shook his head slightly. Then, without further warning, he drew her close against him and took her mouth in a kiss which was as uninhibited, as sensuous and demoralising as the one with which he had marked their first meeting.

After a long moment of mindless, instinctive response, she found the strength to push at his chest, and gasped. 'You—You claim not to be a hypocrite! You, who said that a female prisoner was to be treated with respect, and threatened to punish Rupert Runcorn for assaulting me. And now you . . .'

'It was not an assault,' he interrupted calmly. 'It was an experiment, with no other purpose than to establish the truth.' His eyes laughed at her. 'It has not yet been established to my full satisfaction, so . . .'

She retreated hurriedly towards the cabin door. 'I may be inexperienced, but I am not a fool! I accept the reason why you placed the cap on my head, but you cannot claim to identify any female by kissing her and comparing it with a previous and totally different assault upon her person! It was just one more example of your warped sense of humour!'

'But a thoroughly enjoyable joke,' Trelawney agreed lazily. 'You may leave now, Genevra Shaw, and try to persuade Miss Pascoe that it would be pointless to continue her charade, as I am more than satisfied as to the identity of each of you.'

Her cheeks burning, Genevra hurried from his cabin, but it was with reluctance that she entered the one she would be forced to share with Abigail. The latter had fully recovered her hard inner resolve, and glared balefully.

'Why did you say nothing to the renegade about your uncle?' she demanded.

Genevra made her voice bland. 'What uncle?'

'Do not play games with *me*!' Abigail raged. 'You told me all about him, and how you were to have joined his household. But you were also unwise enough to tell me that he would not recognise you, and even though you may be too squeamish to apply to him for a ransom, I shall certainly do so!'

Genevra did not trouble to respond, but she almost found herself feeling sorry for Abigail. Even if it were possible for her, as a prisoner, to track down the unknown Mr J. McDonald among the British community in Algiers, she would speedily discover that he had no connection whatever with a Genevra Shaw. Mildly, she observed, 'You still intend, then, to continue with the masquerade?'

'Even with the last breath in my body I shall insist that *I* am Genevra Shaw!'

Something kept Genevra from pointing out that it would do her no good, and from recounting that Trelawney had no doubts as to who was the mistress and who the maid. Instead, she said, 'I cannot help admiring the presence of mind with which you saved yourself when we were all tipped into the sea.'

Arrogance flashed into Abigail's eyes. 'Did you imagine it was an accident? I planned the entire incident. I had intended that the rowing-boat should capsize, but in the event it did not matter. A sufficient number of people had fallen into the sea for me to escape attention when I grabbed hold of the rope-ladder and submerged myself. I let go of the valise, for I guessed it would send the Corsairs off on a false trail.'

And she had, Genevra thought, clearly not cared whether anyone else might drown as a result of what she had done. Silence stretched between them for a while, broken by Abigail, brusquely. 'I am willing to make a pact with you. This uncle of yours has never seen you. If you allowed me to be claimed as his niece, I would arrange for a ransom to be paid for myself as speedily as possible. Then the "mistake" could be discovered as soon as I was safely out of Algiers, and I should send money for your own ransom.' Genevra did not respond. After a moment Abigail tried again, frustrated rage and desperation in her voice. 'If you would tell me how I might contact your uncle, Mr . . . ?'

She paused to brush a hank of salt-stiffened hair from her forehead, but even though she had tried to make the gesture a casual one, understanding suddenly dawned upon Genevra. Abigail had forgotten even the false version of Uncle John's name that she had been given. No, Genevra amended to herself, it was not so much that she had forgotten the name as that she had discarded it from her consciousness. As soon as she had established that Uncle John was not likely to interest himself in Genevra's affairs, and therefore to oppose her own plans, he had ceased to be of any importance. But the unknown Mr J. McDonald, Genevra thought, had been spared a great deal of embarrassment and aggravation because of Abigail's self-interest.

'How silly of me,' Abigail tried again. 'I have the name of your uncle on the tip of my tongue . . .'

Genevra gave her no time to finish, or to offer more false promises. She went out of the cabin and up on deck. Shivering, she thought of Trelawney. If he really did wish to buy her, what could his true motive be? Was he, perhaps, hoping to extract a ransom for her from Abigail? She sighed. Having had experience of Abigail's parsimony, it was difficult, if not impossible, to imagine her parting with a penny on behalf of anyone else. If only she could discover why Abigail had set out for Algiers in the first place, she might possibly turn the knowledge to her own advantage . . .

Her thoughts were interrupted by the appearance on deck of Rupert Runcorn, who joined her, and made a deep bow, saying, 'I have to thank you, ma'am, for speaking in my defence to the Rais, and particularly for making no mention of the jewellery inside the trunk I threw overboard.'

She looked at him, and discovered that the scar on his face was no longer shocking and intrusive. Indeed, now that she was becoming used to it, she felt it added an intriguing element to what might otherwise have been a too perfect beauty in a man.

'You will doubtless know,' she said, 'that the real Abigail Pascoe has survived, and is also on board, still insisting that we exchanged clothing. I cannot see that it would be of any advantage to her to mention the jewellery, so it seems that you will escape the punishment you mentioned, the name of which I have forgotten.'

'The bastinado, ma'am. The merchants and Janissaries who have invested in the sea-raids would certainly have insisted on such a punishment if they had learnt about the jewellery. As it is, Rais Trelawney Grant has confined my punishment to a night spent inside a bagnio—a prison, in this country.'

She frowned. 'So many strange terms! What do they all mean? And now that I think of it, the Rais said you were a *paga lunar*, but beyond confirming that it was a category of slave, he did not explain it.'

Runcorn sighed. 'I fear, ma'am, you will become only too familiar with all the strange terms employed in Algiers. As for myself—a *paga lunar* is a slave who is more privileged than most. He is allowed the freedom of living in his own establishment and is exempt from forced labour, but he can be called upon to take part in sea-raids, as I have been. The argument is that his special status will make him less likely to attempt an escape, but even so he is watched at all times by the Moors and the Turks while involved in a raid.'

Genevra's frown deepened. 'But what causes such special privileges to be conferred upon a *paga lunar*?'

Rupert Runcorn gave her that smile of his, rendered enigmatic by the scar, but which she sensed was one of cynical humour. '*Money*, ma'am. It is the key to everything in Algiers! Because they know I have a wealthy family in England, the moneylenders extend me credit in the expectation that they will be repaid with interest one day when all the lengthy negotiations for my ransom have been completed. They are not . . .'

He broke off as Ahmed appeared on deck, and added hurriedly, 'I had best leave you, ma'am. It will not do for the Rais to be told by his personal servant that we have been seen together, apparently on friendly terms.'

'It has nothing to do with the Rais . . .' she began angrily, and hesitated, faced by the reminder that Trelawney held absolute dominion over both of them.

Rupert Runcorn coughed, and said with obvious embarrassment, 'You had better know, ma'am, that they are referring to you on the ship as Rais Trelawney's woman.'

'*What?*' Colour flooded her cheeks.

'It is no more than ship's gossip, ma'am, and obviously fostered by the fact that you are known to have dined with the Rais in his cabin. But . . .' Runcorn stopped as Trelawney himself, resplendent in his robes, appeared on deck, and hastily he made Genevra a bow. 'If I can ever be of service to you, ma'am, find a way of sending me word.'

'There *is* something you might do for me!' Genevra exclaimed on a sudden inspiration. 'Try to find out what business took Abigail Pascoe to Algiers.'

He nodded, and moved swiftly away, and she stood defiantly facing Trelawney as he approached. How spectacular he looked in his robes . . . But she angrily cut off the thought, only to be assailed by one far more outrageous and repugnant.

Trelawney's woman. Was he aware of the label that had been attached to her? She cringed at the thought of the vast amusement it would cause him if he were aware of it.

He surveyed her in silence, before speaking smoothly. 'Do not allow the fact that I intend buying you to go to your head, Genevra Shaw! Until you do belong to me, your status is that of any ordinary prisoner, and you do not have the privilege of roaming the ship at will.'

Trelawney's woman, she thought again. His possession, his chattel, his . . . his bondmaiden! At last she was forced to face the fact that he did, indeed, plan to buy her, and for the most obvious and simple motives. If even his ruffianly crew had guessed what he had in mind, she could no longer refuse to accept it.

'Return below, and stay there,' he went on.

Deliberately, with a defiance born of desperation, she made no immediate move to obey. 'I came on deck for a breath of fresh air,' she retorted insultingly instead. 'However, now that it has become defiled, I have no wish to stay.'

Trelawney pretended to have misunderstood, and said reflectively, 'Yes, Rupert Runcorn has a similar effect upon me. In spite of his scar, or perhaps because of it, not only the pieces of muslin attracted to Algiers but also the genteel womenfolk in the Christian quarter find him irresistible. As for myself, I have met too many of his type not to have recognised him immediately as being a flat-catcher.'

Genevra understood the term, because she had heard it being used by youths in Sussex who had learnt it from their more sophisticated, worldly elder brothers in London. It described a habitual trickster, someone who lived by his wits. To hear such a sweeping, groundless calumny coming from the lips of someone as totally beyond the pale as Trelawney almost took her breath away. Giving him a contemptuous look, she left the deck and went below. She spent the remainder of the afternoon and evening in parrying all Abigail's attempts to extract the name of her uncle, but at least this mental exertion kept her from thinking too often and too deeply about the hideous situation that faced both of them in their different ways.

Just before the light faded, Ahmed came to their cabin bringing a night-shift wrapped in tissue, which had been taken from one of Abigail's trunks. He offered it to her, but she rejected it angrily.

'If you understand English at all,' she snapped, 'then tell your master that I am not to be trapped so easily! I am Genevra Shaw, and this does not belong to me!'

Ahmed had obviously understood her attitude, if not her words, and withdrew politely, taking the night-shift with him. Like Genevra, Abigail settled down to sleep in her clothes. So much had been crowded into one devastating day that Genevra felt herself, against all her expectations, surrendering to sleep.

Both of them were woken by a knock on the door. It was Ahmed again, accompanied by another young Moor, and this time they had brought not only one of Abigail's gowns but also a pitcher of water and a basin. It was made clear that the water was for her sole use, but once again sensing a trap, she refused to wash and rejected the offered gown.

Guiltily, Genevra recognised again that she had only to tell Abigail about her own original meeting with Trelawney in Gibraltar to convince her of the futility of insisting that she was the maid and not the mistress. But if Abigail were told about the meeting, she would also have to be told about that kiss, and it was something about which Genevra could not bring herself to talk, least of all to her.

Her thoughts were interrupted by a fearful sound that echoed through the ship; jarring thuds which shook the vessel. Thinking they were under attack, Genevra recovered herself and ran to the door, through which the grey light of dawn was flooding. The thudding noise was now joined by the sound of hurrying footsteps, and, without discussing the matter, the two girls sped up on deck to find out what was happening.

They were not under attack after all. A Moorish sailor was hammering on a block of wood by the mainmast with an enormous iron bar, and it soon became apparent that this was the customary manner in which the ship's company were woken up each morning, for the sleepy crew appeared on deck and were soon joined by the other prisoners under escort. There was no sign of Trelawney, but a small number of Turks appeared to be in charge. They handed out a breakfast of oranges, dates, dried figs and strong, sweet coffee. Genevra ate her rations and then went to stand by the rail, staring with the deepest despair and fear at the drab brown hills for which they were heading. It could only be the North African coast, and Algiers.

Trelawney, accompanied by what seemed to be senior Turkish officers, came on deck, followed by Negro slaves carrying their masters' belongings. The ship's ensign, a huge green flag with strange lettering on it, was hoisted to the masthead. He strolled up to join Genevra, looking immaculate in pantaloons striped in scarlet and white, worn with white stockings, a scarlet burnous and a white silk turban. The grooves flickered beside his mouth as he studied her.

'You look reassuringly unkempt,' he said with approval.

She flushed. 'Since *I* was given no other choice but to sleep in my clothes, and *I* was prevented from washing myself . . .'

'Miss Pascoe, I see,' he interrupted, glancing at Abigail who stood some distance away, 'chose not to avail herself of the amenities offered. It is of little consequence. But you . . .' He tilted his head to one side, studying her with greater care. 'The other shareholders will not be greatly impressed with your potential value, and would be prepared to sell me their shares by private treaty at an economical price. You look as I had intended you should look, Genevra Shaw.' Before she could utter the furious retort trembling on her lips, he went on, 'We are about to enter Algiers harbour.'

She was momentarily struck dumb by the alarming sight

of Algiers, viewed from inside the harbour. Every available space seemed to be occupied by strangely dressed men seething with excitement. The Corsair vessel had anchored close to several large sailing-ships, the crews of which were loading or unloading cargoes into flat-bottomed boats, and had she not had bitter reason to know otherwise, she would have thought it a normal scene such as could be witnessed in any harbour in the world. Several large rowing-boats came alongside the Corsair vessel, and the prisoners were ordered into them. The crews began to row them along the harbour. The boats tied up beside a flight of steps leading to the top of the mole. The Moorish oarsmen leapt out and ran up the steps to mingle with the excited crowd.

The prisoners were ordered to disembark. Trelawney, Genevra noticed, had already gone ashore and was talking to several Turks, and several of the Genoese and Sicilian women were weeping bitterly as they stood awaiting their fate. When she glanced at Abigail beside her, her expression was quite impassive.

Two of the Turks came towards them. One approached Abigail, the other advanced upon Genevra, and she stifled a shudder of revulsion at the sight of his pock-marked face and broken teeth. She forced herself not to react as he pulled the cap from her head and threw it on the ground, and pushed her hair away from her face so that he could study it. One hand pulled her jaw down and he peered inside her mouth, and she fought against waves of nausea at the foulness of his breath. Already humiliated and degraded, she was totally unprepared for what he did next. He put out his hands and cupped her breasts, his fingers exploring their contours and examining their nipples between thumb and forefinger. This was the final debasement, and more than anyone could have been expected to endure. She kicked viciously at his shin, and at the same time slapped his face as hard as she could.

A concerted hiss went up from the encircling crowd, and the Turk put his hand to his curved sword. Trelawney shouldered his way towards them and muttered something in his ear, which caused him to hesitate. He drew Genevra aside. 'You damned fool!' he said grimly. 'Why could you not have controlled yourself as Abigail Pascoe did? Or did it escape your notice that she, too, was examined in a similar way?'

It had escaped her notice. But even if it had not, she could not have stood meekly while that repellent Turk touched her in such an insulting, intimate manner.

'The man you assaulted is one of the major investors and owns shares in all the prisoners, including yourself,' Trelawney continued. 'By Algerian law and custom he had every right to assess your potential market value for himself.'

'I don't care,' she muttered wretchedly, tears stinging her eyes. 'I wish I were dead!'

'Your wish may be granted more speedily than you imagine! For an Unbeliever even to touch a Turk without his invitation or consent is a punishable offence. To attack him physically is an outrage—*punishable by death.*'

CHAPTER SIX

As if to add dramatic emphasis to what Trelawney had said, gunfire suddenly thundered through the air, and a spasm of terror tore through Genevra. But of course it could not possibly have been aimed at herself, common sense told her. And, indeed, it was followed by another volley, and must clearly be a salute of some kind. Since even more crowds were hurrying down the mole, the salute was obviously in honour of Trelawney and his crew for having brought yet another cargo of human merchandise with which to enrich Algiers.

As the last echoes died away, Genevra found that she was once again the focus of attention. Among the alien figures she spotted a man of middle years, dressed in European clothes. He was looking directly at her and his shocked expression told her that he had witnessed the incident and realised all the implications. He was obviously a member of the Christian community, and for a moment she thought he meant to thrust his way through the crowd and attempt to intercede on her behalf. Instead, he turned away, clearly washing his hands of her and of the situation she had created for herself.

'Abject remorse might help,' Trelawney commanded. 'So throw yourself down on your knees.' When she did not obey, he added, 'They have many forms of execution, including burning the victim alive—slowly.'

This time she did not hesitate. Trembling, she sank to her knees and touched her forehead to the ground. She had discovered that, no matter how wretched one's circumstances might be, death, particularly such a death as Trelawney had described, was *not* an alternative to be embraced eagerly.

He and the Turk began a heated exchange, and she realised, with astonishment, that she could understand much of what they were saying, for they were using French. She had spoken French only with her father, and had read aloud to him from the classics in that language, and it took a while for her ears to become attuned to the accents of Trelawney and the Turk.

'I say to you again, Rais el-Trahni,' the Turk was insisting, 'that this dog without soul should be put to the sword.'

'But what of the other shareholders?' Trelawney argued. 'Why should they, who have not been insulted, suffer financial loss through her death?'

She heard the Turk spit. 'Their loss would be insignificant. Her value can be no more than ten gold sequins. Not only is it clear that she has no wealth, but she is a scrawny wretch, with breasts scarcely fuller than those of a boy.'

'So *you* say,' Trelawney returned smoothly. 'But you, Seremeth Ali, are the only one who has examined her. Even I, who hold a fifteen per cent interest in her, have not yet had an opportunity of looking at her teeth or examining her breasts. The others who have shares in her should at least be allowed to judge for themselves as to whether avenging your honour should outweigh their loss of profits.'

To Genevra it seemed like an unreal nightmare, being forced to maintain her attitude of grovelling humility while she was being discussed in such terms, with the threat of death hanging over her.

Trelawney's next words confirmed this. 'Let us go and speak to some of the other shareholders, Seremeth Ali, and discover their views on the matter.'

'Agreed, Rais el-Trahni.'

Genevra lifted her head and peeped through her lashes. The Turk, with his servants and slaves, began to move away, accompanied by Trelawney, to where another group of robed Turks were standing. She stood up, trembling violently. The crowd's attention was focused upon Trelawney and the Turks and they were ignoring the prisoners. Abigail moved to her side, and addressed her with a mixture of tension and pleading in her voice.

'You heard what the renegade said. You will pay with your life for what you did! They are obviously discussing the manner in which you are to be put to death. It can no longer matter to you which one of us should be accepted as Genevra Shaw. You have nothing to lose or to gain by telling me the name of your uncle.'

Genevra looked at her, stunned by such further evidence of blatant self-interest. A disconnected part of her mind realised that Abigail had wrongly interpreted the reason for Trelawney's consultation with the Turks, and she slowly became aware that she was unfamiliar with French, and did not even realise it was the language which had been used.

She saw that Trelawney was pushing his way towards them again, and that the Turks and their entourages were departing. She managed to ask with only the slightest of tremors in her voice, 'What . . . is to happen now?'

'The prisoners will be marched into the city,' he replied briskly. 'The women and children will be taken to the Spanish Hospital, where their value will be carefully assessed. The others will be taken to the fort and will be similarly valued.'

She could scarcely believe that he was capable of mocking her so cruelly by pretending to misunderstand her question. 'I meant,' she said tensely, 'what is to happen to *me*?' She was about to ask whether she would have to submit to an intimate physical examination by all the shareholders before a decision was taken about her fate. But it suddenly occurred to her that Trelawney could not have realised, either, that she could understand French, and blind instinct urged her to keep that knowledge from him. It was the only small advantage she possessed in this whole nightmarish situation. So she went on unsteadily, 'You told me that what I did was punishable by death.'

His eyebrows rose. 'Did you really believe that I would go to all the trouble of having you captured, only to submit to your being put to death?'

Tears of confusion and despair filled her eyes. 'If—If this is another of your macabre jokes . . .' she began in a whisper.

'It is no joke, I assure you! I do not give up that to which I lay claim.'

He spoke with such confidence that everything began to swim before her gaze in a giddiness of relief, but not before she had seen the disappointment flash across Abigail's face. When she recovered, Trelawney's arm was about her waist to steady her, and his eyes were glinting at her. 'Perhaps,

Genevra Shaw,' he drawled, 'you will not object quite so much to my owning you, now that I have saved your life.'

She did not respond. Relief was ebbing, and she could not forget Trelawney's conversation with the vengeful Turk, which he did not know she had understood and of which he had given her no hint. 'Are you telling me,' she asked, 'that I am to escape punishment altogether?'

'I did not say that,' he countered. 'But I am confident that any punishment will be a mere token. It has been agreed that you should be taken to appear before the Dey of Algiers, and that his decision will be final.'

Before she could question him further, he turned away to speak to his officers, leaving her filled with greater unease. How could he be so confident that the ruler of Algiers would order no more than a token punishment? The very fact that she was to appear before the Dey himself seemed to argue against Trelawney's claim that he had saved her life. If only she could have listened to his conversation with the Turks who owned shares in her.

Trelawney raised his voice to address the thronging crowd which again threatened, in their eagerness to inspect the human cargo, to push the prisoners into the sea. She understood enough of the *lingua franca* to follow the gist of what he was saying: The crowd must disperse and allow the prisoners to be taken into the city. But it was not until one of Trelawney's officers produced a pistol and fired above their heads that they began to retreat.

The prisoners were being ordered, through interpreters, to proceed towards the fortified gate that led into the city. Genevra was aware that Rupert Runcorn, who with the other slaves on board the Corsair vessel had been the first to be disembarked, had returned from wherever they had been taken—presumably to be counted. He would know nothing about the drama with the Turk, Seremeth Ali, and when he attached himself to Abigail and tried to engage her in conversation it was clear that he had begun to honour the promise he had made to herself—to try and find out what he could about her. From the snatches of their conversation she was able to overhear, it was obvious that Abigail meant to cling steadfastly to her role as a humble maid-servant, but all the same Genevra's heart warmed to Rupert Runcorn.

Trelawney had fallen into step beside her, and the enormity of her situation suddenly overwhelmed her. She was a prisoner in this barbaric country, with only the dubious word of a renegade that she was not to be put to death, and the only person whom she could regard as any kind of friend was the slave who had captured her on the orders of the man beside her.

'I never thought that I could ever hate anyone as much as I hate you,' she whispered, fighting back tears.

'Such ingratitude,' he reproached her, 'considering I saved your life!'

'But for you, I would not be in this situation, and I don't know that you have saved my life.' She stopped, cautioning herself not to betray that she understood French, and then went on, 'The Turk did not sound as if he would allow himself to be mollified. What took place between you?'

He raised an eyebrow at her, as though she were quibbling over trifles. '*He* said you should die; *I* argued that you should not. We compromised by agreeing that you should be brought before the Dey.'

'And why do you believe that the Dey will not order me to be put to death?'

He said evasively, 'I have every confidence in the success of the arguments I mean to put to Dey Osman Pasha.'

Genevra looked about her, and thought miserably of the prospect of being owned by Trelawney, of being his *woman*, his slave for the rest of her life, because there was no one who would pay a ransom for her.

'I really don't know that I care very much what the Dey decides,' she muttered.

Trelawney's hand was suddenly on her arm, biting into her flesh, forcing her to halt in her tracks. He looked down at her, his eyes darkened to the cobalt colour of clouds before a summer storm, and no sardonic grooves flickered in his cheeks.

'Listen to me!' he rapped, with anger in his voice. 'You will not survive—or deserve to—in this city if you take such an attitude of defeat! You should fight, and refuse to give in or lose hope!'

Genevra stared at him. But for him, she would not be in this dreadful position. The alternative to death was to be bought as his chattel, and she had few illusions left as to why he wanted her. And he spoke of not losing hope!

She shook off his hand, and they walked on. His bracing rebuke had had one effect: it had reassured her, as much as anything possibly could, that he meant to plead successfully for her life. It must be because his wish to own her had ceased to be a whim and had become a challenge, and he was not a man to balk at such.

They had reached the gate by now and as she glanced at Abigail she thought of those trunks full of beautiful clothes and the valise of jewellery, and it seemed even more unbelievable than before that she could have wished to visit a ruffianly country like Algeria.

The procession of prisoners had come to a halt. As they waited in the heat, Genevra could see other gates separating the city from the sea. Outside one was a stretch of beach that appeared to be for the use of fishermen, judging by the nets lying in heaps on the sand.

'That is the Gate of the Fishermen,' Trelawney confirmed. 'The entrance through which we are to pass is the main one, called the Marine Gate. There is only one principal thoroughfare, and as long as you remember that, Algiers will not seem quite so bewildering.'

Genevra stiffened, staring at him. 'Are you trying to mock me? Behaving as if this were a tour . . .'

'No,' he interrupted bracingly. 'I am trying to reassure you. The Dey will spare your life, and I shall buy you. You will, of course, lead a sheltered life, but there will inevitably be occasions when you have to go into the city—to visit the public baths, for example.'

She was unable to respond. Did he really think he was reassuring her by painting such a picture of her fate as his *woman*? Death would be preferable . . . No, an inner voice contradicted immediately. Life was precious, whatever its quality, and the sooner this slow, nerve-racking prelude to the moment when she would be taken before the ruler of Algeria was over, the better. Suddenly she was confused. She had assumed that she was being taken straight into the presence of the Dey. But now that she thought about it, she could see that, even for an audience with the ruler of such a ramshackle country as Algeria, one would have to endure a lengthy process of protocol.

She asked Trelawney in a tense voice, 'How long shall I have to wait until I am taken to the Dey?'

To her surprise, he replied, 'An hour; perhaps two. Very soon, I shall take you to the Jenina, the Dey's palace.'

'I see. The Dey thinks so highly of his English renegade that he is prepared to grant him an audience without formalities?'

'The Dey does think highly of me,' Trelawney agreed urbanely, ignoring the sting in her remark. 'However, granting me an immediate audience is not a special privilege. Even a prisoner has the right to take his grievances direct to the Dey, who will see him there and then if it is convenient.'

She digested this curious piece of information. That her fate would be decided quickly should have relieved some of her anxiety, but it did not. If she had not understood what passed between him and the Turk, she might have been able to accept Trelawney's blithe assurances at face value, but she dared not insist too much without making him suspect that she had understood the conversation in French. For her own peace of mind, she thought bleakly, it might have been better if she had *not* understood it!

Her unspoken dread had obviously communicated itself to him, for he lifted a hand and cupped her chin, tilting her face so that he could look into her eyes. 'Do not fear, Genevra Shaw. I know precisely how to argue the case for your life with the Dey.'

Perhaps because of the unreality of her situation, standing there among a motley crowd of wretched prisoners and ragged Mussulmen and waiting to enter an alien city where her fate was to be decided, the touch of his hand and his low, intimate voice had a shatteringly demoralising effect. As if hypnotised, she found herself staring into those curiously coloured eyes of his. She was glad when the spell was broken as the crowd of prisoners, guards and onlookers began to move forward again, and she was swept along with them, Trelawney remaining at her side.

He called out, in French, to one of his Turkish officers,

'Sidi Hassan, the *paga lunar* and I shall pass through the gate first with the English prisoners. You and your brother officers follow with the rest.'

Genevra made her voice as guileless as she could. 'Did it take you long to learn Arabic?'

Trelawney laughed. 'No, for I have not learnt above a dozen words of it. Fortunately the Turks, who are the cream of Algerian society, consider it to be a mark of sophistication and superiority to have some fluency in French. As for the rest of the population—there is a local polyglot tongue called Algerine, which is understood by almost everyone.'

She made no comment. It gave her some comfort to know that she would be able to follow any conversation he held with anyone of power, but she would have to school herself not to betray her knowledge. They had now reached the gate, followed by Rupert Runcorn and Abigail. Trelawney exchanged pleasantries in French with the officials, and took her arm.

'We'll wait here,' Trelawney said, 'while the remainder of the party pass through the gate and join us.'

From here, outside the city with its jumbled whitewashed houses, the scene was so familiar that, if she could blot out the many strange smells and the jabber of different tongues, she might have imagined herself staring at any pleasant European settlement. The houses were graceful, with flowering shrubs trailing against their walls, and gardens in which lemon trees bearing fruit grew among exotic flowering bushes and ornamental pines. The men wore fashionable European breeches and coats, while the women were as elegantly gowned and parasoled as one would expect to see in any well-to-do English community.

'The European quarter,' Trelawney said, 'where the various consulates are and where the free Christians live. They don't approve of me,' he added sardonically. As if to illustrate the point, he made a deep, mocking bow in the direction of the watching Europeans, and the men stiffened and the women turned their heads away. But the younger women hesitated before they looked away, and it was quite clear that, disapprove of him as they might, they were also fascinated by this striking English renegade.

Somehow the sight of Europeans living freely in Algiers had heightened her despair. Surely they must know that she was a prisoner, destined at best to become a slave? And yet there was no pity or compassion in their faces, and they avoided looking at Abigail and herself, as though the sight was embarrassing. Just as that well-dressed, middle-aged European man among the crowd on the mole had turned his back upon her plight, unwilling to become involved.

Two of the Turkish guards had moved up and gone ahead of herself and Trelawney. The other prisoners had been formed into a long line, walking two abreast. The guards turned into an alley, and the procession followed along a flight of stone steps leading to a broader road. Several women were among the crowd here; they were not veiled, as she had assumed females in a Muslim country would be. Most of them were amply curved and bold of eye, and she remembered Trelawney's reference to the 'pieces of muslin' who were attracted to Algiers.

The leading pair of Turkish guards passed inside an enclosure open to the sky. Trelawney turned, and addressed Rupert Runcorn. 'You will leave now, and report to the Guardian Pasha of the Bagnio de Belique.' His voice took on an edge of hard cynicism. 'You have had ample opportunity of assessing the extent of Miss Pascoe's fortune, and how it might be diverted to benefit you.'

'My name is Genevra Shaw!' Abigail screamed. 'I *have* no fortune!'

Trelawney affected not to have heard, and Runcorn ignored his unjustified jibe. He bowed to the two girls and withdrew.

As soon as all the captives had been gathered inside the enclosure, a huge oak door studded with brass was firmly shut in the faces of the crowd, and the prisoners were alone with their guards in a courtyard.

'The other women will now be taken to the Spanish Hospital,' Trelawney told Genevra and Abigail, 'where they will be examined and valued. As soon as I have given instructions to my officers, I shall take the two of you to the Jenina, to appear before the Dey.'

'Why do I have to appear before the Dey?' Abigail demanded with shrill suspicion. 'I have done nothing wrong! Indeed, I am the victim of my mistress's cunning and trickery . . .'

Trelawney interrupted her, his voice very smooth. 'Then, surely, as the humble maid-servant, you would be expected to accompany your mistress, to attend her and act as her chaperon?'

Abigail swallowed visibly. 'I . . . Yes, of course.' She moved away, and pretended to study a drinking fountain in the shape of a marble fish, from which many of the other prisoners were drinking.

Tension was rising inside Genevra again. No matter how effectively Trelawney might lull her fears from time to time with confident, positive reassurances, she still had to appear before the Dey. That moment was almost upon her, and she had a right to know what arguments Trelawney meant to put up in her defence.

'What will you say to the Dey?' she demanded. 'How will you persuade him not to hand me over to the Turk, to be put to death?'

He sighed, as though she were persisting in making a great fuss about a trifle. 'One of my main arguments will be that to put you to death would create a dangerous precedent. I shall make the point that, at present, you have no owner but are merely an investment . . .'

'An *investment*!' she could not help interrupting in a tone of abhorrence.

'Had you possessed a specific owner,' he continued, 'and Seremeth Ali insisted on your being put to death, he would then have been obliged to compensate your owner for your loss. While you remain an investment, he cannot be compelled to pay compensation. I shall point out to Osman Pasha that this is manifestly unfair to the shareholders, who would be entitled to nothing in return. I shall also tell him that your execution would lead to all kinds of abuse in the future. If someone had a grudge against a shareholder, for instance, he need only goad a prisoner into attacking him for that shareholder to lose financially by the prisoner's death. The whole of Algeria's economy would suffer as a result of the Dey ruling in Seremeth Ali's favour.'

'Oh . . .' She replied blankly.

Trelawney moved away and called his Turkish officers

together, speaking to them in a rapid undertone.

A short while later, they left the courtyard. Some of Genevra's fear had abated, now that she knew how Trelawney meant to plead her cause. The very fact that his arguments would be based upon the commercial exploitation of prisoners, instead of on humanitarian grounds, persuaded her that they would be effective. Here, it would have been laughable to expect a plea for mercy to succeed.

Suddenly the Turkish officers halted, and Trelawney said, 'This is the Jenina, the palace of Dey Osman Pasha.'

It looked no more imposing than any other building she had seen, although its main entrance was a little larger than others, and on the marble benches on either side of it Turkish soldiers were sitting. Across the doorway, quite low to the ground, was looped a heavy iron chain. Trelawney stooped and took hold of it, and as if it had been a signal, two of the seated soldiers rose and heaved open the door.

Trelawney confirmed her thoughts. 'That is all that is required for anyone to gain an audience with the Dey.'

But the chain also served another purpose, she found, for no one entering the Jenina could do so without bending, and so automatically bow the knee before appearing before the Dey. A short flight of stone steps took them through yet another door which led into a large courtyard, and Genevra caught her breath. Until now, there had been nothing to prepare her for such exotic splendour. In the centre of the courtyard a beautiful ornamental fountain played, its fine spray lightly sprinkling the vivid flowering plants that surrounded it. The galleries all round were supported by exquisite spiral columns of marble which reminded Genevra of twists of barley-sugar.

The people inside the courtyard were either strolling about idly or deep in conversation, and most of them were richly dressed. Women were conspicuous by their absence. Genevra was bemused to see, in complete contrast to so much splendid elegance, a group of slaves sitting in one corner, plucking fowls. They continued along a wide gallery with rooms leading off it. The door of one of them opened, and a man with sandy hair, in a collarless shirt of embroidered silk and deep-blue pantaloons, came towards them.

'Welcome back, Rais Trelawney,' he said in English. 'Osman Pasha is expecting you, for Seremeth Ali has already been to put his own case.'

Trelawney nodded, and turned to the two girls. 'Allow me to present to you the Christian Secretary of Dey Osman Pasha, Mr Hywell Llewellyn. Miss Abigail Pascoe, Llewellyn, and Miss Genevra Shaw . . .'

'*I* am Genevra Shaw, sir,' Abigail put in swiftly, dropping a curtsy. 'My mistress forced me to . . .'

'Exchange clothes with me,' Trelawney finished for her in a mocking falsetto. He touched Genevra's shoulder. 'This is the true Miss Shaw.'

Llewellyn held out his hand, but while Abigail shook it, curtsying again as she did so, Genevra stared stonily at it. 'I do not shake hands with renegades.'

'Mr Llewellyn is not a renegade,' Trelawney said gently. 'He is a Christian, a privileged prisoner who works inside the palace, but a prisoner for all that.'

Genevra glanced at the man's ankle, and saw the thin silver chain which encircled it. She flushed, and took his hand. 'I beg your pardon. I . . .'

'It does not signify, ma'am.' He looked at her with compassion. 'From your description, you must be the young lady who attacked Seremeth Ali. If you will excuse me, I shall announce your presence to the Dey.'

She was scarcely aware that he had turned away and moved towards one of the other doors leading from the gallery. That look of compassion on his face had produced a deep trembling, and faintness threatened her.

Suddenly Trelawney's arm was about her waist in support. 'Listen to me,' he murmured. 'You have nothing whatever to fear from the Dey. A fifteen per cent share in Genevra Shaw may be worth little, and a hundred per cent not much more, but I hold the one, and I aspire to the other. What I hold I keep, and what I aspire to I achieve. *Always!* So remember that, and trust me.'

In spite of what he was, in spite of his crude assessment of her worth in financial terms, and although he meant to fight for possession of her so that she would become what the gossips called his *woman*, she found that she was indeed trusting him, and her fear began to melt away.

Llewellyn returned, and ushered the three of them inside the Dey's audience chamber. The soldiers had been ordered to wait on the gallery. Genevra had a swift impression of the room as they entered it. The floor was of fine marble, and the walls were glazed for part of their height with blue and white ceramic tiles.

On a low wooden platform covered with Persian rugs and scattered silk cushions sat a man who looked to be in his early forties. He was of medium build, olive-skinned and with keen flashing eyes. His robes and turban were made of fine silk, and he wore many jewelled rings on his fingers. He was flanked on each side by an extremely handsome young man who was holding a fan of peacock feathers with which he stirred the air gently above the Dey's head.

'Prostrate yourselves,' Trelawney commanded Genevra and Abigail.

They did as directed. Then Genevra stiffened with shock as he began to address the Dey, for he was speaking not in French but in some language quite unfamiliar to her, and the Dey was responding in a similar tongue. Had Trelawney been lying to her about his ignorance of Arabic? She relaxed a moment later as it became clear that they had been exchanging ritual greetings in which the name of Allah had figured several times, and which Trelawney must have learnt, parrot-fashion, for he switched to French.

'*Effendi*, I shall make my report later about what I discovered in Gibraltar. For the moment, I believe you know why I am here, for Seremeth Ali has already had an audience with you.'

'Yes, indeed.' The Dey's voice held curiosity. 'I must confess, Rais el-Trahni, that I am puzzled, first of all, by your reason for bringing *two* female prisoners before me. I understood from Seremeth Ali that the wretched creature who assaulted him is the one with black hair, dressed as a Genoese peasant. What the other is doing before me escapes my understanding.'

'All will be revealed, *Effendi*. They are mistress and maid-servant, and had been travelling together . . .'

'Yes, I have been told that. I have also been told that it was the maid-servant who attacked Seremeth Ali, an important Janissary, in full view of the lowest of Moors and

Jews and slaves, and for that there can be no defence.'

'In the ordinary way I would agree, *Effendi*. But there are special, economic, reasons why her life should be spared.'

'Then I wish you would explain them to me, Rais el-Trahni.' There was a note of deep puzzlement in the Dey's voice. 'For myself, I can see only that she is a wretched creature who is not likely to attract a ransom, or to be of the slightest use to anyone. So tell me why you feel I should not allow justice to take its course, and hand her to Seremeth Ali for execution.'

Genevra swallowed hard against a sudden rasping dryness in her throat. She remained motionless, scarcely breathing, as she waited for Trelawney to explain all the far-reaching economic effects that her death would entail.

Instead, with a feeling of blank, numbing shock, she heard him say, 'You are mistaken, *Effendi*, about the true identity of the prisoner who assaulted Seremeth Ali. She has been masquerading as her own humble maid, Genevra Shaw, and for reasons of my own I have been pretending to believe her.'

Genevra forced herself to remain still as Trelawney continued, 'In truth, she is Abigail Pascoe, the mistress—a very wealthy young woman who forced her maid to exchange clothes with her. By keeping her alive, there is every chance of separating her from much of her fortune. On the other hand, the only ones who would benefit by her death would be her heirs in England.' He laughed grimly. 'Any grief they might feel at news of her death, *Effendi*, would be greatly relieved by their triumph as they shared out her wealth, congratulating themselves that you, and I, and the coffers of the Belique of Algiers had been fooled and cheated of every last *sou* of it!'

CHAPTER SEVEN

MENTAL IMAGES FLASHED through Genevra's brain. Herself, dining with Trelawney, trying to deny to herself his over-powering attraction, her rage at his mocking sense of humour serving to minimise the grotesque fact that she was a prisoner. She remembered his kiss, his then-baffling announcement that he meant to buy penniless Genevra Shaw, her own outrage and—yes, it had to be admitted now—her secret, shamed excitement at the news that she was being talked about as Trelawney's woman. And all of it had been based upon the cruellest of lies. She wanted to cry out to the Dey that Trelawney was wrong, and that she was not wealthy at all. But some protective instinct kept her quiet.

'Both prisoners, *Effendi*,' Trelawney said, 'have been laying claim, from the moment they were first captured, to the identity of Genevra Shaw, a penniless young woman employed as a maid-servant. From what the captain of the Portuguese vessel told the *paga lunar*, Rupert Runcorn, we know that one of them is the mistress, Abigail Pascoe, whom Gibraltar gossip described to the captain as a con-siderable heiress. The fair-haired prisoner insisted, from the beginning, that her mistress forced her to exchange clothing as soon as Corsairs boarded the vessel.'

'A trick often employed by the wealthy who venture to sail on the waters of the Barbary Coast,' the Dey observed. 'But I am bound to say, Rais el-Trahni, that neither prison-er gives any sign of possessing wealth.'

'Appearances can be deceptive, *Effendi*. I had better explain to you from the beginning what happened.'

Only half of Genevra's mind took in Trelawney's account of the sea-raid; the other concentrated with sick despair and disillusionment upon his total betrayal. She remembered that scene in his cabin, when he had jammed a peasant's cap upon her head and kissed her as a supposed 'experiment' to verify that she was indeed the girl he had met in Gibraltar.

He had noticed so little about her then that nothing could have caused him to recognise her afterwards, for he had been far too preoccupied. His next words to the Dey confirmed this.

'The real Abigail Pascoe is a very clever young woman with a quick wit. She described to me a chance encounter she claimed we had had in Gibraltar. I remember such an encounter, but nothing about the young woman involved. It could be that the prisoner had merely happened to witness the meeting while she herself was visiting the waterfront to enquire about passages for herself and her maid to Algiers. But she was swift to turn it to her own advantage and use it to convince me that she was really Genevra Shaw, the maid. But consider the evidence, *Effendi* . . .'

'I am waiting for that evidence to be presented to me, Rais el-Trahni.'

'In the first place, we have the very different behaviour of the two young women after they had been captured. The one with black hair displayed the kind of arrogance one would expect of someone accustomed to thinking of herself as superior to others. According to Runcorn, she remained in total command of herself and questioned his right to take prisoners sailing on a Portuguese vessel. Not once did she give way to hysteria or to tears . . .'

'None of that,' the Dey put in, 'is positive evidence of identity, Rais el-Trahni.'

'It is, *Effendi*, if one contrasts it with the behaviour of the other young woman, the one whom I believe to be the true Genevra Shaw. *She* became hysterical when confronted by Corsairs; she insisted that her mistress had forced her to exchange clothing. She made a wholly senseless and potentially fatal attempt to escape. When delivered to my presence later, she sobbed and maintained that she was Genevra Shaw. She became hysterical again when she learnt that the shabby trunk which she said contained her own belongings had been lost overboard, and she resisted fiercely any suggestion that she should change into one of the fine gowns she claimed belonged to her mistress. I believe it to have been a desperate attempt to avoid being trapped in the role of the wealthy mistress.'

'But, presumably,' the Dey commented, 'the black-haired young woman also refused to change into a fine gown for the same reason.'

'Indeed not, *Effendi*. She resisted only when Rupert Runcorn tried to force her to do so, but that reaction would have been typical of someone of her superior social class. Arrogance, together with the fastidiousness one would expect from a young woman of wealth and position, made her wish to change out of the peasant clothing for which she had been forced to exchange her own wet garments. She demanded several times to be allowed to wear the elegant gowns that, she said, belonged to her mistress.'

How thoroughly, Genevra thought bitterly, she had allowed herself to be taken in. His single, cursory, and mocking attempt to question the fact that she was a penniless servant ought to have put her on her guard. She forced herself to remain motionless in her position on the floor while she listened to him.

'To return to the prisoner with the fair hair, *Effendi* —when the Janissaries arrived this morning to examine both of them, *she* offered no resistance. In short, she behaved throughout in the manner one would expect of someone accustomed to a subservient position. Faced with a frightening, unknown situation and tricked by her mistress, she allowed panic to overcome her. Once it had been spent, she became cowed by terror, merely repeating, over and over again, that she was the true Genevra Shaw.'

How triumphant Abigail would be feeling at that moment if she could have understood Trelawney's devastatingly plausible arguments, Genevra thought with numb despair.

'Do not rely upon my word alone, *Effendi*,' he was continuing. 'Ask Mr Llewellyn to recount to you his meeting with the prisoners, and the difference in attitude between the two of them.'

The Christian Secretary cleared his throat. 'I am bound to agree, *Effendi*, with Rais Trelawney's conclusions about the two prisoners, now that I know all the facts. When he introduced me to them, the fair-haired young woman identified herself as Miss Genevra Shaw; she curtsied and called me "sir". The lady with the black hair reacted by scorning my offered hand at first, and declaring with considerable hauteur that she did not shake hands with renegades.'

'Hm . . .' the Dey mused. 'Command her to rise, so that I may inspect her more thoroughly.'

Genevra was careful not to make the slightest movement until Trelawney addressed her, and in the meantime she schooled herself to assume an impassive expression. She pretended to start when Trelawney said in English, 'Please stand up, Genevra Shaw.'

At the same moment as she rose, Abigail did so too. She might have understood nothing of what had been said, but self-interest had clearly not deserted her for a moment, and her instincts had remained alert. Not once, Genevra remembered bitterly, had Trelawney addressed herself as Miss Shaw, or even as Genevra. He had always used her full name, because he had been secretly mocking her as he employed the name which he believed she had assumed. She found the Dey's dark eyes examining her minutely while ignoring Abigail, and she concentrated on keeping her face blank and staring over his head.

Trelawney's interest in her, from the beginning, had been purely financial. 'What I hold I keep,' he had said, 'and what I aspire to I achieve.' What he aspired to was a one hundred per cent share of a young woman with a fortune in England, and he would have no interest whatever in her penniless maid. If he had not believed herself to be Abigail Pascoe, he would not have made the slightest effort to save her from the Turk's vengeful wrath. Considering who and what he was, why should she be experiencing such a personal sense of betrayal?

'If you were convinced from the start, Rais el-Trahni, of the true identity of each of the two prisoners,' the Dey demanded, 'why have you pretended to believe the mistress was the penniless maid?'

'Because,' Trelawney said coolly, 'it suited me that she should appear to have no value. I perceived a way of making a profit, *Effendi*. I wish to buy her myself, and obtain ownership at as low a price as possible.'

Genevra felt hot tears threatening behind her eyelids, and blinked rapidly so that they would not fall and betray her. 'Trust me,' he had told her. And, like a fool, she had done precisely that, swallowing all his lies.

The Dey gave a crack of amused laughter. 'You are to be congratulated, Rais el-Trahni, on your sharp business instinct!'

Trelawney went on, 'You know as well as I do, *Effendi*, what happens when prisoners from the richer countries of Europe are brought to Algiers. The brokers ask questions and sniff out all there is to be known about them, and the merest suggestion that there might be a fortune in the background will set the value soaring. But in this case, with both prisoners claiming to be a humble maid-servant, and with myself pretending to believe the one who is really the wealthy mistress, the merchants will pay her scant attention and I shall be able to buy her cheaply—if you agree to spare her.'

'Hmm . . .' Once again, Genevra found that the Dey was studying her intently and it came to her with a shock that, because of the arguments presented to him by Trelawney, only the Dey's unreserved belief in her identity as Abigail Pascoe was likely to save her. No defence whatever had been offered for humble Genevra Shaw!

'Even if I were prepared to waive the just punishment for what she has done,' the Dey continued, 'why should I help you, Rais el-Trahni, to cheat the other shareholders by keeping quiet about her true worth?'

'Because,' he replied smoothly, 'I expect to raise a very substantial ransom for her, *Effendi*, without the usual exorbitant commissions payable to the brokers. After deduction of the tax due to the Belique, I would share the remaining sum equally with you.'

The Dey placed the tips of his many-ringed fingers together. 'I have given the matter serious reflection,' he said after a moment, 'and I have decided to spare the prisoner's life.' He added piously, 'We in Algiers are not savages who lack all qualities of mercy.'

'Indeed not, *Effendi*,' Trelawney returned gravely.

Osman Pasha addressed his Christian Secretary. 'Your presence will no longer be required, and you will make the appropriate entries in the record books. But remember that none but the three of us is to know which of the prisoners is Miss Genevra Shaw and which is Miss Abigail Pascoe.'

Llewellyn bowed and withdrew. 'We come now,' the Dey told Trelawney, 'to the matter of the prisoner's punishment. Something will have to be decided upon—not only because of Seremeth Ali's position as a Janissary, but also because a good deal of suspicion would be aroused if she is let off. I know I can rely upon my Christian Secretary's discretion, so nothing that has been said in this chamber will become known outside. But the brokers would wonder what there is about the prisoner to merit special treatment; they would probe and question, and it would not be long before they realised that she is in fact the wealthy mistress. The value of the shares in her would rise so that no one person would be able to afford to buy her, and she would have to be sold to a syndicate of merchants.'

'That is true,' Trelawney conceded.

'I shall have to decide her penalty, but in the meantime you may tell her, Rais el-Trahni, that I have graciously agreed to spare her life.'

The corruption, the betrayal, the hypocrisy and the greed to which she had been a witness filled Genevra with a revulsion so strong that it almost blotted out all relief at the knowledge that she was not to be condemned to death. Even her punishment, it seemed, would be less for her own chastisement than cynically designed to keep her price low so that Trelawney would be able to buy her cheaply.

He bowed to the Dey, and then turned to her, and the grooves deepened beside his mouth as he gave her his devastating, dangerously beguiling and treacherous smile.

She bent her head and stared at the floor, for her hatred and contempt were so overwhelming as she listened to his intimate, lying voice that he could not have failed to read it in her eyes. 'Did I not tell you,' he said in English, 'that I always get what I want? Dey Osman Pasha has accepted my arguments, and your life has been spared, Genevra Shaw.'

For once, she almost welcomed Abigail's parrot-cry, '*I am Genevra Shaw!*' Not only did it absolve her of the necessity to respond to Trelawney or indicate her gratitude to the corrupt ruler of Algiers, but it focused all attention upon the other girl.

The Dey was frowning at Abigail. 'The maid-servant,' he told Trelawney, 'may be taken to the Spanish Hospital, to join the other women prisoners and have her value assessed.'

'With respect, *Effendi*,' Trelawney demurred, 'I think she should, in the circumstances, be accorded special treatment. From what she has told me, her employment by Miss Pascoe was only temporary, and I understand that she has an uncle in Algiers to whom she is a poor relation, and in whose household she was going to work for her keep. This is by no means uncommon in English society.'

'What difference does that make to her status as a prisoner?' the Dey demanded impatiently. 'Indeed, it simplifies matters, for the uncle can be made to pay a ransom for her.'

'Consider, *Effendi*. She would not tell me her uncle's name; obviously she considered it to be the only slim advantage she possessed. I would guess that he is one of the British merchants. Apparently he has not seen his niece since she was very small, so that she is a virtual stranger to him. If he were forced to pay a ransom for her, do you not think it extremely unlikely that he would remain silent if it came to his ears that I was trying to buy a *second* Genevra Shaw cheaply?'

'Hmm . . . Yes, yes, I understand. He would be required to co-operate.' The Dey frowned thoughtfully for a moment. 'I shall have to consider,' he said at last. 'Remove the prisoners to the Christian Secretary's office, Rais el-Trahni, and then return here with him so that we may discuss what is to be done.'

As soon as they had withdrawn from the Dey's chamber, Abigail began to bombard Trelawney with feverish questions, wanting to know whether the truth about her identity had been revealed, and what was to be done about her.

'All in good time, Miss Pascoe,' he returned abstractedly, and led them into another room leading from the gallery.

But Hywell Llewellyn was not there alone. Facing him, and obviously on the point of taking his leave, was a middle-aged man dressed in European clothes. As he turned, Genevra recognised him as the man who had watched her assaulting Seremeth Ali, and had then turned his back upon her.

He bowed to herself and Abigail, and addressed Trelawney with a politeness that seemed to her to mark distaste. 'For whatever good it might do, I came to see whether I might plead on behalf of the prisoner whom I understood faced the death penalty. However, I am relieved to hear from Mr Llewellyn that she is to be spared.'

Trelawney inclined his head in a somewhat off-hand manner and addressed the Dey's Christian Secretary. 'Osman Pasha requires our presence. No doubt the prisoners may be provided with refreshments while they wait.'

Llewellyn looked slightly harassed. 'Please beg the Dey's indulgence on my behalf, and tell him that I shall join you in a moment or so. As you can see . . .' He made a slight gesture towards the Englishman, who was still hovering as if waiting to take a formal leave.

Trelawney nodded, and returned to the Dey's chamber. Genevra was aware that Llewellyn had pulled at a bell-cord, and that two men who were obviously slaves had emerged from an antechamber in response. But most of her attention was concentrated upon the man who had witnessed her assault upon Seremeth Ali and who had come, belatedly, to try to help her. In spite of her own despair, in spite of the futility of his gesture, she felt she ought to thank him, and was about to approach him when Abigail burst out hysterically.

'No one cares about *me*! I am innocent, but all everyone seems to have been concerned about is saving *her*!' She burst into tears, probably of frustration and rage as much as of desperation.

The middle-aged stranger hesitated, perhaps feeling that it would be insensitive of him to leave at such a moment, even though it was obvious that Llewellyn was impatient for him to go.

The truth struck Genevra with a blinding flash of clarity. Why would any Englishman in Algiers come to risk the Dey's displeasure by attempting to intercede on behalf of a fellow-citizen in danger of her life—*unless he were the British Consul?* She steadied herself by holding on to the back of a bench. How ironical it was that she could not make herself known to him and appeal for help. He had been expecting a poor relation who had been requested to slip discreetly into Algiers without drawing attention to any connection with him. How could she inflict upon him, instead, a niece who had committed an offence punishable by death, and who had escaped such a fate only because it was believed that she was wealthy Abigail Pascoe? Even if he were able to help her, it was impossible to estimate at what diplomatic, financial and social cost it would be to himself.

Llewellyn, clearly disconcerted by Abigail's tears, looked relieved as the slaves created a temporary diversion by bringing in a tray containing cups of coffee. But Abigail refused the offer of refreshment, and as if a happy thought had struck him, the Christian Secretary turned to the Englishman, clearly perceiving a way in which he could be of use instead of an inconvenience.

'I must not keep the Dey waiting any longer. I am sure you would wish to keep the ladies company until my return . . .' Llewellyn broke off, and turned towards Genevra and Abigail. 'Forgive me. I have quite forgotten my manners. Please allow me to present to you the British Consul, Mr John McDonnell.'

With that, he hurried towards the Dey's chamber. Abigail's voice caught in the middle of a sob, and she raised her head to look at the Consul. Horrified, Genevra realised that the other girl's memory had been jogged into recalling the slightly different version of her uncle's surname. Abigail rushed to fling herself into his arms.

'Uncle John! Oh, heaven be praised! I knew we would not be able to recognise one another, and I hesitated to make our relationship known except as a last resort . . . But now you are here, and it has all been such a living nightmare . . .'

For a moment, the Consul appeared to be stunned. Then he said weakly, '*Genevra* . . . Good God, it did not enter my head that *you* might be one of the prisoners involved! I did not expect you to come on to Algiers in the present circumstances!'

'Nor would I have, Uncle John,' Abigail assured him feverishly, 'had I not foolishly offered my services to Miss Pascoe here. As her maid-servant, I had no choice but to obey her order that I should accompany her on board the Portuguese vessel.'

As she listened, Genevra was passing her tongue over her dry lips, in a torment of indecision. Ought she to tell Uncle John how he was being tricked, and that Abigail was using him for her own ends? On the other hand, if she did so, would the Dey be prepared to waive the death penalty if he knew that she herself was a penniless poor relation?

'Oh,' Abigail cried, 'what is to become of me, Uncle John? Even at this very moment that dreadful Turk and his renegade and his secretary are, I am sure, discussing my fate. *I* am not rich, so am I to be doomed to a lifetime of slavery?'

The Consul put her aside, and chewed at his lower lip. 'I shall demand to be present at the discussions. The Dey can scarcely refuse, when my own niece is involved, and I shall use my official status to plead on your behalf.'

Genevra felt as though an invisible net were enmeshing her ever more tightly. If Uncle John joined in the discussion inside the Dey's chamber, he would merely be confirming in all innocence everything Trelawney had told Osman Pasha. He would be helping to transfer the identity of Abigail Pascoe to Genevra herself for ever. And without doubt Uncle John would also be told that, in exchange for his 'niece's' freedom, he would be required to keep quiet about the fact that Trelawney was planning to buy *another* Genevra Shaw.

She came to a sudden decision. Uncle John could not be allowed to compromise his conscience and his professional ethics in that way. Whether or not the result were to prove catastrophic for herself, she would have to tell him the truth.

She stepped into his path as he turned to approach the Dey's chamber. 'I . . . There is something . . .'

Her voice died in her throat as she recognised the expression in his eyes. *She had no need to tell him who she was, for he already knew.*

'Something I might do for you, Miss Pascoe?' he prompted her in a polite, impersonal voice. 'As British Consul, I would naturally endeavour to assist you in any way open to me. I am very glad indeed that you have escaped the death penalty, and I shall certainly ask the Dey to impose as lenient a punishment as possible instead.' He bowed. 'Now, if you will excuse me, I had better hurry to his audience chamber.'

Genevra watched humbly as he strode from the room. She sat down and lifted a cup of coffee with shaking hands, avoiding Abigail's triumphant glance. 'You have left it too late to try and stake your own family claim to the Consul!' the other girl taunted. 'He fully accepts me as his niece.'

Genevra said nothing. She was remembering the expression in Uncle John's eyes, the look which had told her quite clearly that if she were to claim kinship with him, he would deny it. And it had not been the look of a man who had suddenly realised that she must be his niece. He had, she recalled, barely glanced at her before she had stepped into his path. That could only mean that he had recognised her when he had first laid eyes on her on the mole. But how? They were strangers. The answer came to her quite suddenly. *The white streak in her hair*. He might not have seen her before, but he had certainly known her mother, who had possessed an identical streak.

When Llewellyn returned to the room, he approached Abigail, and Genevra noticed dully that he took great care not to address her by any name as he said, 'You are please to return to the Dey's chamber with me.'

She leapt to her feet, her eyes shining, and allowed herself to be escorted out. Genevra was left alone to her own tormented thoughts. It was not too difficult to imagine the cynical plotting which would be taking place inside the Dey's chamber, with Uncle John a willing participant.

A while later the others returned. Uncle John, clasping Abigail's arm, entered the room ahead of Trelawney and Llewellyn. He made Genevra a bow, and spoke in the same polite, impersonal tone he had used before. 'I was happy to hear from the Dey himself that you will not be severely punished.'

She muttered something appropriate and turned her head away, half-aware of Llewellyn's voice offering to escort the Consul and his 'niece' to the outer door of the palace. Uncle John, Genevra was thinking, had scrupulously refrained, this time, from addressing her by name.

That meant that he had agreed to the Dey's terms that she was to be sold in the name of penniless Genevra Shaw, but had confirmed that she was Abigail Pascoe.

Her uncle knew who she was, and yet he had allowed himself to be claimed by Abigail as her relative. He must have been anxious to leave the premises before he could be introduced to the two prisoners, and had probably argued that it would create suspicion if the British Consul were to make himself scarce when Abigail began to weep. Only duty had forced him to stay, and he would have preferred to be claimed by neither. But once Abigail had recognised his name, he had settled for the lesser of two evils. He could not have indicated more graphically that he was washing his hands of Genevra, that once he was assured she had escaped the death penalty he wanted no part of such an embarrassing, disastrous niece.

'The one part of Abigail Pascoe's story that I believed was that she had an uncle in Algiers,' Trelawney said. 'I wonder why she kept it secret that he was the British Consul.'

Genevra turned slowly to face him. He wore such a genuine-seeming puzzled look that, had she not known better, she would have been utterly taken in. Without expression, she asked, 'The British Consul confirmed that she was Abigail Pascoe?'

'Oh yes. Initially, he did try to pretend that she was called Genevra Shaw, but that is understandable. He would have known that both of you were laying claim to the name, and he probably feared that the Dey would regard a wealthy niece of the British Consul as too valuable a prize not to be exploited.' He shrugged. 'In the event, the Dey decided that it might bring a swift resolve of the dispute between Britain and Algiers if he allowed the Consul's niece to be set free.'

Genevra lowered her lashes so that he would not see in her eyes the sick contempt and disillusionment at all his lies. He went on briskly, 'As soon as the Dey has considered the matter fully, he will decide upon your token punishment, and then your ordeal will be over.'

Her ordeal would never be over. Trelawney had played her false in the most perfidious way: he believed her to be wealthy Abigail Pascoe through whom he would be able to enrich himself, and Uncle John was allowing her to be used to that end, without caring what might happen to her when it became known that she was not wealthy at all. Turning away, she walked towards a narrow balcony that overlooked a courtyard. She had thought that it could not be possible to feel more deeply betrayed than she had already been by Trelawney, but Uncle John's rejection had come as an immeasurable extra refinement of torment and despair. If she could have known that he would reject her completely, and that she would find herself the subject of a greedy conspiracy between the ruler of Algiers and what was little better than a pirate who wanted to own her as a slave because he believed her to be wealthy . . .

Genevra's shoulders began to heave, and great uncontrollable sobs shook her. She felt Trelawney's hands on her shoulders, and she tried to fight him off, but he drew her against him, holding her while one hand stroked her hair. As she became calmer, she found that it was a very strange and unnerving experience to be held with her cheek pressed against a man wearing silk robes, the material so thin that she could feel the warmth of his skin against hers. Yet he had the ability to divert one's attention and one's senses from his lying and his scheming, from his corrupt profession and his unsavoury past. Even now, his physical closeness had the power to quicken involuntary excitement inside her. She pushed him away. Why could he not have been less complicated, less diverting and less fascinating, she thought with despair.

Almost as if he knew what she had been thinking, he said softly, 'Do not distress yourself, Genevra Shaw. Your life has been spared, and whatever punishment you receive will not be severe, I promise.'

She caught herself believing him, and almost feeling grateful for his promise. Despising herself for having been tricked again so easily, she said in a shaking voice, 'I—I no longer care. This is a terrible place—and I'm not sure that I would not have been better off, condemned to death.'

A bell rang. 'That will be a summons from the Dey, to tell me what your punishment is to be.' Trelawney took her chin in his hand. 'You are right,' he added in a bracing voice. 'Algiers *is* a terrible place. But it is possible to survive in it, and even to prosper, if one is ruthless and clever enough.'

As you are, she thought, watching him move to the door. With a bitter smile she remembered old Reuben, one of her father's parishioners. Each Sunday the old farm labourer attended church in a mood of earnest penitence, swearing never to touch a drop of gin again for the remainder of his life, firmly convinced of his resolve at the time. And yet each Monday afternoon would find him in a stupor, resolve abandoned and driven from his mind by temptation.

Where Trelawney was concerned, she was not unlike old Reuben, it seemed. No matter what vows she might make to herself, he would always be able to disarm her or throw her off-balance with some unpredictable act or an unexpected show of tenderness, no matter how false, or even by a piece of outrageous banter.

Her chin lifted defiantly. She might be powerless to remain strong against Trelawney, but she would not give way to tears or self-pity again. She had no one but herself to rely upon. She, too, would learn to be clever and ruthless. From now on she would fight with every weapon that came to hand. She would grasp any opportunities Algerian society might offer and use them to her own advantage. Since she was doomed to be a slave, she would be a defiant one who fought back!

CHAPTER EIGHT

TRELAWNEY RETURNED to the room, and Genevra addressed him tensely. 'What is to be my punishment?'

'I shall explain it later. But don't be anxious; as I predicted, it is to be a mere token.'

A mere token, she thought, remembering what the Dey had said, would not satisfy that vengeful Turk, Seremeth Ali. Trelawney touched her elbow and escorted her out. He began to steer Genevra in an opposite direction from the one in which they had arrived at the Jenina.

'Where are we going now?' she demanded.

'To my house. While we lunch together, I shall explain what your punishment is to be.'

Several different reactions stirred inside Genevra. She was aware of pangs of hunger, and would welcome a meal. She was also anxious to learn her punishment, and filled with suspicion and apprehension at the thought of being taken to Trelawney's house. They were once again winding their way through one of the dark, narrow alleys, and Trelawney came to a halt. 'This is my house.'

The familiar blank wall brooded over the street, but as he pushed open the door Genevra saw that, as with the Dey's palace, the interior was anything but forbidding. The courtyard was paved with marble slabs, and there were elegant columns and flowering shrubs and plants everywhere, and a pergola of vines shaded much of the courtyard.

Was Abigail Pascoe, she wondered, at this very moment entering the Consulate inside the European quarter? Would Uncle John be introducing her to his wife as his niece-by-marriage, and to Sophie as her first cousin? Then she straightened her shoulders. She would not give way to useless self-pity.

Several male servants were hovering, and she was surprised to discover that none of them was a slave, but all appeared to be Moors, like Ahmed. So Trelawney did not make a usual practice of buying slaves, but preferred to hire paid servants. But then, she thought bitterly, it could not often happen that such a prize as he believed her to be fell into his lap!

He guided her along a flight of stairs, issuing orders to the servants in Algerine, and after walking along a gallery from which she could look down into the courtyard, she was shown inside a cool room furnished only with a few chairs and cushions and a wooden chest. Against one wall stood Abigail Pascoe's trunks.

'The servants will bring you hot water,' Trelawney said. 'You are to wash and change your clothes.'

'Why?' she demanded, surprised and instantly suspicious. 'I thought you wished me to look as unkempt and unprepossessing as possible, so that no one else would wish to buy me.'

'No one else *will* wish to buy you,' he confirmed. 'You will be put on sale tomorrow, and you will once again wear what you are wearing now. But in the meantime I wish you to grace my table, looking as well as it is possible for you to look.' He added tauntingly, 'I want to assess precisely what I am to buy.'

She was torn between anger and a desire to defy him, suspicion about his motives and the very strong urge to wash away her grime and change out of the crumpled, soiled and ill-fitting peasant clothing.

'A servant will wait outside the door,' he said before he withdrew. 'He will escort you to my living quarters.'

After she had washed, she opened Abigail's trunks, remembering the night in Gibraltar when she had packed them. If only she could have known, then, what the future held in store . . . Sighing, she withdrew a gown of white muslin, together with a flowered petticoat. The ensemble fitted her almost perfectly; too perfectly, for it would only serve to confirm Trelawney in his belief that she was Abigail Pascoe. Her lips tightened, and she thought with vindictive pleasure of the day when he would discover that he had bought a pig in a poke and that she was worth nothing, even though that discovery would no doubt have disastrous repercussions for herself.

Standing in front of the mirror, she used one of Abigail's

brushes to tidy her hair, and automatically she concealed
the white streak at the front. The gown, with its bodice cut
low and its blue sash accentuating the slimness of her waist,
was the most beautiful garment she had ever worn, and
for a moment she forgot her own calamitous situation
as she gazed in wonder at the transformation in her
appearance.

She turned away from the mirror and opened the door,
and the waiting servant guided her along the gallery and
into another room. To her surprise, it was furnished with
elegant European pieces, and the only oriental items were
the patterned silk rugs on the floor. The furniture, she
thought, had probably been part of a cargo carried on one
of the ships Trelawney had plundered. A dining-table had
been laid for two and he was already in the room, pouring
some kind of liquor into glasses.

He straightened when she entered, and turned. He, too,
had changed, and now wore European breeches which
fitted tightly across his thighs and were tucked inside white
stockings just below the knee, and his embroidered slippers
had been exchanged for a pair of shoes with silver buckles.
His waistcoat was of figured silk in two shades of blue, and
the cravat at his throat matched the lighter of them. His
shirt was white, with ruffled lace sleeves which fell over his
wrists. He might have been standing inside an English
drawing-room, waiting to receive guests, and to her deep
shame she felt something inside herself melting in response
to his personal magnetism. She had to remind herself
forcibly what he was, and of his treacherous, venal
intentions towards her.

His gaze moved slowly from the top of her head to the
pair of Abigail's white kid slippers which were only slightly
too large for her. His smoke-coloured eyes studied her, the
grooves appearing and disappearing beside his mouth.
'Yes, Genevra Shaw, you will be worth every penny of what
I intend paying for you tomorrow.'

No, I won't, she thought vengefully, veiling her eyes so
that he would not read their expression. She became aware
that he expected some response to his taunt, and she raised
her eyes, glaring at him. 'I suppose that is your notion of a
compliment!'

'Surely you cannot regard it as an *insult* that I am going to so much trouble to buy you?' he returned lightly.

Once again she was forced to look away. She was not supposed to have understood any of the intrigue which had been plotted in the Dey's palace, and she searched her mind for a credible reaction. '*Why* do you wish to buy me? And please do not fob me off again with a vague answer that a use will be found for me!'

He gave her a lazily-tormenting smile. 'You must be singularly lacking in imagination if at least one reason has not occurred to you! It has certainly occurred to others, judging by the gossip which has reached my ears.'

She felt herself flushing. He could only be referring to the fact that people were calling her 'his woman'. But they did not know, of course, that he believed her to be Abigail Pascoe, for whom he had a far more mercenary role in mind.

'Come and sit down,' he said, 'for my servants are waiting to bring in the meal.'

She obeyed, and accepted a glass of liquor, which he told her had been distilled from figs. 'I should have known,' she said bitingly, 'that your conversion to Islam would not have included abstinence from alcohol.'

He shook his head with mock-regret. 'I can see that I shall never measure up to your own strong moral ideals! In a Turkish or Moorish house, you know, one would sit on cushions and eat from a low table with one's fingers. But, as you can see, in the privacy of my own home I prefer to follow European customs.'

She forced herself to ask the question she had been pushing to the back of her mind, because she dreaded hearing the answer. 'How has the Dey decided that I should be punished?'

'You are to be denied purdah.'

'What does that mean?'

'It means that you will be forbidden to wear the veil. I am sure that is a punishment which must please you as much as it pleases me, for it would indeed be a shame if your lovely face were to be hidden.'

She ignored the lightly-mocking compliment, and gave him a look of deep mistrust. 'That does not sound like a punishment to me at all!'

'Perhaps not, but I assure you that it will be regarded as a punishment by Seremeth Ali.'

'Why? I have seen several unveiled women in Algiers. Indeed, I have seen none who *was* veiled.'

'The veiled women rarely appear in public. The unveiled ones are either Jewish, gypsies from Spain, or ladies of easy virtue who make themselves available as mistresses to freed slaves who prefer to remain in Algiers, or to the *paga lunars.*' He added with irony, 'May I continue telling you about your punishment without interruption?'

She swallowed. 'I thought you said my punishment was to be that I should be denied the veil . . .'

'There is slightly more. You are to be put up for sale in public, with the men, instead of being discreetly haggled over inside a harem. Therefore I shall not be able to negotiate your sale by private treaty with the other shareholders, but no matter. No one would want to buy as a concubine someone who has been denied purdah, and whose face may be looked upon by other men. And since you are only a poor maid-servant, no one would wish to buy you in the expectation of raising a ransom for you. In the ordinary way you would be left to earn what you might in one of the bawdy-houses.'

His voice took on a derisory self-righteous note. 'So, in order to save you from such a fate, I shall bid for you myself tomorrow and buy you for a nominal sum.'

She looked down at the table so that he would not see the rage in her eyes. As the Dey had promised, a way had been found in which to punish her which would not only satisfy Seremeth Ali, but make it possible for Trelawney to buy her without competition.

'And that reminds me, Genevra Shaw,' he added in a tone of exaggerated injury, 'that not one word of gratitude has passed your lips for my efforts in saving you from execution.'

She jumped up, pushing her chair back and looking at him with eyes which blazed with rage. 'I owe you nothing! I would never have been in any danger in the first place, had it not been for you! And let me tell you—death would have been preferable to the prospect of being owned by you!'

He had stood up too, and was moving slowly towards her, his lips flickering so that a suggestion of the grooves appeared in his cheeks. He stretched out a hand, drawing her to him, ignoring her attempt to twist away from him. Now he was standing so close to her that she could feel the silk fabric of his shirt touching her skin where it was exposed above the low front of her bodice. He put out a hand and lifted her chin, his forefinger moving slowly over her lower lip. He looked down at her through half-closed eyes, and murmured, 'Tell me honestly, would you have preferred some hook-nosed Turk with bad teeth to own you?'

'I—I don't wish to be owned—by anyone.'

He cocked his head in a considering way, and said, 'I don't believe you would answer in a bawdy-house. You are not the voluptuous kind of female favoured by the Turks and the Moors, and you would very likely starve. Believe me, I would be doing you a kindness by buying you.'

'Dear God,' she whispered, remembering the full extent of his treachery, 'how I *hate* you!'

He smiled, and lowered his head to hers, his lips nuzzling the lobe of her ear. 'I shall have to do something about that, shall I not?'

Her heart had begun to hammer so loudly that she thought he must be able to hear it too. It required every effort of will not to put up her hands and touch the slight roughness of his cheeks.

He turned his head, and spoke with his mouth so close to hers that she could feel the vibration of his lips against her own. 'I shall tease you, Genevra Shaw, and beguile and tantalise you until you are forced to acknowledge that you want nothing more than to be owned by me, to do with as I please.'

She expected the pressure of his lips against hers to increase. She waited for his kiss, all rational thought suspended, wholly caught up in the atmosphere that sparked between them. But in spite of the desire which she instinctively sensed in him, he did not kiss her, and shame flooded her as she recognised the game he was playing. He was trying to force her to make the first move of surrender. From somewhere she found the strength to push at his chest, and he released her readily, uttering a soft laugh.

He said, in a different, matter-of-fact voice, 'I shall have to change into my robes now, for my presence is needed elsewhere. Do not be foolish enough, Genevra Shaw, to attempt to escape while I am gone. The streets of Algiers hold dangers which you would not even be able to guess.'

He strolled nonchalantly out of the room, and she remained for a while, watching as the servants cleared away the dishes from the table. They paid her scant attention; it was almost as if they were accustomed to their master behaving in an eccentric manner. After a while she wandered out to the gallery, in time to see Trelawney, dressed in robes and turban, leave the courtyard and disappear through the door in the blank wall.

She returned to the room in which Abigail's trunks had been placed, and changed back into the ill-fitting, crumpled peasant clothing. Her first, purely feminine, delight in Abigail's gown had faded as bitterness swamped her again at the way in which she had been betrayed on so many sides into having the other girl's identity thrust upon her. Besides, for her own defence against Trelawney, it was best that she should look as unprepossessing as possible. It was beginning to dawn on her that even though he believed her to be Abigail, through whom he would eventually profit financially, he would still own her in the meantime by all the laws of this benighted country. And the terrible part about it was that she herself would be able to put up very little resistance. She would be like old Reuben once the first drop of gin had passed his lips on a Monday morning. Resolve and rectitude would fly out of the window, and like Reuben she would welcome and embrace disaster. Trelawney, unmitigated scoundrel though he was, held the same fascinated lure for her as a candle for a moth.

With time hanging on her hands as she waited for him to return, she decided to explore the remainder of the house. She found what was obviously his bedroom, for the clothes he had been wearing during their meal lay discarded upon a large tester bed which dominated the room. Several other rooms led from it, but none had doors to ensure privacy. Two of them were empty apart from a few scattered rugs, and another led, to her surprise, into the room that contained Abigail's trunks, through an arch which had previously been hidden by a hanging silk rug. The house had obviously been designed for a Turk or a Moor who would wish to have easy access to his wives and concubines.

Her heart beating in her throat, she went downstairs, pacing up and down in the courtyard, the ugly peasant cap protecting her from the heat of the afternoon sun. There would be no safe haven for her in this house. Somehow, in spite of what she knew about him, she did not believe Trelawney would force himself upon her, but the way in which the rooms communicated would inevitably lead to an inescapable intimacy, and make it so much harder for her to fight against surrendering to him.

The sun was low in the sky when he returned, letting himself into the courtyard with Ahmed in tow. She accosted him immediately. 'Where am I to stay tonight?'

His eyebrows rose. 'Here, of course.'

'No!' There was a note of hysteria in her voice. 'You do not own me yet! You may never own me! Something might still happen . . .'

'My dearl girl . . .'

'I am not your "dear girl", and I will not stay here tonight!' Instinct told her that a man like Trelawney would infinitely prefer the challenge of seducing her *before* she became his legal property. 'There must be somewhere else where I can stay until you do own me—*if* you should own me.'

'The Dey has forbidden you to be lodged in the Spanish Hospital with the other women prisoners, and the only alternative for someone who has been denied the privileges of purdah would be one of the bagnios.'

She had heard the term before, from Rupert Runcorn. 'What are bagnios?'

'Prisons,' he said bluntly.

'Then I would sooner go there!' Locked inside a prison cell, she would at least be safe from Trelawney and, she admitted with shame, from herself. He had already demonstrated the power he could exert over her if he wished, and she dared not be alone with him tonight of all nights, when she was in a particularly vulnerable state after everything that had happened to her.

'Listen, Genevra Shaw,' he rapped, 'while I describe precisely what it is like inside a bagnio. First, you would have to run the gauntlet of the taverns on the lower floors. They are leased and staffed by Christian prisoners but frequented by anyone who wishes to seek oblivion in alcohol. Even if you were to escape being accosted, or worse, by drunken Turks or Moors, you would have to be taken up the stairs to be examined by the Guardian Pasha, who would instruct the prison blacksmith to fit a chain on your ankle, heavy enough to prevent you from escaping.'

'Oh,' she managed in a small voice.

Remorselessly he went on, 'Everything in Algiers is dictated by money, and the few cells inside the bagnio are rented out by the Guardian Pasha. Since you have no money, you would have to sleep wherever you could find a space. How soundly or safely do you suppose you would be able to sleep, the only female among male prisoners, many of them quite uncivilised? If you did survive the night, your breakfast would consist of a pint of vinegar and half a loaf of black bread. Now, do you still wish to be taken to a bagnio?'

'No. But . . .' She stopped, giving him a desperate look.

He appeared to consider, and then nodded. 'There is one other solution,' he said, 'and since you are so violently opposed to staying here tonight, we'll take it.'

'What—What do you mean?' she asked unsteadily.

'I'll take you to the British Consulate. John McDonnell said he would be at your disposal if you should need his help, and he would be happy to offer you hospitality for the night.'

No, he won't, Genevra thought. Nothing could possibly appal and embarrass Uncle John more than to be asked to give shelter to the niece-by-marriage whom he had rejected and betrayed.

CHAPTER NINE

GENEVRA WISHED, NOW, that she had not refused so vehemently to spend the night under Trelawney's roof. But she could not object without admitting that the British Consul was her uncle who, rather than acknowledge her as his niece, had allowed Abigail to claim that relationship and had left Genevra herself to her fate.

'Come along,' Trelawney said, taking her arm and signalling to Ahmed to open the door, and she had no alternative but to obey.

Once again they walked along a maze of narrow alleys, and for the first time, she saw women wearing veils. A group of them were crossing their path, all in robes of unrelieved black or white, and were so thoroughly concealed that only their eyes showed. She could not help but be relieved that she had been forbidden to wear the veil, even though purdah was regarded as a privilege in this country.

To emerge from the claustrophobic centre of Algiers city into the European quarter at sea-level was like passing from night into day. Tension produced a dryness in Genevra's throat and a dragging numbness in her legs as she followed Trelawney. Only the British flag fluttering above one of the houses marked it out as the official residence of the Consul. The front door was opened to them by a dark-eyed, olive-skinned maid-servant who was clearly not British and yet could not have been a Moor, for her colouring was too light and she wore a European-style blouse and skirt with a starched pinafore and cap. She stared with curiosity at Genevra in her peasant clothes.

'Good afternoon, Miriam,' Trelawney greeted her. 'Would you kindly tell Mr McDonnell that I request an audience?'

The girl curtsied. 'Very well, Rais Trelawney. Mrs McDonnell is taking tea on the terrace with some of her friends, and she sent for the master to join them, because the baby seems to be about to take his first steps.'

'In that case,' Trelawney said with a smile, 'it would be a pity if Mr McDonnell were to miss his son's first historic steps! My business is not confidential, so if you will lead the way, I shall speak to him on the terrace. Please tell him that I am accompanied by the other English prisoner whom he met earlier today.'

The girl nodded and walked on ahead. As she disappeared through an arched door beyond which Genevra could see flowering plants and well-tended lawns, Trelawney laid a restraining hand on her arm. 'Give Miriam a moment to announce us.'

'She speaks excellent English. What is her nationality?'

'She is Jewish, well educated and from a wealthy family. Many Jewish girls prefer to leave the overcrowded part of the city where they are forced to live, and work in the European quarter as domestic servants.'

Genevra did not comment. It had just occurred to her that Uncle John might misunderstand altogether the reason for their call. He might assume that she had told Trelawney the truth about their relationship, and if so, it was impossible to guess how he might react. If he gave himself away and admitted their relationship, what would happen to her? Would the Dey still be prepared to waive the death penalty for humble Genevra Shaw? Even if he did, it was extremely doubtful that Trelawney would still wish to buy her, and what would her fate be then? Passionately as she might wish not to be owned by him, the only alternative in this dreadful country was even more unspeakable. In spite of his warped sense of humour, she felt certain that Trelawney had not been joking when he had said she would have to peddle her favours in a bawdy-house.

'You could leave me here,' she said aloud. 'I shall explain to the Consul that I need shelter for the night.'

He grinned. 'And deny myself the amusement of seeing the reaction of his guests as they decide whether to leave in protest, or stay out of curiosity? Not to mention the dilemma of Harriet McDonnell, as she wrestles with the problem of whether or not to offer us a dish of tea?'

Genevra hid her dismay, and retorted, 'I might have known you would not have any qualms about embarrassing decent people!'

'The embarrassment would be caused by you,' he pointed out gently. 'The disapproval and the curiosity would be triggered by myself.'

She flushed. 'I suppose you are referring to the peasant clothing you have forced me to wear.'

'If you were clothed in silk and hung about with diamonds it would make no difference! With one or two exceptions—like Rupert Runcorn, who has charmed his way into being accepted by the free Europeans—prisoners are regarded as being socially beyond the pale. That attitude is likely to be even more pronounced towards a female prisoner in your unique position.'

She dismissed the subject from her mind. What she feared far more than being scorned was that, without in any way accepting responsibility for her, Uncle John might be shocked into admitting who she truly was. Trelawney had begun to steer her out on to a pleasant terrace flanked by lemon and orange trees, with a tiled area shaded by a pergola of climbing plants and furnished with a table and chairs.

She was aware that there were several females, and an infant pulling itself to a standing position against one of the chairs, but her attention was concentrated on Uncle John as he came towards her. Before Trelawney could speak, she said quickly, 'Good afternoon, sir. As the British Consul, you offered me your help, and there is a small matter in which you might assist me.'

Apart from a slight nervous flickering of his eyelids, John McDonnell's expression gave nothing away. 'I shall do whatever lies in my power.' He added in a lowered voice, 'Miss—Shaw, is it not?'

Perversely, in spite of her relief, Genevra experienced a renewed stab of betrayal. He had addressed her as Miss Shaw not because he was acknowledging her, but merely as a reassurance to Trelawney that he would honour the perfidious bargain struck in the presence of the Dey, and he had taken care that his guests would not hear him using her name.

She lifted her head, and gazed at the women seated upon the terrace sipping tea. It was such a civilised scene that she longed with a hopeless intensity to be part of it. Then, as she studied each face in turn, she became aware that Trelawney had spoken the truth. Not one of these women would welcome her in their midst. While they gazed at Trelawney with avid curiosity mixed with disapproval and also something like excitement, they were studiously avoiding her own eyes. One rather plump young girl seemed vaguely familiar, although her face was partly cast in shadow by the brim of her bonnet, but there was no sign of Abigail. Genevra toyed fleetingly with the bizarre notion of that arrogant young woman being banished to some nether region of the house, and fulfilling the role of poor relation by mending or sewing in lonely isolation. Only one of the women on the terrace displayed unqualified condemnation and distaste at the arrival of Trelawney and Genevra. She was conservatively dressed, and looked to be in her late twenties or early thirties, and her mouth was grimly set. It seemed obvious that she was the hostess, and therefore Uncle John's second wife Harriet.

In the bitterness of her own rejection, Genevra wanted to punish her uncle. 'I am sorry to intrude upon you at a social gathering,' she said in a clear, carrying voice, 'but this man intends buying me tomorrow, and he insisted on bringing me here for the night.'

'Indeed,' Trelawney confirmed with mock-piety, 'I wanted to ensure that, until she becomes my property, the prisoner will be suitably chaperoned.'

Genevra had the dubious satisfaction of seeing her uncle flush. Obviously for the benefit of his guests, he enquired, 'May I ask why you intend buying her, Rais Trelawney?'

'You may call it a self-indulgent whim,' Trelawney drawled, clearly taking a sardonic delight in the situation. 'I dare say I shall find a suitable role for her.'

A kind of genteel convulsion rippled through the listening women. They stared at Genevra and looked away again, their attitude implying that she was somehow responsible for the fact that Trelawney wished to buy her for what he had clearly hinted were immoral purposes.

The tight-lipped woman stood up and addressed the others. 'Do please excuse me. I must see whether my husband requires my assistance. Sophie, please attend to the needs of our guests.'

Sophie, Genevra realised, was the girl who had seemed familiar, but she was gazing at Trelawney with open admiration and showing no sign of having recognised Genevra. But being so much younger, she probably had no recollection of her cousin.

John's wife had come to join him, but he did not introduce Genevra to her. 'I am sorry that you should find yourself in such an unfortunate situation,' Harriet said to Genevra in a crisp tone.

A moment of silence followed, during which Trelawney gazed pointedly at the women who were sipping tea. John put in awkwardly, 'May we offer you a dish of tea, Rais Trelawney?' He glanced at Genevra, and looked away. 'The—the prisoner, I am sure, would prefer to be served with refreshment in the greater comfort and privacy of the room which she is to occupy . . .'

'Thank you,' Trelawney interrupted. Any amusement he had so far derived from the situation seemed to have deserted him, for his voice took on an unexpectedly hard edge as he added, 'She will fully have understood, just as I have, the social dilemma that faces you in regard to both of us.'

He swept a bow to the assembled company which was so exaggerated as to be insulting, turned on his heel, and addressed the hovering maid. 'I am sure your master will be more than happy for you to see me out, Miriam.'

Genevra half suspected that he had deliberately planned for them to arrive during a tea-party because he had wanted to make her aware of the free Christians' attitude towards slaves. But why? To demonstrate to her, perhaps, that she could expect no practical or moral support from any of them? Or could it possibly have been that he had wanted to be present when she first met free Christians, so that he could warn her about their attitude and soften its impact for her? But no, surely Trelawney Grant, renegade Rais to the Dey of Algiers, would not be motivated by such thoughtfulness.

A taut, uncomfortable silence fell after he had gone. The guests still avoided looking at Genevra, but pretended an exaggerated interest in the baby. Harriet McDonnell spoke abruptly, her voice constrained as she addressed Genevra. 'If you would please follow me, I shall take you to a guest-room.'

'No, my dear,' John interrupted. 'I shall have to ask her a few questions first, to establish whether I might be able to help her.' He turned to Genevra. 'Please come with me.'

Only the fierce promise she had made herself while inside the Dey's palace prevented her eyes from filling with tears. This man was the only person in the world upon whom she might be said to have any claim of kinship, and for the second time he was tacitly denying their relationship. She accompanied him along a flight of stairs and across a corridor, and was then shown inside an office. 'Well,' he said with an expression of relief, 'we shall now be quite private, for my wife will ensure that Miriam does not listen at the door.'

'And discover that I am not the complete stranger you have been pretending?' In spite of herself, Genevra could not prevent the bitter accusation from spilling out. 'I can quite understand how embarrassing that would be to you . . .'

'My dear child!' he broke in, unexpectedly drawing her into an embrace and kissing her cheek. 'You quite mistake the matter! It would not be a question of mere embarrassment, but of dreadful danger for both of us!'

She looked at him, bewildered both by what he had said and by his apparently fond embrace. 'You washed your hands of me . . .' she began.

'It was for your own sake, Genevra!' He pulled out a chair for her. 'You cannot imagine my utter shock and devastation this morning when I recognised you and saw you attack Seremeth Ali. For what you did, an ordinary prisoner could expect the death penalty, but the British Consul's niece could expect far, far worse!'

She frowned, unable still to trust him fully or to understand. 'What could be worse than the death penalty? And surely your position as Consul would have helped rather than harmed me?'

He gave a hollow laugh. 'The Dey, I am afraid, does not share the general attitude towards international diplomacy. At best he regards foreign Consuls as a means of putting pressure upon their particular governments. That was the reason why, at my wife's urging, I asked you not to make it known that you had any family connection. When I wrote to you, matters in Algiers were as normal as they are ever likely to be, but *now* . . .' He made a gesture with his hands. 'You must have learnt that there is a dispute between Algiers and Britain. The Dey is demanding a substantial increase in our annual tribute to him. If he had known who you were, he would have considered you to be a very valuable political pawn. He would have tried to barter your life in return for an agreement to all his demands, and the British government would have continued to refuse to give in to blackmail.'

John leant towards her across his desk, and continued in a sombre voice, 'You asked what could be worse than the death penalty. The Dey of Algiers, Genevra, would have had you slowly and publicly tortured in order to persuade the British government, through myself, to change their minds. In the end you would have been executed by the most hideous means, and from what I know of the Dey he would have felt himself justified in seizing first my daughter Sophie to take your place, and then my wife. Moreover, I have no reason to believe he would have stopped at using our baby son in a similar way.'

She stared at him, coldness sweeping over her as she understood fully the dreadful dilemma that must have faced her uncle that morning, and the situation into which, in her ignorance, she had plunged his entire family.

'Because of your strong resemblance to your mother,' John continued, 'I could not fail to recognise you, but I was unable to think of any way to help you, and so I returned to the Consulate to consider. Later this morning Rupert Runcorn called, in spite of having been ordered to report immediately to the Guardian Pasha of one of the bagnios. Rupert is a frequent and welcome visitor; his family background is impeccable, and he is a fine young man caught up in appalling circumstances . . . But I digress. He told me everything that had happened, and also that he had learnt what you had done and that both Abigail Pascoe and yourself were to be taken before the Dey. I did not dare to trust even Rupert with the fact that you are my niece, and I hurried to the Jenina to discover what was happening. Then I learnt from Mr Llewellyn that you were to be spared the death penalty, and I knew it could only be because you were believed to be wealthy Abigail Pascoe. I cannot describe my relief! Whatever might happen to you, saddled with a false identify, cannot begin to compare with what would befall you if you were known to be my niece. As you know, I was about to leave when you and Miss Pascoe emerged from the Dey's chamber and she claimed me as her uncle. It would have created suspicion and prompted investigation if I had denied the relationship, and it was a good thing for her that I decided to acknowledge it, because it gained her her freedom. The Dey offered to hand her over to me in exchange for my promise that I would turn a blind eye to the fact that Trelawney Grant intended to buy, also under the name of Genevra Shaw, the girl they believed to be wealthy Miss Pascoe.'

'Yes. Yes, I see, and since I understand French, I was already aware of the bargain you must have struck with the Dey.' Tensely, Genevra leant forward. 'But, Uncle John, the day will inevitably come when it is discovered that I am *not* Abigail Pascoe. What will happen then—to both of us?'

He gripped her hand. 'It is likely to take months before the truth emerges. By that time, I hope the dispute between Britain and Algiers will have been settled. In the meantime, while Miss Pascoe is continuing with the pretence that she is my niece-by-marriage, she claims to have met someone in Gibraltar who has offered her marriage, and as soon as it can be arranged, I shall despatch her there. The moment it becomes known that you are not wealthy after all, I shall offer Trelawney Grant a modest ransom for you on behalf of the British government and have you speedily removed from Algiers also. But the Dey must not discover how he has been tricked, and you must do or say nothing, Genevra, to prompt anyone to ferret out our family connection . . .'

'They would not have to ferret very deeply,' a female voice said behind them, and Genevra turned her head to see Harriet McDonnell standing in the doorway. She entered, and ignoring Genevra, addressed her husband.

'I have given Miriam leave to return home until tomorrow morning, so there is no danger of our being overheard. We may thank the fates that both Sophie and your niece-by-marriage had their hair covered during the scene on the patio, for otherwise the truth would have been screamed aloud.'

'Your Cousin Sophie has inherited the same white streak in her hair,' John told Genevra, before introducing her to his wife. 'No one seeing you with your heads uncovered would doubt for a moment that you are related.'

Harriet addressed Genevra for the first time. 'Because it is reasonable to suppose that Miss Pascoe is aware of the streak in *your* hair, I am taking pains to keep her from meeting Sophie. One look at her would immediately tell Miss Pascoe that we have not for a moment accepted her claim that she is Genevra Shaw. I explained that there was never any intention of acknowledging her as part of the family; she is to keep to the servants' quarters, where she is to be known simply as Jenny. If Trelawney Grant should comment that she was not present among our guests, please explain to him that she is required to earn her keep.'

Genevra nodded, bemused at the thought of Abigail banished to the servants' quarters and known as Jenny. 'I do not think you need be too concerned about Miss Pascoe noticing a resemblance between myself and my Cousin Sophie,' she told Harriet. 'Apart from the fact that I have always been at pains to hide the white streak in my hair, Miss Pascoe is not, in general, interested in others.'

Harriet inclined her head, and changed the subject. 'How did you come to travel in company with Miss Pascoe, so that both of you ended by claiming the same identity?'

Genevra recounted everything that had happened to cause her path to cross that of Abigail Pascoe. When she had finished, her uncle exclaimed, 'If only you had not allowed yourself to be persuaded to venture into these waters! I knew that no British vessel would sail for the Barbary Coast until the dispute had been settled, and I fully expected you to remain in Gibraltar until you could safely come on to Algiers.'

'You should have remained in Gibraltar,' Harriet contributed in a stern voice. 'Anyone with any sense would have gone to the Governor's residence and explained the situation, and would have been put up at the expense of the British government until it was safe for you to sail for Algiers.'

It did not help to be told that there had never been any

need for her to hire herself out to Abigail Pascoe. 'I am
sorry to have caused so much trouble, for myself as well as
for you,' Genevra said miserably. 'Apart from everything
else, you have been placed in a difficult social dilemma.
You have to pretend to believe Miss Pascoe's claim that she
is Genevra Shaw, but you dare not introduce her as such to
anyone. Because of the plot hatched between the Dey and
Trelawney Grant, no whisper must reach anyone that there
is a second Genevra Shaw inside the Consulate.'

Harriet shrugged. 'The European quarter and the city
are worlds apart. The need to introduce the girl to anyone
will not arise, in any case. As far as everyone here is
concerned, we have been expecting a maid-servant from
England, and she has arrived safely. Within a few days she
will be despatched to Gibraltar, and I shall explain that she
proved to be unsatisfactory.'

A chill had swept over Genevra as she listened to
Harriet, but she said nothing. Harriet stood up, and told
her briskly, 'Come with me, please. I must ask you to
remain in the room to which I shall take you, because I do
not wish any of the servants to notice the resemblance
between yourself and Sophie.'

When the door of the study had closed behind them,
Genevra addressed her in a quiet voice. 'Uncle John sent
for me against your wishes, did he not?'

Harriet gave her a long, level look. 'My husband is not
wealthy, and his position demands that appearances should
be kept up. He is hard pressed enough, providing for
Sophie and myself in a way which would not shame us in the
eyes of our friends and of the families of other Consuls
—not to mention securing a future for our son—without
having had to take on the added burden of maintaining
someone who has no real claim upon him. But since he
insisted that you should be sent for, I decided that the
family connection should be ignored, and that you should
be regarded as part of the domestic staff.'

She opened a door to a room halfway up the main
staircase. 'Had I known that you bore such a strong family
resemblance to Sophie . . .' she added, and stopped.

*I would not have allowed you to be sent for in the first
place*, Genevra mentally completed the sentence for her.

Harriet's voice hardened. 'But all that has been changed by your own reckless folly! You represent a source of grievous danger to our family now, and if you are ever to regain your freedom you cannot look to us for shelter or support. Indeed, once you have left the Consulate tomorrow, you must not come here again.'

Genevra bent her head in silent acceptance. When she found herself alone, she sat down in the only chair in the simply furnished room and stared wretchedly in front of her. She felt battered and numbed by everything that had happened to her, and she knew with a terrible certainty that the future could only become worse.

Following a peremptory knock on the door, Abigail entered. It was a transformed Abigail, wearing a plain gown that Genevra guessed had been one of Harriet's cast-offs, and with her hair scraped back plainly into a knot in the nape of her neck. She carried a tray containing cold sliced meat, bread and butter and a mug of chocolate, which she set down on the dressing-table.

'The Consul's wife told me to bring this to you,' she said, staring suspiciously and defiantly at Genevra. 'What are you doing here?'

'What brought *you* to Algiers?' Genevra countered.

Abigail ignored the question. 'If you have tricked the renegade into bringing you here so that you could tell the Consul which one of us is his niece, you have clearly failed. His wife told me to take the tray to *Miss Pascoe*.'

'I dare say you are glorying in your triumph,' Genevra commented tonelessly. Abigail was the last person in the world to entrust with the news that far from wishing to claim kinship with the Consul's family, she had to suppress the fact at all costs.

Abigail gave a brittle laugh. '*Glorying* is scarcely an appropriate word! To think I came prepared to seek hospitality at the Consulate during my visit, imagining an impressive social round . . .'

'Your visit to Algiers was connected with my uncle?' Genevra put in swiftly.

Abigail parried the question. 'You were never meant to be more than a drudge here, you know. I can bear witness to that,' she added with feeling, holding her reddened hands out for inspection. 'I was banished immediately to the servants' quarters, and made to scrub pans! Thank heavens I'd had the foresight to invent an ardent "fiancé" in Gibraltar, so that I shall be here only for a matter of days. After that, no one will remember that a female by the name of Genevra Shaw had ever set foot in Algiers—and who in England is likely to learn that a second Abigail Pascoe is languishing in that barbaric city?'

She turned to the door. Clearly and typically, she was concerned only with her own situation. Genevra called out, with little hope, 'I am to be bought tomorrow, because I am believed to be your own wealthy self. *Please* tell me why you came to Algiers!'

Abigail merely gave her a blank stare, and said, 'I have to get back to those beastly pans. The Consul's wife said you were to place your tray outside the door when you have eaten, and remain inside your room.'

No one else came near, and Genevra was left alone with her tormented thoughts for company. Later, she prepared bleakly for the last night of her life when she would not be owned as a slave—and by someone like Trelawney at that.

In the morning, Harriet McDonnell herself brought Genevra water in which to wash, and followed a short while later with a breakfast tray, explaining dourly, 'Miss Pascoe claims to have been stricken down by a mysterious ailment that will necessitate her keeping to her bed. Please take care to hide your hair underneath the cap before coming downstairs to await Trelawney Grant, because Sophie has been displaying a morbid interest in your circumstances. She is such a silly girl that if she were to suspect your relationship she would blurt it out immediately. And, try as I might, I doubt if I shall be able to prevent her from waylaying you when you leave your room.'

Indeed, when Genevra emerged, she found her cousin hovering at the head of the stairs. The familiar white streak in her hair commanded immediate attention, but in spite of it Genevra thought that when she lost her youthful plumpness she would probably be a very pretty girl. However, it was doubtful whether she would ever lose the silliness of which her stepmother had accused her, and which displayed itself the moment she saw Genevra.

'Oh, you poor thing!' she exclaimed. 'I wished to give you a ribbon or something to cheer your spirits, but Stepmama would not allow it. And she has forbidden me to be present when Trelawney Grant comes for you, because he is not a suitable person for me to meet. What is your name? Stepmama said it was of no consequence . . .'

'I . . .' Genevra began, faced with an unexpected dilemma, but she was saved from the necessity of answering by her cousin's grasshopper mind.

'I do think Rais Trelawney is quite the most dashing man, don't you? He is quite beyond the pale, of course, and I shall never be presented to him. But then dear Rupert is dashing, too, even though he is a slave, and should be beyond the pale also, but . . .'

'That will do, Sophie!' Harriet had appeared on the scene. 'Go to the nursery and help with the bathing of your baby brother.' When she had left reluctantly, and was out of earshot, Harriet turned to Genevra. 'Trelawney Grant has arrived. He is waiting for you in the hall.'

In spite of everything, even knowing that he intended buying her cheaply because he thought she was worth a fortune, and disregarding the knowledge that he had promised almost in so many words to seduce her in the meantime, she could not help reacting to the sight of Trelawney with a quickening heartbeat and a stab of sheer sensual pleasure.

He looked magnificent. He was wearing black silk pantaloons tucked just below the knee inside tightly-fitting white stockings, and leather slippers of a pale gold colour. His shirt was plain white silk, and a jewelled, curved sword was tucked in his waistband. His voluminous burnous was black, bordered by a silk fringe in gold and scarlet. Today he wore no turban, and the reason became plain when he turned slightly. Attached to the burnous draped over his shoulders was a large hood hanging down his back, from which trailed a tassel of silk in colours to match the fringe of the burnous itself. The hood was obviously pulled up to cover his head when he appeared in public. John McDonnell, standing beside him, appeared almost to fade into the background by contrast.

Genevra faced Trelawney, and said stonily, 'I am ready.'

Harriet merely nodded to her before turning away, but John shook hands with her in a show of formality, only the pressure of his fingers conveying his compassion and his regret at being unable to stop her from leaving with Trelawney. Even so, she felt bereft as Trelawney took her by the arm and they left the Consulate.

Several faces appeared furtively at windows to watch as they moved through the European quarter. There was no compassion there for herself; she would never be any more welcome in any of their homes than she had been in the Consulate. And yet the thought of leaving the ordered world of the European community and returning to the tortuous alleys of the city where she was to be offered for sale in a slave-market was almost too much to bear.

Trelawney had pulled the hood of his burnous over his head, which gave him a faintly sinister appearance. She became aware that the corners of his mouth flickered slightly, cancelling out the sinister look. She gave him a hostile stare, and demanded. 'Is something amusing you?'

'No. I was merely trying to see you through the eyes of others, and assessing the lowest bid which would ensure me possession of you.'

Rage rose inside her, and died as despair took its place. She tried to allow neither to show, but in spite of her private vow to remain defiant and uncrushed no matter what might happen to her, she could not conquer an inner trembling as they continued on their way. How was she to bear the humiliation, the sheer degradation, of being put up for sale as though she were an animal? And once Trelawney had bought her, he would, quite literally, have the power of life or death over her.

After they had left the European quarter they crossed the stone ramp that led from the Marine Gate into the city. They passed a mosque whose door stood open, and automatically Genevra glanced inside.

'This is the Mosque of the Fishermen,' Trelawney told her, as if he were escorting her on what was no more than a sight-seeing tour. 'Don't ever to be tempted to step across the threshold of a mosque. Unbelievers who do so can be hanged or burnt alive, or turn Muslim. A prodigious number of converts to Islam have been created as a result of a

Christian inadvertently setting foot inside a mosque.'

Although he had spoken in his usual dry, cynical manner, typically finding a source of grim humour in even such a gruesome subject, Genevra had the notion that there had been something more behind his observation than a mere snippet of local information. It was as if he had wanted to direct her thoughts away from her own coming ordeal, and at the same time wished to remind her to take care in this country, that danger lurked in the most unexpected quarters, and that punishment could be brutal unless one were prepared to sacrifice principle to survival. She thrust the thought away. Considering that he was entirely responsible for what was about to happen to her, it was too fanciful to be entertained. The sun was heralding its arrival above the horizon, and she started as, all over the city, high-pitched, wailing cries rang out. She had dimly, from a distance, heard similar cries the evening before.

'The muezzins,' Trelawney explained, 'calling the faithful to prayer.'

'Oh. I thought it was the wailing of slaves being beaten by their masters.'

He looked at her through half-closed eyes, the grooves appearing and disappearing beside his mouth. 'When I am your master, Genevra Shaw, I shall never beat you— whatever else I might do to you.'

She gave him a searing look. To think that she had, only a moment ago, imagined he was displaying some concern for her! Then fear and despair coursed through her at the reminder of what was soon to be, and she had to force herself to remember her resolve never to be a cowed or a submissive slave.

'We have reached the Bedestan, the slave-market,' Trelawney said, and when they entered a large open square, revulsion overwhelmed her.

The prisoners to be sold were, with the exception of herself, all men. In fetters they sat on the outer perimeter, and appeared to be waiting their turn. Inside the square, two Turks whose plumed turbans and rich robes marked them out as men of substance were bidding against one another for a strapping youth. In another section, what seemed to be professional auctioneers were walking prisoners up and down, occasionally prodding them to make them show their paces by running and jumping.

She felt Trelawney's hand upon her arm. 'You will not be subjected to indignities,' he said with unexpected gentleness. 'I have arranged that priority should be given to the auctioning of yourself.'

She stopped herself just in time from thanking him. Thanking him for having her auctioned like an animal, however swiftly! She looked away, and through the dust that swirled and eddied around the courtyard she caught sight of tawny-coloured hair beneath a red cap, and Rupert Runcorn approached.

He made her a deep bow, and turned to Trelawney. 'I was walking along the mole, Rais Trelawney, after having spent the night in a bagnio as you had ordered, when I saw *Caranguejo* enter the harbour. The captain recognised me and had himself rowed ashore. Apart from diplomatic despatches he has brought from Gibraltar, he has also brought communications for Dey Osman Pasha from the Beys of Tunisia and Morocco. Perhaps, understandably, after what happened at sea, Captain Perreira is not anxious to call at the Jenina, and he also wishes to leave harbour again as soon as possible. He wanted me to take responsibility for the official documents he has brought, but I explained that I have no authority to accept such a task. I persuaded him to accompany me to the Bedestan, since I knew you would be here, and he is waiting outside to place the documents in your care.'

A look of frustration crossed Trelawney's face, then he shrugged. 'I shall have to see him, and deliver the documents to the Dey.' A hard note crept into his voice. 'Stay with the prisoner until I return. I am holding you entirely responsible for her.'

Genevra watched him walk away, and then she glanced at Rupert Runcorn. He wore such a look of guilt and distress that she fought an absurd, maternal impulse to touch the scar on his face in a gesture of comfort.

He burst out, 'It torments me beyond telling to see you like this, ma'am, waiting to be sold into slavery, and in the knowledge that *I* am responsible!'

'You were acting under orders,' she told him.

'The thought brings me no comfort at all. It is one thing to take prisoner an uncouth, brutish Jack Tar from England; a refined young gentlewoman is quite another! Believe me, ma'am, had I not been accompanied and watched by Corsairs, I would have turned a blind eye to the presence of yourself and Miss Pascoe aboard the Portuguese vessel!'

'Thank you,' she began, and stopped, studying his face. 'You accept, now, that I truly am Genevra Shaw?'

'Why, yes, ma'am.' He gave her a puzzled frown. 'The matter has finally been resolved, has it not?'

She looked into Rupert's concerned, ugly-beautiful face, and felt an overwhelming impulse to confide in this fellow victim of the Corsairs. But even as she spoke, she was cautioning herself to be careful not to compromise Uncle John in any way. 'I have reason to suspect that Trelawney Grant believes me to be Abigail Pascoe, and that he wishes to buy me cheaply for profit.' With bitterness, she added, 'He does not expect anyone to bid against him.'

Rupert gave her a startled look, but before he could respond, two men, dark and bearded and wearing black silk turbans wound around three-cornered caps, approached, taking care not to come into physical contact with any Turk or Moor. They ignored Genevra, and the elder addressed Rupert. 'My last letter, it was not answered by Lord Blaymore.'

Rupert shrugged apologetically. 'My father is old, Abraham, and all these lengthy negotiations must be taking a toll of his health. Please be patient.'

'Patient I have been for a long time,' the man said, spreading his hands. 'Patient for how much longer, I ask myself?' He nodded, and the two of them walked on.

Genevra watched with revulsion as they approached a small group of prisoners and began to inspect their teeth and hands before ordering them to strip to the waist. She dragged her gaze away, and asked Rupert, 'Who are those men?'

'Jewish brokers,' he replied in a depressed voice. 'They act as middlemen for the negotiation of ransoms, and they are also moneylenders. Abraham is the one who has been allowing me credit, and trying to arrange my ransom. I have been a prisoner for so long that I cannot guess what is

happening at Blaymore Manor, my family home, but . . .'
He broke off. 'You have troubles of your own, ma'am, and
I shall not burden you with mine.'

Impulsively she put out her hands and grasped his, 'If it
would lighten your own burdens, I do not hold you to blame
for anything. I do not know what is to happen to me, but if
possible I should like us to be friends.'

He looked overcome. 'Why, thank you, ma'am . . .'

'Please call me Genevra! And—if it is not too great an
impertinence—may I ask how you came by that scar?'

His smile no longer seemed sneering or sinister to her,
but merely rueful. 'When I was first captured, and too
young and reckless to know better, I attempted to
escape . . .'

He was interrupted by the return of Trelawney, who
looked thoughtful and somewhat grim. His grimness became more accentuated as he saw that Genevra and
Runcorn were still clasping hands. Brusquely, he said,
'Your presence is no longer required, Runcorn.'

Rupert nodded, and after bowing to Genevra, walked
away and became lost in the crowd. Trelawney had been
looking after him, a jaundiced expression upon his face. To
Genevra's consternation, he said abruptly, 'Has it occurred
to you that Runcorn could very easily grow a beard and so
hide that scar on his face?'

She gave herself a mental shake. 'We are not here to
discuss Mr Runcorn's scar! You—You promised to have
this odious business over and done with quickly.' The
dreadfulness of her situation almost overcame her, and she
added with despair, 'For the love of God, buy me and have
done!'

He took her arm, and for once he did not seem to derive
any amusement from the circumstances. 'I am afraid that
you will first have to be fitted with a leg-iron,' he said gently.

She had grown rigid. While she had watched others being
fitted with leg-irons or fetters, it had not once entered her
head that the same fate was awaiting her. 'Dear God!' she
whispered fiercely. 'How I wish I had never heard of
Algiers, let alone sailed for this hellish country!'

Trelawney made no response. He beckoned to a man
who appeared to be a blacksmith, for he was followed by a

slave who was half dragging a heavy trunk, while another
carried an iron bucket containing glowing charcoal. When
the trunk was opened, Genevra blenched as she saw the
blacksmith selecting a thick iron chain from among its
contents. But Trelawney said something in Algerine that she
could not follow, and the man scrabbled inside the trunk,
bringing out a short, slender chain which appeared to be
made of copper. Trelawney nodded, fumbling inside his
robe and bringing out the pouch in which he kept his
money. He threw several coins on the ground, which were
swiftly pounced upon by the blacksmith. She forced herself
to remain rigid as the light chain was welded in place round
her left ankle. It fitted loosely, so that it dropped on to
her instep and caused her no physical discomfort, but the
very fact of its existence and the knowledge of what it
represented was debasement enough.

Afterwards Trelawney led her away to where the auctioneers were waiting. When it was her turn to be sold, she
stood woodenly beside the auctioneer as he obviously
invited bids. The only response he received were remarks
that were clearly ribald or obscene, and which she was
grateful not to understand. From the inflection in his voice,
he was in turn haranguing the crowd for not snapping up a
bargain, and pleading with them. It was not until desperation had crept into his voice that Trelawney held up five
fingers, signalling his bid.

She gave a sigh of mingled relief, resignation and mortification. Five fingers presumably meant a bid of that
number of gold sequins, which apparently was the currency
of the country, and she remembered that the Turk,
Seremeth Ali, had said she could be worth only ten. So
Trelawney was, indeed, acquiring her at a bargain price.
But at least this part of her ordeal was over. Now she would
have to prepare herself for the next.

This thought was cut off as someone else held up six
fingers. Trelawney answered with an offer of seven. It was
immediately topped by a bid signalling eight gold sequins.

Genevra stood there in bewilderment and trepidation. It
was not just one person who was bidding against Trelawney, but several. *Why?* It had been hammered home to her
repeatedly that she had no value as Genevra Shaw, a

disgraced female who was not allowed to wear the veil. So who wanted her, and for what purpose? A possible answer suggested itself: had Rupert Runcorn, in the belief that he was helping her, spread the rumour that she might be Abigail Pascoe instead? If so, he had done her no service. She balled her hands into tense fists. It had been enough, knowing that Trelawney wished to own her. Even though he was a renegade, he was English, and she would have some insight into his thinking; she would have none into that of a Turk or a Moor who might become her owner.

'Twenty-five gold sequins,' Trelawney said in French, and she held her breath. But this time no one offered a higher bid, and after a moment the auctioneer closed the bidding, and Trelawney stepped forward to pay five times as much as he had originally bid for her.

'Well, Genevra Shaw,' he said with a grim smile, 'you are mine now, and a pretty penny you cost me.'

His remark cancelled out her relief. 'Do you expect me to apologise, or to be flattered that you did not withdraw from the bidding?' she retorted.

'I have come to expect very little from you! I am sure you are as anxious as I am to leave the Bedestan, so let us be on our way.'

He took her arm, and hurried her away through the maze-like alleys and the archways of the city. I am now Trelawney's possession, she told herself with growing despair. I am his chattel, his slave. He may do whatever he pleases with me, and there is no one in the world to whom I could appeal for help.

They had stopped outside a door set into one of the many blank walls facing the narrow alleys, and she did not recognise it until Trelawney opened it, and she could remember from the courtyard with its pergola of vines that they had reached his home.

He gave her a long, unreadable look. 'The Dey wishes to see me, and I shall have to leave immediately for the Jenina. Ahmed will provide you with hot water, soap and towels, and you will wash and do whatever is necessary to your hair. He will destroy the clothes you are wearing, and when I return, I shall expect you to be awaiting me, suitably dressed in something appropriate chosen from Miss Pascoe's trunks.'

'What—What do you mean by *suitably*?' she asked in an unsteady voice. 'Suitable for what?'

His lashes veiled his eyes. 'Suitable for the company of a Rais, of course! I want you to look as I know you are capable of looking—like a beautiful young lady dressed in a fine gown.'

After they had climbed the stairs he left her on the galley, and Ahmed indicated with gestures that she was to enter the room in which Abigail Pascoe's trunks had been stored. The room looked exactly as it had the previous day. No attempt had been made to furnish it as a bedroom.

She bit her lip as she gazed about her. Trelawney had paid far more for her than he had expected to, but his main motive in buying her was for profit. He might be planning to seduce her; indeed, he had made it clear that he meant to do so. But his first priority, now that he owned her legally, would be to delve fully into the background of Abigail Pascoe and discover who held the strings of her purse in England.

The Jewish brokers, Rupert had said, negotiated ransoms for prisoners. And although Trelawney had told the Dey that he did not intend paying exorbitant commission charges to middlemen, he would need expert help in assessing the likely amount of her ransom. Therefore he wished her to be richly dressed so that a Jewish broker could examine her and give his opinion on what Trelawney might expect in return for his twenty-five gold sequins. But whatever his reasons, it would be a relief to be rid, at last, of the ugly, soiled and ill-fitting peasant clothing, and since Abigail had thrust her own identity upon Genevra, she had no qualms whatever about wearing the beautiful garments inside the trunks.

Ahmed carried a tub into the room and other servants followed with hot water, soap and clean towels. She washed her hair first, and after she had bathed she rummaged through Abigail's trunks. Recklessly she selected what must surely have been the most inappropriate ensemble to wear in the home of a renegade Corsair Rais, in a ruffianly country like Algeria and for the benefit of a Jewish broker come to assess her financial worth as a slave. But Trelawney had ordered her to wear a fine gown and look like a young lady, and it was vitally important that he should go on believing her to be Abigail Pascoe, who had no connection whatever with the British Consul in Algiers.

She examined her reflection in the hanging mirror after she had dressed. She had chosen an under-dress of cream-coloured lace, with ruffle upon ruffle of it falling over a half-hoop to her ankles. Over it, caught up at the sides with small sprigs of artificial flowers, she wore a gown of brocade in an apricot shade, its bodice cut low. She arranged her almost dry hair in becoming curls that cascaded from the top of her head on to one shoulder, with wispy curls on her forehead hiding that tell-tale white streak. A pair of brocade slippers to match the apricot of the gown completed the effect, and only the copper slave-chain round her ankle struck a jarring note of reality.

Ahmed came to the room a while later, and gestured to her to follow him. He led her into Trelawney's drawing-room, where she was quite disconcerted to find him sitting alone and with no sign of a Jewish broker.

Trelawney was wearing European clothing, and as he rose to survey her, the grooves deepened in his cheeks. 'I perceive that you have chosen to make a celebration of the occasion,' he drawled. 'I had no notion that it meant so much to you to become my possession.'

She flushed, feeling angry and foolish. 'You ordered me to dress as a fine lady,' she retorted. 'I thought you meant to bring a Jewish broker, and that you wished him to make a judgment of my val—' She stopped, dismayed at what she had just said.

His smoke-coloured eyes were boring into hers. 'Your value? I do not need a Jewish broker to tell me that Genevra Shaw is worth precisely five gold sequins! What made you imagine that I believed it to be more?'

'I . . . Nothing. I did not . . .'

He took hold of her shoulders. 'There can be only one explanation,' he said in a menacing voice. 'You understand French, do you not?'

'Y—Yes.' Her heart had begun to hammer with fear.

Unexpectedly, he threw back his head and gave a roar of

laughter. 'By God, I cannot help admiring your courage! You understood everything! Every single word exchanged with Seremeth Ali and with the Dey, and you never once betrayed the fact!' He released her. 'Go and sit down.'

She obeyed, her thoughts furiously racing. The fact that she understood French, she told herself, would not tell him that she was not Abigail Pascoe, but merely that she had been aware from the outset of his true reason for wishing to buy her.

She faced him defiantly. 'I cannot tell you how glad I am that you have been forced to pay such a high price for me, after the way you have been scheming with the Dey to cheat your fellow shareholders. Obviously others must have begun to suspect that I am the mistress and not the maid.'

'Allow me to tell you precisely why I was forced to bid far more for you than I had anticipated,' he said suavely. 'But I am bound to warn you that the reasons will infuriate you when you learn what they are. In the first place, you have become widely known as my woman . . .'

A sound escaped her, and she felt herself colouring. Why had it not occurred to her that as Trelawney's woman she would naturally have a value over and beyond that of a penniless maid-servant?

He nodded, his mouth curving in a sardonic, self-mocking smile. 'Interest was added by the fact that I have lately been a puzzle to the men in Algiers. I had a long-standing affair with the beautiful wife of the previous French Consul, but unfortunately he found out about it and asked to be posted elsewhere, depriving me of my mistress . . .'

'I could believe anything of you!' Genevra put in, disproportionately outraged. 'You are obviously not in the least ashamed of your behaviour, or concerned about the pain you must have caused the woman's husband!'

Trelawney laughed. '*His* over-riding objection was that I was an Englishman whose country was at war with his own! But, as I've said, the men here were puzzled that I did not frequent the bawdy-houses after the departure of my mistress, or seek to marry, or even display the slightest interest in acquiring a *garzon* . . .'

'What is a *garzon*?' she interrupted.

'It would be quite improper of me to explain,' he said severely. 'To continue—the news spread that you were my woman, the replacement for my French mistress. The other shareholders reasoned that I could therefore be persuaded to go far higher in my bidding than I had intended, and they forced up your price as high as they dared.'

With a total lack of logic, she found herself feeling oddly guilty that he should have been compelled to pay so much more for her than she was worth. She gave herself an angry mental shake. He believed her to be Abigail Pascoe, who must be worth far more than twenty-five gold sequins—and as for being his woman, and the reason why he had been forced to pay an inflated price, was that not precisely what he had in mind for her?

Ahmed came to the door and said something, and Trelawney rose, holding out his hand to her. 'Our meal is about to be served. It will not, I fear, do justice to that magnificent gown you have chosen to wear . . .' His voice tailed away as he studied her, and unexpectedly he lifted his hands and cupped her breasts. 'Seremeth Ali lied,' he said softly, with laughter in his voice. 'They are not in the least like a boy's.'

The blood was drumming in her veins, and a sudden weakness had taken hold of her. She ought, she told herself, to slap his face. But then he bent his head and took her mouth, and as she yielded to him she felt like someone who was drowning and did not have the slightest wish to be saved.

He lifted his head, and smiled into her eyes. 'For all her wealth and her shrewd calculation,' he said softly, 'I don't think Abigail Pascoe would have displayed half the spirit and the courage with which her maid-servant has been acquitting herself.'

Genevra stiffened as she took in the full import of what he had been saying. Dear God, if he knew that she was Genevra Shaw, he must also know that she was John McDonnell's niece. How and when could he have found out? Should she insist, with all the conviction she could command, that she *was* Abigail Pascoe?

Then he said, 'In spite of everything, Miss Pascoe is extremely lucky that the British Consul chances to be her uncle, but even that would not have saved her fortune if the

Dey had not happened to need McDonnell's co-operation at the time.'

The only thing Genevra fully understood from that statement was that both Trelawney and the Dey truly believed Abigail to be Uncle John's niece. She tried not to show her relief. 'So you knew all the time who I really was?'

'Of course.' Trelawney raised an eyebrow at her. 'I may not have noticed what the girl I kissed in Gibraltar looked like, but I did recall that she had been poorly dressed. I had also had a very good view of those on the deck of *Caranguejo* before my men boarded her, and I saw you standing there with your mistress. There was no question at all about your relationship to one another. And while she had fair hair, her maid's was delightfully raven-hued.'

'Then—Then why?'

'Why did I pretend to believe that you were Abigail Pascoe? Because it was the only argument that would have persuaded the Dey to spare your life. Seremeth Ali is a Janissary, a member of the ruling body in Algiers, and assaulting him was a very serious matter.'

She thought of the interview that had taken place inside the Jenina, and said fearfully, 'The Dey agreed to spare my life only because he thought I was Abigail Pascoe. He'll change his mind when he learns who and what I really am.'

'You really must learn to trust me, you know,' Trelawney said. 'The Dey already knows your true identity. I persuaded Captain Perreira to accompany me to the Jenina, to hand over the official despatches and letters he was carrying, and the captain confirmed that the young lady with fair hair was wealthy Miss Abigail Pascoe.'

'Oh . . . Surely the Dey was furious to have been tricked, and that there will be no ransom forthcoming for me?'

'The Dey accepted that I had made a genuine mistake in assessing your identities. As for the loss of his share of a ransom,' Trelawney added evasively, 'the Dey perceived that there were other compensations to be derived from the situation.'

Genevra was still puzzling as to what those compensations could possibly be when Trelawney changed the subject with a light laugh. 'Come, let us go and celebrate my purchase of Genevra Shaw.'

She accompanied him into the dining-room, her mind busy as she tried to assess all the implications of what he had been saying. And then, slowly, her mind filled with dismay as she faced the reality of the situation. He had known from the start that she was Genevra Shaw, who was worth nothing, yet he had paid a very large sum of money for her. It was only too obvious to everyone, including the gossips of Algiers, why he had wanted her. He had already demonstrated it by that uninhibited kiss in the drawing-room, and by the intimate way in which he had caressed her. She was to become the mistress—no, the *woman*—of a renegade Englishman who had turned Turk! And what was even more deeply shaming was the fact that the thought produced a lurching excitement inside her.

As they seated themselves at the table, and the servants began to carry in the dishes, she gazed at the knife that had been laid for her and gave silent thanks that Trelawney did not follow the Algerian custom of eating with his hands. She would secrete it in the folds of her gown after the meal, and keep it with her at all times. He had the power to have her put to death if she attacked him, and the death of Genevra Shaw would not be the financial sacrifice that the death of rich Abigail Pascoe would have meant. But death would be preferable to a lifetime of self-contempt for what her own weakness and his right of possession had turned her into.

Trelawney was pouring liquor into glasses, and was offering her one. 'Shall we drink a toast?' he invited.

'To—To what?'

Smiling, he reached into a pocket of his coat and withdrew a document. 'This is called a *teskere*. Keep it safely, because its value in this city cannot be over-emphasised. There are people who would kill for it.'

She gazed at the document, penned in Arabic script. 'What does it mean?'

'It means that I have renounced my ownership in you. I have bought you so that I may return to you all rights in your own person and in your own identity.'

He raised his glass. 'The toast is to Genevra Shaw—a free woman who belongs to no one but herself!'

CHAPTER TEN

'I—I DON'T BELIEVE you,' Genevra stammered, when she was able to speak at all.

Trelawney bowed his head, and agreed gravely, 'Yes, there are times when I astonish even myself with my capacity for benevolence and chivalry! However, I assure you that it is true.'

She stared at him. 'But why? Why should you have gone to so much trouble and expense to buy me, merely to give me my freedom?'

'The expense was unforeseen, and forced upon me,' he disclaimed modestly. 'Please do not shower me with undeserved credit!'

'Will you stop treating everything as if it were a joke?' she said with exasperation. 'The main purpose of your loathsome profession is to take prisoners and turn them into slaves. I was one of those prisoners, so how can I possibly believe that you would then have set out to buy me simply so that you could give me my freedom?'

He appeared to consider the matter. 'I can only conclude that it was because you amused and entertained me. Had you wept and pleaded with me, I would not have cared in the least what became of you.' The grooves flashed in his cheeks. 'Instead, knowing that I had complete power over you, you turned on me while dressed only in your shift and with your hair tumbling about your face, and you read me a severe lecture on the morality of my profession. After that, how could I have allowed you to end your days in someone's harem? Particularly,' he added with amusement, 'when it was quite plain that those days would be limited to a very few, for I could not imagine you submitting to any Turk or Moor who bought you. This view was fully confirmed when you slapped and kicked Seremeth Ali, and would certainly have suffered the death penalty had I not lied to the Dey about my reasons for wishing to buy you.'

She was silent, staring at the document he had called a

teskere and which he said was evidence of her freedom. If he had been speaking the truth, then she had cost him far more than the twenty-five gold sequins he had paid in the market-place. By lying to the Dey and saving her life, he had also forfeited any ransom which might have been extracted for Abigail Pascoe.

'I simply don't believe you,' she muttered. 'If you had intended all along to give me my freedom, why did you not tell me so? Why did you do your best to make me believe that . . .' She stopped, flushing.

'That what, Genevra Shaw?' he pressed her, his smoke-coloured eyes glinting at her in knowing amusement.

'Why do you always call me that?' she parried.

He raised his eyebrows. 'It is your name.'

'I know. But . . .'

'Would you prefer the formality of Miss Shaw?'

Her flush deepened. 'Genevra would sound more—more natural.'

'I agree. But Trelawney would sound equally natural from *your* lips. Apart from an assortment of insulting epithets, you have scrupulously avoided addressing me by any name. Now,' he added pleasantly, 'to return to your original question. I did not tell you what I intended for fear that you might unconsciously give the truth away. If you did not believe that I wished to buy you for some obvious, personal reason, how could I have expected others to? Besides, how tame the whole matter would have been if you had known the truth. You would not have afforded me half as much entertainment as you did, Genevra, had you known that I had no evil designs on you, and that I intended presenting you with your freedom.'

So many different reactions were pounding through her that it was difficult to hold on to any one for long enough for it to be examined properly. Her disbelief was fading, and it was beginning to seem that this contradictory and wholly baffling man had intended, from the beginning, to set her free. He had been playing a game with her, and the game was now over.

'Tell me about yourself,' he said. 'The arguments I put forward to persuade Dey Osman Pasha that you were Abigail Pascoe were all true, you know. You *are* too well-spoken, too impossible to cow, to have been born to the servant classes. And whoever heard of an English serving-wench being familiar with French? Only a few English blue-stockings of the leisured classes would be at home in that language, and even Miss Pascoe is patently unfamiliar with it.'

'My father was a very scholarly man, and he taught me everything I know, including fluent French and a little Latin. Unfortunately, he was also very poor, having been a Rector . . .' She stopped as she became aware that he was shaking with secret laughter. 'What is funny?'

'Nothing. It is just . . . How I wish I might have known that you were a Rector's daughter! It would have lent such an exquisite edge to what was already a richly entertaining situation.'

She glared at him. 'I am extremely grateful that you did not know!'

'*Trelawney,*' he prompted, his eyes dancing. 'Force yourself to say it.'

'Tre—Trelawney.' As soon as it was out, she knew why instinct had hitherto prevented her from addressing him by name. Now that she had done so, something had changed between them. She could no longer regard him primarily as a renegade Corsair, an Englishman who had turned Turk, someone worthy only of condemnation and contempt. By calling him Trelawney she had evoked a man who had no connection with Algiers or with what he was doing here; someone with a background in England, and with a family and parents who had chosen such an unusual Christian name for him, perhaps because it was a family name.

'Why did you desert from the Navy?' she blurted out. 'Even if you disagreed with your commanding officer, there must surely have been other courses open to you?'

'Do not try to find the good in me, Genevra. You would be sadly disappointed.' He grinned. 'Besides, you were the subject under discussion, and not myself. You said your father was poor. Go on.'

She shrugged. 'I kept house for him until he died, and then I found myself penniless and homeless.' Remembering how vital it was not to betray any connection between herself and Uncle John, she embroidered, 'I needed to earn my own living, and so when Miss Abigail Pascoe visited our village and we discovered that we were very distantly related on my father's side, I accepted the post she offered me as her personal maid.'

'And I wager that she made sure she received the value of the money she paid you many times over,' Trelawney said shrewdly. 'She certainly had no scruples about trying to burden you with her own identity. She could not have guessed that it would work to your advantage instead.'

It worked to my advantage, Genevra thought with deep gratitude, only because you made it do so. You may deny that there is any good in you, but the fact that you sacrificed any ransom which could have been extracted from Abigail Pascoe so that I might live speaks for itself.

A lump had formed in her throat, and it thickened as Trelawney leant across the table and took her hand in his. 'You are free,' he said. 'The *teskere* bears witness to that.'

She was still trying to form the words with which to thank him, when his manner changed and he became brisk. 'When we have finished our meal, I shall take you to the British Consulate. That was what I meant when I said you should be suitably dressed. I did not want you to have to face the same kind of scorn to which you were subjected yesterday.'

Shock tore through her, and she kept her glance riveted on the *teskere* so that he would not read it in her eyes. She dared not allow herself to be taken to the Consulate, where her relationship with Sophie would be glaringly obvious to everyone, and give the lie to the fact that Abigail was the Consul's niece. Uncle John and his family would be thrown into the most deadly danger, which would extend to include herself. Unless—Unless the fact that she had been given her freedom meant that the slate had been wiped clean of all her past misdeeds.

She picked up the *teskere*, and asked, 'Can this be revoked, declared void?'

'Only in very exceptional circumstances.'

That the British Counsul's niece had committed an act punishable by death, and that he had lied to the Dey about her identity, would indeed be considered very exceptional circumstances . . . She dared not return to the Consulate.

But what alternative was there? As a free woman, she was discovering with awful irony, her fate was likely to be far more fraught with danger than if she had remained a slave.

Desperately, she said, 'You spoke of my being free. I shall be nothing of the sort. Miss Pascoe will exploit my situation as a former slave, and expect an even greater degree of servitude . . .'

'She will do no such thing,' Trelawney interrupted. 'You may remember that among the documents which Captain Perreira had brought to Algiers were diplomatic despatches addressed by the British Government to the Consul. The Dey is no respecter of diplomatic niceties, and he ordered Mr Llewellyn to read and translate the despatches to him. He was thrown into a fury because the British government continues to refuse to pay an increased annual tribute, but then he perceived how Miss Pascoe might be used as a lever against the government, through the Consul.'

Genevra remembered how Trelawney had said, earlier, that the Dey had discovered other compensations for Abigail's lost ransom. She remained silent, her glance averted, as he continued.

'The Dey decided that, because both the Consul and Miss Pascoe deceived him about her identity, he was fully justified in having her arrested. She is languishing inside a harem in the Jenina, where he intends keeping her until her uncle persuades the British government to agree to his demands. The Dey has whipped himself into a state of righteous rage about the deception, and had he not been mindful of Miss Pascoe's wealth, and that it might still be put to his use, she would have cause to fear for her life if the British government does not respond swiftly to the Dey's demands.'

Oh, dear God, Genevra thought, clenching her hands tightly under cover of the table. How much more cause for fury would the Dey have when he learnt of the Consul's double deception! His *true* niece had not only been a so-called legitimate prisoner-of-war, but she had committed a crime punishable by death, and he had lied about her identity. If the whole truth came out, the repercussions would be too dreadful to contemplate. Could she confide in Trelawney, and explain why it was out of the question for

her to return to the Consulate? Almost too late, she realised how disastrous that would be. Just because this man
possessed charm, and because he had saved her at the
expense of a ransom for Abigail, it did not alter the fact that
he served the Dey. He might cheat him in relatively small
matters, but his very status in the hierarchy of Algiers
meant that his ultimate loyalty would belong to its ruler. He
could not afford to betray the Dey by withholding from him
the vital information that Genevra was related to the
British Consul, and that he had been unwittingly tricked
into letting such a potentially valuable political pawn slip
through his fingers.

'I am thinking of ordering a sedan chair to be strapped to
the back of a camel, so that you may arrive at the British
Consulate in state!' There was laughter in Trelawney's
voice. 'That is how the wives and daughters of important
Janissaries travel through the city. Just think of the reaction
among the free Christians who turned their noses up at you
before!'

'Indeed!' Desperation was adding considerably to
Genevra's sudden anger. 'It is all one vast joke to you, is it
not? You thought it hugely amusing to play games with me,
and now you are relishing the further amusement of forcing
me to go to the British Consulate, making a show of
myself . . .'

'My dear Genevra,' he interrupted, his eyebrows raised,
'If you would prefer to creep anonymously into the
European quarter after the scorn with which they regarded
you yesterday, you are not the young woman of spirit I had
thought you to be!'

'You know nothing of me at all! And you have not given
one single thought to *my* feelings! Miss Pascoe has been
arrested and I, her known maid-servant, am to be taken to
the Consulate, wearing her rich gown, and you expect me
not to be utterly mortified and humiliated by the reception I
shall receive? No, I will not go to the British Consulate with
you—whether on foot or in a sedan chair strapped to a
camel!'

He had lost his air of lazy amusement. 'Very well,' he said
tersely, 'the game is over. But you *will* go to the Consulate.
There is nowhere else you can go.'

'Then I'll stay here!'

'I do not want you here!' He was beginning to wear a harassed look. 'Good God, Genevra, I thought you would be relieved, if not grateful, to be given your freedom!'

'Did you? Relieved and grateful to be made a gift of what you had no moral right to buy in the first place?'

His face was grimly set now. 'Whether you are grateful or not, you will go to the Consulate. As a free British citizen and a young woman without means, it is the only logical place for you, because you certainly cannot stay here now that I have obtained a *teskere* for you.'

'I will not be treated as a discarded joke, Trelawney!' she cried, desperation lending the right note of moral outrage to her voice. 'You set out to acquire a slave, and it is a slave you are saddled with now!' She snatched the *teskere* from the table and tore it into small pieces, allowing them to flutter to the floor.

He stared at her in stunned silence for a moment, then he strode towards her, his expression frighteningly austere, and caught her by the shoulders. 'Do you realise what you have just done? A *teskere*, once issued, cannot be duplicated. You have, literally, thrown away your freedom!'

'Then—Then so be it.'

He regarded her, his jaw set. 'You will remain a slave by your own choice,' he told her, 'and the chain will remain on your ankle. But you are going to the Consulate, just the same.'

She had not bargained on such a stalemate. Desperately, she said, 'They would not take me in!'

'They would be obliged to take in any British subject upon request.'

'This British subject does not, and never will, request it!'

Unexpectedly, he moved closer to her and lifted a hand, trailing his fingertips lightly and slowly over her cheek. He murmured in a totally different, seductive voice, 'I am flattered that you should wish to remain my slave and stay here with me, and entertaining though I find the thought of a renegade Rais and a Rector's daughter living together in intimacy, I really have to refuse to consider it. It would be far too inconvenient to have a female slave underfoot in a male household.'

She knew that he had changed his tactics in order to goad her into agreeing to be taken to the Consulate, and she forced herself not to react with the outrage he had hoped for, or to reveal that his merest touch had set the blood coursing hotly through her veins. Instead, while she tried to rack her brains as to what to do next, she sneered, 'It has not escaped my notice that you have been referring to me as a slave, instead of a prisoner-of-war!'

'Yes, damn you, you are a slave!' he snarled, his mood switched to one of angry impatience. 'Destroying the *teskere* has made you one. And since you are my slave, and I say you must go to the Consulate, you will obey me!'

Feeling cornered, she grabbed at the only threat that occurred to her. 'Rather than go to the Consulate, I shall insist upon my right to seek an audience with the Dey! I shall tell him how you deliberately tricked him into believing that I was Abigail Pascoe when you knew, from your first glimpse of us together on board *Caranguejo*, that she was the mistress and I the maid, and that you entered into the deception for no other reason than your own amusement!'

Trelawney's expression changed from one of bafflement to grim suspicion, his eyes narrowing to slits. 'Why are you so desperate not to be taken to the British Consulate, Genevra?'

She knew that her answer would have to be utterly convincing. 'Because I would not be able to hold up my head among free Christians, after the particular attention you have been paying me!' she said with passion. 'It would have been bad enough to have to go to the Consulate as a slave and the maid-servant of Miss Pascoe, who would be resented and fit in nowhere. But after the performance you gave yesterday I would be totally ostracised and kept in isolation, for fear that I might contaminate others!'

'You are talking nonsense,' Trelawney began.

'I wish I were! Because it amused you, because it was part of the joke you were enjoying at my expense, you left no doubt in the minds of anyone present at the Consulate as to your reasons for wishing to buy me. *They* do not share your warped sense of humour; *they* would not believe it was all a joke! Neither would they believe for a moment that you intended from the outset to buy me so that you could set me free. What, they would ask themselves, really happened? What gave you such a disgust of me that it caused you to discard me? It must have been something really depraved, they would say.'

'That is all highly-coloured and quite improbable speculation,' Trelawney said, but there was a note of unease in his voice.

'If you believe that, you cannot know very much about any average, moral, respectable community! You introduced me to them in the first place, wearing soiled, ill-fitting garments, and you made it very clear why you wished to buy me. And now you propose returning me to their midst, totally transformed by Abigail Pascoe's expensive gown, suddenly and inexplicably rejected after buying me, and you imagine it will not cause rumour and speculation of the worst kind? Do you really expect me to welcome being treated like a leper for years, perhaps for the rest of my life?'

Trelawney had been watching her with a look of growing frustration on his face. 'If you had not torn up the *teskere*,' he said harshly, 'the Consul would have been able to put you on board the first available vessel and send you home to England!'

Deliberately she put aside her vow not to weep again and summoned tears to her eyes. She was able to do so by reflecting that, whether as a slave or a free human being, there was no sanctuary for her anywhere in the world.

'It—It is too late to think of that,' she said brokenly, allowing the tears to roll down her cheeks. 'I *have* torn it up, and now—now I am doomed, and I would rather confess to the Dey and—and have an end put to my miserable life than go to the Consulate where—where I would be an outcast, an object of contempt and disgust.'

She heard him swear under his breath. 'If I had known, Genevra Shaw, what a millstone round my neck you would turn out to be, I would have left you to the tender mercies of Seremeth Ali!'

Was he, she wondered, signalling capitulation? She

allowed her tears to subside, and watched him staring into space, his fingers drumming upon the table. After a moment he spoke abruptly. 'Go to the drawing-room and stay there.'

'Why?'

'Because I want to be left in peace to decide what to do with you,' he said sourly.

Another unwelcome possibility occurred to her, and she asked in a small, unsteady voice, 'Will you sell me to someone else?'

He gave a bitter laugh. 'Without the slightest hesitation, if I could find anyone fool enough to take you off my hands!' His voice roughened, and he growled, 'Do as you are told, Genevra. Shut yourself up in the drawing-room and keep out of my way, for I do not trust myself alone with you at the moment!'

CHAPTER ELEVEN

AFTER SHE HAD closed the door of the drawing-room behind her, Genevra sank into an armchair, feeling completely drained. She had had to fight so hard, and throw away the freedom which had been offered to her, simply in order to avoid being taken to the very place that had been her destination throughout the whole fraught voyage from England!

She waited for Trelawney to come and tell her what he had decided, but he did not join her. A great deal of noise was going on elsewhere in the house: the banging of heavy objects, and the sound of hammering, accompanied by voices issuing what sounded like orders. But it could hardly have anything to do with herself, and so she remained where she was, a prey to anxiety and to her own confused thoughts.

She could not help but be aware of a new and different feeling towards Trelawney. There had been something in his expression, both when she tore up the *teskere* and when she threatened to betray him to Osman Pasha that had suggested that he was—not hurt precisely, but . . . She struggled to find the right word. *Disillusioned*. That was it. As if he had once again received confirmation of the cynical realities of life.

After what seemed like hours, the noises began to fade, and a while later the drawing-room door opened. But it was Ahmed who appeared, not Trelawney. With gestures, he indicated that Genevra was to follow him. Unable to imagine what to expect, she found herself in the room in which Abigail's trunks had been kept, and was amazed at the transformation. It was now furnished with a bed, a dressing-table and a hanging chest, and she wondered where the furniture had come from. Perhaps Trelawney owned a warehouse where he stored pieces of raided cargoes, but it must have been a considerable feat to carry the furniture through the narrow alleys before manhandling it up the stairs. A closer inspection showed that the doorway that had previously led into Trelawney's bedroom had been firmly boarded up. She drew a long, unsteady breath. She had been told, as clearly as if it had been spelled out in words, that she was not to be sent to the Consulate or put up for sale again. She was to stay here, and she need not fear unwelcome attention from the man who was her owner and her master. She remembered how Trelawney had told her that it was possible to survive in Algiers if one was ruthless and clever enough. She had been cunning and desperate, rather than ruthless or clever, in her battle to prevent the fact that she was the true niece of the British Consul becoming known, but she had succeeded. She was beginning to learn how to survive!

As she unpacked the contents of Abigail's trunks to put the clothes away, she tried to spare some pity for the girl imprisoned in a harem inside the Jenina. But it was very hard to do so in the face of her many past acts of treachery, and at least her own life was not likely to be in any danger.

When she had changed into a simpler gown of figured muslin, she went to look for Trelawney, but he was no-where to be found. The blank outer walls of the house had the effect of shutting out much of the city's noise, but now she could hear clearly the wailing sound of the calling to prayer by the muezzins. She went out to the gallery, and realised that the calls were coming from all directions inside the city, echoing through the alleys and filling the air. It had brought the servants out into the courtyard, and she watched from the gallery as they opened the street door and disappeared. It was closed behind them, and she knew she was quite alone in the house.

She had been too preoccupied and tense to do justice to the meal earlier in the day with Trelawney, and now she felt an acutely growing hunger. It would be some while before the servants returned from their prayers and could prepare supper. There must be something to eat in the kitchen. It proved to have several larders and pantries and cold rooms leading from it, and its baking-oven was unlike any she had seen before. It was heated by glowing charcoal spread upon a recessed area on top of the oven, and she guessed that much of the cooking was done by grilling over the live coals.

The charcoal had been allowed to burn down to a dull glow. In the adjoining rooms, among unfamiliar dry goods and pulses, she found flour, sugar and rice. One of the cold rooms held part of a sheep's carcass and several unplucked fowls. In a dish upon a shelf, and protected against flies by a piece of muslin, was what looked like mutton cut up in cubes. She debated for a moment whether to take some and grill it over the charcoal, but her hunger was too immediate, and when she found, inside another larder, some black bread and what she suspected must be cheese made from goats' or ewes' milk, she decided that it would suffice for her supper.

She had slept very little since her capture, and everything that had happened to her since had been emotionally and physically draining. Almost as soon as she had finished her simple meal, sleep threatened to overwhelm her, and she decided to retire. After undressing, she was asleep almost as soon as her head touched the pillow.

The wailing of the muezzins awoke her, and she sat up, blinking, with memory returning fully. It was very early, and dawn could only just be breaking, but already she could hear the bustle and noise going on inside the house. Of course, she remembered, the servants would be answering the call to prayers, and would have been up and about for some considerable time, preparing breakfast. A jug of hot water had been placed outside her door, and she washed and dressed and pinned up her hair before making her way to the dining-room, her heart beating fast at the prospect of sharing the meal with Trelawney, and wondering what kind of reception to expect.

Breakfast could hardly have been described as a meal, she found. The table had been set with plates and cups and a bowl of fruit, and a jug of coffee was being kept hot on a small oil-stove. Trelawney, dressed in robes, rose and gestured to her to help herself to fruit and coffee.

She sat down, and silence stretched between them. Then she began, 'I—I have to thank you for my bedroom, and for . . .'

'Genevra,' he interrupted grimly, 'don't try my patience too far. You know perfectly well that if I could have thought of a way of ridding myself of you, I would have taken it. I don't want to be thanked for acknowledging that I'm hoist with my own petard.' He pushed his cup aside and stood up. 'If you will excuse me, I have duties awaiting me.'

She ate some of the fruit and washed it down with coffee, and then returned to her room to tidy it and make the bed. A while later she heard the servants coming back, and she went out to the gallery. They treated her with polite indifference, and went about their duties. She wandered down into the courtyard, wondering how to fill in time. It struck her suddenly that she was in the bizarre situation of being a slave, bored almost to distraction because she had nothing whatever to do. She picked armfuls of flowers in the courtyard and carried them upstairs, arranging them in bowls, making the task stretch for as long as possible, aware that when it had been finished only idleness awaited her.

Ahmed came to summon her to the meal which was served before noon. She was, it transpired, to eat it in solitude, for there was no sign of Trelawney. Luncheon consisted of grilled cubes of mutton threaded upon skewers, served with rice. And when she had eaten, more long, empty hours stretched ahead of her.

The dullness of enforced inactivity, after all she had been through, brought with it a sense of anticlimax and then one of grievance. Since she was to be totally ignored like this, why should she remain imprisoned within the house or the courtyard? She put on one of Abigail's bonnets and made her way unhurriedly to the street door, defying any servant to stop her. But they had either not noticed her, or else they did not care what she might take it into her head to do.

She had not meant to venture beyond safe and swift return to the door, but it was not long before she realised that the men who passed her in the alley looked at her, and quickly averted their eyes again as they walked on. She became aware of a muttered Algerine phrase which was repeated by groups of men passing her, and she had no difficulty in understanding, because the most significant words happened to be in French. Her colour high, she heard the men reminding themselves and one another that she was the woman of Rais el-Trahni, and that anyone touching her would have his hand chopped off. It was quite safe, obviously, for Trelawney's woman to appear alone in public. Emboldened, she began to walk on, exploring the alley, and beginning to recognise landmarks such as earthenware pots of different flowering plants arranged upon the flat roofs of the houses.

The alley opened into the main broad road of Algiers, and here Genevra stopped to watch an astonishing sight. Young, good-looking men, some of them scarcely more than boys, were parading slowly along, richly dressed in embroidered silks with gold thread glinting in the folds of their turbans. Wealthy-looking Turks and Moors approached them stroking their cheeks, gazing soulfully at them while kissing their hands, and offering them beautiful bouquets of flowers. She heard the word *garzonés* mentioned several times, and remembered that Trelawney had once made reference to it.

She decided to turn back, and began to retrace her steps, hoping that she had not mistaken the alley which led to Trelawney's house. It was a pleasant surprise to see the familiar figure of Rupert Runcorn coming towards her. He was dressed in pantaloons and shirt of blue and white striped silk, the sun glinting on his tawny hair.

'Why, ma'am!' he exclaimed. 'You should not be abroad like this, quite unaccompanied!'

'I am in no danger,' she reassured him, flushing slightly. 'You are perfectly well aware that I am known as Trelawney's woman, who must not be insulted or harmed.'

He sighed, and shook his head. 'That degrading title! I had hoped, ma'am, that you would not learn how widely you are now known by it.'

She did not respond immediately. It had come to her, with a stab of shame, that she had ceased to feel degraded at being known as Trelawney's woman, and felt instead . . . No, she would not allow herself to examine her complex emotions. She changed the subject. 'Please do not address me as "ma'am". I have asked you to call me Genevra.'

'Only if you would do me the honour of calling me Rupert in return.'

She smiled at him. 'Very well—Rupert.' Now that she had become used to it, it struck her that his scar added to rather than detracted from the appeal of his physical appearance. It reminded one that he had come by it in a brave, reckless attempt to escape from this hellish country.

He had fallen into step beside her. 'They are saying other things about you, Genevra, which you ought perhaps to know. Even though I did not repeat what you told me at the Bedestan, others now believe the Consul innocently identified the wrong young woman as his niece, and that *you* are wealthy Miss Pascoe. They are convinced that is the reason why Trelawney Grant bought you.'

She remained silent for a moment. Neither Rupert nor the gossips would ever believe the truth—that Trelawney had set out to buy her, in the first place, on a self-indulgent whim for his own amusement. 'The rumours are wide of the mark,' she said at last. 'Believe me, if I had been Miss Pascoe, I would have lost no time in authorising my man of business to pay a ransom for me!' The stark reality of her situation crowded in upon her suddenly, and she asked, 'Rupert, if one were to obtain a *teskere*, and—and lost it, would one ever be able to obtain a second one?'

He gave her a startled look. 'What a strange question! What on earth inspired it, Genevra?'

'When I was taken to the Consulate,' she embroidered, 'I overheard people talking of such a case. I gathered that a *teskere* was a document proclaiming one's freedom.'

'It is, and one would have to be criminally negligent to lose it! It is issued by the Belique, or Treasury, and it certifies that the twenty-five per cent tax on a prisoner's ransom has been paid into the coffers. If one lost a *teskere*, another ransom would have to be paid so that the Belique could collect tax on it and issue a fresh document as proof of a prisoner's freedom.'

Genevra was silent. So Trelawney had had to pay for that *teskere* which she had torn up. Freedom, at the moment, was to be avoided at all costs, but life would be totally unendurable if it were not a goal to be strived for. 'If only there were someone who might one day pay a ransom for me,' she muttered wretchedly, half to herself.

Rupert touched her arm in a gesture of sympathy. 'If only you had been a man, Genevra, it might have been possible for you to earn your own ransom.' When she looked at him in disbelief, he pointed to an arcade of open-fronted shops in which European men were busy, fashioning leatherwork

or metal goods. 'Those are all slaves who have borrowed
money from the Jewish moneylenders and have invested it
in businesses of their own. They are saving towards paying
their own ransoms. I myself have been saving whatever I
can from the money advanced to me by Abraham so that I
might buy the lease of a tavern and so help to contribute
towards the massive ransom which is being demanded from
my family . . .'

He broke off, staring beyond her, and when she turned
her head she saw that Trelawney was approaching, the folds
of his turban casting part of his face into shade and giving
it an extremely forbidding expression. He nodded
coldly, dismissively, at Rupert and addressed Genevra in
a curt voice. 'You are to return home with me.' He took
her arm in a bruising grip and propelled her along the
alley.

'Home!' she echoed bitterly. 'It is a prison . . .'

'If it is,' he interrupted tersely, 'you are there by your
own choice.'

Neither of them spoke again until they had entered the
courtyard of his house, climbed the stairs and stood facing
one another inside the drawing-room. 'How dared you
wander abroad by yourself like that?' he demanded with
cold rage.

'I was in no danger! You are perfectly aware that no one
would lay a finger upon me, because I am known as your
woman . . .'

He moved, jerking her against him, holding her so
closely that she could feel the tautness of his thighs against
her own involuntarily responsive body. 'Yes, you are
publicly known as my woman!' he snarled. 'And that being
so, I will not have you seen wandering abroad unescorted,
and I will certainly not allow meetings between yourself and
that smooth gammoner, Runcorn . . .'

'I am not your woman, Trelawney,' she flung at him,
'whatever people may say, and if I choose to make a friend
of Rupert . . .'

His grip on her tightened. 'You are my slave!' he snarled.
'Remember? To do with as I choose, to command as I
wish . . .' His anger appeared to evaporate suddenly as he
looked into her eyes. He bent his head, and she waited,

with a drumming heartbeat and a melting of her entire being, for his kiss.

It did not come, for the spell which held them was broken by the wailing call of the muezzins, followed by the clattering of the servants down the stairs. Trelawney moved away, and she searched her mind for something mundane with which to change the subject.

'Would you please tell me what time dinner will be served?' she asked at last, with unnatural politeness. 'I was too tired last evening to wait up for it.'

He looked at her with grim amusement, all desire wiped from his expression. 'If you had wanted the ordered routine of British breakfasts, luncheons and dinners, you should have gone to the Consulate. Because the servants respond to the calls to prayers, the only meal cooked and served in an Algerian household is the one before noon. In the evenings one generally eats in one of the taverns leased by Christian slaves.' He frowned. 'Obviously you cannot frequent a tavern, and I shall have to arrange for the servants to prepare supper for you in advance. As for this evening —I shall bring something in for you before returning to a tavern for my own supper.'

She thought of the dreary prospect of more hours spent on her own, with nothing to do. 'I could make mutton pies for both of us,' she suggested diffidently. 'I visited the kitchen and the larders last evening, looking for something to eat, and I know there is everything I would need. My father used to say that my mutton pies were by far the best he . . .'

'My dear girl,' Trelawney interrupted with a short laugh, 'the servants would rise up in revolt if a female, and an Unbeliever at that, were to meddle in the kitchen!'

'Oh . . .' She was about to turn away when he spoke again, abruptly.

'How long would it take you to make mutton pies?'

'If the oven is still hot enough, not much above an hour.'

He stood up. 'Then let us go and see how hot the oven is.'

It was hot enough, and while Trelawney leant against the dresser and watched, Genevra set to work, improvising by using oil instead of fat for the pastry, and moulding it inside small earthenware plates before adding the filling of diced mutton and onion and potato and the covering pastry lids.

While they waited for the pies to bake, she remarked, 'I saw some *garzonés* today.'

'Indeed?' His voice was expressionless.

'The Turks and the Moors treated them as though they were girls. Why was that?'

'It is not as far as I am aware, the duty of a master to instruct his slave in the ways of the world,' he said with evasive acidity.

'I gather it has to do with something improper?'

'Highly improper, and not a subject I intend discussing with a Rector's daughter. You had better see if the pies are ready.'

They were cooked to perfection, and Genevra and Trelawney sat down in the kitchen to eat. 'Your father was right,' he remarked approvingly. 'I had forgotten the delights of ordinary British fare. But now we had better remove all traces of what we have been doing.'

They worked together, with Trelawney fetching water so that they could wash and put away all the receptacles that had been used. Afterwards, they made a thorough check to ensure that nothing had been overlooked, and in their zeal both of them attempted to enter one of the larders at the same time, and collided bodily. He put his hands on her shoulders and looked down at her, and her heart gave a leap of happiness as she saw the grooves flickering in his cheeks again for the first time since she had torn up the *teskere*.

'Who would have thought that I would ever find myself in such a ludicrous position?' he said with rueful amusement. 'Conspiring with a slave I don't want to remove the incriminating evidence of illicit pie-making from my own kitchen!'

She laughed too, rather shakily, overwhelmed by his touch. His hands slid slowly down her arms, and hovered unsteadily on her breasts. Her heart beat thunderously in her temples as she waited, for surely this time there would be no interruption to prevent him from kissing her. But he had required no interruption. With an abrupt, almost violent movement, he stepped back. She felt the colour rising in her cheeks, but she tried to bring back a semblance of light-hearted normality by asking, 'What would you like me to cook for our supper tomorrow night, Trelawney?'

'Nothing.' His voice was austere and remote. 'There will be no repetition of this evening's activities.'

She turned away, and concentrated on wiping away a small amount of flour she had earlier spilt on the larder shelf. Apart from the stimulus and—yes, it had to be admitted, the excitement of his company—making the mutton pies had satisfied her need for something to do and had given her the opportunity of exercising one of her skills.

'From now on,' Trelawney told her, 'if you wish to wander about the city, you will be accompanied by Ahmed. And I want you to promise, Genevra, that you will not seek Rupert Runcorn's company, or encourage him in any way, and that if you should encounter him in the street, you will nod politely and walk on.' She turned to face him, her pulse racing with excitement at the thought that had suddenly come to her. 'Well?' he asked. 'Do I have your promise on that?'

She regarded him with unflinching defiance. 'No, you have not, Trelawney.'

'In that case,' he said grimly, 'I shall have to make certain that you are unable to come into contact with Runcorn.'

She lowered her lashes so that he would not read the expression in her eyes. She would contrive to meet Rupert somehow, for she had the strongest of all motives. The making of mutton pies had given her an idea. Why should she not make mutton pies for sale to the public, and so work at raising a ransom for herself one day in the future?

But she would need practical help and advice for such a project, and Rupert was the only person in Algiers to whom she could turn for it.

CHAPTER TWELVE

TRELAWNEY REMAINED TRUE to his word, and Ahmed became Genevra's shadow during the days that followed. Life was frustrating, intensely boring and empty, and she seldom saw Trelawney. She suspected that he was deliberately avoiding her. With Ahmed accompanying her everywhere, it was impossible for her to stop and speak to Rupert on the few occasions when she spotted him in the street, for she was certain the servant would tell Trelawney, and then she suspected that he would stop her from leaving the house altogether. As it was, whenever the servants were away at their prayers, she found the outer door locked and herself a prisoner within the grounds.

Then, by a stroke of good fortune, she learnt of the existence of the public baths. She had seen people emerging from substantial stone buildings adjoining furnaces being stoked by slaves, and when she idly brought up the subject on one of the rare occasions when Trelawney was at home, he explained what they were.

'The men use them during the morning and at night, but during the afternoons they are reserved exclusively for women.'

'Would I be barred from using them?'

'No.' Trelawney took coins from a pouch and handed them to her. 'One of these will gain you admission to any of the public baths in the city.'

At first, it was no more than a welcome diversion to spend part of the afternoon in a public bath, with Ahmed waiting patiently for her outside. One removed one's clothes in an antechamber, Genevra discovered, and handed them to a large, friendly Negress slave for safe-keeping. A room led from the antechamber, so filled with steam that it was sometimes difficult to see anything clearly. Several copper pipes ran round its walls, from which vigorous jets of water gushed at intervals. The room was furnished with cubicles situated directly beneath the water-jets; one received a clean towel and a piece of soap from another attendant and then entered the cubicle where cold water spouted from one jet and steaming hot from the other, mixing as they cascaded into a shallow copper basin fixed to the wall and overflowed to shower one with pleasantly warm water.

By chance, she discovered that the sophisticated baths, so unexpected in a country like Algeria, offered more than an invigorating and pleasant diversion. They also possessed an exit into an alley at the rear, so that she could slip outside without being seen by Ahmed and return later, to re-emerge from the front door. It was not long after she had discovered this escape route that she saw Rupert walking along an alley, and hurried to join him. He clasped her hands in his.

'I feared you had thought better of forming any friendship with me, for when I saw you on previous occasions you appeared to give me the cut direct!'

'I am sorry about that, Rupert. Trelawney has forbidden me to associate with you, and has ordered his servant to be my watchdog. But I must speak to you urgently.'

He listened intently as she told him what she had in mind, but shook his head when she had finished. 'It would not do, Genevra, to make the pies secretly inside Trelawney Grant's house, and smuggle them out for sale to the public. The idea of marketing them is a good one, but you would require premises in which to bake the pies and sell them while they are hot. For that you will need considerable capital.' As she made a sound of hopelessness, he added, 'Allow me time to consider the matter. I may be able to think of a solution.'

She had to leave him then, and slip back inside the bath-house so that she could emerge from the front door and join the waiting Ahmed. Several frustrating days went by, with no sign of Rupert, even though he knew which of the bath-houses she used and at what hour he could expect to see her.

Then, one afternoon, he was waiting for her. 'I have not been neglecting you, Genevra,' he greeted her, 'but I have been busy on your behalf. I think I may have persuaded Miss Pascoe to put up the money you will need, although, of course, she believes it will be for *my* benefit . . .'

'*Abigail!*' Genevra cut him short. 'But she is kept imprisoned inside the Jenina . . .'

'Not any longer. Mr McDonnell has raised a large loan from the merchants, which she will of course repay, and has offered it to the Dey to secure her release. She has been safely back with her uncle and his family in the Consulate for some days.'

She had, Genevra thought cynically, been wise not to waste too much pity on Abigail. It occurred to her that, in spite of the girl's initial reaction at the first sight of Rupert's scar, he must have made a great impression upon her later, if she was considering lending him money. Rupert obviously had not the slightest doubt that Abigail was truly Uncle John's niece; but then, she thought, even though he was a regular visitor to the Consulate and must be familiar with the white streak in Sophie's hair, it was such an ingrained habit for herself to hide her own streak that he had never seen it.

She was about to question him further about Abigail's release when he gazed beyond her, and asked with a frown, 'Is not that the servant who has been shadowing you?'

She turned her head in alarm, but could see no sign of Ahmed. Rupert shrugged and decided that he had been mistaken, but Genevra judged it prudent to return to the bath-house, and when she emerged, Ahmed was waiting for her as usual.

That evening she discovered that Trelawney had decided, for once, to remain at home. He shared the cold supper the servants had prepared for her and she studied him secretly, alarmed at her joy at the sight of him sitting across the table. She made her voice acid. 'It is indeed an honour to have your company, although I am quite sure it was not the thought of my being left completely alone in the house, night after night, which has prompted you to join me.'

He pretended to have taken the remark literally. 'No. I have duties which require my attention this evening, because tomorrow I have to go to sea again.'

She looked at him, so impressive and compelling in his cut-away European coat, the ruffled white sleeves which foamed over his wrists and the sky-blue cravat at his throat, and had to remind herself forcibly *why* he would be going to sea again tomorrow. He would be raiding the ocean, plundering more unsuspecting vessels, taking more prisoners so that they could be turned into slaves. But even more appalling than all this was was her own bereft feeling at the thought of him going away, so that her days would not contain even the faint hope of catching a glimpse of him as he entered or left through the countryard.

Almost as if he were aware of what she was thinking and feeling, he said, 'You will, of course, come with me in the morning and watch the Corsair fleet as we leave the harbour.'

'Why?'

His eyes rested mockingly upon her. 'Because you are known to be my woman, and it would be expected. Retire early tonight, for we shall have to leave for the harbour at dawn.'

As she lay in bed that night she tried to assure herself of the many advantages to herself in Trelawney's absence at sea. She would be free to meet Rupert . . . But she was already free to meet Rupert while Ahmed believed her to be inside the bath-house. Sighing, she attempted to blot the whole matter of Trelawney's leaving from her mind, and settled down to sleep.

The air was chilly the next morning as she left the house with him, and she was glad of the protection offered by Abigail's lilac-coloured velvet cloak. As they reached the Marine Gate they were hemmed in by Turkish officers, sailors and onlookers, and Trelawney explained briefly that the entire Corsair fleet had been ordered and was being financed by the Divan, or government of Algiers, so that all prisoners taken would be the property of the Dey.

She shuddered. 'What a despicable country this is, and what a despicable career you pursue!'

He did not trouble to react, and as the masses swarming over the mole made way for them she could see the preparations for sailing. She could pick out the Corsair fleet by their shape, but there were other ships, too, flying the flags of their respective nations. A party of well-dressed men and women were waiting to board a Dutch ship, *De Merel*, their luggage piled about them. They were obviously free Christians from the European quarter about to visit their homes, travelling onwards from Rotterdam. Something seemed familiar about one of them, and while Trelawney's attention was engaged elsewhere, she crossed over to join the passengers waiting to board *De Merel*.

The young woman dressed in a plain stuff gown with a small bundle at her feet *was* Abigail. She studied Genevra with a jaundiced expression. 'That cloak was a particular favourite of mine! Once I realised the Consul knew that I was not his niece, I petitioned him repeatedly to reclaim my luggage from you, but he refused. He obviously wants nothing whatever to do with you, or he would not have allowed me to claim him as my uncle in the first place. But while it suited me to remain in obscurity inside the Consulate until a passage home could be arranged, I do not see why I should be the loser by sacrificing all my beautiful clothes to you.' She gave a bitter, triumphant laugh. 'If your uncle imagines I will repay the fine demanded by the Dey for my release from that stifling harem, he is sadly mistaken!'

'My uncle is not a wealthy man . . .' Genevra began, appalled at the thought of his suffering such a heavy financial loss.

Abigail swept the subject aside with a gesture. 'I am glad of this opportunity of speaking to you, for there is something else you had better know: I have heard it rumoured that you are the true Abigail Pascoe. That suits me very well, for it means that you will inherit the problems that brought me to Algiers in the first place. Just in case you should take it into your head to forge my signature, I have written in advance to my man of business in England and told him under no circumstances to allow anyone to draw upon my funds, even if the instructions should seem to him to be genuine.'

Genevra was still torn between curiosity about Abigail's unspecified problems, alarm that she herself might inherit them, and indignation at the suggestion that she might try to forge her signature, when the party for *De Merel* were instructed to board the rowing-boats to take them to the vessel, and Abigail turned away without a backward glance.

Trelawney, in his turban and robes, would be difficult to spot among the crowd. Then he came striding up, and as he reached her, the sound of a single cannon-shot made her jump. He placed a reassuring hand on her shoulder. 'It is the signal for the crew to go aboard the Corsair ships. I have to leave now, Genevra. Ahmed will accompany you home.'

She nodded, and waited for him to remove his hand from her shoulder. Instead, with a soft laugh, he pulled her against him, holding her so closely that she was demoralisingly aware of the warmth of his flesh beneath the thin robes. With one hand he tilted her head back. 'You are, after all, known to be my woman,' he said softly.

She wanted to point out that it would be highly improper for him to be seen embracing her in public, particularly with his turban and robes underscoring his conversion to Islam, and that even a Corsair Rais must run the risk of punishment for flouting strict Muslim moral codes. But something kept her mute, and it was only partly because she knew it was the very element of risk that would encourage him to behave in a reckless and outrageous manner. Then his mouth fastened on hers, and there was nothing remotely circumspect about the way in which he bid her goodbye. While the tip of his tongue probed and caressed the inside of her lower lip, his hands, hidden from public view by the velvet cloak she was wearing, caressed her body in its thin muslin gown until she felt engulfed by bitter-sweet sensations.

When he let her go, she said in a tone which even she recognised as being totally unconvincing, 'If—If I had not been your *possession*, and if I had not known from bitter experience what could happen to me in this barbarous country, I would have slapped your face!'

The grooves flickered beside his mouth and his eyes danced. 'That goes without saying! Goodbye, Genevra. Try to behave yourself while . . .' He broke off, his expression hardening, and when she followed his gaze she saw that Rupert Runcorn was watching. He, clearly, was not about to go to sea with the Corsairs this time, or he would have mentioned it the day before.

Trelawney turned away from Genevra and addressed Ahmed in a low, rapid tone. He must be giving his servant instructions to make certain that she did not come into contact with Rupert. Since she knew that she would be able to see Rupert whenever she wished to, she paid no attention to their exchange. Trelawney returned to her side, and took her arm. For a moment she thought he meant to kiss her again, but then he began to bundle her through the crowd towards the steps down to the water, his grip upon her like a vice, and when she tried to protest, he told her roughly to be quiet.

'I will not be quiet!' she cried as he began to force her down the steps to where the rowing-boats were waiting. 'Have you taken leave of your senses? Will you tell me what you are about, and why?'

'I am taking you with me,' he answered grimly, 'because I have discovered that you are not to be trusted out of my sight!' He stooped, lifting her bodily and depositing her inside the rowing-boat in which his Turkish officers were waiting. Trelawney countered their jokes by replying curtly that he had practical reasons for taking her on the voyage.

Her bewilderment and humiliation began to fade, but her agitation was increasing. It must indeed have been Ahmed whom Rupert had seen the day before, and the servant had clearly warned Trelawney that she had been deceiving him by slipping out of the bath-house through the rear exit. If she were forced aboard the Corsair ship, she would never again be given the opportunity of asking Rupert for help and advice in earning her own ransom.

'I wish to have no part in your detestable sea-raids!' she flung desperately at Trelawney. 'And you cannot possibly expect me to accompany you for an indefinite period, when the only clothes at my disposal are those on my back!'

'If I had had notice of your treachery,' he told her coldly, 'I would have made provision for your wardrobe to be taken aboard. As it is, you will have to manage as best you can.'

With helpless outrage and dismay, she saw that they were approaching the Corsair ships riding at anchor. There was nothing she could do to prevent herself from being taken aboard the one commanded by Trelawney. *He* could talk to *her* of treachery? If she had indeed been his woman in anything but name, he might have had cause to be jealous of her friendship with Rupert. And now, because of his totally unjustified action, she would have to watch the hideous spectacle of victim ships being plundered, and in the close confines of the ship it was only too likely that she might in truth become his *woman* . . .

With a shock, she recognised the melting excitement inside her. She was in love with the man!

She stood on the deck, ignored by everyone as each vessel in the Corsair fleet hauled up her anchor and hoisted her large triangular sail. The ships began to follow each other out into the open water, firing cannon-shot. It was answered by salutes from other cannon coming from the harbour fortifications.

It was, Genevra thought, her mind fixed with desperation upon her own dilemma, a totally impossible situation. It could never be otherwise. She—the daughter of an English Rector who had always hoped that she herself would one day marry into the clergy and help her husband with his pastoral work—in love with what was little better than a pirate, an English renegade who had turned Turk, and who *owned* her!

She shook her head. The fleet, she realised, had safely cleared the inshore reefs and each vessel was hoisting her ensign, a large green pennant with Arabic script embroidered on it, and then turned her prow towards land in what looked like a ritual salute of some kind, before pointing out to sea again and sailing in formation with all the lateens billowing in the breeze.

Genevra was vaguely surprised to find Ahmed at her side. He had obviously come aboard on another rowing-boat, and was now signalling to her to follow him. Her mouth dry, and shamed excitement throbbing through her, she recognised the cabin to which he led her as the one belonging to Trelawney. How long ago, it seemed, since she had dined there with him, and he had told her calmly that he had a fancy to own her . . .

She waited for him to appear, but he did not join her. After several hours Ahmed brought her food, and withdrew again. As darkness fell and Ahmed returned to the cabin to light the lamps, it became clear that Trelawney had sought other accommodation. She tried to whip up a feeling of relief, but instead there was only a sense of anticlimax as she prepared for bed.

This sense of anticlimax grew as the voyage progressed. When she went on deck the next morning there was no sign of the rest of the Corsair fleet, and she supposed each vessel must operate independently. Chewing at her lip in perplexity, she returned to the cabin and found Ahmed there. He had brought with him a selection of robes and girdles and he explained to her, with a mixture of Algerine and mime, that she was to change into one of them and that he would return later to collect her gown for laundering. Resignedly, she arranged one of the robes into a toga, holding it in place with a girdle. But, to her frustration and fury, Ahmed did not return her gown. He pretended not to understand when she demanded it, just as he feigned incomprehension when she insisted upon being taken to see Trelawney. She was forced to go on wearing the robes, and the voyage which she had faced with so much dread and shamed excitement became one of boredom and frustration instead.

She woke up one morning to the realisation that they had dropped anchor, and that a great deal of noise and activity was sweeping through the ship. Was a sea-raid at last taking place? Then Ahmed knocked and entered the cabin, carrying a pitcher of hot water and her laundered gown over his free arm. Bewildered, Genevra washed and dressed, and was about to go on deck to see for herself what was happening when Trelawney knocked and came in.

He was impeccably and magnificently dressed in European clothes, and she looked away quickly so that he would not see the helpless hunger in her eyes. She was glad when Ahmed entered too, with coffee and fruit for their breakfast, and created a brief diversion. After she and Trelawney had seated themselves on cushions by the low table, he dismissed Ahmed.

Trying to hide her joy at the sight of him, Genevra asked scathingly, 'Is this by way of a celebration, because you have successfully tricked and plundered some foreign ship?'

'No,' he replied curtly. 'I do not attempt a sea-raid while on the way to Gibraltar. There would be no point in cramming the hold with prisoners when we might need to make a swift departure.'

'*Gibraltar!*' She stared at him. 'Is that where we are?'

'Not yet. But you and I shall leave shortly in a rowing-boat, with two of my officers at the oars dressed as Genoese peasants. We shall step ashore on one of the moles, and if anyone should notice us particularly, the implication will be that a Corinthian and his lady had indulged a whim to be taken for a morning excursion in a rowing-boat. You and I shall promenade slowly along the mole, and from time to time we shall stop while I chat to seamen, asking questions about vessels due to depart shortly.'

This, Genevra thought, must have been the 'practical reason' he had given to his officers for taking her on the voyage. Aloud, she asked tartly, 'Are you not afraid that I might take the opportunity to escape?'

He gave her a grim look. 'I am *counting* on it, Genevra! For what other reason do you imagine I might wish to take you ashore? I want to rid myself of you for once and all!'

'Oh,' she managed, and tried to conceal from him that she felt as if he had dealt her a body-blow.

'The two oarsmen will be watching us from the rowing-boat,' he continued, 'so we must not appear to be in collusion. I have explained to them that your company will lend me added credibility. I think you will admit that you owe me a debt, and you can repay it by making it appear that I had nothing to do with your escape. So, while I am speaking to the seamen, you will take the first convenient opportunity of melting away into the crowd. I recommend that you apply to the Governor for shelter and assistance, and ask him to help you to find some kind of post in Gibraltar. Whether you choose to acquaint him with my identity and my description I shall have to leave entirely in your hands.'

She was seized by an insane impulse to wail, 'I do not wish to escape! *Please* do not ask me to do so!' She fought it, putting her hands to her face to hide her expression. He was offering her the solution to every one of her problems. She would regain her freedom and be helped to find paid employment; she would cease to be a danger to Uncle John and his family, let alone be a charge upon them, and most of all she would be able to fight and hopefully overcome her impossible love for a man like Trelawney. A love that was not even remotely reciprocated, she reminded herself with pain, for had it been, he would not wish her to escape. It was not out of jealousy that he had opposed her friendship with Rupert, but because his pride would not allow the girl known as Trelawney's woman to be gossiped about in connection with another man.

'I dare not arouse my crew's suspicion by asking the ship's blacksmith to remove the chain from your ankle', he went on. 'But if you would avoid holding up your skirts, it would escape notice as we promenade along the mole.'

She nodded dumbly, and he stood up. 'If you are ready, Genevra, we may as well go.'

She forced herself to dwell upon mundane matters, such as whether to wear the lilac cloak. But even though its hood would give her protection from the sun, the cloak itself would be unbearably warm, and she decided to leave it behind. On deck, she discovered that they were anchored close to the unscalable side of Gibraltar's fearsome rock, well out of the path of other shipping. Trelawney climbed down the rope-ladder first, and helped her into the rowing-boat after she had also descended. Neither of them spoke as the two oarsmen in their peasant clothes began to row them round the side of the rock. Trelawney broke the silence only after the two of them had stepped on to the mole, which was crowded with seamen, naval officers, fishwives and gentlemen promenading with their ladies. 'Genevra,' he began, and stopped.

'Yes?'

He looked away. 'Nothing. Just . . . make sure that you go directly to the Governor for assistance.'

'Very well. I—I have to thank you . . .' Her voice froze in dismay. Among the crowd, coming towards them on the arm of a man, was one of the three service wives with whom she had shared a cabin on board *Kite*. She was talking animatedly to the man and had not yet seen Genevra. And the man with her, although he wore no uniform, could only be her husband, a naval officer whom she had told Genevra had served under Sir Edward Pellew during the war. *And so had Trelawney!*

The officer might not recognise Trelawney immediately, if at all. But his wife would certainly recognise Genevra, and stop to speak to them. Even if she could somehow avoid introducing Trelawney, the very recklessness which brought him to Gibraltar would cause him to do so himself, and the officer would certainly know his name. All round them were other Naval officers and ordinary seamen who could be called upon to help overpower Trelawney. He would be arrested as a deserter, a thief and a renegade for whom there could be no sentence other than death.

Genevra's mind was working at lightning speed. There would not be time enough for her to warn him of the situation. Calculating its probable consequences, she perceived only one thing she could do. She pretended to stumble, and as Trelawney unthinkingly let go of her arm, she pitched herself headlong over the side of the mole and into the water. It hit her with an icy shock, and when she surfaced momentarily she saw that he had done precisely what she had calculated he would, and had dived in after her. As she came up for the second time, her arms flailing wildly, he grabbed hold of her and cursed her roundly. Common sense and instinct had told her in advance that he would have to make for the rowing-boat, because they could hardly pretend in their sodden state to promenade along the mole.

He pushed her roughly aboard the rowing-boat before pulling himself into it as well, snapping a command at the oarsmen, who began to row furiously. A cheer had gone up from the crowd on the mole, who appeared not to find it strange that they were rowing away from the mole instead of towards it. This had been the one uncertainty in Genevra's mind when she formulated her swift plan, but now she remembered there were several moles and bays, and the crowd must suppose that they were making as swiftly as possible for the one closest to home.

She sat there, shivering and coughing, aware of Trelawney's fury and aware that Fate had forced her to throw away yet another chance of freedom. She felt wretched and close to tears, and was trying to contain the nausea induced by the sea-water she had swallowed. With shaking legs she obeyed Trelawney's order to climb the rope-ladder once they had reached the Corsair vessel. He followed her, and marched her inexorably to the cabin which she had never expected to see again.

'*Why?*' he demanded, folding his arms across his chest and glowering at her.

'I—I . . .' She brushed a strand of wet hair from her brow, and saw that the rage was slowly leaving his eyes; in its place was a darkening of desire as he studied her. Flushing, she realised for the first time that the wet muslin gown was clinging to her body, clearly defining every curve.

He moved, and caught her to him, and she could taste the salt on his lips as he took them in a violent, punishing kiss. He thrust her aside, and reached for the lilac cloak, and said jerkily, 'Put—Put it on. Cover yourself!' She managed to obey, and heard his voice, weary and puzzled now instead of enraged. 'For the love of God, Genevra, *why*? Why did you do such a thing?'

She could not tell him that it had been necessary, to save his life. To do so would be an admission that she loved him. She looked away. 'It was an accident.'

'It was not!'

With desperation, she said, 'It was your fault! You ordered me not to hold up my skirts, remember? So, after tripping, I caught my toe in the hem, and pitched over the side of the mole before I could regain my balance.'

She watched uncertainty spread over his face. After a moment he shrugged resignedly. 'Well, there'll not be another opportunity like today. Indeed, too much attention was drawn by that incident and I dare not go ashore again this time, so I have given the order for the anchor to be hauled up and the sails hoisted. This visit to Gibraltar has proved totally pointless, and my men now regard you as a jinx and will object to you joining us on any future voyage.'

It came to her that there must be other Naval officers, apart from the one with whom he had almost come face to face today, who were stationed in Gibraltar and would recognise him. He risked appalling danger each time he called there. 'Trelawney,' she blurted out, 'why do you visit Gibraltar? I cannot accept that it is simply to discover which departing ships might be worth plundering! We passed any number of vessels during the voyage here, and you could easily have harassed them!'

The grooves in his cheeks made their most sardonic appearance. 'I am a spy for the Dey, of course. There is a growing movement afoot to launch an attack upon Algiers, and I gather information in order to help Osman Pasha prepare for it if it should come. You may add that to everything else you already know to my discredit!'

She lowered her eyes. The appalling and shameful truth was that it made no difference to her feelings for him. She doubted whether anything would.

Three days later she was offered the chance to put that doubt to the test. A ship was sighted, and immediately the activity on board the Corsair vessel warned her that she was about to witness a raid ordered by Trelawney. Sails were furled and all identifying flags and ensigns were hauled down. She did not have the courage to witness these preliminaries to a raid, and hurried to the cabin. It was not long before she heard the firing of guns, accompanied by blood-curdling shouts. *Mena pera!* The command rang out from the Corsair vessel, and Genevra, shivering as she sat on the bunk, had learnt enough Algerine to know that it meant, 'Surrender, dogs!' That the victim ship *had* surrendered was made clear by the noise of prisoners being brought aboard, weeping and screaming in terror. She clapped her hands to her ears and tried to shut out the sounds.

But the noise made by the prisoners had scarcely begun to die down when terror and a cacophony of a different kind convulsed the vessel. They were caught in a storm of such ferocity that they must surely sink. The wind howled like all the devils of hell and the ship was tossed about as helplessly as a piece of driftwood. Any thought of preparing for bed was driven from her mind, and as she clung to anything inside the cabin that offered support and listened to the crew shouting to one another above the violence of the storm, her thoughts went with helpless compassion to the terrified prisoners on board.

Some hours later the storm seemed to have lost the worst of its force, but it had by no means blown itself out. Genevra decided to risk lying down, fully dressed, on the

bunk, and had just done so when the door opened and
Trelawney entered, carrying a storm-lantern. Caught un-
awares by the elements, there had been no time for him to
change into robes after the raid, and his immaculately-cut
coat was wet, and water glistened in his hair.

'What . . . do you want?' she asked unsteadily, sitting
upright and watching as he shrugged off the coat.

'A bed for the night.' His voice was grim. 'I dare say it has
not occurred to you to wonder where I've been sleeping.
Until tonight I have been using the cabin put at the disposal
of yourself and Abigail Pascoe when you were first captured. But I have ordered it to be offered to the two female
prisoners who are most in need of its extra comfort, and I'm
damned if I'll seek a hammock inside the officers' quarters.
So move up, Genevra, and make space.'

She swallowed. 'Should—Should you not be doing something about the ship?'

'There is nothing more I can do. There is little more
anyone can do, and I've left my first officer in charge. Most
of the sails and rigging have been destroyed by the storm.'
He pushed her to one side of the bunk and stretched out
beside her, and at that moment the ship rolled on the
turbulent sea so that he had to clutch at her to prevent her
from being pitched violently on to the floor.

She felt the warmth of his hands on her body, and the
wetness of his hair against her cheek, and an overwhelming
surge of emotion swept through her. Then a picture came
into her mind of the prisoners being thrown inside the hold,
and she thought with anguish, Oh, Trelawney, why do you
have to be what you are?

'The crew are blaming you for the storm,' he said. 'As I
feared, they are calling you a jinx. And that is another
reason why I decided I'd best spend the night with you.
They are taking it in turns to keep watch and bail out water,
but if the storm causes more damage and we are holed, their
last act before we go down will be an attempt to kill you.'

She shivered, and felt his hold upon her tighten. 'All you
and I can do,' he went on, 'is to hope we'll be able to ride
out the storm safely, and to pray there will be enough sail
and rigging left to enable us to limp home.'

'*Pray?*' she echoed. 'To whom do you pray, Trelawney,

when you have renounced Christianity, and are totally insincere about your conversion to Islam?'

'It was a figure of speech,' he replied curtly. 'Try to go to sleep.'

But sleep would have been impossible, even without the violent movement of the ship and the fear that they might go down—but not before the crew had tried to kill her. She was far too achingly aware of Trelawney's closeness to be able to relax, although she did pretend sleep. And although he lay still and silent beside her, she could tell by the rigidity of his arm which anchored her to the bunk that he was not asleep either. Gradually she became aware that the storm was abating. She knew the precise moment when Trelawney fell asleep, for his arm suddenly relaxed, and he moved slightly so that her head was nestled against his chest. She heard him mutter something unintelligible in his sleep as he cradled her, and she lay quite still, afraid that if she made the slightest movement he would withdraw his arm and turn his back towards her. This moment of illusory intimacy, meaningless though it was on his part, was the most she was ever likely to have. He did not love her, and he had already made it more than clear that he was well able to resist her. As the storm blew itself out, exhaustion overtook her and she drifted into sleep. She woke up suddenly to find that it was dawn, and that she must have turned in her sleep for she was now facing Trelawney, whose hand rested upon her shoulder as he slept.

With a great, aching void in her heart, she studied him. Why had she never noticed before how absurdly long his eyelashes were, and that they curled upwards at the tips? In sleep, he had the innocent, vulnerable look of a boy. There seemed no trace of Trelawney the ruthless renegade, who lacked all scruples and could turn even his loathsome profession into a macabre joke.

Seized by longing, without stopping to think what she was doing, she reached for his hand upon her shoulder and brought it to her breast instead. Perhaps the contact became woven into a dream he was having, for his fingers began to move slowly over its curves. She could no more have stopped breathing than she could have prevented herself from moving closer to him, pulling his head gently down to the level of her own, and laying her mouth upon his. She felt his lips part beneath her own, and suddenly his eyes were open and he was staring into hers. She often wondered afterwards what would have happened next if the ship had not suddenly echoed with the sound of hammering, the signal to wake the crew.

Trelawney swung his legs over the side of the bunk, running his fingers through his hair. Neither of them spoke for a long moment, and when he broke the silence it was to say prosaically, 'We have obviously suffered no further damage during the night, else my first officer would have come to alert me.'

'Yes.' She searched for something equally safe; something to push back the knowledge from both their minds that she had been the instigator of what might easily have developed into far more than he really wanted, or than was wise for herself.

'Those prisoners you took yesterday,' she asked at last. 'What nationality were they?'

He shrugged. 'The storm prevented a detailed inventory being made, but I have been told they are a mixed bunch, including some Britons. The ship had been picking up passengers from ports along the Barbary Coast and was on her way to Rotterdam.'

'A Dutch ship . . .' Genevra began, and stopped. No, it could not possibly be. But to make quite certain, she asked, 'Can you remember her name?'

'Certainly. Her first port of call had been Algiers, and you may even have noticed her. Her name was *De Merel.*'

Genevra scrambled upright, stifling the sound of hysteria which had bubbled into her throat. How could Abigail ever have guessed, in her wildest fantasies, that she was setting out on a voyage which would end in her being returned to Algiers for the second time as a prisoner of Corsairs? Considering her declared intention to defraud John McConnell of the money she owed him, it almost seemed like poetic justice. Genevra meant to contrive a way of sending her uncle a message, warning him not to place himself in further debt to secure Abigail's freedom for the second time until he had in his possession a written guarantee from her man of business that the money would be repaid in full.

Then she remembered something that placed an entirely different complexion on the matter. Abigail had written to her man of business in advance, ordering him not to release any of her funds, not even if he should believe the authority had come from herself. With her obsession to hold on to her fortune, with her overpowering instinct to preserve her own interest at no matter what cost to anyone else, Abigail had been well and truly caught in a trap of her own making!

CHAPTER THIRTEEN

GENEVRA DID NOT see the prisoners being taken ashore once the vessel had limped into Algiers harbour under makeshift sails and improvised rigging later that morning.

'Many of them suffered injuries during the storm,' Trelawney told her, 'particularly the women, some of whom are unconscious, although no one has been seriously hurt. Litters will be brought to the mole so that they may be conveyed immediately to the Spanish Hospital. The injured men, too, will receive treatment before they are assessed and valued.'

Genevra shuddered. Nothing would ever accustom her to this trade in human beings. She decided not to tell Trelawney that Abigail was among the prisoners. He would undoubtedly discover it for himself soon enough, but the longer it could be kept from becoming public knowledge, the more time there would be to warn Uncle John not to plunge himself into further debt on her account. For her own sake, Genevra hoped that Abigail might be among those who were unconscious, so that she would at least be spared the experience of stepping ashore in the city she had thought to have escaped.

'You will go ashore with Ahmed,' Trelawney continued, 'who will escort you home.' He added, 'And you will not visit the public baths in future. The facilities at home are more than adequate.'

As she was lowered into a rowing-boat which took herself and Ahmed to the mole, she became more determined to defy Trelawney in some other way. She had been forced to throw away her second chance of freedom, and the only hope now left lay in the possibility of earning a ransom for herself. She would find some means other than at the public baths by which to seek advice and help from Rupert. But as the crowd on the mole automatically and respectfully cleared a path for Trelawney's woman, it came to her with an unpleasant shock that there no longer was a way in which

Rupert would be able to help her. The last time they had met, he had spoken of the possibility of obtaining a loan from Abigail. But since then she had not only left Algiers; she was about to enter the city as a prisoner once again, and this time she would not be able to raise funds to help herself, let alone to lend money to anyone else.

Genevra sighed heavily, and remembered her vow to fight and turn every opportunity she received to her own advantage. Such opportunities as had been offered to her had been snatched away by Fate, and what was left? Nothing, it seemed, but acceptance of her impossible position as Trelawney's woman, in love with him and vulnerable, destined to remain a slave to the end of her days . . .

She realised that they were approaching his house. As usual, the alley was thronged with people of all descriptions: Turks, Moors and slaves carrying burdens, all passing by.

But one was not passing by. A young female dressed in an austere black gown and with a black scarf covering her head was waiting, motionless, beside the door, her eyes cast down. As Genevra approached with Ahmed, she looked up, and Genevra saw that her eyes were an attractive light brown and set in a face whose glowing beauty could not be quenched even by her drab clothes.

She curtsied, and addressed Genevra in immaculate English. 'Please, miss, may I speak to you?'

Genevra stared at her in bewilderment, and heard Ahmed make a sound. He was staring at the girl with a spellbound expression, as if hypnotised by her beauty. She turned her attention to the girl. 'Who are you?'

'My name is Rebecca Josef, miss. I have a message for you from my father.'

Genevra frowned. 'A message? I don't . . .' She stopped as a passing Moor rudely jostled the girl, and then said, 'You had better come inside.'

'Oh no, miss. I couldn't do that! I am Jewish.' She spoke as if that were the only explanation required. 'My father would have come himself,' she went on, 'but he has been very ill after a heart seizure, and is still not able to leave his bed. When I tell you that his name is Mordechai Josef, I am sure you will understand why he is most anxious to see you.'

Genevra's frown deepened. The name meant nothing to her. Rebecca had misunderstood the reason behind her frown, for she said apologetically, 'I realise that it is an impertinence, expecting you to visit the *hara* where we live, but my father would not be able to leave it for some considerable time, and something has to be done about the business that brought you to Algiers in the first place.'

Genevra's face cleared as understanding dawned. Rebecca and her father had obviously heard the rumours about mistaken identity, and they believed her to be Abigail Pascoe. She was about to tell the girl that she and her father were mistaken, when it occurred to her that here, at last, was an opportunity to discover why Abigail had set out for Algiers. Mordechai Josef had clearly been expecting her, and Genevra could tell him that she had just been returned, for the second time, as a prisoner. 'I'll come with you, Rebecca,' she said.

Ahmed followed them like a sleepwalker, scarcely taking his eyes off Rebecca. As they approached the part of the city she had called the *hara*, he stopped, and Genevra guessed at the inner conflict which consumed him. He seemed unable to turn his back on Rebecca and yet his expression said that Trelawney would not approve of him permitting Genevra to enter this place.

Here, the jostling, closely-packed houses were not whitewashed but had the drab look of sunbaked bricks, and there was a complete absence of any softening touches such as pots of flowering plants. Rebecca gave Ahmed a pleading look, and he was lost. The spell she had woven over him at first sight overcame his sense of duty, and he signalled that they should walk on. Rebecca led the way into a courtyard filled with shouting children; the entire place was filled with a babel of noise. The house seemed to be occupied by different generations and branches of the same family and was desperately overcrowded.

Rebecca cleared a path for them, with curious eyes following their progress. Genevra's first impression, when the door had been opened, was of a splendour in startling contrast to the outward drabness of the *hara*. The walls of the room were hung with silk, and the tester bed in the centre was carved and gilded. An old man with sharp, hooded eyes lay propped up on pillows, and he extended a bony hand to Genevra.

'Miss Pascoe, at last we meet.'

Rebecca was drawing up chairs to the side of the bed. Genevra sat down, but Ahmed elected to stand where he could keep Rebecca in view without her father noticing his fascination with the girl. Genevra took all this in subconsciously, and she also suspected that Ahmed would not, in other circumstances, have dreamed of entering a house occupied by Jews.

Genevra shook the old man's hand, and said, 'I am afraid, Mr Josef, that you are mistaken. I am not . . .'

'My friends call me Mordechai.' He smiled. 'Come to that, so do my enemies. It's a pity, Miss Pascoe, that you would not be guided by me and make use of the brokers and middlemen I appointed, but insisted on coming yourself.' He spread his hands. 'I have no doubt that the other young lady, whom the British Consul identified as his niece and who is now on her way back to England, has gained possession of the jewellery which was to have paid your half-brother's ransom. But he is still a prisoner, and so are you now, and I have been denied my just commission and the reimbursement of all my expenses.'

Genevra had been listening to him in dawning enlightenment. No wonder Abigail Pascoe had been so frantic when she first found herself a prisoner of the Corsairs! She had been bound for Algiers to pay a ransom for a member of her family, and suddenly she had found herself facing the prospect of having to pay *three* ransoms instead of one. It was also obvious now why she had tried so desperately to cling to Genevra's identity.

'You are mistaken, Mordechai,' she said. 'I am not Miss Pascoe. I am her maid, Genevra Shaw.'

The old man regarded her shrewdly. 'Yes, I have been told that is who you claim to be, and believe me, I understand your reasons. But Rais el-Trahni would not have paid twenty-five gold sequins for a serving-girl. I have visited England, Miss Pascoe, and I have never heard a servant speaking as you do.'

'If it comes to that,' Genevra pointed out, '*you* do not speak English like an Algerian Jew.'

Mordechai smiled wryly. 'In my business it is an advantage to be fluent in as many languages as possible. And, talking of business—until the complicated matter of negotiating a ransom for you and for your half-brother has been completed, I am prepared to lend you money on the same terms as those extended to him.'

'I am *not* Abigail Pascoe,' Genevra repeated, deciding not to tell him that Abigail had been returned to Algiers as a prisoner. He would probably discover it for himself before long, and in the meantime she had no wish to add to the trouble in which her 'mistress' already found herself. Genevra went on, 'You have only to produce her half-brother, and he will confirm that we are not related.'

Mordechai chuckled. 'Very clever, Miss Pascoe! Since the two of you have never met, how could he confirm or deny your identity?'

Genevra wondered how Abigail could have possessed a half-brother whom she had never met, and was even more curious about why she had been prepared to pay a fortune in jewellery to gain his release, since generosity was not part of her nature.

'Thank you for coming to see me, Miss Pascoe,' Mordechai said. 'I wished you to know that your credit is good as far as I am concerned. Now I am sure you will want to meet your half-brother, who is expecting you. Rebecca will escort you to where he shares an apartment with other *paga lunars*.'

'Oh . . .' She was curious to meet Abigail's half-brother, and at the same time she did not relish having to tell him that the girl was now in a position in which she would be unable to pay a ransom for herself, let alone for him.

She was still hesitating when Mordechai ordered his daughter, 'Take Miss Pascoe to see Mr Daniel Blake, Rebecca.'

Curiosity won, and Genevra offered no objection. The three of them left the bedroom and squeezed their way past the press of people on the gallery, and made their way across the courtyard to the door.

Once again, they walked along twisting alleys after they had left the *hara*. Rebecca stopped outside an oak door and pounded on it. It was opened by a Moorish servant, who began immediately to engage Ahmed in an animated exchange. Several people were inside the courtyard, and Rebecca pointed to an arched doorway to the left which led from it, saying, 'You will find Mr Daniel Blake awaiting you in there, Miss Pascoe. I suggest that you introduce yourself.' She gave a smile which succeeded in being both shy and calculating at the same time. 'I shall stay here, and talk to Rais el-Trahni's Moorish servant, and persuade him not to tell his master of this visit, or of the one to the *hara*.'

Genevra nodded. Rebecca would be able to persuade Ahmed into almost anything! Then, squaring her shoulders and taking a deep breath, she walked towards the arched doorway to introduce herself to Abigail's half-brother.

The doorway gave access to a pleasant, airy room furnished with rugs and cushions and a few low tables. A male figure rose from one of the cushions, but after the bright morning sunlight in the courtyard, it took a moment for Genevra's eyes to adjust to the shaded room. Then she found herself staring, in dumb and total confusion, at Rupert Runcorn's beautiful-ugly face.

It was not until after he had pushed her gently down on to one of the cushions that she found her voice. 'I—I simply do not believe this,' she said weakly. 'You *can't* be Abigail's half-brother!'

'No, of course I am not,' Rupert admitted in a soothing voice. 'The real Daniel Blake, who was Abigail's half-brother, is dead.'

'But—But surely Mordechai must know that? And even if he didn't, you have been a prisoner in Algiers for too long to be able to pass yourself off as someone else?'

Rupert nodded. 'You, Genevra, are the only one who is supposed to be deceived into believing that I am Daniel Blake.'

'I don't understand anything,' she said helplessly.

'You will, when I have explained. Even though they had never met, and did not even know of each other's existence until Mordechai ferreted out the truth, Abigail's half-brother was a prisoner of the Corsairs, owned by the Dey himself. Mordechai contacted his agents in England, as a matter of course, and they investigated the backgrounds of all the recently-acquired British prisoners at the time, and he learnt of the connection between Daniel Blake and Abigail Pascoe.'

As the story unfolded, Genevra acknowledged that everything Rupert told her fitted only too well with the facts she already knew about Abigail. While the latter's mother was still alive, and herself only a child, her scapegrace of a father had gone through a bigamous marriage with Blake's mother, a respectable middle-class woman whom he had subsequently abandoned in most shameful circumstances. When he grew up, Daniel Blake, believing his father to have died before he was born, had found employment as a clerk, but after his mother's death he had decided to go to America in search of opportunity and hopefully a fortune.

'Instead, he found himself a prisoner of the Corsairs,' Rupert went on. 'There appeared to be no one who would pay a ransom for him, but the Jewish brokers with their international agents are thorough. They discovered who Blake's father had been, and they also discovered that he had a half-sister who had become an heiress. At first she flatly refused to pay a ransom for Daniel Blake, but she had underestimated Mordechai's persistence when he has the smell of money in his nostrils. He ordered his contacts to investigate further, and discovered that Abigail had been at great pains to gain respectability and that she was hoping to marry a titled man. Mordechai threatened to make public the facts of Blake's birth. To avoid a scandal in England, Abigail agreed to pay a ransom after all, but she refused to do it through middlemen, and insisted on coming to Algiers herself.'

'But why?'

'She was afraid that either Mordechai or Blake would extort money from her again. She did not trust the middlemen, and before she parted with any ransom, she wanted all the evidence of Daniel Blake's birth which had been sent to Mordechai handed over to her.'

'Yes, I can understand that . . .' Genevra was silent for a moment. 'But why did Mordechai insist on her paying the ransom in jewellery?'

'He didn't. It was Abigail's own decision. She must have made a point of learning all there is to be known about

Algiers, and she was aware that the Jews not only fix the monetary rate of exchange but they also control the market in gold and precious stones. So, any jewellery would be worth as much or as little as the Jews decide. I believe she meant to use this knowledge in order to haggle over the amount of the ransom. By paying in jewellery, she hoped to save herself money.'

Poor Abigail, Genevra could not help thinking. Saving herself money had been her downfall. She was about to tell Rupert that she had once again been returned to Algiers as a prisoner, when he went on, 'I promised I would do all I could to find out the truth about Abigail, but there did not appear to be much to discover. As far as I could see, she was simply the Consul's wealthy niece who had come, with her jewellery and her fine clothes, to lord it over her poor relations. Then, when she was captured, she realised her folly and tried to claim your identity, and her uncle helped her by pretending, at first, that she was Genevra Shaw. I cultivated her friendship during visits to the Consulate . . .' Rupert stopped, smiling that enigmatic smile of his which one could never quite identify, because of his scar. 'She did not confide in me, but she did hint that she might lend me money—which I intended passing on to you. Then, unexpectedly, I found that John McDonnell had obtained a passage home for her. I saw you in company with Trelawney Grant, on your way to the mole, and followed, so that I could tell you I had been forced to admit defeat. Instead, he took you with him on his sea-raid.'

Genevra looked down at her hands. 'We went to Gibraltar. I almost had a chance to escape, but . . .' She shrugged, deciding not to pursue the subject.

Rupert stared thoughtfully at her. 'During your absence,' he went on, 'I discovered through the grapevine between *paga lunars* and the Jewish middlemen who lend them money the real reason for Abigail's visit. I also learnt that, just before she was brought to Algiers as a prisoner, Daniel Blake had died in a tavern brawl. Mordechai had been left, therefore, without a half-brother to ransom, and Abigail could have saved herself a great deal of money and grief by never setting out for Algiers! Then I remembered all those rumours that you were the real Abigail Pascoe, and I saw a way in which the situation could be exploited to your advantage.'

'To *my* advantage?' Genevra echoed blankly.

'Yes, indeed. I went to see Mordechai, and I made him believe the rumour that you are the real Abigail Pascoe. I persuaded him to pass me off as your "half-brother" for whom you had undertaken to pay a ransom.'

'But how can that benefit me?' Genevra cried.

Rupert touched her arm. 'Isn't it obvious? I'll wager my entire debt to my own moneylender, Abraham, that Mordechai has offered to lend you money.'

'Yes. Yes, he has . . .'

'No one would have considered lending a farthing to Genevra Shaw,' Rupert said. 'But wealthy Miss Abigail Pascoe is an entirely different matter. Accept the loan Mordechai has offered you, Genevra, and allow Rebecca to help you to establish a shop in which you will be able to make and sell pies to the public, and so earn your own ransom.'

She put a hand to her forehead. Too many things had been happening for her to be able to think coherently. She did wish to earn her own ransom, but in such a devious way . . . ? Something else occurred to her. 'If I were to establish a pie-shop, Mordechai will know immediately that I am *not* Abigail. If I really did have money in England, why should I wish to earn my own ransom? Mordechai will refuse to lend me money for such a venture . . .'

'No, he won't. I have explained to him how very reluctant Miss Pascoe is to part with a penny of her money—a fact which he had already learnt for himself. He also saw, immediately, what a good business proposition a pie-shop would be. There are many slaves who would welcome the opportunity of eating supper in a place which is not also a tavern, but where they would be safe from drunken Turks and Moors.'

'I don't know,' Genevra sighed. 'My head aches abominably, and I am unable to think clearly. Allow me time to consider.'

Rupert stood up, helping her to her feet at the same time. 'Don't take too long to make up your mind, Genevra. Trelawney Grant will be personally supervising the repairs to his vessel, and far too busy to concern himself with what you are doing. Once you have established your shop, there would be little he could do about it, for every slave has the right, by law, to earn a ransom if there is no one else to pay one.'

She nodded, and he accompanied her to the courtyard where Rebecca was talking to Ahmed. The Moor did not seem surprised to see Rupert, and Genevra wondered what lies Rebecca had been telling him to account for this meeting between the two of them. Whatever they were, Ahmed already seemed so enslaved by the beautiful Jewish girl that he would probably have been prepared to believe anything.

Soon after Genevra and Ahmed arrived home, Trelawney returned, but he stayed only briefly to change his robes and eat a hasty meal. It was obvious that Ahmed had made no mention of their visit to the *hara* or to Rupert's lodgings, and Trelawney appeared not to notice his guilty expression. Genevra, asking a few judicious questions, discovered that all the female prisoners had indeed been taken to the Spanish Hospital but had not yet been assessed and valued. Clearly, it had not yet become public knowledge that Abigail was among them.

After Trelawney had left again, announcing that he meant to spend the night aboard his stricken ship, Genevra wrote a letter to John McDonnell, addressing him formally as 'Sir' and asking him to call upon her as she wished to consult him. She asked Ahmed to have the letter delivered at the Consulate, and settled down to wait.

But Uncle John did not come, either that day or the next. In the meantime, no news percolated through Algiers of Abigail's recapture, and Trelawney did not mention her as being among the female prisoners. It began to seem, more and more, that she must have left *De Merel* at one of its ports of call and continued her voyage in another vessel.

Slowly Genevra forced herself to face the fact that Uncle John had, no doubt at the urging of Harriet, decided to ignore her letter and have nothing further to do with her. The knowledge added sharply to the rest of her inner conflict. Deeply grateful though she was to Rupert for having gone to such lengths to help her, she shrank from cheating Mordechai by allowing him to lend her money in the belief that she was Abigail Pascoe. The fact that Mordechai richly deserved to be cheated did not salve her conscience.

It might have been a little less difficult to endure her warring emotions and the knowledge that Uncle John had finally cast her off, if life in general had not been so frustratingly tedious. Trelawney did not come home until late each evening, and almost invariably went straight to his study, closing the door firmly behind him, making it clear that he did not wish to be disturbed. Her own days were without purpose. It would have been futile to leave the house in search of diversion, because all that was available would have been a visit to a public bath, and Ahmed would make certain that she did not enter one of them. He would, she thought sourly as she looked at the mooning expression on his face, have agreed with alacrity to another visit to the *hara*, or even to Rupert's lodgings if he thought Rebecca might be there.

But at present Genevra had no desire to see Rupert and confess to her own doubts and misgivings after all he had done to help her, and neither did she wish to be influenced against her better judgment by his arguments. She had still not come to a decision when one was finally thrust upon her. Aimlessly one evening she entered Trelawney's study and was leafing through some French novels in search of one that appealed, when he came in earlier than usual and long before she had expected him.

She laid the book down, her hands trembling. In spite of his rich robes and his habitual air of authority he looked tired and disillusioned, and she wanted to go to him and ease the lines of strain from his forehead with gentle fingers, and remove the grim cast from his mouth with a kiss. She wanted to ask him what particular problem had cropped up during the day, and offer him comfort in any way she could. In short, she wanted to behave as his wife, as his woman. She began to walk slowly towards him. 'Trelawney?'

'Yes?'

The inside of her mouth was dry, and she had difficulty in forming the words. 'I—I have been thinking of my position.

You yourself said that there would be no future opportunities for me to escape. I face years, perhaps a lifetime, of remaining in the same situation. So it seemed to me that you . . . that we . . .' She stopped.

'Go on.'

Colour swept into her face. 'I don't quite know how to put this. But I am known as your woman, and . . .'

'I shall save you the embarrassment of spelling out what you have in mind, Genevra.' His voice was totally devoid of emotion. 'I admit that I have given you just cause to believe that I am attracted to you. But any normal man in close proximity with any personable young woman would be aroused to desire. It is a basic law of nature, intended to ensure the survival of the human race, and not something uniquely between you and me.'

She stared at the ground, flayed to the soul by the cold, analytical way in which he was rejecting her. But he had not finished.

'It would be no hardship at all for me to make you my mistress, Genevra, if I could believe for a moment that matters would remain as uncomplicated as that. But you were not reared to be a mistress. You would not be content to be available when wanted, and remain in the background at other times. In short, you would make emotional demands which I am not prepared to fulfil. It is for that wholly selfish reason that I have imposed restraints upon myself, and fought the temptation to take advantage of our relationship.'

Stripped of every shred of pride, she could not look at him. From somewhere, she found the courage to lie, 'You . . . have completely misunderstood what I wished to ask. I merely wanted to know whether there was any likelihood of my situation changing at some time in the future.'

'There is every likelihood, Genevra. I cannot apply in person for another *teskere* for you. When you tore the first one up, I explained to the Dey that *I* had destroyed it, because I had changed my mind and wished to keep you as my woman. Suspicion would be aroused if I were to pay, once again, for your freedom. In Algiers one does not expend money on a discarded mistress. So all that remains to me is to pay a ransom for you through the agency of a middleman. This I intend to do, as soon as enough time has elapsed to make it seem believable that I had tired of you, and when I have found a middleman I can trust.'

She flung her head up at that, staring at him with glittering eyes. Allow him to pay another ransom for her, when he had just rejected her in a way which made her feel as if her entire being had been peeled away in layers, nakedly exposing her very heart and soul?

'I would sooner take my chances in a bawdy-house, Trelawney,' she said icily, 'before I would accept freedom paid for by you.' Giving him no chance to respond, she walked out of the room.

She had no need to fall back upon the horrors of a bawdy-house. She would accept a loan from Mordechai, and make and sell mutton pies, and earn her own ransom.

CHAPTER FOURTEEN

ESTABLISHING THE pie-shop proved to be astonishingly swift and easy. It would probably not have been achieved at all, had it not been for the spell Rebecca had woven over Ahmed. He accompanied Genevra to the *hara* to arrange the terms of her loan with Mordechai, and afterwards went with Rebecca, a glazed look of adoration on his face, to purchase and arrange for the delivery of a baking-oven and all the cooking utensils and serving dishes Genevra would require. A former coffee-house, complete with benches and tables, was leased with such speed that Genevra suspected her decision had been anticipated.

From the moment the first batch of pies came out of the oven it was clear that the shop would be a resounding success. Because alcoholic liquor was not offered for sale, only the more civilised of the slave population flocked to it, but there were enough of them to keep Genevra very busy, and she was grateful for Rupert's occasional help. Because all slaves were free to follow their own pursuits during the hours before sunset, there were usually crowds of eager customers spilling out into the alley as they waited for a seat inside.

Trelawney appeared to be quite unaware of what Genevra was doing, which puzzled her at first, until she decided he must be too preoccupied with the repairs to his ship to have learnt of her venture. Because sheer fatigue now caused her to seek her bed early, they seldom caught even a glimpse of one another.

Her days were increasingly exhausting as her business prospered. During the early part of the afternoon she prepared mutton pies and chicken patties in the rear of the premises while Ahmed stoked the baking-oven. The first of the pies would be ready by the time she opened the shop in the late afternoon, and then batch after batch would be put into the oven until the time came, just before sunset, for her to lock up and return home with Ahmed. He would place the pies she had brought home for her supper inside the oven in the kitchen to keep hot while she bathed and changed her clothes; then, with all the servants having left to answer the call to prayers, she would sit down alone to eat before preparing for bed.

One evening Trelawney walked in unexpectedly as she was about to start her supper. The news of what she had been doing must have reached him at last, and she waited, her heart beating thunderously, to defend her business venture with every defiant argument at her command. But he merely said, 'I see you have been making illicit use of the kitchen again.'

She hid her relief, and responded with stilted politeness. 'You are very welcome to share my supper. I have already eaten,' she lied, 'and was about to pour coffee for myself.'

He did not answer immediately. 'Thank you, no. I shall take supper in one of the taverns as usual.' He began to leave the room and stopped, turning. 'Do you remember . . .' He did not complete the question but looked away, and left her.

Oh yes, Trelawney, she thought with pain, I remember only too well when we made pies together, and you were about to kiss me afterwards, but thought better of it. I remember far too much altogether for my own comfort. His ignorance of what she was doing and his assumption that she had made the pies for herself in the kitchen gave her an illogical feeling of guilt at deceiving him, but it did not deter her from continuing her business.

As she made and sold pies, she learnt not only the Algerine *lingua franca* with fluency, but also many strange ways of the city. With considerable shock, she discovered what *garzonés* were. Sodomy was not only rife, but considered perfectly respectable, and she, who had never dreamed that male concubines existed, was astounded to learn of the high regard in which their masters held them. Then she learnt something else that was even more shocking. Rebecca had called at the shop to tell Rupert that Mordechai wished to see him, and while she waited for Rupert to finish his supper, she and Ahmed were deep in conversation. It was becoming clear that the Jewish girl was beginning to return the young Moor's feelings, and

Genevra said as much to Rupert.

'Yes, poor devils,' he agreed. 'But nothing dare come of it.'

'Why not?'

'Because, if it did, he would be burnt alive. She would be sewn up in a sack, also alive, and he would be forced to throw her into the sea before his own execution.'

Genevra shivered, and was about to express her horror when the sound of cannon-shot reverberated through the air and she gave Rupert a startled, questioning look.

'It means a fleet has been sighted, making for the harbour. It must be the return of the massed Corsairs.' He wiped pie-crumbs from his mouth. 'I'd best go and see what Mordechai wants. But you might as well shut the shop, Genevra, since everyone will be streaming to the mole.'

The shop began to empty, proving him right. When only Genevra and Ahmed remained she decided to take Rupert's advice, and on the spur of the moment she suggested, afterwards, that the two of them should also go to the mole and watch the Corsair vessels enter the harbour.

When they reached the Marine Gate, the crowd pouring down to the mole was so great that the officials guarding the gate were allowing people to pass through in groups of no more than six. Genevra had temporarily become separated from Ahmed and was looking around for him when she saw John McDonnell coming straight towards her. She tried to make her face as expressionless as she could, reminding herself that she owed her nothing. She would merely nod politely and move on in search of Ahmed.

But he touched her arm, and said in a low voice, 'My dear Genevra, I am so sorry that I dared not respond to your letter in any way.'

Gratitude swept over her at the knowledge that he had not abandoned her after all. Then she frowned. '*Dared* not, Uncle John?'

'Let us continue towards the mole in a manner which will not draw undue attention to us.' They fell into step, and he went on, 'Shortly before I received your letter, I had called at the Spanish Hospital, as a matter of routine, to enquire after the welfare of the British subjects among the prisoners, and those of other nations for whom Britain has taken responsibility. Imagine my horror when I discovered Miss Pascoe to be among them . . .'

'So she *was* recaptured!' Genevra put in. 'I had become quite convinced that she had changed vessels during the first part of her voyage home.'

'No. I found she had suffered a blow to the head, and she was either rambling incoherently or else lapsing into bouts of unconsciousness, but I was assured that her condition was likely to be temporary. There had been nothing among her possessions to identify her and no one else had recognised her. I simply did not know—and I still do not know—who she will claim to be when she has recovered and has taken stock of her situation.'

'You mean that she might once again claim to be Genevra Shaw?'

He nodded. 'In the meantime, relations between myself and the Dey have become strained almost to breaking point. Because the British government will not agree to his demands, I have been forced to walk a very dangerous tightrope. There are spies everywhere who report my daily movements to the Dey. So I felt it would be far too dangerous, both for yourself and for me and my family, if I were seen to be paying you particular attention by doing something as unusual as to call at Trelawney Grant's house, to see his—forgive me—his woman, who would seem to be the last person in Algiers requiring my diplomatic services.'

Genevra flushed, but this was neither the time nor the place to tell him how hollow and false was the title bestowed upon her. 'My note was simply to warn you that Abigail was once again a prisoner of the Corsairs, Uncle John, and also to tell you that she has no intention of repaying the money you borrowed on her behalf. Indeed, she cannot now repay it.' She went on to explain how Abigail was caught in a trap of her own making.

'My main fear is that she may threaten to tell the Dey how I have tricked him by pretending that she was my niece.' He shrugged. 'However, let us try to be optimistic. Lord Exmouth's arrival may alter matters.'

Genevra looked at him in surprise. 'It is not the Corsair fleet that has arrived in the harbour?'

'No. Lord Exmouth's mission is to try to negotiate a new

peace treaty with Britain, and end the dispute between us and Algiers. Look,' he added, as they passed through the Marine Gate and could see down into the harbour, 'that is his flagship, HMS *Boyne*, followed by his ships of the line, and his frigates and sloops sailing at the rear.'

They agreed that they had better not be seen in conversation any longer, and while John walked on towards the mole, Genevra decided that the crush of people was too great for comfort, and once she had found Ahmed, the two of them turned back.

The following day, business returned to normal. For the ordinary slave in Algiers, there was little in the arrival of the British squadron to arouse interest or excitement. Instead, it was a cause for irritation, Genevra discovered. Because the British did not return escaping slaves to the shore, one of her customers explained, the owners of many slaves, who normally required them to wear no more than their ankle-chains, forced them to wear heavy shackles as well to prevent them from swimming out to one of the British vessels in the harbour.

All the benches in the shop were occupied by customers eating their pies while the remainder of the premises was crowded with men patiently waiting. Suddenly her heart bounced in her throat as a new sound came: Trelawney's voice, firm and clear but also scrupulously polite.

'Gentlemen, this shop is about to close. Those of you who are waiting, please leave immediately. The rest of you, have the kindness to finish eating as quickly as you can.'

She stared at him as he towered over the slaves, in a white burnous with a cowl-like hood against which his skin appeared golden-brown from exposure to the sun after all the time he had spent in supervising the repairs to his ship. His eyes were the cobalt colour they had assumed before in moments of rage, and she shivered. She had expected his displeasure when he discovered what she had been doing, but not this blazing fury.

She forced herself to meet his gaze with defiance as he shouldered his way through the fast-departing crowd, and then saw his glance fall upon Ahmed, who had just emerged from the interior of the shop. 'Ahmed is not to blame for any of this . . .' she began.

'I know,' he cut her short in an arctic voice. 'I am very well aware precisely where the blame lies.' He nodded to Ahmed. 'Stay behind and lock up.'

Trelawney took her arm, and then he was sweeping her out of the shop and down the alley. He said nothing at all, but stared ominously ahead of him, the set of his mouth harsh.

It was not until they were inside his drawing-room that he broke the silence. '*How dared you?*' he demanded in a cutting voice.

Part of her mind was glad that he was in such a rage, and that he was stirring an answering anger inside her, for otherwise she would have been totally defenceless against him, looking so magnificent with the white burnous and cowl forming an almost theatrical contrast to his dark hair and sunbrowned face.

'I dared,' she replied crisply, 'because I have learnt that every slave has the right to work towards earning his or her own ransom . . .'

'With the consent of that slave's owner!' His voice was biting. 'Do you imagine for one instant that I would have given my permission? That I would have allowed you to exploit the feelings of homesick, love-hungry Christian slaves by baking and serving them with pies? You cannot be so naive, Genevra, not to realise that you could sell them *anything* simply by playing on their vulnerability and their longing to exchange a few words with a beautiful, young, Christian girl. I consider your behaviour to have been utterly indefensible!'

Her anger was tinged with guilt now. It had never entered her head that the men who flocked to buy her pies had been attracted by anything more than the appeal of eating appetising fare away from the danger of drunken Turks and Moors.

'You dare to call *my* behaviour indefensible, considering who and what you are?' she cried hotly.

'We are not discussing my activities!' he snarled. 'No one has had the courage to tell me what was happening, but how my enemies must have been crowing behind my back! Rais el-Trahni's woman, reduced to borrowing from a Jewish moneylender so that she might display herself in a shop, selling pies!' He caught her by the shoulder. 'How dared you do such a thing to me?'

'I am not your woman, as you are more than well aware!'

'They believe you to be, so it amounts to the same thing!'

Trelawney's woman. Suddenly the title, which had become so familiar to her that she had ceased to dwell on it, seemed to take on a new meaning and caused a clutch of excitement in the lower part of her stomach, so that all she wanted to do was allow her body to relax against his and feel his arms about her.

'Lending yourself to Rupert Runcorn's devious schemes . . .' Trelawney went on furiously, 'allowing your name to be linked with his . . . How could you have betrayed me like that, Genevra?'

'*Betrayed* you?' she echoed. 'Betrayal is not possible in the relationship between a slave and her master, and I am your slave, Trelawney, and nothing more!'

With a sudden movement he pulled her against him, and she felt his breath stirring her hair. 'We both know,' he muttered, 'that there is more between us than that.'

'You—You said . . .' she began to remind him unsteadily.

'I lied.'

She remained utterly still, her heart thudding in her breast. She was intensely aware of everything about him; the way he smelt of the sea and the hardness of his muscles underneath the silk of his robes, the strength of his arms about her and the warmth of his fingers against her shoulderblades. Recklessly she moved, putting her hands to his face to tilt his head, and stood on tiptoe so that their lips would meet.

For an instant he stared into her eyes. Then, abruptly, he removed her hands and turned away. His voice held a curt note of finality as he said, 'Go and pack your things. I am handing you over to the British Consul without further delay. I don't want you under my roof for another night.'

She stepped backwards from him, feeling as if he had just thrown a pailful of cold water at her. 'You—You know why I cannot, why I will not, go to the Consulate,' she began.

He gave her a frosty smile. 'I know why you *pretended* you did not wish to go there. Among all your other qualities you are also a very skilled liar, Genevra. I have discovered the true reason why you tore up the *teskere* and refused to accept your freedom when I offered it to you.'

'Oh?' She watched him warily.

'One of several reasons which have kept me from home for the past twenty-four hours was a visit I paid to the Spanish Hospital, where I interviewed Abigail Pascoe. I had not been aware, previously, that she had been among the prisoners taken from *De Merel*. She was more than ready to admit to her true identity, and to the fact that *you* are the British Consul's niece.'

Genevra looked at him in utter dismay. 'I know you are the Dey's spy! I know you have cast off all loyalty towards Britain! But once the Dey learns how Uncle John had tricked him, his life and those of his family will be in mortal danger. Even if you were to decide to remain silent, the mere fact of your taking me to the Consulate . . .'

'The Dey already knows the truth,' Trelawney put in curtly. 'Osman Pasha is on cordial terms with John McDonnell again, now that Lord Exmouth has announced his intention to negotiate a new treaty between Algeria and Britain. You no longer have any value as a political pawn.'

She shook her head in disbelief. 'I spoke to my Uncle John yesterday, and he said . . .'

'The situation has altered dramatically since then.' Trelawney's voice roughened. 'Go and make yourself presentable, and let us leave for the Consulate. Your trunks will be sent on later. I shall be very glad indeed to be able to wash my hands of you,' he added with force.

Could she believe his assurances, any more than she could now believe those words he had muttered into her hair? Would he be sending her away if they were true? Then instinct and logic told her that he would not send her into danger when he had previously taken personal risks to save her life. Mechanically, in her room, she washed and then put on a silk gown in a delicate shade of magnolia. Her heart was heavy as she thought of the reception she was only too likely to be accorded at the Consulate. Even if she no longer represented any danger to her family, Harriet

McDonnell would not want her there. She might not be able to turn Genevra away, but she would not make her welcome. Pinning up her curls, she was about to follow the ingrained habit of years and cover the white streak in her hair. Then, defiantly, she exposed it to full view. She might be a poor relation who would be expected to labour for her keep, but she would not allow Harriet McDonnell to pass her off as nothing more than an anonymous servant.

She covered her shoulders with a shawl, and went to rejoin Trelawney. He, too, had changed into formal European clothes in which he looked elegant, striking and unapproachable. Her heart sank, but even so she tried to express some of the doubts that had been building up inside her as she had been preparing to leave for the Consulate.

'Trelawney, I don't think the McDonnells will welcome . . .' she began.

'I am not prepared to listen to any more lies or arguments, Genevra.' He cut her short. 'I do not want you here. I have never wanted you here. You have been an embarrassment and a source of irritation to me ever since you stopped being an amusing diversion. Now you may go and plague the life out of your family instead. They, at least, want you and have offered you a home.'

It would have been too humiliating, after that, to try and tell him that she had been sent for by the McDonnells only to be a servant, and that Harriet would find it utterly galling to have to treat her as a part of the family instead, now that it was widely know that Genevra Shaw was the Consul's neice. They did not speak as they picked their way downhill through the alleys.

It was only when they reached the road leading to the mole that Genevra remembered something which had entirely escaped her before. 'If I wrote letters of explanation to Mordechai Josef and to Rupert,' she said, 'would you undertake to see that they are delivered?'

Trelawney uttered a sour laugh. 'It would be wasted effort on your part! How do you suppose I discovered what everyone else was too afraid to tell me to my face—that you were making and selling pies, and why, and how you had come by the capital for the venture?'

She stopped, and stared at him in confusion. 'I—I hadn't thought . . .'

'Then I shall tell you exactly what happened! You were tricked, my dear Genevra, by the smooth-tongued Rupert Runcorn, just as he tricked Mordechai!'

She made a sound of disbelief. 'Not Rupert! He had no reason . . .'

'No? Let me tell you what I have discovered about him. He is the black sheep of a wealthy and proud English family who wanted only to be rid of him after a particularly scandalous episode during which, by the by, he came by that scar on his face.' A cynical note entered Trelawney's voice. 'I have no doubt that he offered you some romantic reason to account for it.'

'He came by it when he tried to escape from Algiers . . .' Genevra began.

Trelawney laughed shortly. 'It was inflicted in England, by the mother of a simple-minded heiress, a girl with the limited mental powers of a child, whom Runcorn seduced in the hope of gaining control of her fortune. Yes, I can tell by your expression that you don't believe me, but it is nevertheless true. His family decided to pack him off to Venice as soon as he recovered, but the ship on which he sailed was captured by Corsairs. Because he was obviously a member of a wealthy family, a Jewish merchant called Abraham lent him money against the day when a rich ransom would be paid for him.'

This last statement she knew to be true, but she shook her head in a blind gesture. 'None of what you have been telling me proves that he'd tricked me, or explains remotely why he should have wanted to.'

'I am coming to that,' Trelawney assured her. 'Of his entire family, only Runcorn's father was disposed to pay a ransom for him, but the negotiations were lengthy and complicated. After Abigail had been released by the Dey and she was returned to the Consulate, news came that Runcorn's father had died; his elder brother had inherited the title and the estate, and he flatly refused to pay a penny for his odious brother's freedom. Runcorn knew that Abraham would continue, for a while, to try and persuade the new heir to change his mind, but he could see the writing on the wall. He began to cast about for a solution, some other means by which he might continue to live the easy life of a *paga lunar*.'

'If you are suggesting that my pie-shop . . .' Genevra began.

'Not at that stage, no. Runcorn concentrated on paying court to Abigail Pascoe, who showed distinct signs of falling under his spell. To you, he appeared the selfless, generous, gallant friend. To Abigail, he was the dashing charmer. Unfortunately for him, the Consul announced that he was sending Abigail home, and Runcorn began to explore how *you* might be exploited to his advantage instead.'

'He knew I had no money,' Genevra muttered, desperately wanting to go on believing in Rupert's friendship. 'Indeed, *he* was trying to raise capital for *me*.'

'That was certainly what he made you believe!' Trelawney's voice was dry. 'Already, he had realised how he might use you. He had learnt the truth about Abigail's half-brother, and he saw a way of persuading Mordechai to finance his continued style of life. It was Runcorn who deliberately started the rumour that you were the real Miss Pascoe, and he made Mordechai believe it implicitly, and agree to pass him off as your "half-brother". But Runcorn needed your co-operation. I would stake my life that it was *he* who put the thought of starting the pie-shop into your head.'

Genevra said nothing. The pie-shop had been entirely her own idea, but it would never have occurred to her to start such a venture if Rupert had not made a point of explaining to her that it was possible for a slave to earn his or her own ransom. And it had been Rupert who had urged her to accept a loan from Mordechai and tacitly allow the Jew to continue believing she was Abigail.

'Suddenly Runcorn's entire scheme collapsed about his ears,' Trelawney went on. 'Abigail had recovered inside the Spanish Hospital, and began to clamour to see her uncle, the Consul. The news that she was once again a prisoner in Algiers became known through the grapevine and reached Mordechai, who has spies of his own inside the Spanish Hospital. One of them succeeded in obtaining a specimen of her handwriting, proving beyond any doubt to

Mordechai that she was the true Abigail Pascoe. But her fortune was beyond even her own reach, and he was furious at the way in which he had been tricked. He sent for Runcorn, and announced that he was cutting off all financial support forthwith.'

Rupert, Genevra remembered suddenly, had not been near the pie-shop since Mordechai had sent for him, and now she was beginning to understand why.

'He has obviously been forced to give up his apartment,' she said, 'and accept, instead, the dreadful conditions of one of the bagnios. I now believe that he did deceive me, but I understand why, and I can forgive him.'

'You will not be quite so forgiving when you learn how Runcorn next attempted to raise money,' Trelawney observed dourly. 'Far from meekly entering a bagnio, he asked for an audience with the Dey, and told him that *you* were the Consul's niece. He explained to the Dey how he might use blackmail against John McDonnell and the British government by seizing you, and threatening to torture and kill you!'

Genevra grew rigid, stricken to the heart. She would have sworn that Rupert was her friend, and even now it was hard to believe in his perfidy. But had Trelawney not warned her against him from the start? And she had dismissed all the warnings as baseless prejudice . . .

'Naturally,' Trelawney's voice cut into her painful thoughts, 'the Dey sent for me, and I was forced to interview Abigail Pascoe inside the Spanish Hospital, where she admitted freely, in front of witnesses, that the Consul had been party to the original deception. Matters looked black indeed for both you and your uncle, not to mention his family. But fortunately for everyone other than Rupert Runcorn, Lord Exmouth announced that he had arrived to negotiate new terms, and that placed an entirely new complexion upon everything.'

'I see,' Genevra said in a small voice, and they walked on. She had not believed it possible to feel more crushed than she had already been, and now to learn that the only one in Algiers she had looked upon as a friend had used and betrayed her . . . After a while, she forced her thoughts to follow a different track. 'I am still a slave. What . . .'

'The British Consul and I will come to an arrangement over the matter.'

With a flash of returning spirit, she cried, 'I have told you that I shall not allow you to pay a ransom for me!'

Trelawney shrugged, and said coldly, 'Then you will have to remain as a slave in your uncle's household.'

Her spirit died, and she felt too depressed to say any more. She could see Lord Exmouth's squadron in the harbour, flying their British flags and ensigns. Then she realised that the British Consulate was at hand, and a sick feeling settled in the pit of her stomach. The sun was low in the sky, casting long shadows. In another hour or two the sudden darkness would have fallen, and Trelawney would have left for the city of Algiers. She would never again be allowed to enter, it, and she supposed bleakly that she would in future be joining her Cousin Sophie in watching the mole for glimpses of Trelawney as he went to sea or returned from a raid. Miriam, the Jewish maid, opened the door when they arrived at the Consulate. From inside the house the strains of music reached them; someone was playing a violin. She spread her hands at Trelawney's request to see the Consul.

'I couldn't disturb him now, Rais Trelawney,' she said. 'Lord Exmouth is here, and will be staying to dinner, and the mistress has invited other guests who are entertaining him with a musical performance before they dine. Mr McDonnell is to play a duet on the pianoforte with one of the lady guests, and it would be very embarrassing for everyone if he were not there to perform when the times comes.'

'I'm afraid my business with him is a matter of some urgency, Miriam.' Trelawney thought for a moment. 'Go and approach Mrs McDonnell instead, and whisper to her that she is wanted. No one will consider it strange if she leaves, since it would be assumed that some domestic crisis requires her attention. I could then explain my business to her, and she would be able to relay it to her husband at a convenient moment.'

'Very well, Rais Trelawney. Please follow me.'

Miriam led them into a small drawing-room that appeared to adjoin the room in which the musical entertainment was taking place, and Genevra caught a glimpse of seated guests before the girl slipped inside and closed the door behind her.

She returned, a short while later, with Harriet McDonnell. The latter froze at the sight of Genevra and said in an expressionless voice, 'Very well, Miriam. That will be all.' She waited until Miriam had left the room, and then checked to make certain she was not listening at the door. She turned, facing Trelawney and Genevra. 'What is your business with my husband?' she demanded in an arctic voice.

'May we sit down, Mrs McDonnell?' Trelawney asked. She inclined her head. When they were seated, he said, 'It is common knowledge now that Miss Shaw is related to your husband, and I have brought her to join her family since there is no longer any danger to you in acknowledging her . . .'

'Do you really imagine,' Harriet interrupted, her voice seething with passion, 'that you can rid yourself of her, now that she has served your purpose and you are tired of her, by thrusting her on to us?'

Through waves of mortification and shame, Genevra heard Trelawney say stiffly, 'You are not only extremely insulting, Mrs McDonnell, but very wide of the mark.'

'Indeed! Do you imagine that talk from the city does not reach us here in the European quarter? That we are not aware of the fact she has been known as your—your *woman*?'

'Allowing her to be known as my woman was the only means of ensuring her total safety in Algiers. It was never true in any meaning of the word.'

'Even if I were to believe that—which I don't . . .' Harriet bit off, 'do you imagine anyone else will? It is not even possible to pass her off as a servant, or as some stranger to whom we are forced to offer sanctuary because of my husband's position . . .'

'Mrs McDonnell!' Trelawney broke in, his voice harsh. 'As soon as I had bought Genevra, I paid the Belique an appropriate sum and obtained a *teskere* for her. I explained to her what it was, and told her that I intended taking her to the Consulate. She tore up the *teskere*; she destroyed the evidence of her freedom, *and she did so to protect your family*! She knew what danger there would have been for your husband, for yourself and your children if the Dey had become aware, at that time, that *she* was the Consul's niece and not Miss Pascoe!'

Harriet's eyes darkened. 'Yes, it is also due to her that we had Miss Pascoe inflicted upon us, and that my husband was forced to beggar himself! We owe Miss Shaw nothing; we were not responsible for her capture in the first place nor for her deliberate rejection of her freedom, or for the fact that she lived with you under your roof and was known by all as your woman—not to mention the fact that she baked and sold pies in the city like a common costermonger! She has become the talk of Algiers, and if you think that I will have her under my roof, Mr Grant, a source of scandal and ridicule, a contaminating influence . . .'

At that moment the other door opened, and the strains of harp music which had been coming from the reception room grew louder before it was closed again. A tightly-corseted middle-aged man with a ruddy complexion stepped into the anteroom, fanning himself vigorously with a lace handkerchief.

Genevra, gratefully seizing on the interruption, stood up and went to stand by the window, staring unseeingly out at the garden. To have been rejected in such insulting, humiliating terms by her uncle's wife was bitter enough; what made it infinitely more unbearable was the fact that it had been done in Trelawney's presence. Trelawney, who desperately wanted to be rid of her, and would insist on the McDonnells taking her in, whether Harriet wished it or not.

The newcomer explained, 'I was in sudden need of some air, Mrs McDonnell, and I would be grateful if you would explain to the lady harpist later that I intended no slight —although I must confess that the harp reminds me uncomfortably of the hereafter . . .' He paused, and seemed to be waiting for introductions, which Harriet pointedly failed to carry out.

Trelawney said in a hard, cynical voice, 'Allow me to do the honours myself, Lord Exmouth. You may remember me as Post Captain Trelawney Grant.'

'*Trelawney Grant!* I do not remember you, but I am well aware of your reputation throughout the Mediterranean!'

Lord Exmouth's voice had risen in pitch.

'I am sorry you should have forgotten me,' he said with irony, 'but honoured that my reputation has reached your august ears.'

Lord Exmouth was silent for a moment. 'You would not care to visit me on my flagship tomorrow, and join me in a glass of canary while we renew the acquaintance you claim, and which I have forgotten?'

Trelawney laughed. 'And find myself overpowered, and bundled below the hatches as you make ready to sail? Thank you, no!'

'How I should have liked to return you to British soil, and see you shot for the deserter and blackguard you are!' Lord Exmouth said with feeling.

'I am sorry that you have found yourself face to face with the man, Lord Exmouth,' Harriet said in a hunted voice. 'I shall ring for one of the maids, who will show you into the garden, where there will be a breeze.'

'Do not trouble yourself, Mrs McDonnell. I feel better already, and presently I shall slip back into my seat.'

A silence followed, and Genevra knew instinctively that she was the subject of Exmouth's scrutiny and speculation. She forced herself to turn round slowly. The earth was not likely to open up and swallow her, and therefore she would have to satisfy the man's curiosity and allow Harriet to introduce her in whatever insulting terms she chose, and concentrate on not giving way to the weight of shame and degradation inside her. Lord Exmouth was indeed staring at her, but his look of curiosity changed to a startled frown. Too late, she remembered about the revealing streak of white in her hair, so similar to Sophie's. Harriet had flushed deeply, and seemed incapable of speech.

It was Trelawney who said, 'Miss Genevra Shaw—Lord Exmouth.'

Exmouth moved towards her, still wearing a frown. He shook his head, and made her a bow. She dropped an automatic curtsy, and as she did so the chain on her ankle tinkled unmistakably. When she straightened up she saw that Lord Exmouth was staring at it. His glance went to her hair, and he drew a shocked breath, turning to Harriet.

'My dear Mrs McDonnell, this unfortunate young lady

cannot be other than related to your husband's family! Apart from a general resemblance, it *cannot* be a coincidence that she has precisely the same distinctive streak in her hair as your stepdaughter!'

'They—They are cousins,' Harriet confirmed in a strangled voice.

Exmouth gave his attention to Genevra. 'My poor young lady, what happened? How did you find yourself in this unspeakable situation?'

Harriet would never forgive her for this! Genevra was thinking. Her uncle's wife would believe she had deliberately drawn Exmouth's attention to herself, instead of waiting for him to return to the other room.

She realised that he was waiting for her reply, and swallowed. 'I—I was sailing for Algiers when—when the vessel was boarded by Corsairs . . .'

'Yes, I understand. You were coming to visit your family, of course. Well, you shall not remain a prisoner, enslaved by this turncoat, this renegade!' His voice softened. 'Do not look so cast down, Miss Shaw. A member of my own family was held as a slave for many years by the dastardly Algerians during the last century, so that I have very strong feelings on the subject.'

Genevra said nothing. Lord Exmouth turned to Harriet again, and exclaimed, 'What a shock it must have been to you, to find your husband's relative enslaved like this! The renegade has obviously come to demand a ransom for her. Mr McDonnell is clearly ignorant of what has befallen her, else he would have mentioned the matter to me.'

Harriet looked more hunted than ever, and shot a sidelong glare of venom at Genevra. 'My husband does not know that his niece-by-marriage has been brought here by Trelawney Grant,' she said evasively.

'Well,' Lord Exmouth assured her in a bracing voice, 'all of you may rest easy. I am to see the Dey tomorrow, and I shall use British government funds to pay a ransom for Miss Shaw, and restore her to the tender care of her family!'

'No, Lord Exmouth, you will not,' Trelawney put in smoothly. 'This particular slave is my property, and she is not for ransom—*at any price*.'

CHAPTER FIFTEEN

GENEVRA DID NOT trust herself to speak after Trelawney, without further ceremony, had removed her from the Consulate. Sweeping Harriet a bow, and giving Lord Exmouth a mock-salute, he had taken Genevra's arm and hurried her from the room, with Exmouth calling heatedly after him, 'My God, you have not heard the last of this matter, you black-hearted rogue!'

Trelawney too had remained silent, for reasons known only to himself, and once they had entered the city any conversation would have been impossible. The sun was nudging the horizon; the alleys were thronged with slaves on their way back to the bagnios for the night.

At last they were at the house, and had barely entered the courtyard when the muezzins began to wail and the servants spilled out to respond. Trelawney and Genevra climbed the stairs to the gallery, and for the first time he spoke.

'We have matters to discuss. Come into the drawing-room.'

In silence, she obeyed. Because she knew that she would otherwise have broken down and wept, she whipped up anger against him instead. 'You wanted to be rid of me, so why did you not leave me at the Consulate? Uncle John would have overruled his wife. He is a kind man, and besides, as Consul, he would have been obliged to give me shelter. You were willing enough to come to an agreement with him about a ransom for me. But now it seems that I have suddenly become an amusing diversion to you again because an important man like Lord Exmouth displayed an interest in me!'

'The situation has certainly acquired a new piquancy,' Trelawney confirmed coolly. 'Lord Exmouth pretended not to have recognised me, but he knew me as well as I knew him. As Sir Edward Pellew, he was Commander-in-Chief in the Mediterranean when the British were blockading the French fleet in Toulon harbour.'

'Sir Edward Pellew!' Genevra exclaimed. The man under whom Trelawney had served before he deserted, stealing the vessel he had commanded.

'And now he would like nothing better than to see me shot and he wants something—your freedom—which I am in a position to deny him. Even *you* must agree that it is vastly diverting.'

Rage shook her at this bland confirmation of what she had been suspecting. 'You cannot keep me a slave for ever, Trelawney, for the sake of a malicious whim! I would die rather than have *you* pay a ransom for me, but the British government is an entirely different matter! I shall appeal to the Dey, and tell him how you are standing in the way of my chance of freedom.'

He studied her for a moment, and the nonchalant manner which he had been maintaining ever since he had told Lord Exmouth that she was not for ransom was replaced by something she could not identify. He moved towards her, placing his hands on her shoulders. '*Freedom* . . . What does freedom mean to you, Genevra?'

She frowned at the question as much as at his change of mood. 'To begin with, it means the removal of this degrading chain about my ankle . . .'

'If the chain were removed,' he put in, 'your name would be scored out of the official record of prisoners in Algeria. There would be nowhere for you to go other than to the Consulate, not only because you would be a free British citizen but also because McDonnell is your legal guardian. I would have no further power or right to interfere in your fate. Lord Exmouth had nothing to do with my removing you from the Consulate. I had intended doing so before he ever appeared on the scene.'

She gazed into his eyes. They were no longer unreadable but had darkened with a passion which instinct told her he would have preferred to continue hiding behind a flippant façade.

'But why?'

His fingers tightened on her flesh, and he answered in a rough voice. 'Because I know now what that fate would be! Harriet McDonnell made it more than plain. You are the shameful family skeleton she would wish to have bricked up in a cupboard as soon as she could. If you were freed, she would persuade her husband to send you back to England. Do you know what happens to former slaves who return to England, and who have no money, and no family or friends to whom to turn?'

She began uncertainly, 'I—I do not believe Uncle John would send me home, totally penniless, knowing that until I obtained work of some kind I would not be able to survive.'

'No,' Trelawney agreed. 'But he is not a rich man, and is already in considerable debt. He would be forced to write on your behalf to one of the so-called charitable organisations which make a speciality of "helping" former slaves. Their representative would be awaiting you when you step ashore. A former slave is not without commercial value in the civilised world, and so you would be offered assistance—at a price.'

'What on earth do you mean?'

His reply was blunt. 'You would be paraded around the country, drawing paying crowds to stare at you. You would be made to look the part, and so you would be forced to wear shackles and rags. In order to touch the pity—and the pockets—of the crowds, your "benefactors" would require you to give lurid accounts of your life as a slave. In short, you would be treated as a sideshow freak for as long as your attraction as a novelty lasted!'

She drew a shuddering breath. It was impossible to doubt the accuracy of the picture he had been painting. 'So,' he continued, 'by allowing you your freedom, Genevra, I would be giving you the freedom to be thoroughly degraded and exploited by predators in England, and afterwards left to starve in obscurity.'

She looked up at him. He did not resemble in the least the Trelawney she was most familiar with; the man who regarded life as a wry joke. Instead of the usual mocker, the smoke-blue eyes were dark with raw emotion and there was a vulnerable cast to his mouth.

'Why—should you care?' she whispered, already sensing the answer but needing to hear it from his own lips.

Instead, he made a sound deep in his throat and drew her against him. 'Why indeed? It all started as a joke, and since then every instinct has urged me to cast you off and wash my hands of you. Never can a joke have turned more sour on a man!'

Her heart was beating in a suffocating rhythm as she tried, once again, to force him to say the words 'Trelawney, are you . . . Could you possibly be suggesting that you—have fallen in love with me?'

He did not reply at all this time. Instead, his mouth fastened on hers, forcing her lips apart with anger at first and then with a hopeless hunger that provided its own answer to her question. She clung to him in unreserved response, moulding her body against his, but she sensed the very instant when he called on all his powers of self-restraint before he lifted his mouth from hers and let her go.

When he spoke again it was as if that brief, emotionally charged and illuminating scene had never taken place. 'Until Harriet McDonnell made herself so plain, I did not understand how matters stood. I knew only that her husband was your uncle and your legal guardian, and I welcomed the opportunity of removing you from under my roof. But if you ceased to be a slave, Genevra, legally owned by me according to the laws of Algeria, you would have to go to the Consulate and most certainly be sent back to England, to the fate I have described. Do you still want your freedom?'

'What else is there, Trelawney?' She took a deep breath. 'What else but to— to become your *woman*—in truth as well as by reputation . . .'

'I have told you why I do not wish to become entangled in such a relationship,' he said roughly.

She swallowed. 'I—I would not make emotional demands, or do any of the other things you feared . . .'

'*Stop it, Genevra!*' He had almost shouted the words. 'You know who and what I am. Have you no pride?'

'No,' she replied simply.

'Well, *I* have! Far too much pride to take a *slave* as my mistress!'

'I see.' A jumbled mixture of humiliation, shame and anger seized her. 'The wife of a French Consul would, of course, be entirely different.'

'Yes, it would,' he agreed bluntly. 'We would be equals.'

Genevra despised herself for the tears which had sprung

to her eyes. It was the second time she had offered herself, and the second time he had rejected her quite brutally. 'It—It is a pity, Trelawney,' she said unevenly, 'that you were not always so fastidious—on past occasions . . .'

'Yes. God knows, I regret each moment of weakness. But it was more than flesh and blood could . . .' He broke off and reached for her, holding her in a hard and almost punishing grip. His voice was muffled as he went on, speaking with his face buried in her hair. 'Even a renegade, a thief, a deserter, a maker of slaves—has peculiar standards of his own. Can you not understand why I refuse to make you my mistress? You are my chattel to do with as I wish, totally in my power. What you are offering me I could take by force if I had a mind to. It is *because* I have such complete power over you that it would shame me deeply to take advantage of it.'

He released her, and she let her breath out in a long sigh, not truly understanding his attitude but recognising the sincerity and conviction behind it. 'So—what is to become of me, Trelawney? Am I to go on living here for ever, a slave with nothing to fill her time, belonging to you according to Algerian laws of property but in no other way?'

'There is no other way. You are a slave and a Christian. Even if you ceased being a slave, I would still remain a Corsair Rais who has taken the turban and who has sworn allegiance to Dey Osman Pasha.'

'But I dare not cease to be a slave,' she reminded him dully.

He hesitated. 'Some day, somehow, I shall find a way of freeing you and sending you home to England which would not involve you in the degradation of being hawked around and displayed as a former slave. To make you my mistress in the meantime would not only blight your own future, but would leave me with an abiding sense of shame and self-contempt.'

A long silence stretched between them. He broke it in a totally altered voice, brisk and impersonal. 'Since the chain round your ankle protects rather than degrades you, it would be pointless for you to try and earn a ransom for yourself. I shall go and see Mordechai tomorrow and repay what you owe him.'

She decided to follow his unemotional practical lead. 'Please allow *me* to call on Mordechai and apologise for tricking him, and assure him that he will be repaid.' She would think of some proposition to put to the Jew, she told herself, some way in which Trelawney would not have to repay the money she had borrowed from Mordechai.

'Very well,' he relented. He moved to the door, and stopped, giving her a long, unsmiling look. 'I am going out after I have changed my clothes. Make sure that you retire, Genevra, before my return.'

In other words, she was not to offer him provocation. He had all but admitted that he was in love with her, but his strange sense of honour would not allow him to make her his mistress. What kind of man was he, that he could take prisoners and enslave them, and yet scruple to make a reality of what the whole of Algiers believed to be true? She sighed. Her future looked bleak, desolate and empty, and she would no longer even have the pie-shop with which to occupy her time and prevent herself from dwelling on her situation.

But by the morning, after an almost sleepless night, she had spied a glimmer of hope. All the servants had responded to the call of the muezzins, but she found Trelawney breakfasting on coffee and fruit. He was wearing turban and robes, and it struck her again how the robes somehow emphasised his masculinity even more than did the tightly-fitting European breeches and coats. Then she thrust the thought from her mind. In the arid future which lay mapped out for her, it would not help her to dwell on his physically compelling qualities.

'Trelawney,' she said, 'if I kept myself out of the public eye, and if I behaved discreetly, would you allow me to continue keeping at least a share in the pie-shop?'

He looked at her with raised eyebrows. 'What have you in mind?'

'If I could arrange for someone else to bake and sell the pies, while I merely prepare them for the oven, with only Ahmed knowing that I am in any way involved in the venture—would you object?' Before he could reply, she added quickly, passionately, 'It would give me something to do, something with which to fill the time! You have no notion how utterly dreary it is to have nothing whatever with which to occupy myself!'

He looked away, and agreed not to stand in her way, and she gained the distinct impression that he, too, would welcome any diversion that would remove her from under his roof for part of the day. A while later Ahmed was eagerly accompanying her to the Jewish *hara*, and she sensed his excitement at the prospect of seeing Rebecca. She felt a little guilty, for she realised that if her scheme did work it would inevitably draw the Jewish girl and the young Moor deeper into a doomed, potentially disastrous relationship.

As she entered Mordechai's silk-hung bedroom and sat down, the old man said, 'Well, Miss Shaw. You have come, perhaps, to mock poor foolish Mordechai?'

'No, I have come to suggest to you a way in which the pie-shop could be made to benefit both of us.' As he waited with raised eyebrows, she went on, 'As you know, it was a success, and I believe it could become an even greater one. While the excellence of the pies was largely responsible, Rais Trelawney assures me that . . . well, that customers were also attracted because they were being sold by a personable young woman.'

Mordechai's slight, cynical smile confirmed that Trelawney had been quite right. 'I would not have lent you sufficient money for such a venture, Miss Shaw, if you had been old and ugly. Not even when I believed you to be Miss Pascoe.'

'Rais Trelawney will not allow me to go on selling pies,' Genevra told him, 'but he will allow me to continue preparing them for baking. And there is someone far more beautiful than I who could continue to attract customers to the shop. I am thinking of your daughter Rebecca.'

Mordechai shook his head. 'Rebecca is beautiful, as you say, but she is Jewish. I could not expose her to the dangers a Jewish girl would face, presiding over a shop in Algiers.'

'There is unlikely to be any danger,' Genevra reassured him. 'Because no alcohol is sold, the customers are the peaceful, civilised members of the slave population, and no Turk or Moor patronises the shop.'

'Hmm . . . And how do *you* expect to benefit from such an arrangement, Miss Shaw?'

'I expect my debt to you to be wiped out. All the assets of the shop, and all the profits received, would go to you and to Rebecca. The work I did in preparing the pics would represent payment of interest on my original loan.'

Mordechai was far too shrewd a businessman not to recognise the commercial potential of such a proposition, and he agreed with reservations. At the slightest hint of danger to Rebecca, he said, he would close the pie-shop and demand financial compensation from Trelawney. Since Genevra felt quite sure that Ahmed would not be far away from the shop during the three hours every afternoon when it was open, and would keep a jealously watchful eye on Rebecca, she did not feel there would be the slightest danger to the girl, but she judged it prudent not to tell Mordechai this.

The following day Lord Exmouth sailed from Algiers. The peace treaty he had negotiated with the Dey was officially marked by the running up of the British flag on the palace and the harbour battlements, to a salute of gunfire from the Algerians.

It was also the day when the shop re-opened under the new arrangement. Accompanied by Ahmed, Genevra left the house to prepare the many different pies for baking, and just before the shop was due to be opened to the slave-customers, Rebecca arrived. Ahmed escorted Genevra home before he returned to stoke the oven and mount guard over Rebecca.

At first, Genevra had dreaded the thought of an unexpected meeting with Rupert. How he had traded on that beautiful-ugly face of his! She did not know how she would react if they were to meet, but she did not glimpse him even among the excited crowds who gathered when the Corsair fleet returned to harbour with their human and other plundered cargoes. She watched in pity as the new prisoners were being paraded through the alleys, just as she herself had once been paraded, and revulsion for the system rose anew inside her.

Only a week later, on the 14th of May, Lord Exmouth

returned to Algiers harbour with his squadron. Genevra was filled with unease, for she had supposed him to have sailed to England. She had been surprised but relieved, at the time, that he had apparently given up so easily any attempt to force Trelawney to accept a ransom for her. Had Exmouth's return something to do with his vow to restore her to her family?

That evening she deliberately waited up so that she could speak to Trelawney. She had barely set eyes on him for so long now that she was momentarily overwhelmed by his sheer physical presence as he stepped on to the gallery. The overhead lamp played on the shimmering white silk of his turban, which was the most ornate she had yet seen; a very wide, long piece of fabric swathed several times around his head in such a way that its long, draped end fell down one shoulder, almost as if it were a half-cape. Beneath the turban, his face was thrown into dark shadows and sharp angles and planes by the lamplight.

'Genevra,' he said expressionlessly, 'why have you not retired?'

'I wanted to ask you about Lord Exmouth's return.'

He hesitated. 'You had better come into the drawing-room.'

As he opened the door for her, she tripped on the edge of a rug, and he put out his hands to steady her. For an instant his fingers lingered, with the merest of tremors, on her upper arms, and she thought, breathlessly, that he meant to draw her against himself. Instead, he moved away, and said roughly, 'Sit down.'

Deliberately he chose to seat himself as far away from her as possible. 'It is late, Genevra, and I am tired. Tell my why you are concerned about Lord Exmouth's return, so that we may both seek our beds.'

'I wondered if he might have come back to try and negotiate for my freedom. I thought he had gone back to England . . .'

'He sailed from here for Tripoli,' Trelawney interrupted, 'and his return to Algiers has nothing whatever to do with you.'

'Oh!' Even sitting in the same room with him, separated by as great a distance as he could put between them, was something to be clung to and spun out for as long as possible. 'How can you be sure that Lord Exmouth does not intend asking the Dey to free me and send me to the Consulate?' she asked.

'Because Exmouth has what he considers far more important matters on his mind,' Trelawney said with a short laugh. 'The news that more prisoners have been brought into Algiers sent him back here to complain to the Dey. I have just come from the palace, where I was present at his meeting with Osman Pasha.'

'What happened?'

'Exmouth was sufficiently naïve to suggest to the Dey that Algeria should turn to international trade instead of continuing to rely for its economy on sea-raids. It would be like urging a successful highwayman to turn stable-lad instead! I could barely contain my amusement.'

Genevra forgot to keep the conversation on an impersonal plane, and burst out, 'You are every bit as corrupt and despicable as the Dey and all his other henchmen, and I don't know why I . . .' She stopped, recognising the absurdity of what she had been about to say.

Trelawney gazed at her for a moment, his eyes unreadable dark hollows in the lamplight. Then he laughed again, with cynicism this time, and when he spoke it was almost as if he were wishing to punish her for something. 'Shall I tell you, Genevra, about the gifts Lord Exmouth has offered to send to the Grand Signior of Constantinople in exchange for his agreement to end the Corsair system? Apart from the usual items of jewellery and weapons, he will also be presenting the Grand Signior, on behalf of the British government, *with forty Austrian slaves!*'

'That—That is nonsense! The British do not take slaves!'

'No. They agree to buy them from the Dey of Algiers and hand them over to Constantinople instead.' Trelawney stood up. 'Nothing is ever black and white, Genevra, and few things are precisely what they seem.' He sketched her an ironic bow. 'Good night. Think of those forty Austrian slaves the next time you are moved to condemn me and my profession.'

She went to bed, disturbed by what he had told her, and relieved that Exmouth's return had had nothing to do with herself. And then, inevitably, her mind began to dwell on the way Trelawney had looked in the lamplight and she was once more overcome by the painful longing and hopelessness that were never far from her mind.

She did not see him the following morning before she left for the pie-shop. To her surprise, she found Rebecca there already, waiting for her. The girl looked as if she had been weeping, and she was accompanied by two stern-faced, bearded men dressed in black.

'These are my cousins, miss,' Rebecca said, and swallowed visibly. 'My father ordered them to come with me, so that I might tell you the pie-shop is to be closed.'

'But why?' Genevra demanded, dismayed and at a loss.

Rebecca said nothing; instead, her tortured glance fell upon Ahmed and then she looked away. Now Genevra understood. Mordechai had obviously learnt, through his spies, of the growing feeling between his daughter and the young Moor. Her head bowed, and accompanied by her cousins, Rebecca walked away.

Genevra explained to Ahmed in Algerine what had happened. He escorted her home, looking bereft, and she felt certain they shared the same thought—that he would never see Rebecca again.

The day stretched aimlessly ahead, and after a while Genevra decided, on impulse, to go and see Mordechai. There was a remote possibility that she might be able to persuade him to change his mind if she gave her promise that Ahmed would be kept away from the shop and another servant installed in his place. She slipped out secretly, and made her way along the narrow alleys to the Jewish quarter.

There was no sign of Rebecca when she reached Mordechai's home, and she hoped he was not keeping her in confinement as a punishment. None of the old man's family tried to stop Genevra from squeezing her way along the crowded stairs and gallery towards his room. She was about to knock on his door when she realised that it was not completely shut, and that he already had a visitor.

'. . . if you would only give me a little time,' Rupert Runcorn was pleading, 'I know I could raise the money!'

'As matters stand, you already owe me more than enough, my friend! And now you ask for more credit, and you make vague promises, and you will not even hint at the source of this money you say you expect to raise!'

Genevra was about to beat a retreat, fearful of coming face to face with Rupert, when she heard him say, 'Very well. I shall give you a hint. I have important information to sell to the Dey. His favourite Rais, Trelawney Grant, is a spy for the British, and I have evidence to prove it.'

Genevra shook her head in disbelief as she hurried from Mordechai's house. Rupert must be desperate indeed to imagine that Mordechai would swallow such an absurd story. And yet . . . She chewed at her lip. Trelawney had better be warned that Rupert would stop at nothing in his efforts to raise money. He might well fabricate convincing 'evidence' and make trouble for Trelawney.

She waited for him to come home, her tension increasing as the hours went by. The sun touched the horizon, and the muezzins wailed the familiar chant to all Believers to come to prayers, and she was alone in the house as the servants went to answer the call. The hours seeped away, and at last she was forced to admit defeat. She went to her room and undressed, and put on one of Abigail's silk nightgowns. She had just unpinned her hair and was brushing it when she heard footsteps on the stairs. Trelawney had returned at last, and she would have to tell him immediately what she had overheard, for she knew he would probably have left the house before she rose in the morning.

She grabbed a shawl with which to cover her shoulders, and opened her door. Trelawney had just gained the gallery and moved straight towards her, and before she could begin to explain why she needed to speak to him, he put out his hands, drawing her against him so roughly that the shawl fell from her shoulders and she was left clad only in the thin silk nightgown.

His hands moved warmly, insistently, over the contours of her body. He gave a ragged little laugh, and she recognised the smell of liquor on his breath. 'Damned little millstone—round my neck,' he muttered, drawing her closer.

His own silk robes were so thin that she could feel the warmth of his flesh against her own, and her senses raced in chaotic abandon, so that she lifted her hands and pushed the cowl of his burnous from his head, burying her hands in his hair, feeling its springy texture beneath her fingers. His lips fastened on hers, and if his kisses had been uninhibited before, this time they held no restraint whatever. Her mouth opened under his as she responded in instinctive female generosity and surrender, and it was only when he picked her up bodily and carried her, still with his mouth fastened on her own, into her bedroom that some sanity began to return to her.

She moved her hands to the sides of his face and forced his mouth from her own. 'Trelawney, no . . .'

'I am foxed,' he said in a thick voice, 'and do you know why, my dearest thorn-in-the-flesh, my slave, my *woman*? Because I dared not risk—coming home early—and finding you underfoot again . . .' He dropped her on the bed, and sat down beside her, reaching for her once more.

'Trelawney,' she warded him off. 'Listen! You must listen to me! This may be important. Rupert Runcorn says he has proof that you are a spy for the British, and that he means to sell his information to the Dey . . .'

She stopped as she saw him stiffen with instant alertness. If he had been inebriated a moment before, he appeared to be completely sober now.

'Do you know what precise proof Runcorn possesses?' he demanded in a sharp voice.

'Then . . .' she faltered. 'Then you really *are* . . .'

'A spy for the British.' He laughed shortly. 'As I told you before, things are seldom what they seem, and there are many different shades between black and white, Genevra.'

CHAPTER SIXTEEN

GENEVRA WAS TOO dazed by Trelawney's revelation to react for a moment. Then he said, 'It is past midnight. By five in the morning Algiers will be awake and taking to the streets. We therefore have less than four hours before I shall have to deliver you to the British Consulate. Get dressed, Genevra, and pack your trunks, and then join me in the dining-room.'

'The—The Consulate?' she stammered. 'But you said . . .'

'I know,' he answered her unspoken protest. 'However, it is the only place where you will be safe. When Osman Pasha learns that I have been spying for the British, his rage will extend to everyone closely linked with me.' His mouth twisted. 'Especially to *my woman*. So please do as I tell you.'

He left her room, and she dressed and then went to join Trelawney. He had lit the portable oil-stove in the dining-room and heated up the large jugful of coffee that had been left there for him, and was methodically drinking cup after cup of the strong brew.

The grooves appeared briefly in his cheeks. 'I wish I had known, when I set out to get foxed, that I would have to concentrate twice as much effort into sobering up.' He poured a cup of coffee for her, and went on, 'Now tell me everything you learnt from Rupert Runcorn.'

She sat down, and recounted her visit to Mordechai, and what she had overheard. 'I did not believe what Rupert had said, and I had no desire to come face to face with him, so I left before I could learn any more.'

'Hmm . . .' Trelawney drummed his fingers on the table. 'Runcorn is not without intelligence. He would have questioned my reasons for visiting Gibraltar so often, and remembered that I had chosen to take, in wartime, the wife of the *French* Consul as my mistress. It must have been he whom I saw in the moonlight, before Algiers was awake this morning, lurking on the mole. He would certainly have realised the significance of what he in turn had seen.'

'What *had* he seen?'

'He watched me being rowed ashore. I had been on board the British flagship, in conference with Lord Exmouth.'

Terror clutched at Genevra's heart. 'If only it had been anyone other than Rupert . . . But I suppose he must have been spying on you deliberately to be there at all.' She looked fearfully at Trelawney. 'Once Rupert has spoken to the Dey, what will happen?'

He considered for a moment. 'Runcorn has no real proof to offer, and it would be his word against mine. He was alone on the mole, and I shall simply deny the entire episode. Besides, I doubt if he will be able to gain an audience with the Dey while Lord Exmouth is in Algiers, and the Divan is preoccupied with British demands that the slave system should be brought to an end. When Runcorn does tell his story, the Dey will not believe him at first, but the seeds of doubt will have been sown, and I would be closely watched. My usefulness as a spy would therefore be over, and life would become increasingly dangerous for me here. So, when Exmouth leaves Algiers, I shall be on board his flagship.'

She looked pleadingly at him. 'In that case, I do not have to be taken to the Consulate yet.'

'Yes, you do,' he put in firmly. 'When news of my betrayal reaches the Dey, the longer the two of us have been separated, the safer you will be.'

After a moment, she asked, 'Trelawney, when you kissed me in Gibraltar, it was not because you had seen a former slave who would have recognised you, was it?'

'No. I needed to report to one of the Naval officers strolling along the harbour, but my officers had arrived too early with the rowing-boat that was to return me to the Corsair ship, and could see me. I needed to create some kind of diversion which would have led to my "arrest". Giving in to the impulse to kiss an unescorted, un-chaperoned girl was something which would have been accepted as being within my character.'

'And—it was you who tried to prevent me and Abigail from sailing on *Caranguejo*?'

He looked deep into her eyes. 'Would that I had succeeded . . . The Portuguese vessel was an obvious target for a raid, but I had no wish to take two Englishwomen prisoner.'

She studied him. 'I know so little about you, and there are so many questions . . . *Why* did Britain want a spy in Algiers? How could you bring yourself to do all the things you have been doing—sea-raiding, taking prisoners, watching them become slaves? How did you feel about abjuring? Who and what are your family?'

He smiled wryly, and poured another cup of coffee. 'As you have said, there are too many questions. At heart I am an adventurer, Genevra, a man with few scruples.'

'But not so few that you would make me your mistress,' she reminded him softly.

He met her glance, and looked away. 'Was that a scruple? I don't know. Perhaps it was merely male pride that insisted that *my woman* should be free, and not someone for whom I had paid twenty-five gold sequins . . .' He broke off, and then continued in an altered voice. 'You asked about my family. They live in Devonshire and I am the second son. Apart from my elder brother, I have two sisters, and I followed family tradition by making the sea my career.' He went on to tell her about his home, describing it with nostalgia, and about his widowed father and his elder brother who would have made the Church his vocation if family tradition had not demanded that he inherit the estate. He stopped talking as the clock in the drawing-room chimed four times. 'We shall have to leave. My servants will deliver your trunks to the Consulate later. I shall put out a rumour that you had continued your involvement with the pie-shop without my knowledge or consent, and that I cast you off in anger.'

They made their way together along the gallery and down the stairs, the moon lighting their way. It was a strange and eerie experience, Genevra found, winding through alleys which were completely deserted and ghostlike in the light of the moon. The silence, too, seemed unreal and unnerving. Then everything else was swept from her mind as she faced the knowledge that this really was the last she would be seeing of Trelawney. After he had left with Lord Exmouth, he would not dare to return to Algiers. She tried to push the knowledge aside.

As the European quarter came into view, dark and silent in the moonlight, Trelawney stopped and turned to Genevra. He took her face in his hands and said in a sombre voice, 'You tried, once, to force me to say it, but instinct told me that it would be wrong for a spy who had taken the turban to speak of love to the Rector's daughter he had enslaved. I still know it to be wrong, but there it is. I do love you. I wish I didn't, for it is not likely to bring me comfort in the months and the years ahead.'

'Oh, Trelawney . . .' She buried her face against his chest and clung to him. 'Take me with you when you leave with Lord Exmouth!' she cried in desperation.

'I cannot.' His hands went to the back of her head, tilting up her face. 'Apart from the fact that I still serve the Navy, who will doubtless find other work somewhere in the world for a spy with my special qualifications . . .' He paused, his mouth twisting. 'Even in the unlikely event that Exmouth would allow you to be smuggled aboard his flagship, I could not take you with me, Genevra. You are no ordinary slave, but the British Consul's niece. The Dey will be angry enough when he learns who and what I was, and that I had gone beyond his reach. If I were to take you with me, his rage would focus on Mr McDonnell and his family. I know how the Dey's mind works, and I know he will seek scapegoats. I could not live with that on my conscience. Could you?'

'No,' she whispered.

He nodded, and sighed. Then he lowered his head and sought her mouth, and this time there was the sadness of farewell mixed with hungry, unfulfilled emotion in their kiss as they clung together.

In silence, they walked the rest of the way to the European quarter. Behind them, they were aware that Algiers was beginning to stir into life. Through the windows of the European dwellings lamplight was flickering also, heralding the day's early start.

Trelawney rapped the knocker on the door of the

Consulate, and a short while later it was opened to them by a startled, sleepy-looking Miriam. Genevra felt his hand on her arm, the pressure of his fingers conveying a warning.

'Good morning, Miriam,' he said shortly, and gave Genevra a push so that she almost stumbled over the threshold. 'Tell Mr McDonnell that I make him a present of his niece, whether he wants her or not.'

Following his lead, Genevra injected an abject note into her voice. 'Trelawney, please—I meant no harm . . .'

'Be quiet!' he snapped, and turned to the bemused but avid Miriam. 'On second thoughts, I had best speak to the Consul myself. If he is still abed I shall wait, because I have too many other matters demanding my attention to come back later.'

'No, Rais Trelawney,' she said. 'Both Mr and Mrs McDonnell have been up for some time. The master is doing some work in his study before breakfast.'

'Then take me to him. No, don't trouble to announce me.'

They followed Miriam along the corridor, and waited while she knocked on a door. Genevra did her best to look both crushed and defiant. At a summons from inside, Trelawney opened the door and stepped forward. 'Good morning, Mr McDonnell. I have come to hand your niece over to you, whether your wife cares for it or not. Perhaps she had better be sent for so that she, too, may hear why I no longer want this young woman under my roof.'

Genevra saw that John had risen to his feet. He looked tired and perplexed, and after a moment's hesitation, he said, 'Miriam, please fetch your mistress.'

When he was certain that the girl was out of earshot, Trelawney said rapidly, 'Could you find an excuse to get rid of Miriam for half an hour, Mr McDonnell? She listens at doors, and what I have to tell you must be said in the utmost confidence.'

John's perplexity grew. He nodded, and gazed at Genevra, his expression helpless. 'My dear, how I wish I had been able to be of more assistance to you!'

'You may help her, sir,' Trelawney interposed swiftly, 'by persuading your wife to accept her as a member of the family. After I have left Algiers you may tell the truth to everyone, which will help to vindicate Genevra in the eyes of the free Christians. Until then . . .' He stopped as the sound of approaching footsteps reached them. The door opened, and Harriet entered, her eyes hostile, while behind her those of Miriam were bright with curiosity.

John frowned before addressing his wife, apparently on impulse. 'My dear, it has just occurred to me that Mrs Deverel may have some soothing syrup that will ease the baby's painful gums. The Deverels' own baby is only a few months older, and its mother will have experienced the problem that plagues our little Christopher. Send Miriam to go and ask Mrs Deverel's advice and help.'

Harriet stared at him, but something in her husband's expression must have communicated itself to her, for she nodded, and turned to confirm that Miriam was to leave for the house of Mrs Deverel immediately.

While the others seated themselves, John remained standing by the window, staring outside. After a few minutes he reported, 'Miriam has just gone by. The Deverels live at the far end of the European quarter, so we should be quite private for a while.'

'What is all this drama about?' demanded Harriet in a stony voice.

'Mrs McDonnell,' Trelawney said rapidly, 'I have brought Genevra to you for safety. When Lord Exmouth sails from Algiers, I shall be aboard his flagship, and the city will then be swept by the news that I have been working as a spy for the British since my arrival here.'

'*What?*' Both Harriet and her husband looked at him in disbelief.

'I could not tell you before. I could not tell *anyone*. The truth is that my so-called desertion from the Navy was a deliberate ruse. Lord Exmouth—or Sir Edward Pellew as he was at the time—could foresee that the war with France would not last for much longer, and when it was over, he and others wished to turn their attention to Algiers and end for good the taking of Christian slaves. Sir Edward was a member of an organisation called the Knights Liberators of the Slaves in Africa . . .'

'Yes, of course, we all know of its existence,' John put in.

Trelawney nodded. 'It was felt that, if reason and

diplomacy continued to have no effect upon the Algerians, we would have to consider hostilities against them at some time in the future. But the position of Algiers, as you know, makes it almost impregnable from the sea, and we needed to know everything we could about the city's defences. So I was chosen to come here as a British Naval deserter, sailing my stolen vessel into the harbour. My credentials as a renegade had to be perfect. For that reason, too, I was forced to abjure and take the turban, and I had to go sea-raiding to prove myself as a renegade Rais.'

His glance rested on Genevra for a moment. 'When I found that one of my prisoners was a penniless young Englishwoman, I knew there was only one way in which I could secure her freedom: I would have to buy her myself. But when I offered her her freedom afterwards, she tore up the *teskere*, and I discovered later that it was because she realised that if she had at that time come to the Consulate as your niece, Mr McDonnell, she would have placed all of you in danger. Now,' he shrugged, '*her* life would be in danger if she were still living in my house when the news comes out that I left with the British squadron, and that I had therefore been spying for them all this time.'

A silence followed when he had finished. It was broken by Harriet. 'Will—Will there be hostilities? A war between Britain and Algiers?'

'I don't know, Mrs McDonnell. Lord Exmouth is trying as hard as he can . . .'

Genevra spoke for the first time since they had entered the study. 'Where will you go next, Trelawney?'

His gaze held hers for a moment. 'Wherever the Navy chooses to send me.' I shall no longer be able to concern myself with your welfare, his expression added. He looked at John. 'The story that will spread through Algiers today will be that I have turned Genevra out in anger, because she defied my orders. I am to be present at the audience you and Lord Exmouth are to have with the Dey later this morning, and I think it might be as well if you and I were to enact a little drama for the benefit of the Dey, Mr McDonnell.' He thought for a moment. 'I shall demand a ransom for your niece, saying that I no longer regard her as my woman. You will refuse to pay, claiming that she is connected to you only through your first marriage and making it clear that you find her presence at the Consulate a personal embarrassment and that you are sheltering her only in your capacity as British Consul. I shall make it clear that I will continue to press for a ransom, and in the meantime I will insist that you pay the monthly sum to the Belique, exempting her from work. That should convince the Dey that I have genuinely cast Genevra off, and it would also prevent him from suspecting, when I leave with Lord Exmouth, that you and I had been in collusion in any way.'

John frowned. 'Lord Exmouth once offered to pay a ransom for Genevra. What if he should offer to do so again?'

'He won't,' Trelawney said. 'I shall have a private word with him beforehand.'

John nodded, and Trelawney stood up. 'I had better leave now. Remember, until I have left Algiers with Lord Exmouth, what I have told you must remain strictly between the four of us.'

As they emerged from the study together, Genevra saw Sophie hurrying towards them. The girl's flushed, excited glance moved slowly over Trelawney, resplendent in his robes and turban, and then she looked at Genevra. 'Miriam told me and the nurse that you have been brought to the Consulate, to stay,' she said. 'Is it true?' Without waiting for a reply, she rattled on, 'How elegant you are looking! I don't believe I would have recognised you, had Miriam not told me who you were. I cannot see any resemblance between us . . .'

She was forced to pause for breath. Genevra became aware that Trelawney was studying her cousin, taking in the plump figure and the pretty face with its somewhat vacuous expression. 'Neither can I,' he said softly. He seemed to remember abruptly that he was meant to have quarrelled bitterly with Genevra, for he added deliberately, 'You, Miss McDonnell, are so obviously a young lady of impeccable gentility.'

He nodded to John, swept a bow at the females, and then turned away to leave the house. Genevra's glance followed him from sight, her eyes stinging with unshed tears. She would truly never see him again.

'Well,' Harriet said with a frown. She seemed not to

know quite how to deal with the situation, or what to do next.

'I think we should go in to breakfast,' John suggested.
'Come, my dear,' he invited Genevra, taking her arm. 'I
dare say you are hungry.'

The breakfast was very British, and for Genevra, it was a
difficult and tense meal. Physical hunger compelled her to
eat, but she gained no enjoyment from the food. The
knowledge that Trelawney had passed out of her life for
ever continued to pound inside her, and matters were not
made any easier by Sophie's inane chatter.

John excused himself and stood up with a sigh. 'I have a
difficult morning ahead. I shall have to leave immediately,
to join Lord Exmouth at the palace.' He kissed his wife's
cheek. 'I shall be home for luncheon as usual, my dear.'

After he had gone, Harriet ordered Sophie to go and help
the nurse with the baby. Once alone with Genevra, it
seemed clear that she still retained a large measure of her
former hostility and reluctance to have her husband's niece
staying at the Consulate. At last she said, 'The knowledge
that Trelawney is . . .' She broke off, obviously remembering Miriam's habit of listening at doors, and reframed her
original sentence. 'Perhaps the altered circumstances will
change people's attitude towards you, and make it easier
. . . That is, many of the scandalous rumours may be
disbelieved. I don't know what we are to do with you in the
long term, but in the meantime, it would be as well if you
were to keep to your room, and have your meals served to
you there. Later, perhaps, when . . .' She did not complete
the sentence.

Genevra understood perfectly. If her own reputation
were to improve after the news came out that Trelawney
had been a spy, she might cease to be treated as an outcast.
But until then she was a social embarrassment who had to
be isolated. At least, she thought with dreary humour,
incarceration in her room would save her from Sophie's
incessant and irritating questions. Aloud, she asked, 'Is
there anything I might do for you while I keep to my room,
Mrs McDonnell? Mending or sewing, perhaps?'

Harriet looked surprised at such willingness to help with
the domestic tasks, and as she showed Genevra to the room
she had occupied before, she announced that she would

send Miriam with a sewing basket and some mending to be done.

Sewing, Genevra found later, was not the most effective way of blocking out painful thoughts. An hour or so after the sun had risen, Trelawney's servants carried in her trunks, and their expressions as they looked at the sparsely furnished room and then glanced at her, sitting hollow-eyed over the bundle of sewing in her lap, showed that they believed she had been cast off in anger and had been received by her family in disgrace.

At noon, Miriam brought her luncheon on a tray. Genevra picked at the food, and then thought of the meals she had shared with Trelawney in the past. She remembered the evening when she had made mutton pies for their supper, and how they had cleaned the kitchen together afterwards so that the servants would not be aware of their intrusion, and she swallowed hard against the knot in her throat. Little more than an hour after Miriam had removed her barely touched tray, she knocked on the door again and imparted the surprising information that Mrs McDonnell wished Genevra to join her for dish of tea in the garden. As she followed Miriam from the room, she could hear scales being practised on the pianoforte, presumably by Sophie.

On the terrace, Harriet was seated alone by the table that Genevra remembered from her first visit to the Consulate, when she had been wearing peasant clothing and had been filled with fears and suspicions against Trelawney. She forced herself to thrust the ever-encroaching thoughts about him from her mind, and went to join Harriet.

'You sent for me?' Genevra asked uncertainly. 'I mean, Miriam did not mistake your . . . ?'

'No. Please sit down, Genevra. Miriam, you may bring the tea now.'

Harriet waited until the Jewish girl could no longer overhear, but even then she pitched her voice low as she said, 'John did not come home for luncheon, as he promised, and there has been no word from him. I—I wondered whether you, with your knowledge of Algiers, might be able to think what could have occurred?'

Genevra shook her head slowly. 'No, I'm sorry.' She was silent for a moment. 'Would you like me to visit the city, and see if I can discover anything?'

Harriet chewed indecisively at her lower lip. 'I don't know. You might not be safe there any longer, now that people know Trelawney Grant has abandoned you . . .' She stopped talking as Miriam appeared with the tray of tea things

In a thoughtful, anxious silence, they drank their tea. 'The European quarter might be a world apart from the city of Algiers!' Genevra said suddenly. 'There, whatever has happened will be common knowledge to everyone by now, or at least there would be rumours. Whereas here . . .' She looked up to see Miriam approaching them once again.

'Mrs McDonnell,' she announced. 'There is a young Moor at the door. He says he wishes to see Miss Shaw. He says he has brought something she left behind in the house of Rais Trelawney.'

'Bring him out here, Miriam,' Genevra ordered quickly, before Harriet could respond. As the girl left them to obey, Genevra said in a low voice, 'I am sorry, Mrs McDonnell, to have appeared so presumptuous. But the Moor can only be Ahmed, Trelawney's personal servant, and since I know I left nothing behind in his house, this must be an excuse to deliver a message, and out here we can at least ensure that Miriam does not overhear.'

Harriet's offended expression left her, and she nodded with something like gratitude. Genevra guessed that it was in her mind, too, that Trelawney was to have been present at the Dey's meeting with Lord Exmouth and the Consul, and so he might know why John had not returned home as expected.

A few moments later Miriam was showing Ahmed out to the terrace. He made them a respectful salaam, and handed Genevra an emerald pin. 'You left this is the house of Rais el-Trahni,' he said in Algerine, presumably for Miriam's benefit, since he knew as well as Genevra did that Trelawney had often worn it in his turban.

She thanked him in an unsteady voice, and waited for Miriam to return reluctantly to the house. She sensed that Trelawney had genuinely wished her to have the pin as a keepsake in remembrance of himself, and had not merely seen it as a means of conveying a message. With fingers that shook slightly, she pinned it to her fichu.

When Miriam was out of sight, Ahmed continued speaking in Algerine, his voice pitched low. Genevra heard him out, and tried not to allow her expression to reveal her reactions. It struck her that Ahmed was far too loyal to Trelawney to be left safely behind in Algiers and that he, too, would have to leave with Lord Exmouth. When he had finished speaking, she addressed Harriet. 'Would you please ring for Miriam to see Ahmed out?'

Miriam responded so quickly to the handbell that it was obvious she had been hovering close to the door in the hope of hearing something useful. But since she would have to see Ahmed through the house and to the front door, there were a few minutes in which Genevra could safely translate his news to Harriet.

'Please try not to be too alarmed,' she said swiftly. 'According to Trelawney, there was an angry exchange of words inside the palace during the audience with the Dey. Lord Exmouth threatened to break off diplomatic relations with Algiers and to withdraw the Consul. The Dey said Uncle John would not be allowed to leave the country until he had paid his debts.'

'The debts,' Harriet observed with bitterness, 'incurred on behalf of Miss Pascoe.'

Genevra nodded, feeling guilty, because if she had not attacked Seremeth Ali Uncle John would not have been forced to allow himself to be claimed as Abigail's uncle. 'Trelawney intervened in the quarrel,' she went on, 'and it appeared to have been settled. Uncle John then left the palace with Lord Exmouth. But Trelawney says the Dey suddenly flew into a renewed rage as he reflected on Lord Exmouth's demands and issued orders to his soldiers. Lord Exmouth was walking in the street with Uncle John, on their way from the palace, when they were arrested.'

'*Arrested!*' Harriet echoed with horror. 'Where are they now?'

'Lord Exmouth was released, and allowed to return to his flagship. But Uncle John . . . I'm sorry, Mrs McDonnell, but he was taken to one of the bagnios.'

Harriet covered her face with her hands. 'Oh, dear Lord above . . . Whatever am I to do?'

Genevra decided not to pass on another piece of information Ahmed had conveyed—that the Dey, in his rage, had ordered all British citizens found inside Algiers city to be rounded up and imprisoned. 'I suggest you do nothing,' she said. 'The Dey is a very volatile man, and any action on your part would probably make matters worse. There is, however, one thing which Trelawney recommends most strongly you *should* do. Get rid of Miriam. She is not to be trusted, especially while conditions are so uncertain. The position of Jews in Algiers is so precarious that one cannot blame them for being alert to situations they can exploit to their own advantage.'

Harriet frowned anxiously. 'But how am I to do that, without making her suspect my reasons, and causing her to carry wild tales into the city?'

Genevra glanced up. She could tell, from the shadowy movement she had noticed, that Miriam had returned to the door which led to the garden, and was trying to hear. She turned her head, and mouthed at Harriet, 'I know how.'

She picked up her now cold cup of tea, took an angry sip, and placed it forcefully down on the table again. Raising her voice, she cried hotly, 'Well, let me tell you, Mrs McDonnell, *I* have no wish to be a financial burden to you either! In fact, I insist on earning my keep, and by that I do not merely mean doing a little sewing in my room! Whatever you pay Miriam to do, *I* shall do gladly for no more than my meals and a roof over my head. And after what you have been levelling at my door, I shall refuse to eat another crumb in this house unless you do make use of my services in that way!' Then she rose and marched with apparent burning anger inside the house, affecting not to notice the obviously chagrined Miriam as she passed her.

Almost an hour later, Harriet came to her room and asked whether she might sit down. She looked anxious and careworn, and her voice shook slightly as she said, 'I hope, Genevra, that you meant what you said about doing Miriam's work, because I told her that her services were no longer required. I said I would not be held responsible by my husband for your starving yourself unless you were allowed to earn your keep.'

Impulsively, Genevra placed a hand over hers, and said,

'Yes, of course I shall do whatever Miriam used to do. I would be glad to, for the one thing I cannot abide is to be idle.'

Colour washed into Harriet's cheeks. 'I—I can scarcely believe that I could have been so mistaken in your character. The thing is—it is not easy to be a second wife, Genevra, married to a man who is not in the least plump in the pocket, so that economies are always having to be made.'

'I know. I understand. It could not have been easy, either, to be asked to take in a relative of his dead first wife.'

Harriet's flush deepened. 'I confess that I did not want you here, and I agreed to your coming only on condition that you did so as a servant. Then, when you arrived not only as a prisoner but also looking so much like Sophie, with the same white streak in your hair making it clear that you were a relative . . . And then later, all those things I said about you . . . I jumped to the basest of conclusions, and chose to believe all the gossip, and the only excuse I can offer is that I was concerned for Sophie. She is such a silly, impressionable girl, and it is hard enough to be stepmother to someone like that without her gaining the notion that there is something romantic about being a slave, and known as *Trelawney's woman* . . .'

'My dear Mrs McDonnell,' Genevra interrupted, 'please say no more. It is all in the past, and forgotten.'

'Call me Harriet,' she urged, and smiled slightly as Genevra looked up at her in surprise. 'Yes, it is strange, is it not? Only this morning I bitterly resented having you thrust upon us, and now I could not be more glad that you are here, because Sophie would be no comfort at all in this present situation.'

Fear and uncertainty about Uncle John's fate, Genevra was thinking, had brought a change in Harriet's attitude towards herself which would otherwise not have occurred for a long time, if at all. She heard Harriet continue in a tense, strained voice, 'Genevra, what do you suppose is to happen to John, to all of us?'

'I don't know. But I am quite sure that if there is anything we should do, Trelawney will send a message.'

But no further message came from Trelawney, and the day wore anxiously on. Genevra and Harriet kept from

Sophie the news that her father had been arrested, and she did not appear to wonder why he had not come home. By nightfall she accepted without question Harriet's remark that he must have decided to spend the night on Lord Exmouth's flagship.

Perhaps it was as well, Genevra told herself, that her own previous night had been sleepless, and that Harriet's had been disturbed by the crying baby, for otherwise they would have sat up and fretted ceaselessly about Uncle John's fate, while Genevra would also have had to fend off painful thoughts of Trelawney. As it was, sheer exhaustion would give them temporary relief in sleep.

But, the next morning, Harriet looked hollow-eyed and drawn and unrested. 'I think we should drape the furniture inside the reception room in covers, and close it,' she told Genevra. 'I cannot foresee . . .' She stopped, her lips trembling.

Genevra knew what was in her mind. With the British Consul imprisoned, and with the threat of a war looming between Algiers and Britain, it was not likely that the room would be needed for official receptions for a long while, if ever again.

They worked together, with Sophie ostensibly joining in but more of an amiable, chattering hindrance than a help. The front-door knocker caused Harriet to jump, and her fear-shadowed eyes went to Genevra, who nodded, and said, 'I'll answer it.'

Sustained by hope that the caller might again be Ahmed, come with a message from Trelawney, she hurried to the door. She was seized by surprise and then by relief to find that it was John, looking haggard and dishevelled, but otherwise unharmed. On either side of him stood an armed Turkish policeman.

He smiled a tired greeting at her, and stepped inside. 'The policemen will be remaining at the door,' he said quietly. 'We are under house arrest, Genevra, although only the dear Lord and the Dey know why.'

A little later, while he ate the meal which had hurriedly been prepared, he was telling them what had happened. 'Relations have been partially eased between the Dey and Lord Exmouth, it appears. They have exchanged gifts, and

Lord Exmouth is to leave for Gibraltar. In the meantime, I believe the Dey remains suspicious of the intentions of the British, and he is using the excuse of my debts to deny me free movement. Indeed, my entire family is under house arrest.'

Genevra heard the cannon booming out later, bringing the message that Lord Exmouth's squadron was leaving Algiers harbour. She climbed the stairs to the top of the house and stared through an attic window, watching in tearless grief and despair as HMS *Boyne*, with Trelawney on board, took the lead and, with billowing sails, departed from Algiers. She would never see him again.

In the days that followed, she was glad that hard work filled her mind and that exhaustion often left no room for emotions of any kind. She took over the cooking and helped Harriet with the general cleaning, while Sophie's only true usefulness lay in helping to care for the baby. Although none of the McDonnells was allowed to leave the Consulate, visitors were permitted, and it seemed ironical now that Harriet should once have been so concerned about what people would be saying about Genevra's position in the family. There were far more momentous subjects for everyone to think and talk about, for rumours of impending war were rife.

Then, quite inexplicably, the Turkish policemen who guarded the British Consulate in pairs abandoned their post and the unpredictable Dey summoned John to an audience.

'He seemed quite friendly,' he reported to his family afterwards, his expression puzzled and troubled. 'He made no mention of my debts and regretted the "mistake" which had led to our being placed under house arrest . . .' He interrupted his own narrative by exclaiming, 'Who do you suppose I came upon, working in the Jenina? None other than Rupert Runcorn! I have never been more disappointed in a man! He tells me that he has quite given up hope of being ransomed, and is planning to abjure instead and take the turban in the hope of becoming a Rais!' Harriet looked shocked, and Genevra decided not to comment. John went on, 'The Dey assured me that all British prisoners will continue to be well treated, Miss Pascoe in particular. He appears to have it still fixed in his mind that she is my niece. Indeed, the only time he became heated and angry was when he talked about the treachery of Trelawney Grant. Fortunately, it seems to have escaped him completely, Genevra, that you are still legally owned by that man, for otherwise I fear that he might well have ordered you to be handed over to him. Of course I did not dare raise the subject of paying for a new *teskere* to be issued for you.'

The reminder that she was still a legal possession of Trelawney brought an odd and incongruous kind of comfort. It was a link, however barbaric, however tenuous, between them.

Even though they were no longer under house arrest, life continued much as before inside the Consulate. No one trusted the volatile Dey, and rumours of war were still reaching them from the city.

One day John returned home for luncheon, looking white and shaken. 'A Spanish merchant vessel has arrived in the harbour,' he reported, 'bringing newspapers from Europe giving details of a fleet that is sailing for Algiers under Lord Exmouth's command. It seems there *is* to be a war.'

After that, events moved swiftly and ominously. Armed guards once more appeared outside the Consulate, but this time there were half a dozen of them, and as before, they permitted visitors to enter. Their presence seemed to be symbolic more than anything: it demonstrated to all in Algiers the contempt in which the Dey held Britain. When the muezzins called the summons to prayer, the guards left their posts, but none of the Britons would have thought of venturing outside during their absence.

From the attic window, Genevra could see the Algerian crowds daily taking up vantage-points along the walls and the parapets as they waited for a first sighting of Lord Exmouth's fleet. They must have been as puzzled as she was when, instead, a frigate sailed into the harbour, followed by a smaller corvette, both vessels fluttering a white flag of truce beside their British colours. She hurried downstairs to tell John.

'The frigate's commander has obviously arrived with an ultimatum for the Dey,' he said.

But for whatever reason the vessels had called at Algiers, the Dey did not summon John to any audience, and they remained in anxious ignorance. When Genevra returned to the attic window she could see that several uniformed British Navy men had come ashore and were strolling along the mole. The crowds appeared to be jeering at them, but did not offer any physical violence. That evening, she was about to lay the table for supper when there was a knock on the front door. She moved automatically to open it.

The visitor stood on the threshold, tall and lean in his Naval uniform with its gold frogging and epaulets. The last dying rays of the sun against which he was silhouetted gave his black-bearded face a satanic look. He had removed his cockaded hat and stood with it pressed to his chest. She did not know enough about Naval uniform to be able to tell his rank, but it seemed obvious that he must be the commander of the two visiting British vessels come to call upon John McDonnell. The Turkish guards, she noticed, had left to answer the summons of the muezzins.

When the officer did not introduce himself, she said, 'If you would care to step inside, sir, I shall ask the Consul to receive you . . .'

'It would give me much greater pleasure,' Trelawney's lazy, intimate drawl came from the bearded stranger's lips, 'to be received by his enchanting maid-servant.'

Shock and incredulity kept her motionless. He stepped across the threshold and closed the door behind him and then, displaying the same lack of restraint as when he had first pulled her into his arms, he enclosed her in an embrace and brought his mouth down on hers.

It was only when he let her go, and bowed to Harriet, saying, 'Your servant, Mrs McDonnell,' that John's reaction put into perspective what had so far been solely a source of joy and incredulous happiness to Genevra.

'Good God, Trelawney!' he exclaimed. 'Have you quite taken leave of your senses? You have put yourself into the most deadly danger by setting foot on Algerian soil again! The Dey has offered every Corsair Rais an extravagant bounty for your capture, and he means to have you slowly dismembered if you should fall into his hands!'

CHAPTER SEVENTEEN

ICY FEAR SWAMPED Genevra. How could she have been so stupid, exulting at the sight of Trelawney, without another thought in her head? 'Go back!' she cried feverishly. 'Back to the safety of your ship! Quickly, before the guards return from their prayers.'

He touched her cheek lightly, reassuringly. 'You are under house arrest, I know. We deliberately timed our arrival for today, the Mussulmen's Sabbath.'

'What has that to do with it?' she interrupted wildly.

'My dear Genevra, I knew that if the guards had remained at their post at all, which was unlikely, they would have been prostrating themselves to face Mecca, which is conveniently in the direction away from the Consulate and the harbour area. And since the arrival of two British ships flying flags of truce would not have been seen as a threat, they would have ignored my arrival.' He looked about him. 'May we go and sit down?' he asked Harriet.

'Yes. Yes, of course,' she answered in a flustered voice. 'We were about to serve the supper. If you would care to join us . . .'

'I am afraid there will not be time for that.'

'Come into the drawing-room,' John invited, and said in the same breath, 'You spoke of *we*. Who commands the second vessel?'

'Captain Dashwood. An audience has been arranged between him and the Dey for tomorrow, and you, Mr McDonnell, will be asked to attend.'

John shook his head. 'Presumably Captain Dashwood has come to present a final petition to Osman Pasha. But why on earth did Lord Exmouth take the risk of sending you to accompany him?'

Trelawney did not respond until they were all seated in the drawing-room. 'None of you recognised me until I spoke,' he said, 'so why should anyone else? A bearded

Naval officer in uniform will not be associated with Rais el-Trahni, especially as no one would believe he would be foolhardy enough to return to Algiers.'

'Why have you?' John asked again.

Trelawney side-stepped the question. 'Captain Dashwood is supposedly here to make a last appeal to the Dey to cease taking slaves, but no one believes he will agree to end a system that has profited his country for centuries. The real reason for Captain Dashwood's visit is to take you and your family, Mr McDonnell, to safety.'

Genevra wondered tensely why Trelawney had not said one word to explain his own presence. Her every instinct screamed out to him to leave the Consulate immediately and remain in anonymous safety on board his ship. She fought her fears, and gave her attention to what her uncle was saying.

'I cannot leave my post. Apart from my duty towards the British citizens and prisoners still in Algeria, I am also responsible for other nationals. My family, however . . .' He made a gesture, indicating that their safety was an entirely different matter.

'Your attitude was anticipated,' Trelawney acknowledged. 'The plan for taking your family to safety is this —Captain Dashwood will visit the Consulate tomorrow in company with several of his ship's officers and men, and will bring with him the uniforms of two midshipmen. You and your step-daughter, Mrs McDonnell, will put them on and leave the Consulate . . .'

'Oh, what a lark!' Sophie cried with excitement, her eyes shining.

'It will not be a lark at all, Miss McDonnell,' he said in a grim voice. 'If you drew attention to yourself and were caught, well, with things as they are you will not only be arrested, but you might well be burnt alive.'

Sophie made a shocked sound and lapsed into silence. Trelawney turned to Harriet. 'The two of you will accompany Captain Dashwood and his men, and be taken aboard his frigate as midshipmen . . .'

'No!' Harriet interrupted firmly. 'I shall not leave my husband!'

Trelawney's voice was blunt. 'Perhaps you have not fully

understood the situation, Mrs McDonnell. There is going to be a war.'

She wavered, and then cried, 'What of my baby? No mention has been made of him! Does anyone imagine that I would leave little Christopher?'

'No,' Trelawney soothed her. 'There is a plan for taking the baby aboard also. Another party of sailors will call at the Consulate later tomorrow. They will bring with them a basket of provisions, which will make it seem that the Consul's family are preparing for a siege. Among the sailors will be the frigate's surgeon, who will bring with him a safe but effective drug to keep the baby quiet. The child will then be placed inside the emptied basket and rowed out to join you.'

Harriet still protested against leaving her husband, but John persuaded her to co-operate with Captain Dashwood. Then he addressed Trelawney with a frown. 'You mentioned *two* midshipmen's uniforms. What of Genevra?'

'She could not be included in the plan. She is still a slave, and if things went awry, the attempt to smuggle her out of the country would inflame the situation beyond measure.'

Genevra swallowed hard, and said, 'I would certainly not wish to risk bringing danger to anyone else. I shall stay here with Uncle John.'

'No,' Trelawney interrupted. 'You will come with me. That is why I asked Lord Exmouth to allow me to sail with Captain Dashwood. You are my responsibility, my legal possession.' He looked at her, and his smoke-blue eyes held a revealing glitter. '*My woman*,' he added with a twist to his lips. 'So I have come for you myself.'

Her heart gave a tremendous jerk. 'But—But how? When? In what kind of disguise?'

'Now,' he said. 'Before the guards return to the house. And just as you are, your clothes covered by that hooded cloak I remember.'

He went on swiftly to explain what he had in mind. Because it was Friday, only slaves would be abroad, and a few free Christians. The Jewish Shabbat, too, began at sunset, so the hawk-eyed merchants and the brokers would be safely inside the *hara*.

'As I've said,' he went on, 'we deliberately chose today

for our arrival. The hours just after sunset on a Friday will be the safest in which to stroll casually together to the mole, from where we shall be rowed in a gig to my corvette.'

John was urging Genevra to agree to the plan, and Trelawney was telling her to hurry and fetch the cloak, adding, 'As soon as the Dey realises war is about to break out, he will send all slaves into the country to prevent them from doing anything to help the British. Because you have been denied purdah, you would have to go with the men. You would find yourself the only female among a crowd of desperate male slaves and vengeful guards.'

Genevra gave in, and hurried to her room. Since taking over the cooking and so much of the housework at the Consulate, she had stopped wearing Abigail's gowns, and was dressed in a simple blouse and skirt. She put the cloak on over it, and secured the edges with the emerald pin that had belonged to Trelawney. Then, after she had said goodbye to her relatives, she left the house with him.

They stepped out into the dusk. Only now was she beginning to take in fully the appalling danger they would both be in until the moment they stepped aboard the corvette. By himself, Trelawney might be dismissed as no more than a visiting officer from one of the British ships. Together, they would attract a great deal more attention. If only it were dark, she thought with a sick feeling at the pit of her stomach. But if it had been dark, the guards would have been on their way back from prayers.

The Marine Gate would now be manned by some of the freed slaves, and they would be armed. What if one of them recognised herself and Trelawney?

He held her arm, and when she tried to lengthen her steps he forced her to adopt a leisurely pace. 'We are out for a pleasant stroll,' he murmured.

She nodded, her mouth dry with terror, and looked down at her ankle, to make sure that the hem of the cloak was covering the chain. Would anyone recognise her by her cloak? She had worn it only once before in public. The men who had taken over the guard duties at the Marine Gate were scanning the crowds passing through, and she stopped, paralysed with fear. Rupert Runcorn was one of them!

Trelawney had seen him too. 'Courage, my love,' he whispered, putting his arm round her as if to shield her, but in reality to force her to continue walking. She almost fainted with shock when she remembered that Rupert had seen the cloak before. She had been carrying it over her arm when Rebecca first took her to meet Abigail's 'half-brother'. He would remember it, she thought hysterically. But she was propelled along by Trelawney, and it was only when she realised they had passed through the gate that her tensed muscles relaxed slightly. Rupert had not recognised her after all.

At the mole, two midshipmen were waiting with a gig, and Trelawney told them, 'My cousin wishes to be shown over the corvette. Row us out, please.'

Then she was sitting inside the gig, with Trelawney beside her, but danger was still around, for Rupert might suddenly remember her cloak. The guards would easily pick them off if news reached them that the two passengers were Trelawney and his women. At last she was swaying on the deck of the corvette, Trelawney's arm about her waist; he was issuing orders to the men and then they descended, and he opened a door. It was uncomfortably warm below deck, and with shaking hands she took off the cloak before she followed him inside the cabin.

'I'll light the lamp . . .' Trelawney began, and stopped, for to her own dismay she had begun to shake with sobs as tension drained from her. The door of the cabin had swung shut, and she felt Trelawney reaching for her in the darkness, holding her and murmuring soothing words.

As her sobbing diminished and died away, the character of their physical contact altered. His touch became caressing and then urgent instead of comforting, and she gave a shiver of response to his questing hands. In the darkness his mouth sought and found hers. Then he was picking her up in his arms and she made no resistance as he felt his way towards the bunk. He laid her down on it, and with his mouth still upon hers, his fingers worked at the buttons of her blouse, and then at the lacing at the front of her shift. Never before had she imagined such heat and fire as his mouth and his caressing, probing hands were sending pulsating through her. She helped him, with eagerly unsteady fingers, to undo the buttons at the waist of her skirt, and felt his other hand moving over her thigh, his fingertips caressing and then exploring the length of her leg. Suddenly he stopped and remained motionless, and she knew that his hand had encountered the chain round her ankle. With an abrupt movement he released her and stood up, moving away from the bunk.

'Can you get dressed in the dark, Genevra?' he asked in a strange, unfamiliar voice. 'I'll light the lamp afterwards, and have someone bring supper to you.'

Her senses stirred to a previously unknown pitch, she was too confused for a moment to take in more than that she had been rejected and left hungry and unfulfilled. Unsteadily, she protested, 'It—It is only a chain, Trelawney . . .'

'Only?' Now his voice had a rasping quality. 'It is an obscenity! We are in Algiers waters, and that chain is evidence that you are a slave of the Regency, *my* slave. I will not make you my woman in truth while you remain my slave, my possession.'

There had been such implacability in his tone that she knew he would not be swayed. As well as she was able, she dressed herself, and brought some order to her hair. Only when she told him that she had finished did he light a brass lamp suspended from the bulkhead and left her, with nothing more said between them.

A young midshipman brought her a tray later, and she ate alone, with only her thoughts for company, but after a while her intense strain took its tool in fatigue, and she lay down, fully dressed, and fell asleep.

She was awake before dawn, but it was not until she had breakfasted that Trelawney came to see her again, bringing a midshipman's coat and hat.

'Put these on, Genevra. Then, if you should be spotted from land, you will appear to be merely one of the sailors.'

She obeyed, and they went on deck together. 'When do we sail, Trelawney?' she asked. Once they were out of Algiers waters, she was thinking, and he had had the chain removed from her ankle, he could hardly go on regarding her as his slave.

'As soon as we have seen Mrs McDonnell and your

cousin safely taken aboard the frigate.' He seemed to be about to say something more, but obviously changed his mind.

She glanced at him. The beard made him seem not only unfamiliar, but also a little daunting. Something else occurred to her. 'Do you still sometimes wear a turban and robes?'

'No. I am no longer a Muslim. I requested redemptionist rites while I was in Gibraltar.' He glanced at her, and for a moment he seemed like the old Trelawney again. 'I doubt if folks in Devonshire would have reconciled themselves to a squire who wore robes and a turban and was prevented from attending services in the parish church.'

'Squire? I thought you were the second son, and that your elder brother . . .'

'In a letter awaiting me in Gibraltar, my brother told me that he had, after a great deal of soul-searching, decided to join an Anglican order of monks. So I shall therefore have to return and take over the estate, for my father is becoming too old. The Navy has agreed to release me from service in the near future.'

'Will you mind?' she asked, remembering how he had said that he was an adventurer at heart.

'No. I regard it as a new kind of challenge.' He looked at her, and asked deliberately, 'Will *you* mind?'

'I . . . What have *I* . . . ?'

'Coyness does not become you, Genevra. You know very well that I mean to marry you. But not until you have officially ceased to be a slave in the Regency of Algiers.'

'Trelawney,' she asked in despair, 'how can it possibly ever be *official*?'

'By waging war against Algiers,' he returned inflexibly, 'and forcing the Dey to free all slaves.'

She was silent. What if the British lost the coming war? She looked at Algiers, so well fortified, and her heart fell like a stone. Knowing Trelawney, he would go on and on, taking horrifying risks in his determination to have her officially declared free.

He spoke again. 'The original plan was for you to be transferred to Dashwood's frigate once we left Algiers harbour. He was then to continue on to Gibraltar with you and the McDonnells, while I sailed to where Lord Exmouth is anchored, to give the signal for the attack on Algiers.'

It had not even occurred to her that he might take part in the hostilities. Stifling her fears, she tried to speak evenly. 'You said that had been the *original* plan.'

'Yes. But do you have the courage, instead, to remain with me during the fighting?'

She stared at him in amazement. 'I would vastly prefer it to waiting in suspense in Gibraltar! But I would not have thought it would have allowed, let alone encouraged! Why do you wish me to stay?'

'Because, if the battle should not decide matters, I might be able to think of another way of gaining your official freedom. I would start by asking Lord Exmouth to make it part of a new peace treaty with the Dey. Osman Pasha is not likely to agree if he learns that you have already been smuggled out of Algiers.'

Perhaps, she thought, it was because Trelawney himself had caused her to be enslaved that he was so obsessive about her freedom being officially granted. 'I understand,' she said. 'I am more than happy to remain on board with you.'

He touched her hand briefly, and then left her by the railing. A while later, she saw with relief that a gig was approaching, carrying several sailors including two midshipmen who could only be Harriet and Sophie. They were safe, and the baby would be following them shortly. Trelawney confirmed this, and everything was made ready for him to sail to where Exmouth's fleet was waiting.

That night Genevra again slept in what she now knew to be Trelawney's cabin, while he shared the quarters of his first officer. By the following morning they could see the fleet commanded by Lord Exmouth riding at anchor, and Trelawney manoeuvred the corvette into position. She saw little of him while they waited. He made many visits to the flagship for conferences, and was able to exchange only a few words with her before they set their course for Algiers early on the following day.

'We should be within sight of the city again by sunset,' he said. 'Hostilities will not begin until after a formal ulti-matum has been delivered to the Dey. After that, Genevra, you are to remain below. Do you understand?'

She nodded, hardly able to imagine the reality of the coming confrontation.

The following dawn broke without a cloud in the sky, and Genevra's heart was filled with secret dread. Trelawney drew her attention as one of the British frigates, displaying a flag of truce, moved close to the shore. 'Her captain is to deliver the ultimatum to the master of the Algerian vessel sailing to come alongside,' he said.

The waiting which followed seemed interminable, and intensely wearing to the nerves. The frigate remained, awaiting a reply from the Dey. Suddenly Trelawney's corvette was convulsed by the news that the Dey had failed to respond to Lord Exmouth's ultimatum. Then a single shot rang out from the land. The battle had begun.

A hand like an iron band closed upon Genevra's arm. '*Below!*' Trelawney growled.

As she scurried towards the companionway, she knew she would not be able to bear being cooped up inside the cabin, so she made her way to the gun-deck and watched the gunners, stripped to the waist, blackened with powder-stains and streaming with perspiration. Gripped by alternating emotions of fear and hope, she quietly made her way back to the main deck and was in time to watch a flotilla of some forty or fifty Algerian vessels come out of hiding and head towards the British flagship. She gasped as she realised that they meant to board Lord Exmouth's vessel and take it. Even she could guess what a blow to the morale of the rest of the fleet that would be. But a series of broadsides caught the Algerians in a hail of shot. Volley after volley from the flagship added to the slaughter, and within minutes all the Algerian vessels had been destroyed and the few survivors were fleeing back to the harbour.

Sickened by the sight of such destruction, Genevra went down to sit in the cabin, listening to the nightmarish sounds. For the first time she had witnessed the grim reality of battle, and she thought of those in Algiers whom she had known. Not only Uncle John, for whom she had been offering silent prayers, but Mr Llewellyn, the Dey's Secretary, the many slaves who could not possibly have been sent away, and even Rupert Runcorn. Then she thought of

Abigail, shut up inside a harem, who had set out for Algiers to pay a ransom for a half-brother already dead by the time she arrived. Motivated by self-interest and the obsession to hold on to as much of her fortune as possible, it could never have crossed her mind that she might end up in danger of her life from British fire!

Some time during that hellish afternoon, Trelawney appeared briefly. He looked dishevelled and his eyes were reddened by smoke.

'Are—Are we winning?' she asked fearfully.

He gave a tired shrug. 'Difficult to tell. We have inflicted a great deal of damage on the port area. On the other hand, *Impregnable* has reported 150 men killed and wounded, and one frigate became becalmed within a direct line of fire from one of the batteries.' He added grimly, 'I can only pray that all the poor devils aboard were killed.'

She looked at him in shock. 'Why?'

'Because,' he said with bitterness, 'as I know only too well, the Algerians use a mixture of anything that can cause blindness or terrible injuries to those not killed outright.' He left her, to hurry back to his post.

When it began to grow dark, she lit the brass lantern, while the battle continued. It must have been close to midnight when she became aware that their vessel was moving. There had been none of the usual preliminaries to drawing up anchor, and she was wondering what was happening when Trelawney again paid her a swift visit.

'We've received orders from Lord Exmouth to cut the cables and withdraw to seaward,' he reported. 'We have to retreat to beyond the Algerians' guns and there is no time to pull up the anchors. My sails and rigging have not fared too badly, but those of other ships have been shot to pieces. We are all being forced to manage as best we can.'

Genevra drew a grasping breath. 'Does that mean that we have lost?'

He grinned sourly. 'It certainly does not mean that we have won. On the other hand, Algiers has been subjected to heavy fire and much of the city is burning; we have also destroyed a great deal of their shipping.'

So much death and destruction, she thought, and it might turn out to have been to no purpose. The Dey would set slaves to repair Algiers, and the sea-raids would go on.

As the fleet limped to seaward the bombardment continued, but the gunfire seemed to be coming only from the enemy. In the early hours of the morning, a violent thunderstorm broke out, but the morning dawned cloudy and cool. The sea was very calm. Small craft were returning to their own vessels the captains who had, it appeared, been summoned for a conference with Lord Exmouth. Trelawney was one of them, and Genevra hurried to join him when he came aboard.

'What has been happening?' she asked.

He rubbed a tired hand over his face. 'We have sustained heavy losses, and we do not have enough ammunition left to resume the bombardment. Lord Exmouth is drafting a face-saving peace treaty to offer the Dey.'

The news of their defeat left a bitter taste in Genevra's mouth. All the carnage of the past hours had been for nothing, and she herself would remain a slave, her name continuing to appear in the official record books in Algiers. Even if he had the chain removed from her ankle and married her in time, her still official state of slavery that he himself had caused would continue to eat away at Trelawney, and must affect what was between them.

Breakfast was served while the fleet waited for Lord Exmouth to finish drafting a peace treaty which everyone, including the Dey, would recognise as being an admission of defeat. Suddenly, just after noon, three shots were fired from Algiers, and immediately a vessel bearing a flag of truce approached them. The Algerians, totally unaware of their enemy's inability to continue the battle, were themselves surrendering and admitting defeat! A ragged cheer rose from the Navy men, and the vessels began to prepare to return to the harbour.

As they drew near, Genevra could clearly see the damage. She was not surprised, now, that the Dey had admitted defeat, for he must have feared further destruction. Even from the sea she could tell that hardly a house or a mosque had escaped being hit, and the batteries and the port area had also been devastated.

The fleet had hauled down their sails and were gently

bobbing on the water close to the mole. Genevra watched as a party of British officers went ashore in gigs. She heard footsteps behind her and saw Trelawney. In spite of his look of fatigue, his eyes held a glint of triumph.

'Lord Exmouth has torn up his original treaty,' he reported, 'and replaced it with another, demanding as the price of peace that all slaves be freed immediately. It will be presented to the Dey for signature. In the meantime, I am taking you to the flagship.'

'Why?'

'Because the British Consul has gone aboard to speak to Lord Exmouth. I know you will wish to exchange a few words with your uncle.'

'Yes indeed!'

On the flagship, they were escorted to Lord Exmouth's cabin. John McDonnell, looking haggard and drawn but unharmed, stared in astonishment at Genevra, who was still wearing the midshipman's coat and hat that Trelawney had lent her.

'Genevra!' he exclaimed, hurrying to embrace her. 'I thought you would be safely in Gibraltar!'

She smiled. 'There were reasons why I chose to remain with Trelawney. But I was glad that Harriet and Sophie and little Christopher escaped without a hitch.'

'Oh, but there was a serious hitch!' John corrected. 'Harriet and Sophie were transferred to the frigate, disguised as midshipmen. But the scheme to take the baby aboard went awry. The Jewish nurse had told her Rabbi of what was being planned, and he, fearing reprisals against his people if he remained silent, in turn informed the Dey. Poor little Christopher was seized, and the surgeon and the other sailors who had smuggled him out of the Consulate were arrested.'

Genevra gazed at him in shock. 'Where is the baby now?'

'The Dey relented after a while, and allowed Captain Dashwood to take Christopher to join his mother. But, in revenge, the Dey ordered me to be clapped in irons and imprisoned, with the threat of death hanging constantly over me.'

Genevra was glad that she had had no inkling of any of

this before. It would have added immeasurably to her tension and anxiety.

She felt Trelawney's hand on her arm. 'I suggest we return now, Genevra. Your uncle has official matters to discuss with Lord Exmouth.'

They took their leave, and were being rowed towards Trelawney's corvette when he issued an abrupt order to the sailors, who shipped their oars.

Genevra followed his glance. Hundreds of cheering, shouting slaves were being brought down to the mole, chained together as they marched down the road towards the Marine Gate. There had indeed not been time to send them into the country before the battle, and they had, instead, been shackled together and kept locked up. But not all the slaves were shackled in groups. Women, *paga lunars* and domestic slaves wore ankle-chains only. Genevra gave a cry as she recognised two of them.

Rupert Runcorn with his tawny hair, his beautiful flawed face and his ability to charm and disarm was also hurrying towards the mole and freedom, and clinging to him was Abigail in a shabby gown and with no sign of that hard inner core which Genevra had discovered to her cost. The expression on Abigail's face was revealing and unmistakable as she gazed up at Rupert.

'Her father,' Genevra said slowly. 'After all her scheming, after all her efforts to turn respectable and marry a title and hold on to her wealth—she has fallen hopelessly in love with someone who is just like her father!'

Trelawney studied them for a moment. 'They deserve one another.' He dismissed them, and stared at the mole, where blacksmiths were setting up their equipment in preparation for striking off the shackles and freeing the slaves.

Trelawney ordered the sailors to make for the mole, and when they reached the steps, he leapt from the boat and held out a hand to help her ashore. His smoke-blue eyes were alight, and she wished the beard did not hide the grooves which she knew were dancing triumphantly in his cheeks. She did not need to ask what was in his mind. He hurried her towards the nearest of the blacksmiths, and she raised the hem of her skirt, exposing her badge of slavery.

As it fell to the ground, no more than an insignificant piece of broken copper chain now, Trelawney swept her into his arms. He pressed her to him, and the vanguard of the approaching slaves cheered their approval as he claimed her mouth. This time there was something in his kiss that had never been there before.

As she responded joyfully to him Genevra understood, for the first time, the invisible barrier that had held him back before. They were equals now that she was free, and they belonged to one another because each wanted it and not because a law, however barbaric, made her his possession.

His head tossed back in jubilant laughter, his arm about her waist, he hurried her towards the gig, to be rowed back to the corvette and the privacy of his cabin where, she knew, she was to become in truth what she had been for so long by public reputation only: *Trelawney's woman*.

HISTORICAL FOOTNOTE

After the attack by the combined fleet under Lord Exmouth's command, Algiers was reconstructed and the city restored to commercial life within the space of months. The work could not possibly have been carried out with such speed had not the Dey, in spite of his assurance to Lord Exmouth that *all* slaves in the country had been set free, in fact hidden a considerable number of them away before the attack on Algiers.

The Corsair system was gradually resumed and more prisoners were taken, and the trade in human beings continued until 1830, when the French conquered and colonised Algeria.